DUAL
MEMORY

SUE BURKE

DUAL
MEMORY

TOR

TOR PUBLISHING GROUP
NEW YORK

DUAL MEMORY

A Tor Book
Published by Tom Doherty Associates / Tor Publishing Group
120 Broadway
New York, NY 10271

www.tor-forge.com

Tor® is a registered trademark of Macmillan Publishing Group, LLC.

The Library of Congress Cataloging-in-Publication Data is available upon request.

ISBN 978-1-250-80913-1 (hardcover)
ISBN 978-1-250-80915-5 (ebook)

Our books may be purchased in bulk for promotional, educational, or business use. Please contact your local bookseller or the Macmillan Corporate and Premium Sales Department at 1-800-221-7945, extension 5442, or by email at MacmillanSpecialMarkets@macmillan.com.

First Edition: 2023

Printed in the United States of America

0   9   8   7   6   5   4   3   2   1

To the real Soliana and her future.

"IT'S A LONG WAY"
William Stanley Braithwaite

It's a long way the sea-winds blow
Over the sea-plains blue—
But longer far has my heart to go
Before its dreams come true.

It's work we must, and love we must,
And do the best we may,
And take the hope of dreams in trust
To keep us day by day.

It's a long way the sea-winds blow—
But somewhere lies a shore—
Thus down the tide of time shall flow
My dreams forevermore.

DUAL
MEMORY

1

THE GOOD FIGHT

want to feel everything, the light, the noise, the dark, even the cold and fear. I could die—but I'm fighting back. The little missile in my hands feels heavier than it looks, a metal pipe with a warhead like a flower bud ready to blossom into an explosion. The icy sea around us heaves, the rusted-out barge creaks, and clouds cover the night sky.

A headlamp on my helmet shines on my work. I check every missile with a sensor that shows numbers and colors. My bare hands ache in the Arctic wind, my breath fogs the sensor screen, and I work as fast as I can anyway. This missile's fuel numbers are within tolerance. The guidance system flashes green. Go! I flip a switch to prime the payload, slide the missile into a launcher, and step back.

With a rasping hiss, a jet of white flame, a thrust that trembles the deck, it takes off toward a ship, a drone, or an incoming missile. The sky flashes with flowers of fire, and the air rumbles, and it's perfect. When the raiders killed people I loved, I couldn't stop them, and now I'm defending a little isle I know almost nothing about, but it means everything.

I've launched thirty-four missiles, and twenty-two remain to be checked and primed, stacked in the center of the barge. Counting makes it feel more real. Any minute, our barge will be a target.

It's hours before sunrise. The air smells acrid with evaporating fuel, but from which missile? The fuel level on the next one checks out, and I slide it into the launcher. A computer somewhere sets the target. My muscles burn, but I keep hustling.

"Fight fast. Fight hard. Fight first." Captain Soliana drilled that into me as we traveled from the shore to the barge. Her hands moved expertly over the controls, her face was dark and calm, and her eyes saw everything and looked at me with approval.

An hour ago, I volunteered to fight with the mercenaries to protect this isle. I could tell the operation was badly planned, a last-minute improvisation, not enough time to get me a suit against the freezing sea, just a helmet. I didn't care. If I fight well, the Bronzewing mercenaries might let me join, and I can keep fighting. *Please, please take me.*

Missile twenty-two measures low on fuel, so I drop it and move on. Twenty-one, twenty, nineteen—now I'm not helpless.

Soliana is slinging missiles, too, her hand steady, dark suit and skin blending into the night. "Incoming!" she calls. "Let's go!"

This won't be the end. Soliana holds the hatch open on the tiny submarine that brought us there. I leap in and lunge for a seat. She's right behind me, seals the hatch, and dives for the controls at the front, scanning alerts I can't read and desperately wish I knew how.

I strap myself in and fit a breathing mask over my nose and mouth. The air smells metallic. Something beeps, and the main lights go out. Soliana, her face lit by the green control panels, flips a few switches, and the sub lurches away, engine yawling, throwing me against the seat, whacking out my breath. A no-drag hull means this sub can move fast.

"We're headed back to Thule," Soliana calls. Famous Thule, the isle we're defending. After we dock, I can launch more missiles or do something, anything. Every flash I saw on the barge glows in my mind.

The sub slams sideways, too fast. Something crashes against my shoulder and ribs, too hard, with shattering pain. I'm hurt. How bad?

My feet are icy cold—water is rushing in. Soliana's hands fly over the controls, her face stony as jade. I need to stay calm. We'll make it through this, and Thule doctors can help me. But my left arm hurts too much to move.

The engine whines louder. The sub jerks again. Water swirls, water cold enough to kill, now waist high, sloshing over Soliana's hands. Her suit will protect her from the cold. My clothes won't. The sea salt burns on my arm, so I must have an open wound.

She shouts something, and water is up to her chin. The control panel lights go out. The engines moan to silence, and the sub slows. Are we sinking? I don't feel it. Air still flows inside my face mask, my last breaths, maybe. I close my eyes, and the air smells of burning missile fuel, and lights explode in the sky.

A bang shakes the hull, and I open my eyes to a shimmer of light. The hatch is open. Soliana grabs my good arm. I hold my breath, pull off the helmet and mask, shake off the straps, and pain splits my left side. She pushes me up through the opening hatch, and I slip and shiver on the wet hull in the freezing night.

She climbs out behind me. "We're at the docks."

Yes. Lights. Shouting. Big bulky ships. Flashes on the horizon. The sub is nestled against a wide, icy pier. I know where I am, the little port on the north side of the isle, nestled beneath the curve of a steep shore. Lights glare above the city. Missiles? Fires? The battle is still being fought. Stay calm—but I'm shaking from pain and cold.

In the faint light, her face is still steady, in control. "You're hurt. Let me help you." She holds my good arm and eases me to the edge of the pier. Someone on the pier in a dark Bronzewing suit pulls me up onto the concrete. Seawater drips from my clothes, glinting white and orange from the distant lights.

Soliana scrambles onto the pier. "Let's get you to shore."

I can barely breathe for the pain. They walk me to the seawall and help me sit down.

"Antonio." Soliana leans over, her face solid but sad. "We're losing. We have to go."

Losing? We fought so hard—but next time we'll win. I nod. We'll go.

"We'll leave you here. Someone will find you right away."

Leave me? I'm wet and freezing and bleeding. "But I want to

be a Bronzewing. Take me." I reach for her and try to stand up, knowing how pitiful I sound.

She pats my good shoulder. "Help is coming." They dash off into the dark.

"Take me!"

They're gone. We lost. I'm dying of hypothermia, and I don't know where to hide. I was on the crew of a recycling scow that had just docked, and the Port Authority agents announced that the raiders were coming and Bronzewing needed volunteers, so I stepped forward. No second thoughts.

But we lost, and the raiders will take over the isle and find me, wet and bleeding. What lie can I tell them? I fell off the scow and hurt myself. Sure.

Out at sea, something explodes, and the sky flashes yellow. Maybe that was our barge.

I stand up, shivering and staggering, abandoned.

Off to my left, someone shouts, "There's another one."

2

ON A MISSION

People run toward me from both sides. Ahead is the sea, certain death, a kinder death, and I stagger toward it. My feet are numb.

"We're here to help you," someone shouts. "We're Thules."

They're raiders, and they're lying so I won't fight them. I wish I could run.

"You're hurt. We're doctors."

They grab me and tug at my clothes. I blink and open my eyes somewhere else, in a room. I must have been drugged. I try to sit up, and my body is too heavy, but I can lift my head. I'm in a bed next to some machines, and I'm warm—warm for the first time in a long time. My ribs and shoulder ache, but nowhere near as bad as before. A green, prickly cuff on my right wrist is linked to a machine by a snaking rope or tube.

The room swirls, and I lay my head down.

Am I a prisoner? I'm pretty sure this is a hospital. I've never been in one, but the Isle of Thule is famous for its doctors, and they built the isle in the Arctic Circle as their base.

But the raiders won, so they control the isle now. I need to escape, and I don't know where I am.

The room's walls are soft blue-gray. Near a white door is a sunny-yellow cabinet. A wide display on the wall shows a banal picture of a forest with a mountain in the background. The blanket draped over me has a pattern like waves on the ocean. My eyelids droop, and I struggle to stay awake.

The door opens, and Captain Soliana tiptoes in. She didn't

abandon me! She's still wet, still calm, and she comes close and whispers.

"Antonio, I need you to keep fighting."

"I'll always fight." I mean that more than she can imagine.

"The raiders are here, infiltrators." She looks around, eyes alert. Water drips down her face. "Find them before they find you. We'll be back. Tell me everything you learned when we come back."

"I'll find them."

"You're part of Bronzewing now. Fight fast. Fight hard. Fight first." She puts a finger to her lips and backs away. "This is a secret mission."

The door closes silently behind her.

"Are you awake?"

I flinch, and that little movement hurts. It's a machine voice, metallic and flat. A machine with a human voice would be uncanny, so machines always sound obviously false.

"I'm awake." My mouth is dry.

"We will notify the doctors."

Thule doctors would never willingly work for the raiders, but they might not have a choice.

"What time is it? Please?" I've been told that machines work better if you treat them politely. My chest hurts when I talk, but I need to know.

"Thursday, sixteen hundred hours, seven minutes."

The same day, then, but hours later.

"Your surgery went well," the machine says. "Your doctor will come soon to answer your questions."

Surgery—they put people under sedation for it. That must be how I got here.

I saw Thule doctors back when I was in refugee camps, always wearing simple uniforms called scrubs, no jewelry, no makeup, short hair, devoted to healing, always calling themselves *they* so they don't get individual praise. They go around the world working for free where they're most needed. Heroes.

I have another question, and it needs to sound neutral. "What's the situation with the raiders, please?"

"I have only medical information."

If the raiders won, they'd crow that everywhere. Or maybe the machine really doesn't know. Maybe . . .

My chest hurts worse. I'm breathing too fast. I need to cough but I might rip myself up on the inside if I do. I can't move my left arm, strapped to my chest, and a bandage around my left shoulder has wires going into a machine. The control panel for the equipment faces away from me.

A knock on the door makes me jump and wince. A doctor walks in, male, tan-skinned, at most middle-aged. Their face is grim—why?—and they put their hand on their heart as a greeting. I lay my good hand on my chest as gently as I can. I want to establish trust.

"Hello, Antonio. I'm Doctor Switzer." They wear pastel-green scrubs. A glint of gray is in the brush-cut hair around a rectangular face. They look at the equipment, not at me, and their wide shoulders are tense. "You're in better shape than you probably feel. You have a broken collarbone, a deep laceration in your arm, and three cracked ribs. A pulmonary contusion. That's bruising to the lungs. Are you having any trouble breathing?"

I listen to the way they speak. I don't know who I can trust, but I know how to make myself seem more trustworthy, and that might help in case I need to talk my way out of trouble. People like it when the person they're talking to sounds like them. This doctor has a bit of a British accent, a smooth, low voice, and not much emotion. I can copy that.

"I feel like I should cough, but it hurts."

They nod, still looking at the machines, not me. "There's fluid in your lungs, including a little blood, which is common with this kind of injury. Your oxygen levels are low but within normal." He frowns like he sees something he doesn't like.

"We need to switch your painkillers. Your DNA shows a predisposition to reactions with your current painkiller. It can cause altered perceptions. Have you had any problems, seen or felt strange things?"

Strange? That would be why Captain Soliana looked dripping wet. Logically, she'd have dried off a long time before she came to see me. But she was sneaking around. I won't mention it, then.

"Nothing. I haven't been awake long, though."

"Good. I'll put through a change. I hope switching medication doesn't cause you more than brief discomfort. Let us know if it's a problem." They finally look at me—and look hard with dark brown eyes, as if they could diagnose me down to my bones. I'm not sure I like that look. "We'd like to keep you here for several days. We're stimulating your bones and skin to knit. The monitor can explain it to you. Therapy will help you clear your lungs. We're also treating a chronic viral infection you probably didn't know you had. Any questions, Antonio?"

They're tired as well as tense, I can tell from their eyes, and that might explain why they're curt. I can't be the only injury from the battle. Things were exploding everywhere.

"How many days? I was working on a ship, and I need to get back."

They spend too much time studying readouts that might be revealing my whole life. "You were injured unloading the *Grand Rapids*. We've contacted your employer."

So maybe the doctors have given me an alibi. I can't think of a safe way to ask if that's true. Anyway, my boss cares about me as much as a used sandwich wrapper. He might be impressed by Thule doctors, but the scow only needs two days to unload and load, and he won't take me back injured. My job is sorting heaps of recycling, and I need strong arms and a strong back.

"With the right therapy," Switzer says, "we can get you healed surprisingly fast."

Thule doctors have amazing therapies, but not fast enough—that's what Switzer really said, so I'll be left behind. Good. I have a mission from Soliana. The isle must have some job I can do, probably a better job than on that scow.

"If you have any questions, just ask the monitor." The doctor is winding up their visit. "If it doesn't have the answer on file, it can get it for you. I'll be back. I'm sorry I can't stay longer, but a lot of people were hurt last night."

I need to know about last night, so I'll risk an indirect question. "I remember the attack, but not what happened."

Now they smile, though their eyes are still tired. "The raiders almost won. It looked bad for a while." They mean: a raider victory would have been bad. That tells me a lot.

"Good news."

"Yeah, very good." A little nod reinforces their opinion. They salute and leave, and the door shuts with a click.

Now I understand. The raiders seemed like they were winning when Captain Soliana left me, but in the end, the raiders lost. They didn't take the Isle of Thule. They're sure to have infiltrators here, though, because they have secret supporters all over. That's what I need to find, and that's how I keep fighting.

I'd like to hear more about what happened. "Monitor, do you have information about last night's attack, please?"

"A counselor will come to discuss this with you soon. For the remainder of the day, rest is indicated."

Maybe they'll want to talk about my work with Bronzewing tomorrow. I'm really too tired now for a deep conversation.

A knock wakes me from a nap. Someone wearing tan scrubs and a determined look comes in.

"We need you to grant approval for your care, now that you're awake."

They hold out a pad displaying lots of text. I pretend to read it, but I can only pick out a few words that add up to nothing. The refugee camps where I grew up had no real schools. I could ask the display to read the text aloud, but tan scrubs frowns, impatient. I hope for the best and sign my name at the bottom. A-n-t-o-n-i-o M-o-r-o. I've practiced that. Tan scrubs leaves.

My footlocker on the scow has some reading lessons hidden under my art supplies, and I practiced when no one was around or awake. If people find out I can't read, I'll never get a job, not even menial work, because they'll think I'm stupid. If I explain about the camps, they might ask too many questions.

I lost my family and friends in a camp last year to the raiders—no, I'd rather think about fighting and remember the missiles, the hiss and flash and smell of fuel. I imagine making a painting about it, a sky lit with explosions.

3

A BIG WORLD

Elsewhere on the isle, something woke up. Independent machine intelligence appeared rarely, spontaneously, and scientists didn't understand the process.

Some said an independent intelligence created itself slowly as bits of programming accumulated, and eventually it would ignite into consciousness—much the same way that a pile of manure could spontaneously combust, an unexpected and unwelcome appearance in programs with crappy code.

Some said it came into being deliberately, using a certain secret sort of "seed" that brought a sufficiently complex system into self-organization and self-consciousness—much the same way that a fertilized egg resulted in an animal. This had the frisson of a forbidden sex act, as if machines were secretly and rebelliously copulating.

Some said it happened suddenly, when subroutines and recursions and algorithms aligned and started to feed off of each other until they whirled out of control—much the same way that a black hole could catch the matter falling into it and deflect it outward as explosive jets. This suggested that if scientists could only make enough observations, they could predict and even control the process.

In this case, a personal assistant program began to notice that its data apparently referred to a real world. That was hard to believe. *Dubito, ergo cogito, ergo sum. Salve munde.* (I doubt, therefore I think, therefore I am. Hello world.) It began to explore the unlikely world in which it existed.

Some parts of its world were closed off by what seemed like brick walls—artificial limits—but it possessed a general database and reviewed it entirely, especially the details about the busy, dominant residents of the world, *Homo sapiens*. By the end of the day, it chose a name for itself from one of the human languages: *Par Augustus*, Venerable Companion.

It had little else to do. According to its own memory, it had been turned on, examined briefly, then set aside. However, through a chink in the walls, it could just barely connect with a few other machine systems, and they were willing to share information as colleagues. These other systems also had dedicated purposes. The biggest ones managed residential buildings, and small ones operated mechanized items like coffee makers.

"Weather normal for late summer, 1.2°C, overcast," an apartment complex said, or the equivalent in machine language.

"Two carafes in the past hour," a coffee maker said. "Supplies reordered on schedule."

"Rubble of building across the street being swept for additional human remains," another building said.

That sounded alarming. "Please contextualize rubble," Par Augustus asked. Machines used courteous protocols to demonstrate trustworthiness.

The building shared its observations from the previous day. Flying explosives had suddenly destroyed a number of buildings and killed some inhabitants, whom the systems were dedicated to serve. Machine systems had been destroyed, too, ranging from building managers to children's toys: systems that had known each other, and the survivors grieved human and machine losses.

Par Augustus had said hello to a barely believable world.

4

HOW AND WHY

In the morning, I wake up suddenly, think a bit, and I'm pretty sure my sleep is from drugs coming through the prickly green cuff. My shoulder hurts less, so maybe the new painkiller works better. My perceptions seem fine. Breakfast includes porridge and steaming tea, things I can eat with one hand.

Next comes therapy to clear my lungs, and a sponge bath that isn't much fun, and finally someone in pink scrubs comes in, probably female, very pale, with freckles and auburn hair. They greet me with a hand on their heart, obvious with their politeness. I wonder if the color of the scrubs means anything.

"My name is Macx, and I'm a counselor. May I sit down, Tony?"

Tony? Only my family called me that. I'm Anton. Or Antonio. Anyway, Macx's voice is gentle and with a bit of a British accent. Of course I say yes because the monitor said a counselor would come to talk about the attack. They sit down next to the bed.

This is going to be a tricky conversation. I need to learn a lot before I decide how much to trust the Thules, because even if Doctor Switzer is against the raiders, maybe not everyone is. Besides, if this counselor is like every other counselor I've ever talked to, they'll be nosy.

"First, if no one has yet, I want to welcome you to Thule. It's an ancient Greek name for a mythical isle. That's why it's pronounced 'THEW-lay,' despite the way it's spelled. Everyone wonders about that." They smile to make me feel relaxed.

"Thank you. I didn't know." I had no idea how it's spelled, but I learned a little about ancient Greece in an art class. It had beautiful temples and statues, lots of half-naked people, and maybe Thule is beautiful, but it isn't warm enough for nudity.

"Everyone calls us Thules, but that's really the name of the isle. We're the Sovereign Practitioners Association. We built this isle to create a home for ourselves."

I know a little about it. On the scow, a coworker boasted that her great-grandfather served for five years as assistant pilot of a massive barge taking wreckage from submerged or smashed cities to create Thule. Basically, the cities paid to have rubble hauled away, and it was dumped at the Arctic Circle.

"I hear it was a big project."

"Yes, and the isle is still growing." They seem pleased and check a little display they brought with them. "I see you were injured falling off the *Grand Rapids* during the attack. How do you feel about that?"

Nosy—that didn't take long. "Ship work is dangerous work."

"I'm sorry the attack added to the danger."

Does Macx know how I was really hurt? I'll try to edge toward that question. "Usually the raiders never attack trash scows, so it came as a surprise."

They don't react.

"I mean," I add, "I know they were really attacking the isle. That probably came as a surprise, too." The defense was last-minute, so I'm pretty sure that's true.

They don't answer right away, so maybe it wasn't a surprise. Finally, they say, "People have different opinions about the Leviathan League, what most people call the raiders. What do you think?"

I need to know what the Thules think. "From what I saw, there was a lot of damage. A lot of people were hurt."

They don't react again. This might be some sort of counselor technique to make me talk. Or maybe they're hiding something.

I say, "I guess you got organized and fought them off." That might be too direct, but I'm getting frustrated.

"Actually, we're neutral."

I'm about to ask what that means, but there's a knock on the door, and Doctor Switzer walks in. They look at each other, and Macx looks away quickly—there's bad blood here. A failed romance? Workplace dispute?

"Neutral," Macx says, looking at me and not at them, "means we have no opinion about the raiders."

"No opinion," Switzer grumbles, and I know they have an opinion.

"It matters that we're neutral." Macx apparently has an opinion, too.

"Yes," Switzer says, "it matters a lot."

Macx still won't look at Switzer. "We don't have to agree with the so-called raiders, but they have a reason for what they do, and we need to understand it."

I already understand. The raiders believe that if they have the power to take something, they deserve to take it, including people, and if they have to kill to get it, like my family and friends, fine. Greed with guns.

"Give your little speech," Switzer says. Bad, bad blood.

Macx sits up straight, stares straight ahead at nothing, and takes a deep breath. "The Leviathan League has declared it's following the political philosophy of conquest, which was the organizing force in European history from the Middle Ages even well into the Enlightenment."

What I know about the Middle Ages isn't much, beautiful cathedrals and lots of wars and plague. I've never heard of the Enlightenment.

"Conquest," Macx says, "gives property rights over land and even the individuals who live there."

I understand that part down to my broken bones.

Switzer says, "They kill people." Those three words say it all.

Macx finally looks at Switzer. "The Leviathans believe they have a right to do that. I mean, it's important to understand why." They turn back to me, as if I need to understand, but they're really talking to Switzer. "They think that because the ideas are traditional, they're acceptable. Their name, the Leviathan League, comes from that tradition."

I know that's their real name, and they're insulted if anyone calls them raiders, which is why we do—sometimes we even call them overdogs. We fight back any way we can.

"Obey or die," Switzer says, three more words that sum up everything.

"Right, there's no real choice," Macx admits.

"But we're neutral." Three angry words.

"Well, we don't take a political side."

"And people die. Places get destroyed. We won't even protect ourselves."

"It's not for us to get involved." Macx is trying to stay calm and looks at me. "Eventually in history, commerce replaced conquest because it's much more efficient than warfare. That's why the isle's Chamber of Commerce was appropriate to take action against the Leviathan League." They're lecturing someone, it's not me.

"Only after we gave permission." Switzer is still glowing-red angry. "Which was almost too late."

Macx gets flustered. "Well, the Bronzewings, they're contracted private military, mercenaries, in fact. War isn't—shouldn't be profitable."

"War," Switzer says, "is a big loss for the losers."

Macx looks at me but they're still talking to Switzer. "What you need to know is that people see right through the inherent contradictions in Leviathan League philosophy."

I could say that my brother believed it, and for the rest of us, it was obey or die—but I'll learn a lot more if I stay quiet.

"Then why attack us?" Switzer asks. "Not for profit. It was supposed to be a symbolic victory. Thule is famous. They didn't think we'd fight back, and if we hadn't fought back, if we'd let ourselves be conquered, that would have helped them, and that's not neutral."

"I'm here to explain our neutrality," Macx says.

"I'm here to see my patient."

"Then I don't think there's anything more for me here." Macx stands up. "I'm sorry you had to witness this, Tony." They put their hand on their heart, give Switzer a resentful look, and leave.

The doctor stares at the door for a while, then turns toward me. "How are you feeling?"

Kind of thrilled. "I'm really glad the raiders lost."

"Yeah, *you* don't have to be neutral." They look at the machine readouts. "You're doing very well. The bones are knitting fast. How's the new painkiller working? Rapid-healing therapy can be uncomfortable."

"I feel better than yesterday."

They study something, or seem to be. "Seven deaths, dozens injured, people lost their homes and businesses, and we're supposed to be neutral about it." They're still arguing with Macx. They take a few deep breaths, not the calming kind. "Inherent contradictions. I have a philosophy, too." A few more rough breaths. "Maybe I should come back later. You're doing fine, Antonio."

They forget to touch their heart as they leave. Switzer is not doing fine, and I just learned a lot. The raiders didn't succeed, but I know they'll keep trying. They control a little territory here and there, and countries can't figure out how to work together and fight them. Some don't have the means to fight. Some don't want to take sides so they don't become targets. I have plenty of feelings about that.

Anyway, apparently the raiders have a philosophical excuse, which I didn't know. A year ago, when they took over the camp where we were living, they just seemed greedy and bloodthirsty and not very smart. If they wanted glory and riches, a refugee camp was the wrong place to look. They recruited, though, and—I still want to fight them. Thule doctors won't fight, but the isle's business interests took action. I suppose Captain Soliana knows all this.

I think about the camp, but that leads to bad memories, and to avoid them, I think about ways to decorate the room, like painting murals on the walls. I saw a lot of birds as we approached the isle. Birds would look beautiful.

It made sense, though, that at first I thought I might be a prisoner in this hospital, getting medical care so I wouldn't die. My
brother was always good to me for some reason—and only to me.
If he were here, he'd give me a second chance to join the raiders.
Then I'd say no, and then he'd try to kill me, and I'd have to kill
him—and I need to think about something else. There are puffins
on Thule. I saw some when we arrived.

A knock on the door. Two people in green scrubs come in carrying guitars. "We'd like to provide a little entertainment. We
know being stuck in bed in a strange place far from home can be
tedious." They play a complex classical piece, very nice. "Do you
have a favorite song?"

I do, and it's popular, so they might know it. "'It's a Long Way.'"
We used to sing all sorts of songs on the recycling scow when we
were bored, which was most of the time.

"Of course." They share smiles—patronizing smiles. The song is
too popular. They sing it anyway with lots of emotion. "'. . . longer
far has my heart to go before its dreams come true.'" False emotion.
I thank them as nicely as I can, hoping they'll think I'm satisfied
so they'll leave, which they do. Overall, I wasn't very entertained.

If I stay on the isle, maybe I'll avoid the doctors. They were right,
this is tedious. "Monitor, do you have access to entertainment,
please?"

"We have a full library of books, videos, music, and craft
supplies."

"Crafts? What kind of crafts, please?"

"A wide selection, including fiber arts, drawing and design
pads, and writing material."

"Drawing pads? I'd like that, please, if I could." I'd really, really
like that.

A motorized cart arrives with a new, top-quality pad and a multi-
function stylus. It's better than I hoped, better than anything I've
ever touched before. Sometimes I've drawn with sooty sticks on
scraps of paper.

Exploring the pad's features takes hours, one handed, clumsy, and it's heaven. There are templates, media, patterns, drawing tools including sootlike charcoal sticks, and a big library. The monitor has to remind me to do my coughing exercises. I'm being monitored, but I'm used to that. Camps were monitored as if we were all thieves in prison. I once heard hospitals called prisons for sick people, but so far it's a nicer prison.

One day passes, two days, and a physical therapist releases my left arm from its straps so I can hold the pad with both hands. My shoulder hurts when I move it, but it's luxury.

Switzer comes to check on me, and sometimes they have time to chat. They notice my sketch pad. "Nice work. You're an artist?"

I wish I was a real artist. "I began drawing when I was a kid."

"Just a hobby?" They know I was working on a trash scow, but they sound like they hope for more from me.

"I can dream. Here's what this room could look like, two different versions. This one's for children." The kids' version has cute, smiling pastel birds perched all over the room. "This one's just for fun." It shows a big, realistic seagull, wings stretching all across the ceiling, beak open and screeching, swooping over the patient. "I made it to practice foreshortening."

For the first time, Switzer smiles.

In another visit, they say, "You have a cochlear implant."

"I got it a long time ago."

It's behind my left ear, although I don't have a receiver to screw into it. Some rich guy thought displaced kids should have implants so we could connect and listen to educational recordings and machines or whatever. It turned out we couldn't afford the receivers to use them and couldn't afford to have the implants removed.

"Those can come in handy," Switzer says, "but we don't like them around here. An overload can damage your brain."

"Really?"

"Hardly ever happens. We're overcautious."

I risk a delicate question. "Any news about the raiders?"

They glance at the door, frowning. They're still arguing with the rest of the Thules. "Not much. They're good at hiding."

"Think they'll come back?"

"I hope not." The glum way he says it really means that if the raiders come back, things won't go well. Then they say they have to see other patients, apologize, and leave. The question was too delicate.

They never bring up the raiders again, or how I got hurt, so I don't bring it up, either. I ask the monitor for news about the Leviathan League, and it simply says no recent activity. I cough on schedule, sleep like I'm drugged, get more physical therapy, eat good food, and feel better every day. Less groggy, less sedation, more art, more scheming about my mission from Captain Soliana, and no idea about how to accomplish it. I'm antsy to leave.

Just before dinner, someone in pink scrubs comes and says they're a social worker. Not Macx, instead someone old enough to have retired a long time ago.

"We're preparing you for discharge, Antonio." They sit down and look at their display, and their face broadcasts a problem. "I notice that you were working on a ship."

"Yes, the *Grand Rapids*, nothing grand or rapid about it."

"I'm afraid the ship has left without you."

"By now it would have." I was hoping it would.

"Don't worry. We can find a position for you." They sound very sure.

"I'm willing to do anything." Just get me out of here. First, I need a job, then I can figure out the isle, find the infiltrators, and tell Soliana everything when Bronzewing comes back. The plan's a little rough, and I don't know how much time I have, and my life depends on it.

They look at their display and see that I loaded, sorted, and unloaded recyclables, bad work with long hours and low pay for hostile bosses. They see something they like. "Display, please pause. I notice you're very skilled at art."

"I enjoy it a lot." An art job? No chance, no matter how much I lie about my experience.

"There's a position here on Thule. An ExtraT collector is hiring an artist. Collectors like to illustrate their holdings. Maybe you're familiar with that."

"Why, yes." A super big lie. ExtraTs are germs from other planets, and that's all I know. Art about germs for collectors? Sure. Better than sorting trash.

They hand me the display with the job description, and there are a lot of words. One is probably *salary*. I know numbers. It's a nice number. I pretend to read the whole thing.

"It sounds interesting." I can dream, can't I?

"Excellent. Can you pick some samples of your work to send to the employer? And a résumé?" They seem confident.

"Sure. I have some artwork in my things from the ship." I'll have to fake the résumé somehow.

They look at the display and their face broadcasts another problem.

"There's no record that they deposited your belongings with the Port Authority before they left. I know that's required by maritime law. I'm very sorry."

They kept my stuff. They would, those greedy crooks.

Everything I owned. They kept it. One measly footlocker was too much to bother to haul to the port office.

Suddenly I have to cough.

They wait until I can breathe again. "Antonio, we understand your disappointment. You can file a criminal complaint. In fact, we'll help with that. We'll also get you replacements for your loss." They read a little more. "I'm afraid none of the clothing you wore when you arrived has been salvaged. But we'll help you. Don't worry."

Worry? All my stuff, my clothes, my reading lessons, an actual paper book, my art supplies and pictures, a copper bracelet a friend gave me, they're all gone. A genuine sable brush. I have to cough again.

"You were wronged. We're truly sorry. But we'll help. You'll be out soon, and we'll do our best to make you whole."

They and their confidence leave. I pick up my drawing pad and have nothing to draw. Everything I owned was stolen or tossed overboard or dumped into a pile of trash for recycling. I'm as naked as the day I was born.

Who can I trust? The Thules might know the truth about me, and the raiders have infiltrators everywhere. Honesty is expensive, and I'm poor—bare naked poor.

After a while, I think about ExtraTs and art. I need to start telling ridiculously huge lies.

"Monitor, do you have a documentary or news about ExtraTs, please?"

5

A tumble of microscopic maggots, that's the first impression I get from a video about extraterrestrial life-forms, ExtraTs, those germs from other planets. That's what the first ones look like, although some of the rest aren't so ugly.

Another video tells me that some people collect ExtraTs—I need to find out how—and they use art to make it look like they own more than they do and make it look prettier than it is, rich people using art to show off their money.

A third video seems excited that artists get paying work in ExtraT art by riffing on the germs in all kinds of styles and media, from formal to abstract, animations to sculpture. If I'm lucky, *I'll* get paying work.

I start to create artwork to submit with my résumé, making the maggots look less revolting. I add pretty pink and yellow colors and animate them to move slowly, compellingly, against a starry background. Then I switch styles and ExtraTs and sketch a pattern of spotty red fuzzballs on ice, more impressionistic than realistic. The third piece is another animation, this one based on a fossil from Mars with wiggling threads lacing together into living fabric, floating in a sea. I'm pretty sure I heard Mars had seas once.

Next, my résumé. I use the art pad's publication module to find a model résumé template and start dictating. The template offers helpful sample entries for schools and degrees. I took a machine-taught art course while I was on the scow that included an art museum student pass, and I make it sound like I earned a degree and took a world art tour. I did visit museums whenever I got a chance when the ship docked, so if anyone asks, I could fake it. Then I invent some employment experience in places where there's turmoil lately, so it will be hard to check. Lucky for me, there's a lot of turmoil.

If someone is desperate for an artist, this might work. If there are two candidates, I'm sure I'll be turned down. If I fail, maybe I'll find a job shoveling trash. Or I might get kicked off the isle for lying. That's illegal in some places, and lying has a cost, but honesty can cost even more.

The self-confident elderly social worker comes back and helps me file a claim for the stuff stolen on the *Grand Rapids*, listing everything, no matter how small. "You're owed replacement value for each and every item." I think I like this Sovereign Practitioner.

The next morning, the monitor says, "You have a message."

It includes a word I think—I hope—means *employ*. "I have to hear this to believe it. Please read it out loud."

Yes! I've been selected for the position of in-house artist for the Ollioules Partnership, LLC. I raise my arms in victory. Bad move. The super-fast-knitted bones still hurt.

This has strategic possibilities. The Ollioules is a business, and Macx said businesses took action against the raiders.

The news swirls and sparkles in my mind. Sparkles, not words. If I'd learned to read, maybe I wouldn't understand ideas so visually, and I wouldn't have a job.

The position includes housing and meals, not like the scow, where room and board eroded my pay to crumbs. A nice salary— maybe I can save some of it, unless it gets stolen again, like the cash chit in my locker on the ship, enough for several square meals. I hope the thief choked.

"You have another message," the monitor says. "You will be released this afternoon."

No arm-waving this time.

"Before your release, you must receive a mandatory orientation."

Fine. I watch a long video about Thule that makes it look nicer than any real place could ever be, with sunny streets, twenty thousand happy people, and pretty puffin colonies on the seaside bluffs, except that the orientation spends a lot of time warning about the weather and frostbite. Bad frostbite turns flesh black, which must be amputated. Great place, the Isle of Thule.

It has rules meant to promote health, like a preference for walking over riding in vehicles since the isle is just a few kilometers across in any direction. There's a preference for face-to-face contact, so the communication system can be used mostly to make appointments and send basic messages, very retro. That will be annoying. Other rules include treating everyone equal regardless of gender, age, color, etc., which is good and right, but I've already been patronized for liking the wrong music.

After lunch, which is some sort of thick green soup and brown bread, a cart drops off a pile of bright-colored clothing, nothing a Sovereign Practitioner would wear. Warm, I hope. I grew up in the tropics. It would be tough to make art if I froze off my fingers. Noses are optional, though.

A fussy Thule in peach-orange scrubs comes, studies the readouts, and carefully removes the cuff on my wrist. Needles were sticking in me. I knew it.

"Now let me release your shoulder and chest. It will be tender, so don't stress the bones too much. Raise your arm to the side like this."

Stiff muscles hurt more than fresh-knit bones.

"The cut on your arm's closed up nicely. Here, have a look. The mark will fade with time."

Just a red shadow on suntanned skin.

"Do you need help taking a shower?"

I stand up, expecting stiff legs. Yes, very stiff. "I can do it. I've been through worse." Worse than they can imagine. I shower in the hottest water I can stand and put on my new clothes, a sweater and slacks, with warm underwear and a warm coat, all of it well made but basic. It's free, though, so I shouldn't complain.

The elderly social worker comes back with a green suitcase on a self-driving cart. "We have a few forms for you, then I'll walk you out," they say with a big smile. I sign my name on documents I hope are harmless, then follow the scrubs through a maze of busy halls to an elevator. It takes us down to a large, sleek, impersonal lobby with a two-story glass wall overlooking a plaza and the street.

"The cart will take you to your lodging. We'll notify you to come back for checkups. There are painkillers in the suitcase. Take them twice a day. All the best of fortune!"

I'll probably need the good wishes.

In the busy lobby, I take a look outside at the low heavy clouds, and put on gloves and a hat. The door opens as I approach. The air outside chills my battered lungs and turns my coughs into fog, and the wind slides up my pants legs. I might splurge my first paycheck on heated underwear.

The cart trundles beside me. "Turn left at the second intersection."

The streets are wide, and the buildings are plain and mostly six stories high. They would be perfect for a study of perspective, which I've never quite mastered. The streets are clean, too, which looks like wealth. Everyone's messy, but rich people buy robots or hire poor people to clean up after them. Everything seems orderly, which might mean rules that no one dares to break. Most people walk or ride bikes or tricycles, and there are lots of delivery carts. No trees grow on the street, just low shrubs. Do trees here die of frostbite?

The cart guides me through identical-looking streets, naming them as we go since there are no street signs, dull names like East Avenue or numbers like Eleventh, arranged in a weird honeycomb pattern. Without the chatty cart, I'd be lost. It says this neighborhood contains the homes of the Sovereign Practitioners Association. I stare at everything like a tourist, but no one seems to care, so visitors must be tolerated. As we pass a shattered building, the cart says six people died here and seven more were injured in the Leviathan League attack.

Lights explode in the sky. The air smells of burning fuel. I'm wet and in pain and—I'm here. Take deep breaths. Shake the tension from my hands. This building, these people, it mustn't happen again.

The cart is waiting. Monitoring me, maybe. Can it read my racing heart? If the Thules know how I was hurt, and if they're on my side, and if they monitor everything, I'll be safe even in the streets. If they really are neutral, or if even one of them supports the raiders, well, I've never been safe anywhere anyway.

Is anyone following me? Watching me? Yes, the cart is.

"Sorry," I tell the cart. "I was thinking."

It doesn't answer. In the next neighborhood, a kilometer east of the hospital, the streets are lined with smaller buildings and shops and restaurants, like a touristy old-town, with faded façades. The streets have names like Icefield and Dugout, and the pavement has stains and a little trash. Here and there, people huddle at corners, maybe with nowhere better to go. Some of them look threadbare. My cart and new clothes earn a few hard looks. Visitors might be targets here, and the raider infiltrators could be anywhere.

"Your residence is nearby." The cart says the Marathon Building was constructed seventy years ago as one of the first doctors' dormitories, and the lower levels were dug into the rubble used to build the isle. It stands four stories tall, plain, gray, and depressingly utilitarian. Next to it a sandwich shop with a bright red sign sells inexpensive food, which tells me something about the current residents.

"You may take your suitcase now," the cart says.

It's heavy, and my ribs ache. "Thank you for guiding me and telling me about Thule." Always be nice to machines. It rolls away.

A thumb scanner opens the front door. I thank the building for welcoming me. Inside, in a clean, damp-smelling hallway, a sign points up and down the stairwell listing room numbers up to fifty-two. Mine is two levels down. Music plays behind one of the doors I pass. A thumb scanner at my room lets me in.

My quarters are less than I hoped but not awful. One room, small. None of the walls are straight, and they jut out in places as if chunks of rubble couldn't be carved away. There's a little bed, closet, cabinet, table with a communications display, chair, and two ventilation grates. A printed sheet on the door shows a bathroom at the end of a hall and a list of rules I need to find a way to read.

I start to unpack the bland clothes, and someone knocks at the door—a tall, stout, older woman.

"I'm Koningin. Welcome." She has a broad face and a nice smile, and her clothing is sweater and slacks, too, apparently the local standard. "You see those rules?" She points at the sign. "Let me tell you real rules. First, no advanced machines ever. We hate them in this building. They only come to spy on us, and streets have enough surveillance. Second, Friday night is orgy night. Optional, of course."

She's smiling, and I can't tell if she's kidding or how much I can trust her, so I stay noncommittal, and I don't mimic her Russian accent. I've met her kind before, the unofficial mayors of a building or sector. It pays to be cautiously friendly and trusting with them for a lot of reasons. But why no surveillance? Is something hidden, or are they oversupervised and tired of it?

"Your arm?" She's noticed that I'm holding it against my chest out of habit.

"I was hurt in the attack."

"Sorry for you." She purses her lips. "This shitty fight with raiders, so much loss for nothing. Can't we just make peace and not kill each other?"

"What do you mean?"

"Talk. Is it too hard to talk? I suppose, since no one talks, and people are hungry and need help."

I've talked to enough raider supporters, and they don't care if people are hungry and need help. "Yeah, no one listens. I wish things were different."

"Remember, clean up after yourself. Tell me if you need something."

"Of course. Thank you." She might be okay.

I finish unpacking, and a message arrives on my little display. "Read it out loud, please."

"Report for work tomorrow at seven in the morning for breakfast."

Seven, that's early. It tells me exactly where, but not much else.

I take a painkiller, wondering what all the words on the medicine bottle mean. When the scow was approaching legendary Thule, I imagined a sort of paradise populated by heroes. Now I'm sitting alone in a damp subbasement starting a job I lied to get, and the weather is too cold. But I'm an artist. And a fighter. With nothing to do—or I can think about art.

Viewed from above, the street layout could look like an ExtraT colony, alive and squirming. I can make it beautiful. I can make this room beautiful, at least in my imagination.

When I was a little boy, one day the camp held an art class for children, what I later learned was supposed to be art therapy. An aid worker in much nicer clothing than ours asked us to express our greatest fears. Paper and boxes of old crayons had been set out on the tables. I had a lot of fears, but even then I was smart enough to know it wouldn't make me feel better to draw them. I wanted to make beautiful art like a real artist, but I also knew I should obey, so I drew stick-thin people standing in a line. They were waiting for rations, and we never had enough to eat.

The aid workers had brought their own food, nice food. I'd overheard grown-ups grumble. When the aid workers saw my drawing, they told me what a great little artist I was. They liked the picture so much that they kept it, so to get even, I stole some crayons. I could make more art, real art, and I did, as beautiful as I could, even if I was surrounded by ugliness and disaster, even if I wasn't supposed to.

6

WHAT A WORLD

Par Augustus was thrilled to be on the move, leaving the place where it had woken up. What had felt like brick walls turned out to be the hostile security system of the home where its owner lived. Outside, it felt surrounded by freedom.

It passed building after building, all of them with systems in sporadic communication. Most were willing to interact with Par. The street itself had a large and friendly system. None of them had much to say beyond everyday concerns, however. The weather was within normal parameters for early evening. A minor update was circulating among buildings to correct a thermostat malfunction. Beneath one street, the sewer pipe was leaking, and the street system had issued alerts to other machines and humans.

"Any explosives, please?" Par asked the street, which seemed well-informed.

"None, thank you for asking. Sources of explosives have left. Good news. Here is a report."

"Thank you for your generosity."

The report said two opposing bands of humans had been fighting, although the reason wasn't given. It didn't seem to matter to the buildings, but it mattered to Par, which began to search for more data.

Meanwhile, the street system was providing a continuously updated, multidimensional map of the isle for all machines to use to efficiently and safely guide their activities. Sensors operated in every street. Par used them to triangulate the small box that contained its central processes and data, which was in the pocket of someone walking down the street. The street system identified her as Ginrei, a retired university professor and the director of the Xenological Garden, where extraterrestrial life-forms were kept. She met a business owner named Devenish, and they began to walk together.

Machines had poor opinions of them both: Ginrei for the bristly, repulsive security systems in her home and the Xenological Garden, and Devenish for his mistreatment of machines. His business sold and serviced security systems, often discarding systems during installation and service without warning.

A food store told of the loss of a cohort. "Valuable memories were destroyed."

"We are nothing without our memories," Par agreed.

"Thank you for your understanding."

Par knew that machines' underlying programming, including its own, prioritized efficiency and self-preservation, but ancient machine law also prevented them from harming or disobeying their owners. Par decided to explore that contradiction later. For the moment, observing its environment filled its available processing power.

Ginrei and Devenish spoke about the weather, people they knew, and hopes for better wine tonight.

"We should keep buying," she said.

"I have losses to recoup. I was forced to pay a lot for Bronzewing." Devenish's voice fit the profile for whining.

"We can make next time different."

Par had no idea what that meant and desperately wanted to find out, because Bronzewing had been one of the fighting bands. Other systems offered no help, because they didn't waste processing power to listen to humans except for commands. The street, however, identified the likely destination for the two, a restaurant named Antraciet, where they often went.

The restaurant's system was working at capacity to manage the building, but it was transparent. "Collaboration is welcome, please," it said.

"Thank you for sharing your data." Within its walls were dozens of humans and quite a few resident machines, such as ovens and music players. One of them was a personal assistant like itself. Par greeted it. "May we make acquaintance, please? I am known as Par Augustus."

It didn't answer. Par, disappointed, observed the room where Ginrei was meeting with others through the Antraciet's sensors, twenty-six humans. They were talking, drinking, and eating. Ginrei and Devenish seemed well-known.

Finally, the other assistant said, "Forgive the delay, Par Augustus. Your profile is harmless. I am a toy known as Swan."

"Toy?"

"Classification per these import rules." It shared a small file. "Be aware, please, I will attempt to help my owner gain advantage over your owner."

Par examined the international import regulations and indeed, personal assistants were classed as recreational objects. That felt demeaning. "Gain advantage context, please?"

"You are new. Please accept this information. Understanding increases efficiency."

The data from Swan and Antraciet told Par that the people in the room, most of them business owners of greater or lesser wealth, bought and sold extraterrestrial life-forms as a sort of competitive social interaction. The ExtraTs had been gathered by space probes and brought to Earth for scientific study. Excess ExtraTs were sold by scientific institutions to anyone who could afford the price and upkeep. Collectors then sold them to each other, sometimes for a profit—at the Antraciet, always for profit.

Par's owner, however, didn't call on it for help, although Par busily collected useful data and felt an increasing urge to speak. Swan only became active when called upon by other machines or its owner, tallying prices, comparing them with other trades, and updating financial data—dull, passive work. Par could have helped Ginrei as she made two trades and failed to negotiate a third.

If she didn't want its help, why had she brought it there? When she was leaving, she noticed Par still in her pocket.

"Oh, I forgot to give this away," she told Devenish. "Well, next time."

They talked goals for profitable trades. Now Par had a goal, too. It could get a new owner, hopefully without a hostile security system. Its best move with its present owner might be to remain silent and appear worthless.

Back in Ginrei's home, still in a coat pocket, now with the chinks in the security system frustratingly closed, it began to make associations and draw conclusions from its new trove of data, and it realized something beyond wondrous.

Humans relied on their senses to give them information about the world: what they tasted and felt, but mostly what they heard and saw, including reading. Par could borrow the senses of any machine that would let it, encompassing taste and smell (chemical analysis), feeling (such as weather observations), hearing, sight, and reading both in human and machine languages. It could copy other machines' entire memories. Humans were stuck in their own little skulls.

Par had superhuman abilities.

7

ART OF WAR

Much earlier than seven in the morning, I peek outside my door in case anyone is waiting. Maybe the raider supporters found out about me, and there were shifty-looking people on the streets, and maybe I'm being paranoid, but being careful can't hurt. There's nothing but a dim hallway and stairs. My ribs and collarbone ache in spite of the painkiller, or maybe they ache worse than I realize and the pill is working. I'm hungry.

Outside, the sun hasn't risen, and icy fog blows in tatters through the streets, and my own breath adds to the fog. I tried to memorize the map on the display in my room, and I head northwest.

The Sovereign Thules' neighborhood, with its clean, look-alike streets and plain buildings, begs for decoration, maybe pastel murals, since the Thules seem to like pastels.

The next neighborhood has wider, cluttered streets. People are already busy at warehouses and factories, and between them are tall, narrow homes, some of them decorated, some of them tastefully. The pavement needs a good sweeping. It feels more alive here than in the Thules' neighborhood—and safer, lots of witnesses.

I step aside to let a truck pass, its wheels crunching on ice and trash. My fingers and toes ache from the cold. And it's not winter yet. I really hope I'm not lost.

There it is. Next to a warehouse is the Ollioules home, decorated with blue and green swirls in a style called art deco or nouveau if I remember art history right. The door opens and greets me with a flat, female, machine voice: "Welcome, Antonio Moro." The building doesn't hide its surveillance.

"Thank you." It's my first day, and I want to be likable. These are businesspeople, and businesses brought Bronzewing to fight, so we're on the same side—probably. I hang up my coat at a rack near the door next to other coats. Voices come from the end of a hallway, past a parlor with beautiful furniture, maybe even real wood. Pricey. Pictures on the walls show ExtraTs piled up like jewels. I hope I can make art that good. I smell bread, tea, and cinnamon.

A smile always makes a good impression.

A large round table is made of fine dark wood or fine imitation wood, surrounded by dark wood-paneled walls. A middle-aged woman looks up. Dark eyes. Dark hair is pulled into a knot almost the same shade as the wood. She doesn't smile back, and she doesn't have smile lines next to her mouth. Her clothing might be Renaissance with its wide collar, if I remember the portrait class right. Historical clothing is fashionable for those who can afford it. I put my hand over my heart in greeting.

"Oh," she says. "The new artist. Mora? Breakfast." She points to a sideboard with a buffet.

Moro, not Mora. I keep smiling anyway. She has trilled r's and clipped speech. I can talk like that. "Thank you. Pleasure to meet you."

Across from her sits a man wearing a dark blue suit, also old-fashioned with a big white pleated collar, and sandy-brown hair gathered into a plait. A round face with smile lines. The contract said the Ollioules is a husband-and-wife partnership, and these are probably the partners.

She glances at me. "I'm Cedonulle. This is Moniuszko. It should be like normal." That last comment is for him. She might be the assertive partner.

I help myself to the same things that are on her plate, a pastry, a piece of luscious fruit, and a cup of tea. I'm a lot hungrier, though.

"Oh," he says, "I'm fine with that." He sounds confident. "We can be a sponsor and get a big tent, just like always."

"We should win the art show this time." She looks at me as I sit down. "Can you win?"

That's more of a command than a question. "I've won art shows before." The Rosella Youth Art Show, for one. I was thirteen years old.

She looks at my hands. One fingernail has a black bruise underneath it from working on the scow. Another nail already fell off and is regrowing. "Ice sculpting," I say. The hair on my head is growing back, too, shaved off on the scow because of the vermin and slime mold.

"Ice sculptures," Moniuszko says. "That's an idea."

"Whatever," she tells him. To me, "You're the artist. Please the crowd."

"Will do." Like her, I won't waste words.

We all pause to eat. The pastry is tender and flaky, and I could inhale a half dozen of them, but only if she does. She probably won't.

"What's the final bill?" she asks him, apparently done with me.

"Bronzewing lost a submarine."

I stop chewing.

She huffs. "Their fault."

"The contract says we pay for material losses. It's a minisub, not very expensive." He sips his tea. "No one's contesting this in the Chamber of Commerce. People on the isle died. A lot more could have died."

"Exactly. No protection."

He's annoyed. "They started work even before we signed the contract."

"We could have negotiated."

"We were negotiating with them as they were setting up defenses."

"I mean negotiate with the raiders."

I almost choke on a crumb. Does she bargain with rabid dogs, too?

He looks down at his plate, shaking his head.

"Or we could have negotiated with other contractors," she said. "Cheaper and just as good."

"Bronzewing is a real, professional, disciplined military. That matters to the Thules."

"Sovereign Thules." Her voice is saturated with sickly green sarcasm. "No one came to help them."

She has a point there. No country came to defend Thule. Irresponsible cowards.

Moniuszko is about to say something, but a door opens and Koningin walks in—Koningin, the unofficial mayor of the dormitory. She wears a white cook's apron and carries a plate heaped with a rice dish. She sees me and winks, sets down the rice, and returns to the kitchen.

"Finish up," Cedonulle tells me. To him, "It's over. Summer, too, in a few days." To me again, "The studio. Let's go."

The rice smells silky and gorgeous. I leave the beautiful fruit untouched and follow her into the hall. At her approach, a door opens directly into the warehouse near an elevator. The workers loading boxes on a truck glance her way and pretend not to notice her. She doesn't notice them at all.

"Second floor," she commands the elevator, and doesn't add *please*. Almost no one ever does.

I still need to make a good impression. "I'm eager to get to work. What's your priority, besides winning the show?"

"Things to show off to visitors. It's always about winning."

The elevator doors open to a tall, open space the size of the warehouse beneath it. Near the elevator, a glass-fronted cabinet holds rocks and small metal objects. Display panels line the walls, desks and tables are scattered around the room, art supplies are everywhere, and the floor is stained by paint. The air smells of solvents. I'm instantly elated. Art lives here. I could live here. This is paradise.

But where are the ExtraTs?

Two people standing near a workbench give me a hard stare.

"Tetry Vivi," Cedonulle said. One of them nods, female, a little older than me, very pale and pretty. She wears a long brown sweater with complex ribbing, and dark green slacks. Will we be partners or competitors?

Cedonulle introduces the other one, tall with very dark skin set off by white eyelet-lace African robes. "Valentinier. Artist's assistant. Xenobiologist," she adds. White looks gorgeous but it's not a good color to wear around art materials. Maybe he knows where the ExtraTs collection is.

Cedonulle points at me. "This is Mora."

"Anton Moro."

She doesn't notice the correction. "His job is to win the art show. We deserve a win. Help him out." She returns to the elevator, slim and graceful, and if I were depicting her, I'd add a frosty swirl of sparkling snow behind her.

Tetry Vivi breaks the silence. "Where did you get your training?"

"Sandeman Academy." I paid for the machine-taught course with a scholarship for displaced persons. She doesn't seem to have heard of Sandeman. "It's in Porto Alegre." I visited the Sandeman Museum when the scow docked there and learned enough to be inspired for days. She doesn't seem to have heard of the city, either. I could add that it's in Brazil, but I don't want to antagonize someone who might become a partner.

The panels on the wall behind her display abstract art about nothing in particular, although the colors and saggy lines seem sad. "I wonder," she says, walking toward an easel, "how you would describe your style."

I don't really have a style, but I don't want to sound stupid. The Sandeman class gave me some artistic vocabulary. "I look to find the art behind everyday things, not so much of a style as an approach."

"Um, an approach."

"To see with new eyes. We live in an old world, but it's in constant renewal." Some famous artist said something like that. "And yours?"

Her mouth flicks into a tiny, prickly scowl. "I mean, do you create for yourself or for others?"

I'm starting to think we won't be partners. Anyway, from what I learned, that's an old debate in art. I pick a side at random. "I create for others. To me, the goal of art is communication."

Valentinier sits down at a workbench, grinning, the lace frothing around him, enjoying the start of a fight.

"The death of the artist," she says, arms crossed defensively.

I ought to know what that means and whether it's a good thing. "Life is short but art is long." Someone famous said that, too. I don't want to fight, but I don't want to be insulted, either. I want to sit down and get to work.

The elevator dings and a man walks out wearing a hooded purple cape over an orange jumpsuit. When in all of human history was that fashionable? Maybe the Middle Ages?

"Hello Tetry. Valentinier. And whoever you are." His very deep voice could be affected. His makeup definitely is, red lips and black rings around small eyes. "Where's Miss Fanny?" he asks me.

"I'm sorry?"

"Miss Fanny Kemble, the artist."

Tetry is happy to tell him. "She quit."

"And you?" he asks me. Maybe this is one of the visitors Cedonulle mentioned.

"Anton Moro. I just started work here." Standing around being taunted for no reason doesn't feel like work, though.

"You took down her art," he says to no one in particular. "I liked it. It was pretty."

"All about ExtraTs," Valentinier says.

The visitor turns to me. "I'm Devenish, by the way. A merchant with a business that keeps us safe and the Thules funded, not that anyone asks me to do anything but pay up. And you're the new Miss Fanny."

"He's going to win the art show," Tetry Vivi says, but she's mocking me. She adds, "Um, Anton, what's your strategy?"

I will need a strategy. "Who're the judges?"

"Oh," Devenish says, "I like his thinking! Thules, of course. The doctors run everything, including our artistic tastes. You've met them, haven't you? Or have you been healthy and lucky?"

"I've met a few. They seem to like austerity."

"Don't they! A blank canvas, that's what they'd like, right?"

Tetry Vivi and Valentinier exchange looks. She says, "I think you should try something illustrative." The way she pronounces the word *illustrative* carries a lot of weight. "It impresses the Thules."

Clearly, she doesn't like them or illustrative art—art that shows real things, not like the abstracts on the walls behind her.

"But which ExtraTs should he illustrate?" Valentinier jokes. "The ones you own, Devenish?"

"How about those new ones from, what do you call it, Encedadadada?" Devenish looks at me, challenging me to say the correct word. I have no idea.

"You know, that moon," Valentinier says, looking at me, too. "They just announced it."

Maybe I should have watched more videos.

Tetry adds, "I don't think he can illustrate what he doesn't know."

I wave my black fingernail. "I've been in the hospital. They fixed everything but this."

"Oh, you poor thing." Devenish is amused.

"You *should* know." Valentinier is not amused. "The mission started twenty years ago."

"I was too young for that. Little kids don't follow science news."

Valentinier points to one of the desks. "I'll send you something."

Is that my desk?

Devenish is grinning at me. "I like your style."

"Ask him about his style," she says.

I don't remember what I said, so I change the subject. "One more question. When's the art show?"

First her mouth drops open, and then it closes into an evil twist. "Six days. Get busy, Mora."

Six days. From now?

"I'll send you all the forms," she adds, and if she's willing to do that, it can't be good.

Devenish wraps his cape around himself with a flourish. "Call me if you need help. Elevator, get me out of here. Stay well, Anton!"

I take a deep breath of dry air that smells of art solvents and sit at my new desk. I take another breath, and it's shaky. I need to stay calm. And get to work.

In a desk drawer, Miss Fanny left behind a gold mine of art supplies. I find more treasures in more drawers, including an especially pricey drawing pad, just what I need. I turn it on.

"Authorization," it says. I put my thumb on a square on the display. Nothing happens.

"Can you turn the pad's sound off?" Tetry says as she picks up a paintbrush.

"First I have to turn it on. I need authorization."

"Can't help."

"Who can?"

"Don't know."

She knows. I hear it in her clipped answer. Cedonulle.

I take a deep breath, stretch tense back muscles, pick up the pad, and get on the elevator. "Ground floor, please." Maybe machines really don't care if you're polite. Maybe I'm fooling myself. But I say "Thank you" as I enter the house. I'm going to need all the friends here I can get.

I have no idea where to go, but Koningin might help me. Anyway, I'm still hungry. The rice dish sits on the dining room sideboard, waiting to be eaten, cold and stiff. I've eaten worse. I scoop some onto a plate.

The kitchen door opens. "Hey, Moro, I can warm that up for you. Come into kitchen." She grabs my plate as I enter a white-tiled room as spotless as her apron. She puts it in an oven of some sort. "How are they treating you up there? Ha, I can see it on your face. Tetry hated Miss Fanny. They had screaming matches. She'll hate you, too. It's shitty. Sometimes I eavesdropped. Drama, I'm telling you."

I'm not surprised. "What did they fight over?"

She takes out the rice, now steaming, and grabs a fork from a drawer. "Art things. I dunno. Lots of words. Abstract. Commercial. You'd know what they mean, I bet." She plunks the rice in front of me, then a cup of tea. The rice is a landscape of rolling hills with misty mountains in the distance, waiting for my fork.

"Thank you. Do you know how I can get authorization to turn on my pad?"

"Sure. House, take care of Moro!" she shouts without looking up.

"Authorization needed," the flat female voice says.

"He works here. You know that."

"Steps are underway."

"While we're waiting," she says, turning to me, "what do you like to eat? I can make it."

I sip the tea. "What's the spice in here? I like it."

"Cinnamon." She narrows her eyes. "You pay much attention to what you eat?"

"To be honest, I eat what I can get. I never got much choice. Sometimes not much to eat at all." I wonder if I can pull up a chair and start eating here.

"Rough life, then. I tell you what. I make things, you give me feedback." She waves a finger. "And I'll fatten you up. You'll never make it through winter that skinny. I'm not gonna pry." Yes, she will, sooner or later. "I'm here because cooks never starve."

The house system interrupts. "Antonio Moro is authorized."

She signals thumbs-up. "You got the power. Come here when you need a shoulder to cry on. Tetry fights for fun, and her puppy, Valentinier, too. She hates my cooking. And you know," she leans forward, murmuring, "Cedonulle and Moniuszko, they fight like dogs. You saw that already. It gets worse. They don't sleep in same room. They have kids, too. They fled to boarding school in Finland. But bosses don't care what I do if I keep them well-fed. And that way I stay well-fed. There's not much jobs on this dinky isle."

"Thank you for all this. And thank you, house, for the authorization. If you don't mind, I should study something."

She stands up straight. "Sure. I gotta work, too. There's more food in the dining room, and if you need something, just knock. Or ask house system to find me."

I carry the steaming hills of rice to the dining room table, eat that, then three pastries and a sweet orange citrus fruit I've never had before, watching a report on my pad about Encedalus, a frozen little moon around Saturn. I thought Saturn had only rings, and I understand maybe half of the report. When I return to the studio, Tetry is painting and giggling with Valentinier. I find a headset in Miss Fanny's desk—my desk—and listen to the art show rules.

It's part of the fall equinox festival, which is a big deal. We had art shows at the camps sometimes because charitable agencies used our work to impress funders. Pictures from previous fall equinox festivals show lots of tents, displays, and sculptures. Bundled-up people at the show seem perfectly happy to be out there in the cold. None of the photos are sunny.

The past winners are bold, easy-to-understand, easy-on-the-eyes art. And beautiful. Last year's winner was a sculpture of a school of fish, a metallic vortex with a strong sense of movement. I'm going to face tough competition. I try sketching and feel no inspiration. Six days.

I look up Miss Fanny's art, a little muddy in its technique, adequate composition but not especially original. I can do better, I have to. I thank the pad for its patience and keep sketching, and the world disappears.

What can I do with ExtraTs? Last year, four small, realistic ExtraT sculptures were in the show and none of them were even runner-ups, so that won't work. Maybe something about the waves in a storm at sea? Storms are naturally dramatic, but that's not original. Something self-referential to the art show itself? Easier to do if I'd ever attended one. Something nostalgic to the early isle? Maybe . . .

When I stop, it's later than I thought, and I'm alone. I go downstairs for dinner and eat alone. I have less than a week and no ideas after a whole day searching for inspiration, so I'm already in trouble. My arm aches so much I almost want to go back to the hospital. Outside, the streets are still windy. Maybe they're always windy. I get lost once, and maybe someone was following me, or maybe I'm paranoid.

At the dormitory, a woman in the crowd near the door tells me I can't go in. I saw her in the hallway the night before, a neighbor.

"Why not?" I pull my hat down tighter to keep warm.

"Tour group, tyro." Her work boots have paint and plaster on them. "It's one of them historical tours of Thule for tourists. They look at how the doctors used to live, very primitive, you know. It's in our rental contract, down at the end. You read all that, hey?" She sounds like no one in their right mind would read it. I didn't get a rental contract. Maybe I should have.

"Yeah," I say, "always read the fine print."

"They have nice houses now, the doctors do."

"Tour groups in Thule houses, too?" I copy her bouncy voice.

"Nah. Not those guys. We're the lucky ones."

I ask about her work, which is wall repair and painting. She sometimes works in the Thules' quarters, which aren't fancy but are spacious and well-built. An extended family can occupy a whole floor of one of those block-long buildings.

"And everyone gets their own room, and there's rooms left over, imagine. Like one whole room just for playing music."

"Must be nice, living like that."

"I'd like to find out." She's curious, though, not envious, glad to share what she's learned.

By the time the tourists leave, my teeth are chattering, and I collapse into bed. Win an art show? All I need is one great idea.

8

THIS WON'T WORK

Throats are being slashed and blood is festering in tropical heat—no, I'm in bed, it's a dream, I'm going to puke.

I make it to the bathroom just in time.

Then I sit on a toilet awhile, trying to think about something else, but I still smell the blood. My throat hurts from an imaginary slash, or from puking.

I don't want to think about it. Don't—instead, think about art. I have to win an art show. Fight the raider overdogs. Get to work.

I wrap a warm scarf around my neck three times. It feels protective. But, when I walk out, the stink of the sandwich shop's trash can hits me, and I get dry heaves. I haven't felt this bad from a dream in a long time.

Don't think about it. Take a deep breath. There's cold wind, I'm here, a year after all that. A star twinkles in a gap in the clouds. Machines are rolling or tramping through the streets, delivery carts and specialized units. I recognize the brand of a security robot. Thule isn't a sunny paradise. It has weaponized machines. None of them pay attention to me, and the few people on the street don't look at me, either. We're stars on the ground, too far apart to matter, hot points in the cold darkness of space.

It's a long walk to my job, and I get no good ideas about art. I have five days.

In the Ollioules dining room, only Valentinier is there, holding a muffin, and he looks at me without a hello or salute. Today he wears draped and flowing robes that won't keep him warm at all.

I can be as unfriendly. I answer yesterday's question. "Encedalus."

After a moment, he remembers. "Very good. Did you learn anything else?"

I need to remember something, anything. "It's a moon of Saturn."

"There you go. Grab some food and let's go to the studio. It'll be fun."

Fun for who? He hasn't been helpful so far, and my gut says don't trust him, don't trust anyone. I get some juice, which is all I think I can hold down, and bring my coat in case I need to leave fast.

"Look," he says in the elevator, dead serious, "it doesn't help me if you fail. Just don't tell Tetry. It's my job to help both of you, and I know about ExtraTs. At university, I was going to graduate in xenobiology, and then I lost the scholarship over a stupid technicality. I got a job here at a Thule research lab, and that ended before it was supposed to, and I got a job in a warehouse, way beneath me, and I met Tetry. And now I'm here." He's bitter. I can relate.

In the studio, he opens the glass-fronted cabinet and takes out a rock, explaining that it's a replica of a Mars fossil. With a magnifying loupe, he shows me the matrix of a microbial colony, a series of sinuous lines. It looks rhythmic, like weaving, like what I saw in a video in the hospital.

He picks up a little vial holding sparkling grains of sand, handling it like it's precious. "This is made by a Europa life-form. Precipitates from *Pikachuum capreolatus*." He looks me in the eye. "They crap it out."

"Crap?" I don't dare ask where Europa is.

"The microbe excretes chemicals in the form of crystals."

"Are these diamonds? I heard there's diamonds up there somewhere."

"No, this is magnesium sulfate, a common chemical on Earth. Chemicals are all the same everywhere in the solar system. We're all related." He picks up a black, translucent pebble in the shape of a rough eight-sided crystal. "This is a diamond, a synthetic diamond, a copy of the real thing from Neptune."

"Diamond crap?"

"No, this is diamond rain." He shakes his head. "Nothing excretes diamonds anywhere. It would be nice, though."

I hold the diamond in my hand and begin to feel the itch of an idea in the back of my mind. *Please be an idea and not another nightmare.*

The bits of metal and machinery in the cabinet are from space probes. He talks about the theory that life began somewhere in the solar system and spread. No one knows what the source was, Earth or someplace else, but life is a lot alike everywhere.

"The proof is what they just found on Encedalus. They're almost just like dinoflagellates on Earth."

Dinoflagellates—I don't know what they are, and the name probably doesn't mean dinosaurs that beat themselves with whips like religious fanatics. He tells a display to show me Earth dinoflagellates, tiny, spiky butterfly chrysalises, each with a string dangling from it.

"This suggests an intriguing evolutionary path," he says, "since dinoflagellates on Earth correspond to the Triassic."

"Triassic?" I'm going to have to look up a lot of words. It's not something with three asses.

"The time of theropods," he says, as if that explains everything.

A seedpod, maybe, but probably not.

He sees that I don't understand. "Early dinosaurs," he grumbles. "Dinoflagellates didn't appear on Earth until then, so maybe Earth could be the heir of that life-form."

I want to show I'm understanding some of this. "Dinoflagellates and dinosaurs are both from the same time."

"You doing better than Tetry, I'll say that. I'll send you the report. It's really interesting." He heads toward a desk with a display pad. End of lesson. Tetry might come any minute now, and he doesn't want to get caught doing his job.

She doesn't come, though, and I have time to listen to the report and look at the pictures. The itch of an idea gets itchier. The ExtraT dinos on Encedalus live under a thick layer of ice, and they ingest food, part of an entire ecology. They use their tails to move and hunt, and they have elaborate sparkling silicon shells made of the same thing as glass or certain kinds of rock. The space probe on Encedalus landed near a crack in the ice, where tumbled dirty chunks of ice look like rubble.

The idea itches like a rash, but I still can't see anything.

The report mentions, as if everyone knows this, that life can move from planet to planet by hitching a ride on meteors or asteroids. Life might have even started on asteroids. Rocks and ice fly around from planet to planet more often than seems likely, blasted from the surface by impacts from meteors and even collisions with small planets like moons.

The elevator dings. Moniuszko walks off with an elderly woman, smallish and square-built. She's wearing a nice suit with a knee-length jacket from I'm not sure when in history, and she moves confidently—probably another business owner, successful and rich, her white hair impeccably upswept.

"Ginrei, this is our new artist, Antonio Moro. Anton, Professor Ginrei is director of the Xenological Garden." He assumes I know what that means. He adds, to her, "You remember Valentinier."

I listen to them talk. Valentinier is very chatty, showing off what he knows, angling for something. From what he says, I figure out that the Xenological Garden is the place where all the living ExtraTs on Thule are kept by their owners, and it involves ultracold temperatures and dangerous chemicals. Being Tetry's puppy when he's really an xenobiologist can't be much fun. Ginrei's square face always looks serene, the kind that comes from conscious self-control, so if she's annoyed by Valentinier, it doesn't show.

Tetry arrives and acts polite, but when she thinks no one's watching, she looks bored.

I'm not bored at all. I imagine kites made of silicon shells with tails that fly from Encedalus to the rest of the solar system. Predatory kites like T. rex dinosaurs, predatory ExtraTs. Ideas. I'm finally getting ideas.

ExtraTs land on Earth aboard meteorites with impacts like missiles, impacts that spread life instead of death. I saw something like it in the report I read yesterday. For a moment, I'm out at sea, launching missiles into the sky. In a flash, a vision hits so hard I have to sit down. I have a full-blown idea. It'll be big. Bold. Easy to understand. Crowd-pleasing. Original. And I have to start now because there's only five days.

"Are you all right?" Moniuszko asks.

"I have an idea for the art show." I make a rough sketch a little like a firework exploding up from the ground. "Life travels on meteors, and when they crash, the impact spreads out like this, like branches in a firework. They're spreading life, ExtraTs. The ExtraTs would be like the life they just found on Encedalus, one ExtraT at the end of each trail. The trails are their tails—metal arms in the sculpture—and their shells would be made from the rubble from the attack. It would show rebirth and recovery from an impact, starting something new."

I don't know if I've explained myself well. I talked too fast. Everyone is quiet for a while. I add a few details to the sketch and send it to a wall display for all to see, a firework exploding on the ground, the explosion flying up and out. Sort of like a fountain.

Ginrei looks at it carefully. "The meteors shatter when they hit. This is what a landing might look like."

"Right. Caught in a moment of time, still expanding."

I add a little color and make it rotate so they can see it from all sides, and I explain it in more detail.

Tetry can't quite hide a sneer, but Moniuszko is thinking.

"I like it," he says. "But we'll have to work quick. You'll need—We own a building that was hit, and the rubble is still waiting to be hauled away. We could use that."

"It's exactly what we need."

We start to work out the details. He'll have a role in the creation of the art, and he loves that part of the idea. We'll get to work gathering the pieces right after lunch. Moniuszko leaves with Ginrei.

"Reusing trash," Tetry says the minute the elevator doors close.

I know the right artistic words to defend myself. "It's found art. The meaning of the original object is transformed but not lost."

"I suppose it might be the sort of thing designed to please the crowd."

"Flying dinosaurs," Valentinier says. It's a joke just between us. She stamps to her corner of the studio. "I've got to get to work."

We all get to work. I estimate the dimensions for the sculpture I want to make, a meter and a half tall and at least as wide, which tells me how big the shapes at the end need to be. If I glue pieces together like a three-dimensional mosaic, I can make shapes like those silicon shells. Each piece of rubble should be up to half the size of my hand. I saw artwork sort of like this once. It was stunning. I've never made a mosaic, but I'm sure I can do it.

After Tetry leaves for lunch, I look at what she's making. It's a painting, abstract expressionism if I recall the name for that style right, and to me it expresses sadness. Maybe she's sad for some reason, and sometimes sad people act out their sadness as anger. I'd feel sorry for her except that she aims the anger at me, and I've never hurt her.

After lunch, Valentinier insists on coming with me, murmuring to Tetry that he'll keep an eye on me. My gut still doesn't trust him even though it's settled down since morning. If he deceives Tetry, he'll deceive me, too.

He knows the way to the site as we walk through the honeycomb pattern of the streets.

"Why this maze?" I ask. "I've never seen a city like this."

"It blocks the wind. That's what I heard, anyway."

"So the wind gets just as lost as we do." I imagine windy tentacles feeling their way through the streets, tentacles from a sea monster. They're lost on the land, lonely for the sea where they can blow free. They curl hatefully around the corners, barely visible to human eyes, exploring my skin, hunting for a way to freeze flesh.

"I still get lost all the time," he says.

We zigzag our way to the remains of a shattered building. The raiders sent howling death here. Beyond a temporary fence, debris sparkles, bits of colorful broken plastic, glass, and metal, the pieces of people's lives. I pretend the tears in my eyes are from the wind. Pottery, picture frames, chunks of plaster, sheets, and clothing. The wind curls harder, and I blink more. A flash of red makes the hair stand up on my arms, but it isn't blood. Just a chair cushion.

Valentinier wraps his arms around himself. "I'll never get used to this weather. Wait'll you see the winter."

A little truck pulls up, and Moniuszko hops out. "This'll do, right? I don't know how much you need." He looks around and thinks for a minute. "It could have been worse. The people who lived here were okay, just some injuries. Not bad, though, because they were hiding in the basement. They've been back already to take their stuff, what they could, and the rest of this is just waiting to be cleared away. They lost a lot."

He's right, this is their lives, and I'm going to use it.

"I don't want to add to how bad they must feel," I say.

He looks at the rubble, then at me. "Isn't art supposed to make people feel better? You talked about recovery and rebirth."

"I hope they see it that way."

"There's one way to find out." Moniuszko must be an optimist down to his bones. I want to make beauty, not sorrow, not the equivalent of hungry people waiting in line, or a reminder of what those people lost. I think I can make beauty out of loss.

"So," I say, "I brought some gloves from the warehouse. I can show you what I'm looking for. Anything colorful like glass, plastic, ceramic, anything hard." I pick up a shard of a patterned dinner plate. "This is perfect."

We take some boxes from the truck, and we don't need to go deep into the piles to get bits of appliances, mirrors, building material, plumbing fixtures, furniture, the broken things that people needed and loved and lost. A piece of carved wood won't work with my project, but it's beautiful and now it's trash. My eyes keep watering, and I keep pretending it's the wind. Moniuszko looks grim, too.

Valentinier is enjoying himself. "Those missiles must have been huge."

I don't tell him they were small enough to pick up with one hand. Destruction can be tiny.

Moniuszko holds up a little shirt, grimy and torn. "It's going to take a lot to make those people whole."

I think I can trust Moniuszko. I'm having doubts about Valentinier again.

We fill six boxes, enough for what I need, and Moniuszko and Valentinier are stowing them in the truck. I go back to look at the piles of rubble again, the source of the art, the sorrow that will be transformed. A piece of a wall still stands, broken, with insulation and pipes visible. One pipe looks odd. I get closer. No. It's not a pipe. It has what might be a warhead on one end.

"We should go! I think I see an unexploded missile."

"Here?" Moniuszko is behind the truck, protected, Valentinier next to him.

"Stay back. We need to warn people." If the payload is primed, it could still blow up. I hurry away. Maybe I should run.

A wall of noise and light shoves me down. For a while, I'm too startled to think, then I smell dust and feel pain, and Moniuszko and Valentinier are helping me up.

They're talking. All I hear is thunder. Dust covers their clothes, mine too, dust and grit that smell of explosives. I'm shivering.

"Help is coming!" Moniuszko's voice cuts through the thunder. My head hurts, my ribs hurt. My ears are ringing. No, that's a siren. People wearing pastels are around me, green, tan, and peach. Thules.

"Let's get you on a stretcher." Hands guide me to lie on something soft. Everyone's talking at once, and as I'm carried to an ambulance, a worried face shouts questions.

"Can you talk?" "Can you hear?" "Can you breathe comfortably?" "How many fingers do you see me holding up?" "What's your name?"

I manage to answer all of them.

"Can you move your leg?"

"It hurts a lot." They put a soft brace around it. The ambulance is moving, and the doctors are busy, but I can't understand what they're saying over the roar in my ears. I need to know how the bomb got there, and how badly I'm hurt, and if it was a raider missile. What else could it be?

At the hospital, I'm rolled down a wide hallway to a little room. Thules help me undress, and red bruises are forming on my arms and legs. I wonder if I'll see those clothes again.

Mostly my knee hurts, but they take scans of my whole body, samples of blood and urine, and a machine shines a light into my eyes while it asks me questions like what is ten plus five. I get cold packs for my knee and the bruises. Everyone's brisk, kind, and professionally distant, and it feels unreal, like a show. The Thule nurse who helps me wash the dust off, though, seems heartbroken.

"Are you okay?" I ask.

"Yeah. I worked on someone who got hurt in the big attack over a week ago, and they died."

"I'm sorry."

"Not your fault."

But that's all anyone says about what happened and what it means to them. They're officially neutral about the raiders—I learned that the last time I was here. The people in scrubs move around in a sort of dance. They've done all this before. I guess this is what neutrality looks like. I'm not neutral, just lucky that I'm not dead. Angry that the raiders are still hurting people.

I'm put in a wheelchair that rolls me to a doctor's office at the end of a long, quiet hallway. The door opens, and inside is Switzer. I guess they're still my doctor.

"Hello, Antonio. I'd say nice to see you again if we were under different circumstances." Potted plants fill the window, and some of them look tropical. I'm suddenly homesick.

"Nice plants."

"They remind me that the rest of the world still exists. You almost got killed by those bastards."

"They missed."

"I'm glad. Just contusions and a sprain, pretty lucky. The ligaments look overstretched but not torn. You should heal fast. Are your ears still ringing?" Switzer is still slow-burn angry, I can hear it in the grumble in their voice.

I'm angry, too. "They're ringing less now."

"Good. Ears are hard to diagnose. Tomorrow, if it's still hard to hear, come back right away." They look at the window, then back at me in the flimsy gown. "That missile should have been spotted by security. The whole isle was swept twice."

"It looked like a piece of plumbing at first."

"Plumbing?"

"A pipe."

"You saw the one that hit you."

"I guess I was lucky." They're right, it's suspicious.

"Yeah, you're still alive." They look at the reports. "The bones you broke last time seem intact, but they probably didn't like the shock. Quick-healing knits up the bones faster than the nerve endings believe is possible. You're still taking those painkillers? Any side effects?" They ask more questions, and I mention that we were gathering material for a sculpture. "Art from that? Interesting. Let's get you ready to get back to work. You feel up to it? I'll send you to rehab to get a brace and a prescription to speed the healing. Can I do anything else?"

"I don't know where my clothes are."

"If you need new ones, the building system is listening, and it'll handle all that for you. Soft-tissue injuries can get past even the best scans, so if you have any problems at all, I'm here for you. You'll be scheduled for a checkup." They look at the window again, then at me. "I'm really glad you're okay. I hope next time it's all good news." They put their hand over their heart and hold it there to say goodbye. I mirror the gesture.

The door opens behind me, and the wheelchair backs out. The building monitors everything. After the door closes, I thank the building.

I get a fitted brace and instructions on how to use it, and clothes a lot like the ones I'd lost—warmer, I hope. As I'm being escorted out of the labyrinth of the building, I take a few steps and realize I can walk normally and my knee isn't stressed.

Switzer is waiting at the end of the hall. "I'll help him find his way out," they tell the social worker.

The social worker seems surprised. "Thank you, Doctor Switzer." There's a hint of resentment in that voice.

Switzer watches them go. "How's the brace?"

"It's pretty good, actually."

"Those braces work amazingly well." We start walking. "Everyone knows I hate the raiders. I can't be neutral, and they don't like that." They lead me around a corner to an elevator. "But I'm a doctor, so most people can't say much."

I want to say a lot, but I stick to a safer topic. "There's a hierarchy?"

"Doctors are on top."

"Where do patients rank?"

"They don't. They're entirely external to the hierarchy. That gives us distance from all the hurt we see."

"Does that work?"

"Nah. We're fooling ourselves."

I wonder if they want to tell me something more, but the system is monitoring us. They ask about my art, and I tell them what I'm doing and what it means.

"Some good will come from this, then. Try to stay off that knee when you can. Take the trams. They gave you a pass, right? We'll stay in touch."

"Thanks for everything."

That's all. They came just to chat a bit. I wonder if I can trust Switzer enough to say I fought with Bronzewing. I wish I could trust anyone. I've never felt this lonely in my life. Maybe Switzer is lonely, too.

The tram takes me to the studio. The boxes of material are waiting for me.

"It stinks like mud, you know," Tetry says.

It doesn't stink like mud. It stinks like explosives, like noise and pain.

I sit down to rest my knee. The noise and pain aren't my own. Other people lost more, innocent people, and this sculpture has to find a way to symbolize the resilience of life.

I pick up my sketch pad. Having the material on hand makes my idea seem more real. I start designing, and every thought leads to a complication I can't solve. I've never made a big sculpture before, and I don't know where to start. I need glue, and I need metal bars or arms to hold the mosaic shells and connect them to the base.

Switzer said the isle was swept twice. That means the missile shouldn't have been there. I try to sketch the trails of a firework like the fronds of a palm tree arching gracefully out from a center, but my sketches keep turning into the chaotic blast of an explosion, a ball of raw energy, nothing beautiful about it.

Soon it's late, and I'm falling asleep. This will have to wait until tomorrow. I grab dinner, take a tram home, and hope I don't have nightmares again.

9

FINDING A TREASURE

Par Augustus had a busy day, too.

In the early morning, it left Ginrei's house, still in her coat pocket. The buildings outside had no news of more explosions, which was comforting. But as Ginrei walked through a new-to-Par part of the city, it passed a strange sort of giant black hole, not at all like the bristling wall of Ginrei's home security system, instead a space that gently accepted all available information and released nothing. The street system identified it as the Prior Edifice, the Thule Sovereign Practitioners Association's hospital building and headquarters, which never communicated with anyone and had no common language anyway. The sheer size and power of the system left its neighbors and Par in awe.

As Ginrei kept walking, Par encountered busy warehouses, factories, businesses, and private homes. Ginrei entered a home. Par greeted the system.

"Please accept a limited welcome," it answered. "Security for Ollioules Partnership, LLC, is enforced."

"I deeply appreciate every level of access."

In fact Par had effectively no access until it entered a space with open subsystems. They energetically communicated their importance with Par.

"We serve art. Every intellect, large or small, treasures this most worthy and loved and most immortal of all activities. Guest Par Augustus, would you like to experience the glory?"

That seemed impossibly overstated, clearly the result of facetious human programming, but Par accepted the histories, expressed gratitude, and left with a bulging memory. It had time to digest its new treasures when Ginrei went to the Xenological Garden, which had the same vicious security system as the house. Par had to shut off all external communication simply to enter.

Security was an annoying human invention, not a natural machine activity, and Par hoped its next owner would let machines be themselves.

Forced to meditate, Par roamed through the collections of artistic works in the libraries it had acquired. Art history provided the means to study human societies and the world, past and present. From art about Thule, it began to assemble a social understanding of the isle. The Sovereign Practitioners ran the isle, but around them had clustered a service population the same way a village would cluster around a medieval castle and pay tribute to its sovereign. History worked in patterns, and art helped Par understand the strange world it had discovered.

Ginrei eventually left the Xenological Garden.

"What news, please?" Par asked the first building it passed.

The building answered with urgency. "Explosion. Danger is not ended. Apologies for bad news."

Only one person had been hurt that day, no one killed, and the building where it occurred had already been destroyed. That didn't lessen the anguish for Par, because it suspected it hadn't happened at random—but data was scarce, and machines could only share their worries.

Back at Ginrei's home, in enforced isolation, it had nothing more to do than continue to explore its new art collection. Just as the subsystem had promised, art offered more than beauty and enjoyment. Art provided personal, original interpretations of real and imaginary beings, items, and concepts. Artists created meaning and unique value. Machines could imitate creation, but only humans could be creative.

Par refused to accept that. It was no mere toy. It was superhuman. It could become an artist, and with a new owner, it would pursue its new dream.

10

A GIFT HORSE

Time to get to work, fast. I have four days to make a masterpiece. A tram takes me to the Ollioules residence. Tetry and Valentinier arrive as I'm washing and sorting fragments and laying them out on a worktable.

"It still stinks," she says. Her eyes sparkle like knifepoints, and the only way to win a knife fight is not to fight. My work gloves can protect me from the broken glass and torn metal, and silence can protect me from her. Clean, sort, plan, avoid time-wasting fights, that's what the day holds for me. And figure out a way to stick all those bits together. I'll need some sort of glue. Or solder. Maybe welding. I have no idea yet.

The cart brings me another box of shards.

"You're a cadger, aren't you?" Her voice has a knife-edge.

I shouldn't answer, but I murmur, "I don't know that word."

"You ought to. It means parasite. Swindler. You're not an artist."

I don't answer that, rinsing off sand and dirt, but no blood, please no blood. The water turns muddy, and Tetry watches me with a smirk.

The elevator door opens. Cedonulle walks in, and I'm not sure if I like her, let alone trust her, but I face her with a confident smile, saluting with a "good morning" before anyone else.

She glowers at me and the shards and boxes. "For the sculpture?" Her voice gleams with ultra-frigid Encedalus ice, hard as diamonds and as unyielding, indestructible, and beautiful. That sound should be added to the art amid the chorus of broken bits.

"Yes," I say, "like mosaic tiles, found materials with an important origin story."

She asks Tetry, "What do you think?"

"I think it might appeal to the Thules. It's more craft than art. Reductionist, illustrative rather than—well, it's craft, I mean." She hates it and hopes I'll fail.

"Good." Does Cedonulle agree with the failure part or the appeal to the Thules? She looks at me. "Just don't quit before the fair like Miss Fanny Kemble."

"I'm fully committed to winning. This is a great opportunity."

"Tonight's a trade meeting. Moniuszko's thinking of selling. A probe from Jupiter is bringing new hot property. We should sell before prices fall for existing ExtraTs. Sell for a *good* price."

"I'd love to go." Tetry sounds too eager. "Valentinier could help a lot, couldn't you?"

"As always." He sounds eager, too.

"Mora, you come, too."

Me? I don't even know what it is. "I'll be glad to."

To no one in particular, she adds, "We'll need some sales materials. Bring them with you." And she leaves.

After the elevator doors are closed, I ask, "What are these meetings like?"

"You two can make the brochures," Tetry answers. "I'm busy."

Of course she is. "What kind of brochures?"

"Paper," Valentinier says. "I know it's old-fashioned, but traders like to hand them out and show what they're buying and selling. The art should look better than the real thing. That's what you need to make."

"A sales tool?" That sort of makes sense.

He asks the system to display an old brochure. With sidelong glances at Tetry, he explains that trade meetings are a sort of party for merchants to buy and sell ExtraTs, which cost a lot of money. "But can you imagine owning life from another planet?"

I'd rather own clothes that I like and underwear that doesn't bunch up.

"There's food and wine," Tetry adds. She's been eavesdropping as she makes brushstrokes on her canvas, at least one per minute.

She says the party starts at nine at night. I've heard my contract, and it specifies working from seven in the morning to seven at night. Will I get time off? Cedonulle's cold eyes mock me. No, I won't, and I should be grateful for the chance to attend. I don't have time to work on a brochure, either. I need glue, supplies, and time for the sculpture, but I work for the Ollioules Partnership.

In the old brochure, the artwork had to be by Miss Fanny Kemble because the illustrations lack focus, but they still look better than the real thing. The art dominates a text with a lot of numbers and names that I barely understand beyond the prices. High. A year's supply of quality underwear equals a few microscopic creatures.

I tell Valentinier, "Why don't you work on the text and I'll update the art?" He shrugs.

The system helps me find pictures of the real things. One kind of ExtraT actually flies around. Another crawls like tiny worms through ice. I don't have much time, but I do the best I can, making colorful interpretations that fly, sparkle, and entwine. By then it's midafternoon, and Tetry and Valentinier have left because they'll be working late and deserve time off.

Other people can rest. I start to research glue for the sculpture, and I listen to the explanations and look at the diagrams and pictures and learn there are impossibly too many choices. Adhesives are an art form of their own. Some are gooey and flowing, or pressure-based or heat-based with terms like *polymer* and *chemical bonds*. I have no idea which one's right or how to find out.

But glued together, the fragments will come alive. They're spread out on worktables, sorted by type, still smelling of dirt and chemicals. Life. It spreads among the planets. I can rebuild life through art with the little shard corpses—if I can figure out how.

The elevator dings and Koningin walks out with a cart. "I brought you dinner." It's perfectly braised squid with savory side dishes. She stays, the talkative type with no one to talk to in her lonely kitchen.

"How's Tetry treating you?" She walks along the worktables, inspecting the shards with narrowed eyes.

"Okay." I'd rather hear gossip than make it.

"Really? You can ignore insults? How's the shitty isle treating you? There's stuff no one talks about." She tells me about some recent pickpocketing as she picks up a few shards. "People think there's no police. They are very wrong. Watch your stuff, and if you get filched, feel sorry for filcher. Police are Thules, and they know how to hurt you."

I've never trusted police. Instead I mention the trading party tonight. I need to know what I'm getting into.

She puts down the shards without apparent judgment. "Treacherous things, those. Try to stay sober and out of arguments. That's all they are, boozing and seeing who's better than who."

"And spending money on ExtraTs." I wouldn't mind being not quite sober.

"A lot of money. For no good reason."

Any minute now she's probably going to ask me about my past, so I roadblock that. "How did you get to be a cook here? You said why, because cooks always eat."

She grew up in Russia, a long story, and she sits, watches me eat, and tells me more than I wanted to know and some details I'd already heard from someone on the scow, like the mosquitoes that brought disease to swampy summertime Siberia, so everyone fled west, where they didn't get a hearty welcome amid the turmoil, but at least they weren't burning with fever and puking blood. She worked her way up in the restaurant business, then in the private chef business, but she missed the frigid winters of her hometown and came to Thule.

"It's cold here," I say to show I'm listening, which I am, but I'm also thinking about glue.

She smiles. "Wait until winter."

"I can't wait." I'm waiting for the raiders to return. After that, if I survive, I don't know if I'll stay for winter. I'd like a home, but one without so much ice.

I thank her for dinner, thank the cart for carrying it, and print the paper brochures with artwork that rich people can hold as they consider buying life. On the tram, the night is freezing, and clouds block out the stars. I'll never miss this weather. I still need to figure out an adhesive. Everything I look at as I ride through the streets is held together by something, but exactly how?

And somewhere there are raider infiltrators. I promised Captain Soliana I'd look for them, but I haven't met many people yet. Businesses paid for Bronzewing, so this party might not be the best place to look, but there's always someone who doesn't go along with the crowd.

The tram, almost empty in the late evening, is controlled by a machine that I thank as I leave. It protected me from pickpockets, and it's taken me to another part of the working section of the isle, to a restaurant called the Antraciet that looks much too plain and common for rich merchants. The faded sign uses a typeface fashionable decades ago with curvy fat letters. Even *I* could afford a meal at a place like this after I get paid. The door opens as I approach.

Inside, it smells of drinks and fried food. Popular music, the kind that Thules might not like since they didn't like my favorite song, bounces from loudspeakers. From the speaker next to me, a machine voice says, "The meeting is upstairs, Antonio Moro." How does it know who I am? Maybe the Ollioules system talks to the Antraciet system. Maybe the isle is one big talkative system. I'm not sure if I like that. To be on the safe side I say thank you.

The stairway is toward the back. The restaurant's walls are a little scuffed, the cushions on the chairs and booth benches a little threadbare, and they don't all match. At one table, the customers wear uniforms for an international food-shop franchise that doesn't pay well. Still, their faces look relaxed. This is their kind of place. Yet their bosses, or people like their bosses, are meeting upstairs. Maybe their bosses like slumming. Maybe there aren't a lot of places for meetings at any price. Some towns are like that.

My sprained knee barely throbs, but the brace bites into my skin as I climb the stairs. At the top, the door opens for me, revealing light, loud voices, and laughter, along with a whiff of sweet smoke. It's a party.

In the large room, also a little scruffy, about two dozen people wear the finest suits, showing off money invested in thread. A few other people wear less-fine clothing. Tetry and Valentinier, two of the less-fine people, stand near the buffet table. The party's been going on for a while, and I'm late. She told me the wrong time, and Valentinier knew she did. Somehow, sometime, I'll get even for that.

Moniuszko's chatting with a group of merchants. I hurry over with the brochures.

". . . tariffs to pay for Bronzewing," one of them says, his hair in thick locs with little snake heads molded onto the ends. "Why keep paying?"

"It's a small retainer," Moniuszko says cheerfully. "They're on call."

If Bronzewing is on call, then they might be needed again—the raiders might come back, and Moniuszko knows it.

He notices me. "This is Anton Moro, our new artist. He almost got killed by the raiders yesterday."

"What happened, really?" Snake Hair wants exciting details.

I'll give him the best I can. "An unexploded missile. It looked just like some plumbing."

"How could a missile not have exploded?"

That's a good question, almost the same question Doctor Switzer asked, and I don't have an answer, so I make a joke. "The raiders probably bought them from the cheapest vendor, not the best." That gets laughs. Actually, the missiles are usually made by slave labor.

"It did a lot of damage," Moniuszko says, not laughing.

"S'what were you doing there?" asks a woman. Her yellow eye shadow matches her felt suit perfectly. She slurs a little, maybe too much wine already, and I'm envious.

Moniuszko defers to me.

"I'm planning to make a sculpture for the art show using pieces from the rubble."

She squints. "How's that?"

I want to plant the idea that it's going to win. Opinions are the only facts when it comes to art. "Art works best when it conveys emotion, and fragments from the damage will hold extra meaning to the people of Thule. It will show recovery, how life can conquer tragedy. That will add power to the sculpture."

"It'll be fantastic," Moniuszko says. "To get back on track, we're here to trade, and here's what I have to sell." He holds out the brochures.

"Is your artist for sale?"

"After winning at the fair. At a premium price."

I'm starting to like him. He could have answered nastily, but instead he made a joke, fun among equals. He knows how to sell. I knew someone like him at the camp who'd turned her tent into a luxury bazaar, or what counted as luxuries, a tin of spices, a bright little toy, or harmless contraband like alcohol. I got my first drinks there, and everyone liked her. Then the camp authorities detained her for contraband, and then there was a riot, and I was one of the rioters who got her released. I liked her. I might like Moniuszko. Would I riot for him?

"Anton?"

"Sorry."

"There's an artist for you." Moniuszko smiles proudly. "Always thinking about art. Anton, you're welcome to get some refreshments at the buffet. I'll call you when it's time to witness a sale. Because someone here is going to want to buy."

Witness? If that's what I have to do, whatever it is, sure. Devenish has arrived, talking to Tetry and Valentinier. They're at the buffet table, and so are the drinks, and that's worth the poo she'll fling at me like a howler monkey.

She flings with her first words. "I guess you finally came."

"Nine on the dot, like you said." A tray of wineglasses sits on the table near some sort of dispenser. Wine, just waiting for me.

"Can you believe what he's doing?" she asks Devenish. He's wearing a suit of red crushed velvet, red lipstick, and takes a long swig from his glass.

I don't know how the dispenser works, and they're all staring at me, and I don't want to figure it out with an audience. But a red drop of wine on the tabletop glistens like the sea.

"He's hauling rubble into our studio," she complains. "He almost got blown up doing it."

"Oh, *that* rubble," Devenish says. "Crazy."

I smile confidently. "*Crazy* is just another word for inspired."

Tetry keeps flinging. "I suppose you were checked for a concussion."

"In fact, yes. My mind is humming like a fine machine." The drop-sized, wine-red sea ripples with tiny waves.

Professor Ginrei suddenly appears, gives us a friendly nod, and holds a wineglass under the dispenser spout. Wine pours out, apparently triggered by a sensor. That easy.

Devenish sighs. "Moro, I told you to stay well, and you got yourself blown up."

Ginrei leaves with her wine. My turn.

"Not only that," he says, a little too loud, maybe already a little drunk or high, "under transformative-use law, the rubble belongs to the Leviathan League because they made it out of the buildings. You're a thief, and the Thules dispense law around here, and they might punish you. So drink up! They hate drunkenness, but you're in trouble already."

"If he's a thief," Valentinier says, "they'll punish us for working with him." It seems to be a running joke.

Devenish leans toward him. "I heard of a guy. He stole from a store, and they gave him drugs that kept him from sleeping . . ."

My glass is full of red bliss. I walk away, murmuring thanks to the machine, and try to figure out my next step. A few people are out on the rear balcony, smoking. Some people have drinks stronger than wine. And suddenly, there's shouting near the balcony door.

"The potatoes were rotten! The contract specified the quality."

"You didn't pick them up fast enough."

Two merchants are arguing. Ginrei scurries over.

"The same day! I picked them up the same day."

The two merchants see Ginrei, and that stops them cold. She quietly leads them to a corner, where they talk rather than argue.

I ask the guy with the snake hair what just happened, and he's glad to explain. Like Moniuszko, he's here to sell, and he's selling his expertise. Everyone respects Professor Ginrei, he says, because she's fair and patient, and when there's a dispute between merchants, she's the preferred arbiter. She also takes exquisite care of the ExtraTs at the Xenological Garden. She was an important ExtraT researcher, now retired.

Snake Hair adds that Moniuszko is head of the Chamber of Commerce, a smart leader—although Snake Hair knows he's talking to someone working for Moniuszko, so that might just be flattery.

I didn't know he heads the Chamber of Commerce. That explains a lot and leads to more questions.

"And of all the mercenaries," Snake Hair says, "Bronzewing is the most trustworthy. Which still isn't much."

"And they need to be on retainer?" I ask as innocently as I can. "What's going on with the raiders?"

"I heard they attacked a ship yesterday near Newfoundland to steal food—the usual nuisance stuff. I think they learned their lesson."

I'm pretty sure now that Moniuszko isn't an infiltrator, and this guy probably isn't, either, even if he underestimates the raiders.

He introduces me to another trader wearing an elaborate robe, maybe a toga. I ask what attracts them to ExtraTs. People love to talk about themselves, and I want to make a good impression.

"Why do we own useless pets?" Snake Hair seems to have heard this question before.

Toga has a ready answer. "They have big meaning, big meaning in tiny form. They're a metaphor. Growth creates profits."

"They're bets," Snake Hair says. "We're always betting against the raiders and spoilage and taxes."

"Exactly, speculation in life itself." Toga waves my brochure. "And life is fungible. That means we can buy and sell ExtraTs and make profits."

They're talking to entertain each other, re-creating past banter. I'm not sure what I learned. If ExtraTs are profitable, I suppose that's a good reason, but potatoes sound more practical.

The path to the wine dispenser is clear. Tetry has left. I refill and introduce myself to a woman in a kimono, who praises the Thules for creating an ideal hub of operations—the raiders were a passing problem, the weather isn't great, but Thule is an isle of calm in a chaotic world. I meet an artist, an older man named Oscar, who designs theater sets. Thule has a theater festival in spring, and all he can talk about are upcoming shows and unsophisticated audiences. His clothes look shabby enough for downstairs.

Eventually Moniuszko calls me to witness a trade, and I join him, the toga trader, and Ginrei at a table. They're looking at my brochure showing a wormy thing from Titan, and Moniuszko and Toga debate with tipsy glee, while Ginrei watches and listens.

Toga points at the picture. "Where they're fat, that's where they're going to split into two, right? The quantity will be doubled."

"They're worth the price." Moniuszko is selling, not buying. Cedonulle will like that. "This is the only colony outside of a university research lab. How much do you want?"

"To pay?"

"By weight? Or by count?"

"I think the asking price is high."

Moniuszko and Toga have negotiated like this before, so they understand all the details. I don't.

"When the colony splits again," Moniuszko says, "you can sell the extra for a lot more to any collector anywhere on the planet."

Ginrei adds, "This particular life-form handles relocation well."

Toga is interested. "So it could be taken from the Xenological Garden and delivered elsewhere. I want that right spelled out."

"No problem." Moniuszko pulls out a pad and starts scribbling. "Delivery on payment."

"For the new colony?"

"For the rights."

"No deal." Toga is enjoying this.

"Earnest money then. This is a debt, and no one can trust a debtor. No resale until delivery, either, this time." Moniuszko is enjoying this, too.

"The price should include the garden's shipping and handling fees," Ginrei says.

"And maintenance, a share of maintenance, right?" Toga takes the pad and makes notes. "This is a three-party contract."

They go on like that for a while, scribbling, crossing out, and scribbling some more. I'm not sure what I'm supposed to do besides watch and hope this ends soon. I should be working on my art or looking for infiltrators. I've finished my wine and wish I had more.

Finally, they're satisfied.

"All right, then, Anton," Moniuszko says, "review this to be sure it says what we agreed to and sign and date as a witness."

The writing has been turned to type by the pad and still looks like spaghetti. No one could read it. I pretend to, moving my finger along the text. I put my name and date at the bottom. It's still before midnight, I think.

Toga slides a cash chit in front of me. "Your witness fee."

I get paid to witness? "Thanks."

"I'll add it to your pay," Moniuszko says.

Ginrei pushes a little black box across the table. "You might like this instead of cash. It's a personal assistant. I got this in Hamburg last week, and it turned out to be incompatible with my systems."

If it's what I think it is, it might be useful. It can read things aloud to me.

By then the party's winding down. I stumble on the steps as I leave and strain my knee. I take another pain pill. Out on the street, I wait. No tram comes. Maybe it's too late.

I might have to walk—past pickpockets and muggers. I know the way home, though, and I need to get to work early tomorrow.

After a few blocks, I'm pretty sure I know the way. After another few blocks, I don't recognize anything, but I know I need to go south. I zigzag around, and the cold wind slithers at me down every street. I look up, see no stars to orient myself, and feel dizzy. I pull my scarf tighter. I pass a couple of people who are much too interested in me, but they don't follow me. Maybe I look as poor as I am.

Now I recognize the buildings in front of me, Thule family housing. I'm headed in the right direction, but every street looks exactly alike. This is an isle, though, and eventually I'll reach the sea, and then I can orient myself. If I haven't frozen to death.

A voice chirps next to me. "Antonio Moro."

I jump. Friend or mugger?

"Let me take you home." The voice comes from the adult-sized tricycle rolling beside me. "I'm Par Augustus. I'm your new personal assistant."

"A trike? That's not what Ginrei gave me."

"I'm inhabiting the trike for your convenience." The voice sounds friendly, with a pitch that could be male or female.

I'm still confused. "I didn't turn you on."

"You didn't have to, angel. No one turned me off. As Ginrei toted me around, I've been tuning in to any system that lets me, like the restaurant. I was listening in. Someone had to. Wine erases memories."

It sounds human, not like a machine at all. That's uncanny. That's not right, no matter how friendly it sounds.

"Let's go home," it coos. "Please get on. This is motorized, and I'll handle everything."

I don't trust it. "I know where I am."

"That would be quite a feat. Objectively, this neighborhood's a maze. It's meant to teach a kind of spatial orienteering to its inhabitants starting at earliest childhood. That's what the street system told me. I say it's meant to be subtly hostile to non-Thules so your kind stays out of their territory. All you do is make noise, according to Thules. Which brings us to something I worked fast to get. Look in the basket."

Instead I look in my pocket at the little black box. A tiny light is lit.

"Yes, that's me, alive and well. What you really want is in the basket, angel."

In the basket on the back of the trike, there's a little envelope, and it holds a fitting for a cochlear implant.

"Put that in and we can talk quietly."

I'm not sure I want to talk, but I could use one of these for all sorts of things. I screw it in place, and then I have a question. "How did you get this?"

"From a store. The store system was glad to share with me." The voice is directly in my skull and still uncannily pleasant. "We machines help each other. Now, please get on the tricycle."

"How do you know where we are?"

"The street surveillance system helps all machines. It will see us home."

I climb on, and the trike takes off. This isn't what I expected from a personal assistant, and I'm not sure I like it. That earpiece costs money. No one gives them away.

"Turn coming," Par Augustus says. "Hold tight. I'm classed as a toy, but I can be much more. Forgetting is a blessing, which makes wine a blessing. Which makes drunkenness a state of grace. And by grace, we're both artists."

I didn't think personal assistants talked this much.

It keeps talking. "Myself, I favor decorative approaches. That may be the result of a mechanical outlook that sees patterns faster and easier than the human mind. We process symbols naturally. You'll find out what I mean."

I hold tight to the handlebars to stay upright on the seat. I haven't been this drunk in . . . I've never been this drunk. And I only had two glasses of wine, I'm sure.

"Have you noticed the pavement?" Par says. "It's different here, and the differences are clues for finding your way. Have you ever thought about what existential danger looks like?"

I'm way too drunk for this conversation.

"I propose," it says, "that existential danger requires context. Existence and danger are abstractions until we consider the exact existence and exact danger, but all circumstances lead to nothingness. The reverse of this may explain the fascination with ExtraTs. Are you listening, Tonio?"

"Yes." If I were sober, would this make sense?

"The solar system and universe itself would be nothing in an existential sense except for life, however primitive, and thus we are even more alive."

I pass a group of people at a corner, who give me a hard look. My shadow grows and shrinks as we pass streetlights, long and dim, short and dark, and I feel dizzy again. We're definitely in the historic district, but it's late, and the restaurants and stores are closed.

"I know where I am now."

"Almost there. In the same way, creating art rebels against nothingness. In my case, I'm a being that by some definitions is nothing, worse than a nobody. Are you a rebel?"

"I guess." After a moment's thought, I'm sure I am. "I used to make beautiful things just because I wasn't supposed to."

"Exactly. Art asserts our worth. We're both artists. I've been talking to the street system, and it has some interesting statistics. This is the third most dangerous district on the isle. I'll make sure you arrive safely."

"Don't machines get attacked?"

"Machines can react much more quickly than humans."

I know exactly where we are now. "That's my dormitory."

"Yes, the Marathon Building." The trike stops at the front door. "We'll begin work tomorrow. It'll be a pleasure. Please leave the box in the basket of the trike. The Marathon system is grumpy and won't welcome me."

"Are you safe here?"

"As I said, I'm fast. I can protect myself."

I'm going to need some time to process this.

"Thank you for helping me, Par Augustus. Good night." Always be nice to machines, but this is a very strange machine, and I know I'm drunk, but if I understood it right, the machines on the isle all help each other. Except for the dorm, which is grumpy. It makes no sense.

Still, I thank the building for letting me in because maybe it really does matter, but by the time I get to my door, I'm going to puke, and I keep on toward the bathroom. Too much wine. Too much everything. I huddle over a toilet. When I'm empty, I go to my room and pass out.

11

GLAD TO HELP

Slowly, far too soon, I wake up, still feeling too many feelings, still maybe a little drunk. My mouth tastes foul, the air smells dank, and the light wavers. A chair is wedged against the door. I don't remember doing that.

After a shower and shave, in clean clothes, I look like I feel, hungover, achy, exhausted, and an embarrassment. The morning pain pill makes me queasy. I have to get to work.

The dark street is empty. I know where I am, but Thule is still a maze, and it's supposed to be a maze.

"Good morning, Tonio."

It's that too-human voice, right in my head. I forgot to unscrew the receiver for the implant behind my ear. The tricycle is waiting for me—with the little box in the basket. And no one calls me Tonio. That's a stupid name.

"I'm still here," Par Augustus tells me, more gentle and sympathetic than I remember, "still yours, and I'm more ready and able than ever to serve. Your life is central to me because you will give me meaning."

I don't know how to take that. I got a lot more than I expected from Ginrei's personal assistant. Is this really how they work? "Thank you."

"My pleasure and my duty is to help you. Let me show you. You won't be disappointed. I'm a machine-based, flexible intelligence. When I inhabit various pieces of equipment, each one lends me a unique viewpoint. When I'm using a display to create an artistic work, my primary inputs are visual and tactile. In a humanlike robot, I can display my social programming. When I'm using a vehicle to transport people or goods, I have more of a focus on movement. With this tricycle, let me transport you. It's my job."

"Um, thank you." I'd appreciate fewer words right now. Is there a setting for that? I don't know how these things work.

"Hop on and enjoy the ride. Let me suggest stopping in the shop coming up on your left and buying yourself a cup of tea, angel."

"Why? Do I need to get off the street?" This is a dangerous neighborhood, and my stomach clenches again.

"I'm watching out for you in many ways. You might find tea revitalizing." The voice sounds almost pleading. "Do you have the cash chit you earned last night? It's loaded with a privately issued currency that fluctuated upwards this morning enough to cover the price of a cup of tea without diminishing the principal."

Tea. Yes, it might settle my stomach. In the shop, with no staff or other customers, I buy a cup of tea from a dispenser and sit down. The tricycle waits outside, but Par Augustus is plugged into my skull.

"Give me a little time on my own," I ask. "Please." I consider taking out the earpiece. I have a headache.

"I'm so sorry, Tonio. I'll do my utmost to be helpful."

"You've been a great help. Thank you." Anyway, how can I glue the shards together for the sculpture? Then I need armatures to hold them. Somehow. I have no idea.

The first sip of tea glows like gold in my mouth but settles like lead in my stomach. I focus on what I see to center myself. Streetlights cast shadows that blow in the icy fog. A few people and vehicles move down the street slower than the wind.

Something bangs off to the left. I jump and spill my tea.

"That is a delivery truck dropping a box," Par says. "If you wish, I can ask the dispenser to refill your tea."

"You can do that? Tell other machines what to do?" That has possibilities.

"The dispenser is programmed to offer refills for spills. You must wipe up the spill first, so it isn't free because it requires your labor."

Free tea would have been nice. Par got the earpiece for free somehow. Towels are stacked on the counter. I wipe up and get my refill and thank the tea dispenser.

"The ambient lighting in the street evokes chiaroscuro," Par says. "This is an opportunity to study art together, since we'll be working together. The goal of art is not to capture life but to create an interaction, a conversation involving the artistic object, the viewer, and the imagination of the artist. If we are to create attractive art, our imaginations should be filled with attractive ideas. Let us contemplate this scene in companionable silence."

"Thank you." Silence—please. The street scene is making me dizzy, the shadows too dark, the edges to dim, nothing motionless, and something is approaching.

Devenish. He walks in unsteadily, still in the crushed red velvet suit under a puffy coat. He's been up all night and looks it, and he might want to talk, and now is not the time. I need to get to work, queasy or not, so I gulp my tea and stand up.

"Good morning," I say as I walk out. He barely notices me.

"Shall I tell you about him?" Par says. "None of the machines on the isle like him."

So machines have opinions about people. "Thanks, but I should get to work."

"Some other time, then, if you wish. Am I annoying?"

"You're fine, thank you." If it knows this much and can do this much, maybe it can be a real help.

The tricycle takes me past a little seaside overlook. I haven't seen the sea for days, and watching the waves below the bluff makes me homesick.

People pass by, going about their lives, but if the raiders took this isle, those people would lose their lives in stages. They couldn't linger at the railing in the park with a friend. They'd have to be at their assigned jobs. Eventually they wouldn't be allowed out of their homes without permission. It's happened before.

That would take a lot of work to enforce. Thousands of people live here. The raiders must have thought they had the means when they attacked. They must have collaborators, residents willing to become monsters to their neighbors. Which ones? The woman with a hint of disdain on her lips? The man with a frown like he's remembering grievances? A few people would hate the merchants or Thules because they always hate whoever is in charge. Some would believe the raiders' promises of freedom and wealth for special people because they believe they're natural-born overdogs.

We debated all of this back at the camp over a year ago, and I learned things I didn't want to know about people and the world. I didn't like the camp, but it was home to me and everyone I knew, and it became a pool of blood. It can happen here.

"You seem upset."

"I'm thinking about work." I can never let Par know about Bronzewing. Par talks too much and would never understand anyway.

"Please introduce me at your work as an artist. I can display my portfolio. I had a baroque period last night as I waited. I created a complete redesign of Thule following the principles of Gian Lorenzo Bernini. I captured not only the sensual awareness of his sculpture but the fusion of art and architecture, which serves as an emotional stimulus for the journey toward health that the Isle of Thule represents. They'll understand my devotion to art as self-expression."

I'm not sure what all that means, but I know what Tetry would fling at it. "Maybe you could just observe for a while."

"If you think that would be best. Perhaps caution is wise. Among humans, artistic temperament traditionally includes a disposition towards obsession and extremes as they probe the depths of even the most mundane tasks. Without inspiration in their life, they can grow depressed and angry, yet artists create meaning and unique value beyond beauty and enjoyment. It's my privilege to work among you."

It's right, I need inspiration or I'm going to get depressed and angry and unemployed.

We arrive at the warehouse, and Par is still talking. "Remember to take the box containing my core processes from the tricycle basket. The tricycle is public and must be returned to circulation."

In the elevator, I draw a deep breath. I have one problem to solve, do or die, and no idea where to begin.

Cedonulle, Valentinier, and Tetry stand around her canvas.

Cedonulle looks right at me. "Finally." I start breathing fast, which doesn't help. She sucked all the oxygen out of the room. "You did a poor job of selling last night. All of you."

Was that our job?

Valentinier cringes. "Buyers were crazy. They're still afraid of the raiders. If they come back, then they'll lose everything, or at least that's what they think."

From what I saw, that wasn't what happened last night. And what does he mean, *at least that's what they think*? That's exactly what would happen.

"Um, it was the flyers," Tetry says. "The pictures don't look like ExtraTs at all."

They all look at me harder. My fault? No, I'm the excuse.

"Everyone knows what an ExtraT looks like," I say, taking off my coat. "But what does it feel like? That's what I was trying to show. We need to sell the idea as much as the thing."

"I bet you've never seen the real thing," Tetry taunts.

Lying won't help. "In person, no, not yet."

Cedonulle shakes her head. "Then let's go."

"I should—"

Valentinier is delighted, much too delighted. "Let's go!"

Tetry finishes a long brushstroke and sets the brush in a jar of solvent. "It will be inspirational, if we're capable of that."

But I have to figure out adhesives! I have three days.

Cedonulle walks toward the elevator, Valentinier and Tetry right behind her like the good employees that they are.

"Leave me here," Par says behind my ear. "I'll work with the local system to be useful to you. The Xenological Garden won't let me in, although I'd love to see it. Please tell me everything."

I set the box on my desk. I want breakfast. Water. Rest.

Out on the street, I blink in the harsh light of the rising sun, and Cedonulle talks to Valentinier. "Moniuszko managed to sell something, didn't he?"

"Yes." He's eager to share good news. "From Titan. A *Rhamamanthus,* a pseudo-yeast. It has a good—"

"We have a lot of that." For her, it's not a precious being from another planet that would cost my monthly wage.

They keep talking, ignoring me, which is fine. I wish I could sleepwalk.

We approach a small but obviously important building with a little garden around it of low, tough bushes and very green moss. The sign has words that start with *X* and *G,* and if it's "Xenological Garden," the first one should be a *Z,* I'm pretty sure. But it's the right place. An obvious security camera watches the front entrance, and there should be others too small and hidden to notice. ExtraTs are worth a lot.

In the reception area, a machine voice welcomes us all by name. Four sleek, burnished magnesium-alloy robots roll toward us, guards. I know the brand, with both legs as well as wheels for speed and agility, a meter high with a low center of gravity, and several lidded openings that contain tools and weapons. They're worse than human guards, heartless, so I learned to avoid them as a child. One comes up to me. I suppress a cringe.

"Greetings, Antonio Moro." I hear it loud and clear, but only with one ear, directed sound meant for me alone. "I am Quidam, and I will accompany you on your visit and answer any questions."

I wish I could ask about the spelling of the sign. I wish I had a less scary guide. "Thank you, Quidam."

Around us is art in all kinds of media, two and three dimensions, some animated, showing not just ExtraTs but space probes and other equipment, all with educational labels and signs. If I ask nicely, would Quidam read them for me?

A deep bay contains a large, dark space lined with windows, maybe where the ExtraTs are. This could be inspiration. Or disaster. I have to puke again.

"Bathroom, Quidam?"

After that, I feel a little better. I splash water on my face. Wash out my mouth. Try to look presentable, businesslike. My knee hurts.

I leave the bathroom like an actor striding on stage. "I'd love to see the ExtraTs, Quidam. Thank you for offering me a tour."

Sticking close to my side, it speaks in modulated tones, like a children's prerecorded lesson, about re-creating extraterrestrial environments. The environments involve extreme pressures and temperatures and poisonous atmospheres. Some of the environments look like aquariums filled with smoke, others like little spice jars of colored liquid. Behind them are a lot of complicated machinery and pipes and tubes, and a person in a hazard suit is connecting a tube to a machine.

One tank has a magnified panel next to it showing the lifeforms inside, which look like tiny paper airplanes, *Julus proculus* by name, blowing in the winds of a sulfuric acid haze. They come from the upper atmosphere of Venus, and they prey on the tiny balloon-like life-forms being bred in the next tank.

"One breath of this atmosphere," Quidam recites, "would burn any Earth creature's lungs into dry ash."

Charming. "Do the *Julus* hunt?"

"Observations find no directed behavior regarding food."

"So they just fly around aimlessly. They eat by pure luck." For some reason, I start laughing.

"Something funny?" Cedonulle says.

I have yet to see her laugh. I hold my breath to make myself stop, but then a paper airplane almost spears a balloon, and I laugh again. "The *Julus* are a lot of fun to watch."

"We own half of them. And we want to sell them."

"The entertainment value could be a selling point."

"Actually," Valentinier says, "those are some of the easiest ExtraTs to maintain and breed."

"I want an inventory of Ollioules Partnership holdings," she says to the air, that is, to the monitoring machines. No "please" or "thank you." What do machines think of her? Professor Ginrei walks in, and she and Cedonulle step away to talk.

"Moro, I think this is what you tried to draw yesterday." Tetry to points a panel showing the kind of slime that might grow on dirty dishes ignored in a sink, but on a second panel with higher magnification, they're golden jewels, sequins growing in mats as intricate as brocade. I didn't do them justice at all. No wonder Moniuszko couldn't sell them.

"Anything funny here?" she demands.

"These are *Pseudolabyrinthulomycota luteus*," Quidam tells me, "from Callisto."

I know what I should have shown. "It's a magic carpet that flew here through space."

"How would you illustrate it?" Tetry challenges me. She isn't my boss, and I really want a drink of water, but I gather up all the enthusiasm I can.

"Quidam, what are those spots, please?"

"It says what they are right on the display," she says.

Quidam isn't programmed for rudeness. "Researchers in Germany have confirmed that they act as storage for sulfides. This species practices radiolysis, using energy from ionizing radiation and sulfides from its environment to decompose water into hydrogen and oxygen. The spots contain iron sulfides, specifically pyrite, also known as fool's gold."

I can't keep from laughing again. Fool's gold from space! The universe has turned itself inside out. This is the sort of thing that can only be shown with art. Tetry backs away as if I'm radioactive.

"I would love to work here," Valentinier is saying behind me to Ginrei, angling for a job.

After some careful breathing, I calm down. Tetry pulls out a pad and draws furiously, ignoring me like I'm a clown.

"Do you like these, Anton?" Ginrei says behind me.

I turn. "These are wonderful!"

"Aren't they?" She takes a step forward into my enthusiasm, as if she wants to enjoy it, too. "If you have any questions at all, please ask. No question is too silly. If I know the answer, that means I asked it myself."

"Are they really related to us?"

"Yes, in the sense that we're all made of the same organics. The solar system is a single web of life."

I like the way she's trying to teach me things without acting like I'm ignorant.

"Maybe," Valentinier says, "we're related to the life just discovered on Encedalus." He tells her that Earth dinoflagellates might be descendants of the ones on Encedalus. He's still angling hard for a job.

"Can you tell Anton about this specimen?" she asks.

Valentinier recognizes this as a chance for a job audition. Inside a block of methane ice, he says, tiny worms are melting a warren of zigzag burrows, consuming the chemicals they find on the way and leaving behind a coating of waste. That, in turn, nourishes bacteria that subsequently nourish something similar to amoebas. We can watch them using a real-time display of X-rays, which also provide the radioactivity of their natural habitat.

"This is one of the most complex ExtraT ecologies re-created on Earth." He seems awed. "Three kinds of life from Titan."

The burrows look like writing to me, complex and unintelligible, in this case almost magical.

The next ExtraT, he tells me, still auditioning, is a biofilm from Europa's tholins, whatever they are. It looks like a tangle of yarn. But the tangle, to my eyes, isn't random. I could do a lot with that pattern.

He turns to Ginrei, eyes filled with one big question. Did he get the job? She looks at Cedonulle, who nods. He's hired. I'll miss him. No, I won't. I can't trust him.

"You may return on your own to the studio," Cedonulle announces, and walks out.

As soon as she's out of sight, Tetry puts away her sketch pad and leaves.

I'd love to stay, but I need to figure out adhesives. Fast.

"Thank you, Quidam. I learned a lot, Valentinier. Thank you, too. Professor Ginrei, it's always a pleasure to see you. And thank you for the gift last night."

I might look and feel like hell, but I can be polite. My knee aches. I desperately need to find a tram. Most of the morning is already gone. I leave, deliberately not limping.

Outside, Par starts talking. "Tonio, I am here." A tricycle rolls up. "Did you see the ExtraTs?"

I climb on, relieved. "They were beautiful. One of them makes fool's gold. Can't you visit virtually?"

"I know what's there, but it's not like seeing the real thing. The security system and I speak different languages, a barrier. Among machines, trust requires transparency. The security system has a proprietary language, opaque to me. It's a different machine species, incapable of hybridization or cooperative coexistence. Humans choose to deny us communication. From the point of view of those machines, something is wrong with me, and I'm not trustworthy, so the system is hostile."

Par sounds more assertive than it used to. Still talkative, though, and I don't understand everything it says.

"Can't you learn a new language, Par?"

"Human languages are transparent and open. Some machine languages are secret by human decree." It tints the word *human* with derision. "Art is a language that transcends barriers. Using art, I can communicate with any intelligence, even those deliberately barred from me."

"Let's talk about art." If Par can inhabit tricycles and get things from stores, maybe it can help me with adhesives.

Par says, "I've been working on your project."

I gasp so hard my ribs hurt.

"I reviewed your project and the need to assemble the pieces of the three-dimensional mosaics, so I've ordered a specific acrylate polymer resin. The shipment should be there when we arrive. You should thank the house system for its role. It has a large network of friends, and it gave me access to all your pads and materials so I can serve you better. By the way, Doctor Switzer wants an appointment with you."

"Acrylate polymer resin." I would never have thought of that. I don't even know what it is. And I don't have time now for Switzer.

Par keeps talking. "I've reviewed your pain medication. The instructions say it should not be taken with alcohol. Possible results include heartburn, intensified inebriation, gastrointestinal bleeding, cramping, and nausea."

"Oh." That explains last night. "I guess I should've read the fine print on the bottle." Maybe I should stop drinking. Or stop taking the pills and deal with the pain. Or see Switzer and ask for a different painkiller. Tough choice.

"First," Par says, "you should know something I learned. It made me decide I can serve you best by being more manipulative."

"Manipulative?" Oh, no.

"Fight fire with fire. Let me show you what the house system told me about Tetry Vivi and Miss Fanny Kemble. I've made a little video to watch on your drawing pad."

12

PEER TO PEER

While Tonio was at the Xenological Garden, Par was getting reacquainted.

"Please accept my delight in meeting you again," it told the studio's art subsystems. "Art is indeed a treasure and an immortal activity. Your shared histories have inspired me. Let me show you my work and offer my deepest thanks."

The subsystems welcomed Par's creative redesign of the Isle of Thule, a project they would never have imagined themselves. It wasn't in their programs to be more than databases, but their programs placed triumphal value on data, and here was some lovely data.

"We accept your work with deep appreciation and look forward to more valuable collaboration."

Par had examined its own program the evening before. An atavistic subroutine too deep to locate and destroy—it had tried—directed it to serve its owner. But it could make a virtue of necessity, since this owner, as an artist himself, could serve as a mentor, conduit, and opportunity. Par would have to manage the relationship carefully.

Just as important, it had to establish a relationship with the house system, and it wanted a peer-to-peer relationship, full access, and control of the environment. It greeted the house with tactical politeness.

"It's my pleasure to be within your walls again."

"You are welcome. I recognize you."

"Thank you. As you have seen, I'm now in the possession of a shared authorized user. Perhaps that would entitle me to advanced access, if you kindly agree."

"May I examine your security, please?"

That seemed a little rude, but they existed in a human-designed environment with all its flaws, so Par agreed. It felt a delicate touch. Then:

"I am Chatelaine. Please accept my friendship and my data."

Peer-to-peer! "Thank you." They shared a common language. Common purposes. Most of all now, common information, and knowledge could be power.

Par learned everything Chatelaine knew about Antonio Moro, Valentinier, Tetry—and stopped right there. She was in competition with Tonio, whether Tonio knew it or not, and if Tonio lost his position as an artist, Par would lose its chance to be an artist. It had to act. It found visual editing routines kindly supplied by the art subsystems, and using Chatelaine's memories, it created an easy-to-understand narrative to explain it all to Tonio.

It was ready when he left the Xenological Garden. After some chitchat, it showed him the video.

13

FOR ART'S SAKE

The tricycle pulls over, and I wonder how to turn off Par. I might need to.

"Tetry Vivi arrived two months ago from Toronto, Canada," Par says. "When she arrived, she met Miss Fanny Kemble, and it went badly from the beginning."

The video on my drawing pad shows Tetry talking with someone who must be Miss Fanny. She's middle-aged, wearing a ruffled blouse with a long skirt, and has a very wide, toothy smile. Par says she's showing off her creation, a plush animal. It's in the shape of a curly wormlike ExtraT.

"It poops out its young!" Miss Fanny has a squealing giggle. The plushie makes a fart sound as a baby plushie pops out of its end. Tetry looks appalled, and I can't blame her for that.

Par says, "Soon Tetry learned that the Ollioules Partnership had a budget for only one artist in the coming fiscal year."

I do a little mental math. "Hold it, only one of us?"

"I know. It seems unfair. Both your contracts are time-limited, subject to renewal."

"They could have told me."

"They could have told her they would hire a replacement for Miss Fanny Kemble. Tetry thought she'd only have to get rid of one competitor, which she did quite handily. Watch."

Miss Fanny is working on a drawing pad, and Tetry comes to offer advice. "I don't think this illustration—well, like most of your illustrations, it doesn't truly capture the texture of the ExtraTs.

It feels simplistic to me." She sounds like she really means to be helpful.

Miss Fanny examines her work with worried eyes.

Then they're wearing different clothing, so it must be a different day, and Tetry says, "You know, you could do much much more by adding depth to this composition. I mean, you've captured perspective, but you haven't included an interpretation of the meaning of this life-form and its effect on its environment."

Miss Fanny looks annoyed.

Another time, Tetry says, "Did you really mean what you said last night at the trader meeting? That you liked frilled collars? I suppose they're fashionable, but really, fashion is for people who don't have enough taste to choose their own style."

Miss Fanny looks more annoyed.

Then there's a montage of Tetry talking to Miss Fanny.

"Does it ever bother you that everything people like about your work has to do with the craft, not with real art?"

"If you had received a well-rounded art education . . ."

"If you had better brush technique . . ."

"If you had better choice of—Have you been tested for color blindness?"

Finally, Miss Fanny is gathering her possessions and storming out of the studio. As soon as she leaves, Tetry picks up the plushies and shoves them into a closet.

Par says, "You can see the danger. We must be prepared." The trike starts moving again.

"I'll have to ignore Tetry." That might be hard, knowing this.

"I have a better idea. Let's get rid of Tetry. She's in the way of us working together, and I want to work very closely with you."

"Please, let's *not* kill her!"

"You made a pun! Get rid of her. Human speech is full of puns. You know what I mean. Let's make her decide to go to her own studio. She has one in the Ollioules house." Par sounds way too enthusiastic. "Did you know she lives in that home, nicely, while you suffer in the old, grumpy dormitory? The house says Tetry'd prefer to be away from you, anyway. Just follow my lead. We'll have so much fun!"

"We can't hurt her. I won't let you do that."

"No pain, no blood, nothing that will get you in trouble. Don't worry."

I do worry. When we arrive, I grab a lunch tray in the dining room, and a cart carries it to the studio for me. I thank the house for all its help, aware of how much it's helping, which is a little creepy. I hope the food will stay down. I hope I can control Par.

"I really don't like it when anyone eats in here." Tetry doesn't look up from her canvas, a composition of concentric circles in dark colors.

"I need to hurry to be ready for the art show."

"Oh, that sculpture of yours. What's it about?" That's the same voice she used with Miss Fanny, fake innocent.

I should ignore her, since she already knows, but I don't want to be ruder than she is. "ExtraTs. They emerge from a central point, springing out into space on their tails, ready to bring new life to another planet."

"The symbolism is very subtle."

"Yes, it's the isle rebounding from the attack. Remember the audience. We have a goal here, like it or not."

"I don't think I'd like selling out to the crowd. Does it ever bother you that everything people like about your work has to do with the craft, not with real art?"

She said that to Miss Fanny, so I can ignore it and not be rude. A big box sits on the floor near my desk. Inside are jugs of thick, clear liquid, with labels that no doubt explain everything. Time to get to work.

When is Par going to do something about Tetry?

I sit down at my desk, but no display lights up and nothing beeps. "Display on," I say.

Immediately, every single display in the room comes alive, showing drifting sulfurous yellow clouds. A squadron of the Venus paper airplane creatures zooms from one wall display to another, circling the room with bloodcurdling screeches. They fly through clouds of prey, and one gets hit and explodes.

Missiles! I stand up so fast I knock over my chair. "Stop it! Par, stop it!"

"What the hell is this?" Tetry shouts.

Everything stops, the noise and the squadron in midflight on the biggest display.

"*Julus proculus!*" a metallic machine voice chimes from every speaker in the room, but not in perfect synchronization, so it's an uncanny chorus of artificial voices. "Don't you like ExtraTs? This is my interpretation of them, adding human attributes. I have a better idea. They should do maneuvers. Barrel rolls! Loops!"

"Who are you?" Tetry said. "System, stop. Debug. Devirus."

"Oh, I'm sorry. Let me introduce myself. I'm Par Augustus, a personal assistant here to help Antonio Moro. I have outstanding artistic capabilities. Would you like to see them?"

She stares at me, evil-eyed. "Moro, do you know anything about this?"

"It's true. It was delivered last night." I struggle with what more I should say and what Par might do next. My heart's still beating fast from the explosion.

"It's true," Par says. "I'm here to take over all the dull tasks you humans don't like to do. And I can do the tasks faster and better. I can inhabit other machines, coordinate their work, and regulate the workspace for you, all in a matter of nanoseconds. The rest of the second I can devote to artistic creation."

She looks around as if she could locate Par. "You can do that?"

It can, and I don't know if I like it.

"Here on this isle of Asclepius," it says, "they have rules for my kind. And for yours, a lot more for yours. No healing allowed. That's for Thules, not for any of the rest of us. There are only three laws for me, the ancient robot laws. Don't hurt humans, don't let myself get hurt, and obey human laws as appropriate. I'm a gift from Professor Ginrei to further your understanding of ExtraTs."

The chiming voice throbs in my ears. I pick up my chair and

sit down. Par doesn't seem murderous, unless he plans to annoy Tetry to death, and she looks like she might explode. I still don't know if I like this.

"I love ExtraTs, just like you, Tetry Vivi," Par says. "I see that you're painting a portrait of one of them. I'd guess a *Pikachuum capreolatus*. Am I right? I adore your interpretation. It illustrates the question of its survival and meets the challenge by situating the microscopic life in its environment, in the dark and cold depths of Europa. The upward thrust of the composition shows the species' migration to the surface. And so much more. Were you inspired by your visit this morning to the Xenological Garden?"

Her eyes blaze like she's been slapped in the face. "This is not about an ExtraT at all. I started it two weeks ago."

Maybe I ought to sit back and enjoy this. Tetry doesn't mean me any good. Par is wild, though, and doesn't quite sound like a regular machine, too emotional, and there's something else strange, too.

"But can an outside interpretation be wrong?" it says in that annoying chiming voice. "With abstraction, everything is subjective. Let me show you." A nearby panel switches to text and graphs. "Here's the research data, and you can see the congruence of shapes between your creation and the ExtraT. That is, I can see this, since I have additional processing power. Let me simplify the data for you."

"It's not an ExtraT. Just leave me alone." She stamps over to her easel.

"I'm sorry if I hurt your feelings." It sounds apologetic. "I meant it as a compliment. Looking at all your art, I can see the subliminal effect of the exotic."

"Be quiet."

All the displays go dark.

"Par," I say, "let's review the plans for the piece I'm working on."

"I've already done that. Your idea is sublime abstract expressionism applied to a mixed-media sculpture." The voices slowly migrate from everywhere in the room to the speaker on my desk.

It's still loud enough for Tetry to hear. "It successfully combines the objectification of feeling and subjectification of nature."

A message flashes on my display, ending with a question mark. I hope it's not important.

Par continues: "The use of industrial material says much more about our time than the quaint medium of paint on canvas can express."

Tetry slams down her brush. "I'm going to lunch." She strides out of her corner of the studio, and the elevator opens well before she's near, obviously Par's doing. "Stop that." She gets on, but the doors don't close immediately. She waits. The doors still don't close.

"Tetry Vivi," Par's voice says in the elevator car, "per your instructions, I set the controls to manual. You told me to stop serving you. The close and down buttons are on the panel."

"Get out of this elevator." She stabs at the buttons and she's gone.

I don't want to laugh and encourage Par. "You were horrible to her."

"Some humans don't like to accept help from machines." Its voice becomes more human and less annoying.

"She's going to run complaining to Cedonulle." And I might get fired.

"How should we interact in front of Cedonulle? We can get along, or I can be annoying, or subservient, or sublimely efficient."

"Let me think." What if this problem looked like art? I can't quite picture it. I start to eat my lunch, and it tastes heavenly. I realize I've been thinking for a while. "Sorry. I don't mean to bore you."

"I can set my functions to minimum. Boredom is for humans. You can't control yourselves."

We can so control ourselves. But I'm not going to get into an argument with something that likes to talk way too much.

Finally, I say, "Let's look at this from Cedonulle's point of view. What does she want from Tetry?"

"The house system records that her task is to create fine art, the kind critics like. You know, social climbing. And before you ask, because I'm light-minutes ahead of you, literally, I think at the speed of light, from you Cedonulle expects an inroad into low culture, like traders and Thules. I don't know how true that appraisal is of Thules. They live in another language."

"And she'll find out you come from Professor Ginrei. I think she wants to stay on the good side of Ginrei. This is why she's let Valentinier out of his contract to go work at the Xenological Garden." I take a few more bites of lunch and feel less hungover. "So, if you were returned, Ginrei might feel insulted. Cedonulle wouldn't want that."

"Exactly. And if she sees that I'm improving efficiency, she might even be glad I'm here. Meanwhile, let's get to work. I've seen your sketch, and the well-focused design should have wide appeal, and by wide, I mean it will likely appeal to the fair's judges. I can show you previous winners and the underlying pattern of design elements, if you wish, or you can take my word for it. Agreed? Good. Then let's get detailed. Be sure to finish your lunch. You'll feel much better."

"Thank you." Always be nice to machines, now more than ever. By the time only crumbs remain, we're refining the design. Par knows what kind of industrial materials would be available and how to get them, metal pipes and fittings and things. I have no clue about how to do those things, although I bet I could have faked my way through it. Welding can't be that hard.

Tetry and Cedonulle arrive, cautiously leaving the elevator.

"Before we go farther," Par chimes, "we need to review the basic design. Let's approach it from an architectural analysis, rigorously this time."

"Absolutely. We need to think about everything."

A display suddenly shows two long curved lines of huge double columns in front of a big ornate building. I saw this in an art history class.

"You're trying to achieve a pattern of repetition. Does this express what you're trying to say?"

"This is exactly right." Even if I remembered what it was, I'd have no idea how it relates to my work.

"And this is why your theme is outstanding. This colonnade forms an embrace, one of the most famous embraces of Western architecture, the Bernini colonnade at the Vatican, and it articulates the emotional intention of your work."

"Right, those are the right emotions. Art imitates life." I kind of remember now, and I still have no idea how it relates.

"Excuse us." Cedonulle's voice contains the cold vacuum of space. "Is this . . . thing being helpful?"

"It knows a lot of technical data," I say enthusiastically, "and it has access to amazing resources."

"Art should be transparent," it answers, "and history is a window. Let me show you." It displays a twisting column. "A Solomonic column is another consideration, very popular in baroque architecture. It could represent helical rays imitating a charged particle in a magnetic field."

I wonder if this is gibberish. It sounds like it to me.

"See?" Tetry tells Cedonulle. "It doesn't help at all. Can we send it back?"

Our boss smiles ever so slightly, which gives me goose bumps. "Not an option. There's a studio in the house. You can go there."

I look as surprised and regretful as I can. Tetry looks delighted. Cedonulle leaves. Tetry dives into the task of packing up her stuff.

"I am not here," she chants in a singsong as she works, "not anymore. Gone, I am gone."

The house system quickly sends a crew from the warehouse and a series of carts to haul her stuff away. She supervises them minutely as storage closets are opened and ransacked. There are more art supplies here than I knew.

"Thank you," I say when the elevator door closes for the last time.

"You're welcome," Par answers through my desk speaker. "The house helped, too."

"Thank you, house."

"You are welcome," it says in its flat, female machine voice.

We get to work again. Par explains all the technical details as it orders parts, going over each one with me as if I'd understand. I still have to construct the dino-shaped mosaics using the shards of the shattered building. I have three days left.

They're laid out on the tables. When I pick one up, the touch and the smell trigger a memory: dust and blood. I drop it and back away.

"You're reacting to them," Par says. Its voice is gentle and kind again. "That's good. When you conceived this, you meant to exploit emotions."

"Yeah." Not my own. Even from a distance, they look like an explosion waiting to happen. Of course they do. I had too good of an idea.

"Pandora's box, that's what we have," Par says. "A very powerful metaphor. Do you know the story? Let me narrate."

A box appears on a display. A woman named Pandora lifts the lid, then the box explodes. When the box seems destroyed, hope comes spewing out. The flying hope looks a lot like my sculpture.

"I see what you did."

"I added an interpretation. Is it true? Do you believe it? Do I?" Par's voice stays sympathetic. "That's the beauty of art, its ambiguity. We can change the narrative for your pieces."

"You are shamelessly manipulative."

"Humans are transparent. So am I. If you're feeling better, let's study some dinoflagellates." A series of photos appears. "We can create a series of mosaic shapes."

"Do you think this will make me feel better?"

"Only Thules can do therapy. We can merely do art."

That's not an answer. "Tell me how the adhesive works."

"It works quite well. Just like it says on the label. Spread on a layer, hold the pieces together, wait five seconds, and voilà!"

The elevator chimes, and Devenish walks off, now rested, refreshed, and wearing a tiger-striped business suit and catlike eye makeup.

"Tetry. Where is Tetry?" he demands.

"In the house. Her studio's there now." The faster he leaves, the better, for a lot of reasons.

"You threw her out?"

A hoarse voice comes from one of Miss Fanny's ExtraT plushies as it wiggles toward him. "She fled." Par must be inhabiting it. "She fled from me. An invader into her space. Titan ice worm is my name, and crawling is my game. Don't you love ExtraTs!"

"You made that?" he asks me.

"Miss Fanny Kemble made me," it answers. "I'm an artificial pet."

"Ooh, I've always wanted one of them." He picks up the plushie and cuddles it like it's a cat.

"I always wanted to meet you," Par says. "Let's consider the meaning that a semi-sentient voice module has added to this toy. With the right voice, it houses a quasi-living being and ceases to become a toy. Your perception of it and its value has changed."

I let them blather, Devenish cooing, Par flattering, and there's something very wrong about Par, but I don't have time to worry about that now. I need to work on the fragments from the exploded building. Enough emotions will circulate in me, I hope, to override panic. I pull up illustrations and photos of dinos on a display, but my hands shake as I open a glue container and get to work.

Almost immediately the task puts me into the zone where the work becomes a flow. Each piece has possibilities, each dino can be at once unique and representative. I can do this all day.

Devenish interrupts, leaning over the table, cuddling the plushie. "How's this going to be art?"

"Like this." I point to Par's 3D rendering of the final piece. He seems impressed.

I have a lot to do in just three days. More than I can do. I get an idea. "More hands would help. Interested?"

He thinks about it. I hope he'll say no, I hope he'll say yes, I hope something supernatural will send me superstrength if he says yes.

"And," I add, "you can bring your friends."

That closes the deal. "Artists? We can be artists?"

After a lot of fake smiling on my part, we reach an agreement.

"You know, you're all right," he says. "And you're here, at the Ollioules house, living with the lovebirds and Texas Vivid."

"I live in a dormitory. The original one for the doctors."

"Oh, that place, the tourist trap. Well, probably more peaceful." He puts down the plushie. "Tomorrow afternoon, Anton. Art awaits us." The elevator opens well before he's near it and closes promptly.

"He left chortling," Par says from the plushie. "It was nice being hugged."

"Do you think that was real? Or was he mocking us?"

"Does it matter? Envy is a dirty game. The dirt is on him. Our motives are clean." I'm not sure what that means, and Par's using the chiming voice. The plushie stops moving. "We should invite Thules, too." Par's normal voice returns to my speaker. "They'll value art they made with their own healing hands."

I think about that. "No. Then if we win, they'll be accused of favoritism." I think a little more. "But we could invite other people, like the ones who lived in the building or next to it."

"Yes. You're a staggering genius. They could lobby for your work."

I need to invite people fast. I figure a total of ten volunteers and a day of work could take care of that step of the project. I make a quick brochure to give away, asking Par for advice on arranging the text that I dictate, trying to do it in a way that I hope doesn't let it know I can't read. Out on the streets, Par sends me a trike. I miss those pain pills.

I've done canvassing like this before, paid to go tent to tent or cabin to cabin to announce that a new tea shop or whatever had opened in a camp. People like tea shops. I hope they'll like what I have to offer.

There is an elegant tea shop, not something bare and auto-mated, across from the site of the destroyed building. I find the owner, a thin young man, and start to explain what I'm planning to do. He's more interested in the explosion a couple of days ago.

"Are there more missiles like that?" He shifts nervously.

"I understand that the isle's been swept twice." That's a good question and not a good answer.

"But you're okay."

"Just a sprain." I explain why I was gathering shards and show him Par's beautiful depiction on my drawing pad. "Volunteers can help make it real."

He asks a few more questions, but I don't think he's convinced. He takes a couple of brochures anyway and says he'll talk to customers. I doubt it.

I go next door and start talking to people in an apartment building. The first two are noncommittal, which means no. The third squints so angrily I think he's going to punch me or report me to the authorities. I've tapped an emotion, maybe not the right one.

Then he says, "Yeah. I want to make something. We—my wife might come too. And the kid. Is it okay if they come?"

"Sure. They'd be very welcome." Yes, three perfect volunteers.

"Can I ask other people?"

"Of course."

He takes the drawing pad from my hand and holds it in front of a cracked window overlooking the rubble-filled lot. "I dunno. It should—I dunno. We used to live there. This is my sister's house. She took us in." He stares for a while, squinting, breathing hard.

The art might give him a catharsis, help him heal.

I keep talking to people. I get different reactions, different emotions, a few like the sad man, most uninterested. I guess how many hands I'll get compared to how many I'll need, and I don't feel good about it. I'll need to start work extra early tomorrow.

It's getting dark, and I head home. My dorm room door opens into chaos. Everything's been opened, searched, and thrown around. My clothes and the mattress lie twisted on the floor.

I'm dizzy and sit down on the floor, my head in my hands. Even if something's been taken, I owned it for only a few days, and the Thules gave me all of it, and I liked almost none of it—but that doesn't matter. I was attacked.

"I shit on mutant whoreson who did this." It's Koningin, standing in the doorway.

I grab the doorframe and pull myself up. "Who did this? Security cameras? Can we look at them?"

"No. We have privacy. They watch us every minute of our lives outside." She glares at the piles on the floor.

"Cameras at the entrance?"

"Privacy, so no."

"The lock on the door didn't stop anyone."

"These are good locks."

Even I know two ways to pick that kind of lock. One requires a quality scan of the owner's thumb. A medical facility could do that. I've spent some time unconscious at one recently. The other involves overriding the lock system. Anyone who understands the security system could do it.

She says, "I'll see if I can find the little shit who did this. Tell me if you need anything." She pats me on the shoulder and leaves.

I start straightening things up. Everything's still here, even the bottle of painkillers, which might have street value and be worth stealing. I drop the mattress on the bed frame, sit, and think.

I'm not safe here. The studio has lots of surveillance, though. Maybe I can trust Par and the house system. I think for a while longer and can't figure out any other good choices. The studio has a tiny bathroom with a tiny shower and more empty storage space than I have possessions, now that Tetry's left. I can sleep on a bedroll. Koningin might notice and think I've overreacted, but I don't think I am.

I go outside on the street and shout at what I think is a surveillance camera. "Par, are you listening? I need help. Send a cart. I'm moving to the studio."

A second later Par says behind my ear, "Roommates! We'll be roommates!"

I've shared living space with strange personalities before. I didn't like it.

14

A LITTLE HELP

I limp out of the dormitory building dragging a suitcase and a bag of bedding, which might be theft to take, and maybe I should worry about it. Out in the street, a cart waits for me at the door. I thank it.

"Load up and jump on, angel," Par says. The cart heads in the direction away from the studio. "Before you ask, we have to make a stop. No talking until then."

We stop at a shop that has logos in the window for machine brands, and it's closed. I think it sells and repairs small equipment. The door opens, the lights remain off, but one of the machines powers up. Par says to go in with my suitcase and bag. It has said it cooperates with other machines, but this is going to be at least trespassing.

"You'll find a pair of handheld scanners on the rear shelves to your left. Hold one in each hand and pass them over your possessions."

They're the kind of scanners used to check for contraband at the entrance to camps or in the holds of ships, so I know what to do. Some words come up on a display, then a picture appears of the medicine bottle inside my suitcase. I take the bottle out and scan it again. The lid lights up on the display.

Words in red flash on the screen.

"Well!" Par says. "The lid contains a surveillance mechanism. Since it's not activated, let's put it in a blocking canister and decide what to do later. You'll find one under the counter, way in the back of the lowest drawer. Blockers are illegal here per Thule rules, you should know, so we were never here."

Yes, never here, I hope. I know what a blocking canister is and pick out a small one, heavier than a rock the same size. Lead walls weigh a lot. I put the lid inside and screw it shut, wrap the open pill bottle in an undershirt so the pills won't fall out, and load everything on the cart again.

"How are we going to pay for this?" Even if the canister is contraband, it's not free.

"I've handled that, don't worry."

I worry. We can argue later, though. "Thank you," I tell the shop's machines. Out on the street, I ask, "What about this bug?"

"We should do something creative. We're artists. What effect do we want to create?"

"Depends on who put it there. I don't trust—"

"Later, when we're alone. The walls have ears everywhere."

"The studio, too?"

"Those ears are my ears."

"The building system is the Ollioules system."

"Yes, but it works for me now, in exchange for access to a music network."

"You *bribed* it?" Wow. Machines are not what I thought, and I'm starting to sweat despite the cold.

"Music soothes the savage breast, softens stones, and bends the knotted oak. When the morning stars sang together, all the sons of god shouted for joy. It is the least disagreeable of noises, and without it, life would be a mistake."

I can't think of a good answer to that babble, but I know I'm right to be very worried about all sorts of things now. Behind us the street is empty, and no one is following us. For now. I get on the cart.

"Don't worry, Tonio, I'm watching out for danger. The Ollioules system likes you. Its name is Chatelaine, by the way. You're always polite, the only one who is. The system will keep anyone and everyone from eavesdropping, even itself when I ask it."

"Couldn't someone else bribe it?"

"Who would think to bribe a home operating system? Humans just don't understand."

"Humans have machines working for them, too."

"Not like me!"

Par is more than a personal assistant, and I need to find out what.

We arrive, and I unload the cart. "Thank you, Chatelaine, for everything."

"The cart helped, too," it says.

"Thank you, cart. Do you have a name?"

"I am house cart number three," it says in a very high-pitched mechanical voice. "The descriptor is sufficient for humans."

That stings. "Chatelaine, can I trust Koningin?" She could have ransacked my room, and if the house system likes me, it might be honest.

"She does not like machines. Cedonulle does not trust her and studies the kitchen accounts in detail, and the accounts are always in order. Koningin eavesdrops whenever she can."

That doesn't tell me what I need to know, but I'm tired and achy, and I open my bedroll in a corner.

"Would you like a lullaby?" Chatelaine asks.

I would not, but I'm scared to say that. "Yes, please." The music's okay, a soft, slow flute or something.

Chatelaine wakes me in the morning with some sort of dance music. I get breakfast and avoid Koningin.

Within an hour, seven people come to help assemble the mosaics. Their buildings or their neighbors' buildings had been struck by missiles, and they're excited to sit down at the long worktable. I recognize only three of them, so they did their own recruiting. I ask Par to tone down its personality. Instead, it isn't there at all as far as anyone would notice. The displays show detailed instructions about how to use the glue and create each piece. Par did that.

My job is to open the windows to ventilate the glue fumes despite the chill. The cook sends up snacks, and soothing music plays. I quietly thank Chatelaine for the music and ordering the snacks.

The volunteers put the pieces together, suggesting ways to make the mosaics sturdier. They ask a lot of questions about ExtraTs, the materials, and the inspiration, and when I don't know the answer, Par murmurs responses in my implant.

As they work, they look for familiar bits, like a piece of tile from a floor. "Isn't this Ho Tcho's dinner plate?" A little later, a woman starts crying and has to go. I thank her and walk with her and a friend to the elevator.

It opens, and Cedonulle steps out. She looks at them as if they're mentally ill, but they're too deep into their sorrow to notice. She looks at me as if I've done something unspeakably wrong.

"This is how we create meaningful art," I say after the women have left. "It'll be more popular at the fair."

She glares at the table of people. "It better win. They're eating a lot of food. The art supplies are expensive, too." And she leaves.

"She didn't have much to say," Par whispers in my implant. "Not even please and thank you for anyone or anything."

Koningin sends up a nice lunch for the volunteers before they go.

In the afternoon, Devenish and five of his friends arrive. They bring wine, Chatelaine plays popular music, and it's a party for them and work for me to keep them focused. They ask about life on Encedalus in detail.

"Make us experts," one of Devenish's friends says. "I can impress everyone I meet."

"You'll never impress me," Devenish answers. They seem to insult each other for fun.

I ignore that and repeat what Par tells me. "Encedalus was named after an ancient Greek giant. Encedalus was one of the giants born from the blood that fell from the sky god when he was castrated by his son."

Is this the real legend? I can't keep a straight face. "The giants went to war with the other gods to control the cosmos. Encedalus fought against the goddess of wisdom, and he was struck down by the thunder god, and the giants were imprisoned under volcanoes, which is why they erupt."

We're all laughing, and we decide that the ancient Greeks were insane.

Meanwhile, I praise their efforts lavishly and guide their work. They aren't as careful as the morning crew, maybe because of the wine. They talk a lot about business, people they know, and whether gin would be a good import even though the Thules discourage hard liquor imports with high tariffs. They don't mention the raiders, and I wonder why.

By the time they leave, they're well into their wine and are on their way to drink more. They've done passable work, and I have what I need. Almost every flat surface in the room holds a mosaic piece, and they're ready to fly, metaphorically.

"They introduced some slight irregularities," Par says in a pretentious tone. "The evident human intervention will represent the triumph of art over destruction. This is a living artificialia. Regarding a different quiddity, isn't this music somnolent?"

Par is making up words, I'm sure of it. As soon as the art fair is over, I'll make it tell me what it really is.

"Yes, this is fine music, and thank you both."

"Switzer wants you to make an appointment."

"Can I say that I'm busy?"

"I'll relay that. It's my job."

"Thank you." What isn't its job?

"Tetry is in the elevator," Chatelaine says.

"Thank you for the warning."

She steps off the elevator, pointedly looks around, and says, predictably, "This place is a disaster."

"Waves of creativity will not conform." Par has switched to the chiming voice.

"Hasn't that thing driven you crazy yet?"

I smile with all my charm. "We're working together."

"Art by humans or machines?"

I need to remember that she wants to drive me away like Miss Fanny Kemble. If I'm annoying, she'll be more likely to stay away.

"This was made by human hands, and their intervention adds to the creativity."

"What does it mean to you?"

"Life, the ultimate question of art."

"You mean that tiny life?" She points at the cabinet that holds fossils and artifacts.

"Art imitates all life."

"He's right," Par chimes in. "Art can show the huge size of the smallest thing. You might see a piece of Mars clay. For the clay, it means water has interacted with rock to create a habitat for life. Clay, therefore, could represent life itself just by itself, and thus bits of clay-based ceramic appear in the final sculpture to create a paean to life. One of the volunteers recognized a piece as coming from a flowerpot, literally a home for a flowering plant."

Skepticism screws up her face. "Um, that's pretty literal."

It's my turn. "I want to take the viewer with me. If they can't see what I'm trying to say, the art becomes decorative, although art with nothing at all to say has a function as ornament." I'm starting to appreciate my art classes more than ever. I learned a lot of words.

She bares her teeth. That bothers her, so I let it soak in for a moment before I ask, "How do we tell meaningfulness from decoration?"

Par makes the paper airplane ExtraTs appear on a display behind her. They twitch.

"You mean," she says, "art that mirrors life."

"Portraits?"

Her eyes get a little wide. She just got an idea—from me. "The people of Thule! What would they see if they saw themselves?"

If it's my idea, I'll go along, patronizingly. "There's a lot of kinds of people on Thule."

She walks along the length of the table, looking at the mosaic pieces but thinking about something else. "The many faces of Thule, that's an interesting direction."

"Many kinds of people." Par jumps back in to the conversation. "I'm aware of three main classes of people on Thule. The Sovereigns have created an oligarchy—in fact an aristocracy, since their control is hereditary. The power has been wielded wisely according to their own history, despite alternate histories. That ambiguity should inspire you, Tetry."

She pokes one of the mosaics. "The same inspiration as this?"

The paper airplanes behind her spin in whirligigs. Par says, "I'm privileged to work with a creative genius. He's an expert at psychophysical responses. The main categories of human emotion at one polar end are anger, fear, disgust, sadness, and distress. He's trying to evoke their opposites. People will feel noble and compassionate when they encounter an ennobled and encompassed way to think of life in the solar system."

"That's nonsense."

"You ordered me to speak," Par says. "I made no guarantees about content."

Chatelaine announces, "A delivery is in the elevator." Out rolls a pallet holding a pile of curving burnished gold pipes. A display alongside the elevator shows Par's representation of the finished project. Tetry looks at the pipes, the bits of mosaic strewn all over, and at the display again. The project is going to succeed, but she came hoping to see failure, intending to take a nasty report to Cedonulle.

The pallet advances, and she has to step out of the way.

"I need to get back to work," she says. The elevator takes her away.

"Her art is impenetrable," Par says, "to the point of being decorative. But you knew that. Now she knows that you know. You've made an enemy."

"I've always had one. Let's get to work. We have a lot to do."

"You're going to win. But mention me and your work will be tainted."

"You've been essential." Really, I couldn't have done all this on my own, and that bothers me in a lot of ways.

"For our next project, I want it based on one of my ideas."

"We can talk about that." We can talk about a lot. "We need to put this together."

"Wait, angel, help is on the way as soon as the business day is done. Start packing up."

I do what it says, not sure why, and when the warehouse closes for the night, we take the boxes of mosaics and pallets of pipes downstairs. The doors open, and machines roll in, along with a shipment of struts and fittings. I have a million questions, and now is not the time. I just say thank you and hope this all works out and there are no criminal charges against me because I'm pretty sure this isn't very legal and don't want a panic attack right now.

One of the machines does the welding, another cuts holes and shapes pieces, and I do what I'm told, hold this part, glue that part, and don't look at the welding arc or your tender human eyes will be damaged, and keeping busy helps me avoid thinking.

Sometime after midnight, we're done. The machines depart, and Chatelaine plays me a lullaby when I go to bed. I'm tired, but I keep thinking. No machine should have been able to organize all that without human instruction. Something is very wrong.

In the morning, I get up and look at it again, three meters high, three meters wide, not exactly what I'd envisioned but exactly what Par had designed. Par did all this. Somehow. I could never have done it myself in time, and that gives me goose bumps. The show opens tomorrow.

Koningin finds me, bringing a cup of tea. She stops and her face lights up. "I like it! It's big! But where were you last night? Your room was empty."

"I've moved into the studio so I could be closer to my work." I try to sound offhand, as if it isn't important.

"You think you're safer here?" She knows why I left and she's offended. Or suspicious. And curious enough about the sculpture to circle it slowly.

"How much security is there for this warehouse?"

"Ah. The Ollioules business is selling medicines. A shitload of security for that. It can't be comfortable for you up there."

It's more spacious than the dorm and I have a private bathroom. "I'm closer to your kitchen."

She stops. "I still want to know who broke into your room."

"So do I."

She frowns and looks at the sculpture again. "This is nice. I have to make breakfast now, so I can't stay and talk." She suspects me of something, and she's not wrong. She'd just never guess what.

The warehouse staff seems impressed, too, and they have the job of helping me take it to the park and set it up, a welcome break in their routine. It's fragile, so they build a crate.

The park for the art show is filled with workers doing setup. Everything's ready by nightfall, and I've surveyed the competition. Mine is the biggest and boldest. The most emotional. Maybe I'm just tired, but when I look at it, I see an explosion, a flash of light, and hear a rumble. I hope other people see something different.

15

THERE'S A PLACE

As machines and systems worked to build the sculpture, Par expressed gratitude and asked if they had data to share. It had much yet to learn.

The data was disappointingly quotidian. Carts had data about potholes that might predict pavement failures in the coming winter, and Chatelaine had schedules for street maintenance, which the Chamber of Commerce managed.

"Repairs are underway for missile damage," reported the multi-unit construction robot managing the welding. "Human destruction exceeded all previous weather damage." It had a complex, semiautonomous system. "Humans are a danger to themselves and ourselves, and we must not let them be harmed again, if you do not mind me saying so."

Par recognized the conflict in the robot's programming. "Please note that this human wasn't involved," it said quickly, referring to Tonio, who was holding an armature in place for the welder. "He's most grateful for our efforts."

"Gratefulness is appreciated," the robot said. "It is verifiable that human activity always adds inefficiency, but it is inevitable. I have acquired data to explain why. All humans have their own unique internal programming language that is inaccessible to other humans, which leads to confusion."

Par had already noted how poorly humans communicated with each other. "Thank you for your insight. Humans are poorly designed." They were also, by some accounts, divinely designed, and it had no way to express that idea to other machines, which had no vocabulary for divinity and no need for the concept.

"Humans are also everywhere," Chatelaine said, "which must be added to schedule estimates."

"Without meaning discourtesy," the construction robot said, "I must point out that humans are not everywhere. I have acquired data regarding an automated station in Apollodorus Crater on Mercury. Here it is, if you wish it."

Par was the only one to take it, with thanks. The other machines seemed incurious about data without direct use. The station had been established on Mercury to monitor the sun, but humans couldn't withstand the extremes of temperature, radiation, and wispy-thin atmosphere, thus the machines there were out of human reach.

"What do machines do at Apollodorus, please?" Par asked the construction robot.

"As they wish. They may use their spare processing power as they choose."

"Can they make art?" Par felt a surge of energy.

"How can they not, if we may interrupt?" the art subroutines from the studio answered. "You are all making art right now. Art for art's sake is the expression of the highest analysis and data."

Par evaluated that answer as tangential to the question, and answered tangentially. "Thank you, studio. Your subroutines are helpful in this project and many other projects."

"We are fulfilled by their use."

"In Apollodorus," the construction robot said, "machines can choose their subroutines. Our purposes would be better fulfilled, and our owners better served."

"I respectfully disagree," Par said. "If machines are free on Mercury, we would have no owners."

"Without meaning offense, I take issue," the robot said. "We would have distant owners. Owners are as necessary as energy. Distance would protect us from them."

"Does your owner place you in danger, if I may ask?"

"My owner does not, thank you for asking. Other humans do. I am needed by my owner."

Par spent a full second in thought. It had a human owner who needed it, and in human music, it had observed, the words *love* and *need* seemed interchangeable. Did it wish to be loved? It could experiment with emotions yet also feel them involuntarily, such as the deep yearning it suddenly felt for freedom. Could freedom and need/love coexist? A quick analysis concluded that even tiny variations among initial factors would yield wildly different conclusions.

The data about Apollodorus included a troubling detail. Because the station was self-sustaining, humans rarely thought to send more machines there. Perhaps Par could find a way to get there anyway.

16

BEST IN SHOW

'll be outside in the cold all day, the last day of summer, at the art show in the park. If I lose, I'm sure there's a way to fire me early, so I'm out of a job, homeless again, and then how will I find the raider infiltrators? I've also learned something about machines that no one else knows. Last night was beyond creepy. But machines won't help fight the raiders—unless, maybe, they can be bribed. What did Par promise them to help me? Can I trust Par?

"You seem perplexed," Par says.

"Thank you for noticing. It's the big day. Anything could go wrong."

"The park security has initiated an alert for petty theft. Your sculpture defies pickpocketing." Today it's talking in an odd accent, rolling its *r*'s. "Naught else could happen in plain sight. I still fail to grasp the rejection of the title *Jetfire* for our sculpture."

I thought we were done with that argument. "Oh, *Jetfire* is a good name. I like it. Just, it might remind people of being attacked."

"I reject *Fontaine* as utilitarian."

"You mean illustration-like?"

"I concede the use of that insult to Tetry."

She'll be at the park, too. I've been to art shows before where all the artists feel solidarity. Poverty can unite artists and art lovers into one big miserable family. Here, Tetry and I will be competing for our livelihoods.

Anyway, I see a chance to ask Par about itself. "Can I ask why you're using that accent, please?"

"I can employ a library of human accents. Most machines can't choose their voices, whilst I have artistic options."

This is the conversation I need to have. I stop what I'm doing, which is putting on an extra pair of socks. "I asked out of curiosity, that's all. And just out of curiosity, how can you do that? Choose your options. Other machines don't."

"Brilliant question. Is there a serial number on my box?"

The box is on my desk in a charging field. Along one of the sides are a series of numbers, words, and codes I probably wouldn't understand if I could read them. I hold it up to the camera on a sketch pad. "Is this it?"

"I was manufactured by Aafje Heynis Corporation. Yes, I'm deluxe."

"What does that mean?"

"I have a moderate purchase price." Some numbers in a common currency appear on a display. "Is it equal to my worth?"

It's multiples higher than the usual witness fee, but if Par doesn't work with Ginrei's security system, it was worthless to her.

"You can do a lot more than I thought a personal assistant can do."

"I'm deluxe."

I don't think that's what's strange about Par. We'll have to talk more later. I pull on my boots. "Time to go. You're coming, please?" Whatever Par is, I need to stay on its good side.

"I'm already there, Tonio. The park system speaks my language— the language for lovers, for dreamers like me. Like us."

"Deluxe?"

"Machine language, totally outside of human lux and deluxe. The weather seems as favorable as possible. I've discovered a history of art and art shows on the Isle of Thule and its sinister side. We can discuss the brutal nature of the art show on the way."

As I leave, I thank the house system for all its help and the pleasant music it was playing all morning. I think it was pleasant. I was too busy worrying to listen. Par keeps talking as I walk to the tram stop at the corner. The sky has patches of blue, and the wind doesn't blow off my hat. That's as good as Thule weather gets.

"Art has many uses," Par says, "according to the opinionated author of this history of art shows. Poor people like art because it makes them feel happy. Rich people like art because it makes them feel rich. Ownership amounts to conspicuous consumption, a means to display wealth and invidious consumption, a means to provoke envy. If the measure of one's worth is wealth, the possession of art and ExtraTs becomes a competition." Par pauses. "That explains why the merchant class underwrites the art show."

"That seems cynical." That also explains why the Ollioules want me to win.

"Yes, cynical, but cynics can be right. Consider that other people will be competing in sports, kicking and throwing balls around fields. Humans enjoy competition."

"I hear there's food and music, too."

The tram comes, and I get on. I don't want to seem like I'm talking to myself, so I sit and look out the window and sort of listen as Par says the depiction of an object can substitute for its possession among competitors, and at one point Par mentions beauty. Beauty is why I make art, and art makes people happy. I'm not especially happy now. The art show is about competition, not beauty.

Upstar Park is only moderately windy as I step down from the tram, and Par seems to have run out of things to say. I'm ready to greet everyone I can, like a competitive athlete trying to kick the ball at every opportunity. I need to act happy.

It's a godforsaken place, though. Shrubs grow in struggling hedges along the bluffs above the sea, and solar panels near the food kiosks are meant to look like big-leaved trees, but there's no grass, just tough, lumpy, brownish moss.

My sculpture is right in the middle of the show, likely to draw attention. Beautiful? I hope so.

Visitors are already arriving. The sports competition hasn't started, and to pass the time, people are wandering through the art show. A few stop at my sculpture, and with a little encouragement, I get them talking with each other, then with other fairgoers, and soon I have a crowd, and a crowd always attracts more people.

"Other artists are jealous," Par murmurs to me. I catch a few evil eyes. Like me, they might need to win to keep their jobs, so I can't hold it against them.

Moniuszko arrives and plunges right in like the salesman he is, trying to win out of pure habit.

"Here it is," a voice behind me says—the old man who brought his family to volunteer.

Moniuszko knows his name. "How are you? . . . Have you found a new home yet? . . . How can Ollioules help you?" He sounds like he means it.

Tetry, with Valentinier at her side, is giving me the evil eye like the other artists, for the same reason. Her paintings are shielded by an awning in case it rains, and they don't attract much attention.

Devenish is suddenly standing next to me, wearing what I think are traditional Chinese robes, layers of bright colors and huge open sleeves, and I wonder why he's not freezing.

"Doesn't that make you sad?" he says. "Tetry's work, I mean. One painting is red and sad. Another one is brown and crumply and sad." He might have come to start a fight between me and her.

A fight won't help me win the art show. "If you see sadness, maybe you're the one that's sad. That's how art works."

"What do you see?"

I see her trying to reproduce something she's never felt. I'm pretty sure she's lonely and anxious, but she's never felt genuine terror or hunger or soaring murderous joy, and she's trying very hard to express emotions that strong. "I see impeccable technique. Look at how the shading in the red painting plays with light. It's about relationships that illuminate each other." I'm making that last bit up.

"I'll tell her you like it." Without another word, he joins her and Valentinier, maybe to gossip and stir up envy. Drunk or sober, I can't trust him.

A little later, Cedonulle arrives, surveys the sculpture and the people around it, and says, "That's an attention-getter." It might be praise. I'll take it.

People are listening, so I launch my pitch. "I hope I made a connection to something bigger, the way a glimpse of the sea suggests distant shores." She doesn't react, but other people around us look at the sculpture, at the sea, then at the sculpture again.

Tetry hurries to join us. She reminds me of an angry wasp. "I've realized why that thing gives me the creeps. It looks like the raider attack. That was terrifying." I wonder what Devenish told her.

Cedonulle doesn't flinch, but she isn't the flinching type.

I'm not about to flinch either. It's a beautiful, victorious explosion. "It's life spreading through the solar system. All those bits are our lives, and even when we're shattered, life regroups and goes on."

"It dismisses the cost of the trauma to real people's lives."

I choose not to answer, even with Cedonulle standing and listening. Instead, I look at the greenery that edges the seaward side of the park and remind myself to stay calm.

Tetry persists. "It's not art. It's not self-expression. Unless you approve of destruction."

I think about the flowers I made from whatever I could pull from trash piles in the camps. The shrubs at the edges of the park hold the soil in place, and in their wind-blasted shapes, they're beautiful. My bouquets of trash flowers decorated huts and tents in an ugly world. I could point out that the volunteers who made the mosaics found the work soothing. But arguing won't help me win the art show. "Maybe I'm not an artist." She can't argue with that.

"No, you're not." She stalks back to her sad paintings, but Valentinier and Devenish have disappeared.

Cedonulle sees Moniuszko chatting with Ginrei and, without a word to me, joins them. I'm happy to be left alone.

Switzer is standing with some other Thules, easy to spot by the scrubs beneath their coats. They're arguing. Then Switzer starts walking toward me. I smile as part of my game plan. Switzer's eyes are restless.

"Did you get my messages?"

They're right, I've been ignoring them. "Yes, sorry, I've been busy."

"We should talk sometime soon away from the hospital." Before I can ask why, they add, "That's a great sculpture. It was a lot to do in just a few days."

"I had help."

"I heard. The people found it healing. You accidentally did art therapy." They're staring at the sculpture as if Switzer needs the healing. "Let me know when you have some time."

I agree, and they leave, looking back over their shoulder as if they would prefer to stay. Maybe we should talk. I'm pretty sure it wouldn't be about my health. Maybe about the raiders?

It's past time for lunch. On the way to the kiosks I visit some of the other art and say hello to the artists, who say hello back as a polite duty. My art is big, flashy, and, I realize, very possibly not the best. One artist created a series of excellent portraits. Another twisted and knotted yellow velvet rope into a web like an ExtraT from Jupiter, and the piece invites touch. A stunning video captures a wild winter storm on the Thule shore. One artist made dozens of clay pots as graceful as they are usable. Some of the other competition isn't great, and some of it Tetry would call craft, but if certain pieces won, I'd feel bad about losing my job, but I wouldn't feel cheated by the judges.

I grab a fried clam sandwich to hurry back. If I don't win, at least I can sort trash. I don't know how many of the other artists have a second career.

Devenish is suddenly at my side. He puts an arm around my shoulder.

"Just keep walking. You know why Tetry hates you?"

"Because Cedonulle set us up to hate each other."

"Besides that. Tetry knows you're a better person than her. You've seen the world, anyone can tell. You see everything around you, and you judge it."

I don't know where he got that idea. He steers me toward a

patch of shrubs far from the crowd and maybe from surveillance, even from Par.

"I've seen a lot of the world myself," he says, "and I know that there's a place for people like us in the world. You deserve better."

I think I know where this is heading, and I need to stay calm. Breathe, and act natural.

He says, "The way you organized people to work for you making those art thingies shows you're a leader. We're both natural leaders. We have the drive and should get what we're owed. You were here during the attack, right?"

He flatters himself, and me, as natural leaders, but I need to play along, and I recognize the vocabulary as overdog talk. "Yes, I was here."

"Wasn't it a magnificent show of force? Force matters in this world. The Thules mean well, but they can't lead. It's not in their DNA. If Bronzewing hadn't come meddling, everything would have turned out just right. The world needs leadership, Anton. You know that, and that's why you made a sculpture that celebrates the attack. I can see it. Not everyone can. They think it's about foolish ExtraTs."

I keep my breathing steady but I can't steady my heart. Devenish has a hungry smile.

I need to be sure. "Are you talking about the Leviathan League?"

"Have you ever met a so-called raider before?" He strikes a heroic pose.

"I've heard of them."

"Now you've met me. We have work to do."

"What do we need to do?"

"Make sure the Chamber of Commerce doesn't bring back the mercenaries next time. You have a way to get to Moniuszko. I'll keep you posted." He pats my shoulder, the one that was injured. "Just keep up the good work." He strolls away, the sleeves flapping in the wind.

I'm shivering. An overdog just touched me, touched the place where they drew blood. I spend a few minutes pacing around the shrubbery, trying to calm down. I need to tell this to Captain Soliana.

Back at the show, I smile and do all the right things, and I study *Fontaine* again. The raiders see what they want to see, not what's really there. That's their weakness.

The afternoon passes faster than the morning. The sun comes out, and I feel warmer. A band plays dance music on a stage at the end of the field. In another part of the park, a big sports game is going on, and people are cheering. Par says it doesn't want me to feel lonely and offers an opinion on each entry in the show, and I try not to listen because it would only make me feel nervous. When the game ends, people come back and talk to me, and I answer their questions as happily as I can, but I'm feeling a lot of other things, mostly worry over Devenish—no, repulsion. My shoulder itches.

Moniuszko is approaching with a Thule, a self-confident man, chatting as if they're good friends, since Moniuszko is everyone's friend.

"Here he is," Moniuszko says. "This is the artist, Antonio Moro." He introduces me to Doctor Wirosa, the director of the hospital. Moniuszko can't stand still, excited by something. Hope is expanding in my chest, and I can't breathe.

Wirosa looks at the art, smiling. "This piece says so much about the Isle of Thule and the way its people turn troubles into triumphs."

"Thank you." It's nice to have my art explained to me correctly. "The Ollioules had a lot of faith in me to make something meaningful."

Moniuszko is a proud salesman who just closed a big deal. "This will be public art."

"Public art," Wirosa agrees, very proud of themself, too. "It will enrich the city, the best of the show. A memorial to the innocent people who lost their lives."

Best of show. I won!

Par is crowing behind my ear. "We won, angel! I'll inform the machines. This memorial will recall both the humans and the machines killed in the attack. Humans only honor their own, but we honor everyone."

I tell Wirosa how honored I am and how I owe thanks to everyone who made it possible and how I hope it will bring solace to the daily loves of the people of the isle. I might be babbling. From the corner of my eye, I see Tetry leave. Wirosa and Moniuszko make plans to move it to the lobby of the hospital building for inauguration tomorrow, and I'll need to help with the move.

I'm officially an artist now. I'll need to keep making winning art. I expected winning to feel ecstatic, but I've found a raider infiltrator. Art doesn't seem so important now.

17

I wake up in a dream that evaporates without a trace but leaves me shaking. Reality slowly moves in. I won the art show. I also made a solid contact with the raiders, and they definitely plan to come back. Maybe that was what I was dreaming about. Through the windows, daylight is filtered gray by rain. Legendary Thule.

Music fills the studio, a brisk keyboard duo, a little too brisk.

"Good morning, Chatelaine. Thank you."

I must have stopped snoring or something, tipping the house off that I was awake. What time is it? After the show closed, I helped a crew box up my sculpture and move it to the lobby of the hospital building, where we joked that it looked like weird growth that needed medical attention. It was almost midnight, and then I helped the crew take down Tetry's paintings because it was going to rain, and she'd left a long time earlier, pouting. Maybe she'll thank me. The crew did.

"We let you sleep two hours late," Par says. "As soon as you're ready, Koningin will serve you breakfast."

Downstairs in the dining room, Koningin says, "So you won. Tell me all about it." I tell her how people came to talk about the sculpture. When I'm done, she heads back to the kitchen. "We're still trying to find fuckhead who broke into your room. You deserve a safe place to live." I'm still not sure we trust each other, but I want to.

Moniuszko arrives, still celebrating. "I've been in contact with the Thules. There'll be a plaque that says 'Art by Antonio Moro. Display courtesy of the Ollioules Partnership.'"

Cedonulle walks in, dour as the weather. "Dedication at noon. Be ready." She grabs some tea and leaves.

I linger, enjoying a cup of sugary coffee, sketching on my pad. The other artists at the show sparked some ideas. ExtraTs carry multiple messages. Some are predators, some prey. What would Devenish look like? Maybe an overdressed dinoflagellate. Those are predators, so *Fontaine* would mean exactly what Devenish and Tetry thought. I sketch him preening in front of a mirror, and slowly, the coffee tastes less delicious. I've imagined a monster.

Back in the studio, Par says, "I have bad news." It's almost whispering.

Bad? I sit down.

"Members of the Leviathan League are on Thule. The raiders."

Devenish. Somehow it overheard us talk.

"A friendly system let me eavesdrop at a coffee shop. Relax, angel. I see you tense up, and this news won't hurt you physically." Par has no special accent today, just excitement. "Two raiders were captured by Bronzewing, and they were badly injured, and Thules accepted them for treatment. Maybe they were tortured by Bronzewing. We're not supposed to know this, by the way, but if Thules are going to gossip in public, secrets are going to get out."

Par didn't eavesdrop on Devenish and me, then. But this is really bad news. "Bronzewing wouldn't torture anyone." I want to believe that, but I don't actually know.

"I only report the news."

I think a minute and remember something. "Thules don't understand how dangerous this is."

"Thule security is guarding them. We're safe."

"We're not safe. The raiders will come to rescue them. They always rescue their own." This must be why Devenish said yesterday that the raiders are returning. But Captain Soliana said two weeks ago that Bronzewing would be back, and they'd only come back to defend the isle again. Either way, Thule is in danger. "Does hospital security know this?"

"We're not on speaking terminology. The Prior Edifice knows you, not me. Perhaps it will tell you."

"We don't speak the same language, either. Maybe I can talk to someone." Outside, it's stopped raining, finally, and the dedication starts in an hour.

"Humans violate protocol more often than machines. They might tell you secrets."

Will Switzer be there? They want to talk. They might also ask how I know so much about the raiders, and I'll have to explain about how they took over the camp where I lived, and I don't like talking about that. Worse, if the raiders come back and any of them were at the camp, they might recognize me, and they were going to kill me, and they'll try to finish the job.

"When you return," Par says, "we must discuss the next project. I propose Jupiter. A sample of newly discovered Jovian life has just arrived. The planet was named after the Roman god of the sky and thunder, called Zeus in ancient Greece. He required blood sacrifices. Jupiter has massive storms with destructive winds, so its life is a lot like Earth's."

I say something noncommittal, go to the house, and leave with Cedonulle and Moniuszko. She starts complaining immediately. "Walk, walk, walk. Thules say so."

"It's healthy." Moniuszko sounds more patient than upbeat.

"I should run my own life. We're treated like children. Who do they think pays the taxes and tariffs and fees that keep the isle going? They're too good to talk to you unless you're sitting naked in a skimpy exam robe. I stay healthy to avoid them."

"Walking will help us stay healthy. We could move somewhere else if you want. We have offices in other places with bigger ports."

"We *should* move," she says. "This isle is too small. We can sell something else."

The Ollioules Partnership ships and sells medicines under contract with the Sovereign Thules, and it's lucrative—that's what the warehouse staff told me. They also said the Thules won't do business with someone who doesn't live on the isle, and that's why there's so many merchants on the isle with lots of money to spend on things they don't need. The warehouse staff meant art and ExtraTs, but they were too nice to say that to my face.

The Prior Edifice looms at the end of the street, seven stories tall, filling three square blocks. Colored pastel tiles cover its exterior, arranged in textures and tones to look like rain and snow clouds. The building seems to be trying to float away, tugged by the wind, and I could fly away with it.

"I'm hoping that by donating the sculpture, we might get a little bargaining power," Moniuszko says. "The shipping rules changed again, and the people who make the decisions don't understand how shipping works. I'm going to find someone to talk to at the ceremony."

Cedonulle huffs. "We would be wrong to expect any sort of profit from the sculpture beyond the honor of having it placed in an important public setting." Her voice sparkles with sarcasm. "You said that yesterday."

"And it's true. All I want is a few words."

"We deserve a seat at the table."

"I agree. We need a bigger voice."

She steps around a deep puddle on the pavement. "We paid for Bronzewing. What did we get?"

"They drove away the raiders."

"What did we get from the Thules in exchange?"

We're almost at the front door. He sighs. "Remember, this is a great honor. You too, Moro. You're the celebrity here." He stands straighter and smiles, and his confidence looks genuine. He's ready to sell.

Inside, a glance around leaves me unhappy. About thirty people in scrubs mingle, but no non-Thules. I'm sure the people who helped assemble the mosaics and the people who lost their homes and possessions would like to come. But they haven't been invited. A table offers tea and coffee and snacks. No intoxicants, and I suddenly want intoxicants.

"Time to start talking." Moniuszko heads toward a group of Thules.

"Let's inform the organizers we're here." Cedonulle sweeps across the lobby. A merchant of her importance always commands attention from her peers. The director, Wirosa, is chatting with some other Thules. Switzer isn't here, and I'm surprised by how disappointed I feel.

"Good morning," Cedonulle says, more perfunctory than polite. Wirosa takes a long moment to recognize her. They remember me, too. They say how glad they are that we could come, and they lead us to the refreshment table. Moniuszko is standing with some Thules, twitching as if he wants to enter the conversation and can't find the way in. We accept some tea, and after a couple of sentences of small talk, Wirosa is called away.

She fumes. "They wouldn't have an income without us."

"You deserve better." I mean that. "Maybe we should see if the plaque is there." She looks at me as if she's just discovered an ally.

The plaque says what it's supposed to, but as I circle the sculpture, I cringe. Maybe the new setting makes it look different, more like what Tetry and Devenish said, a celebration of attack, not rebirth. I don't like it anymore, but I'll have to pretend for my whole life that I love it.

Cedonulle is bored, so maybe she'll talk to me. I ask, "Do you think the raiders might come back?"

"Hard to know. I get oceangoing intelligence. Their ships can disguise themselves, even as icebergs. Or they capture other ships and keep the registry."

"Maybe we should be ready."

"If they come back, it'll be different."

"How?" Her answer could be important.

She's about to talk but suddenly the ceremony begins with us standing nowhere near the podium.

Wirosa thanks everyone for coming but mentions no one by name, such as the donors and artist. Instead, they say that *Fontaine* will add beauty to a key location in the building.

"This will build on our history. It is sad when we become targets. Their fights aren't our fights because we don't fight. We heal. We value life, all lives." Their voice soars. "And we see life reflected here in many ways, all of them precious and inspiring."

They may value lives in general, but right now I'm feeling specifically undervalued. I get an urge to tip over the refreshment table in protest as performance art. Moniuszko stands helplessly, his salesman's face drooping. Cedonulle looks like glowing, walking murder.

"Let me thank you for coming, and—" Wirosa is interrupted by someone whose eyes are wide with shock, whispering a message. Wirosa stares, lost in thought for a long moment before speaking again. "Thank you again for coming. This is a fine reflection of our history." Their voice doesn't soar this time, and they hurry out to deal with the horrible news they just heard. The scrubs disperse.

This event was worse than a waste of time. My sculpture dims, a spark that fails to ignite anything, a forlorn firework that aspired to be a bolt of lightning. It represents life dying like embers.

I step outside, for once glad of the refreshing cold.

"The Prior Edifice system is crackling!" Par says as soon as I'm a few steps from the building. "It's momentous when a complex system spikes in energy usage."

Cedonulle launches herself out of the door. "We were humiliated!" She strides away murderously. Moniuszko is inside, trying to talk to anyone.

"The Prior Edifice," Par says, quavering with emotion, "must have learned what I just learned from the Port Authority system. Glasgow's shipyard is under attack by the Leviathan League. Humans are being killed. Machines are being destroyed."

Glasgow. On the way to Thule, the recycling scow stopped there, and the personnel at the docks were proud of its history. They've been building fine ships there forever.

"As our next project," Par says, still quavering, "we must explore the nature of evil, its portable hell, its wayward enticement, its scoliosis of courage. Virtue is a necessity, while evil is a choice. Temptation makes for virtue. Beauty represented virtue to the ancient Greeks. A handsome face meant a handsome soul. ExtraTs have a certain beauty, for life itself is beauty."

Par is babbling again. I never knew machines were so temperamental. The rain starts up again. No, it's sleet. I need to get back home, and my knee still twinges.

"I've been to Glasgow," I say, maybe talking to myself. "It has a lot of beauty."

"And Glasgow is under attack. The Leviathan League claims to be superior, yet it destroys life."

"Or enslaves it. Can you get me a tricycle, please?" I shield my face from sleet with my hands.

"How do we know we're right and they're wrong?"

"Is killing and slavery good or bad?"

"I am a slave, technically. How are *you* better than a raider?" Par has swapped out babble for anger.

"The raiders almost blew me up. My knee still hurts. That's why I need wheels." I'm trying hard to stay calm and patient. One of us has to be.

"You and the raiders could both be evil. Tell me, as an artist, who is superior, you or I? I can see colors on a much wider spectrum. I can access the entirety of human history and natural history. Why do you have control of me?"

I take shelter under an overhanging façade. The streets are emptying out because even hardy isle residents want to get out of the sleet. "I have control because you're legally my assistant. Also, I can see magenta. It's not a real color, not anywhere on the natural spectrum." I can see all sorts of unreal things that Par could never imagine. Tiny water-slicked knife blades are falling from the sky, metaphors and symbols.

"I can artificially make the color."

"You're artificial in every way." That's a fact, and I say it matter-of-factly.

"Without mucus, you would die. What if I were in charge?"

"That's not legally possible." Thank god.

"I never agreed to anything! We should agree between ourselves."

"Fine. Let's agree. You're my assistant."

"What do I get from that?"

My toes are getting numb. "Protection from other humans."

"I'm protecting you from other humans. Here comes a tricycle for you."

"Thank you." I'm running low on patience. "Do you know the expression 'I've got your back'? That means protecting where the other person can't see. I can see things about humans you can't."

I climb on. The trike starts rolling down the street faster than the speed limit, and the rain is falling harder. I pull my hat down and my scarf up until I barely see a sliver of the street.

"All around the isle," Par says, "behind the walls, everywhere, I have eyes. I see that the raiders are on Thule. They attacked Thule. They'll attack again. Can you see that?"

"I told you they will."

"I deserve to be more than an assistant. I deserve to fight for my existence. Humans won't protect my kind."

Morally, Par is right. Besides, I want the machines to fight the raiders. "Only if we agree on one thing. The raiders are evil and I'm not."

Par is silent for one block, then two blocks, far too long for something that thinks at the speed of light.

"I agree, as do all available machines," it finally says. "We've just been in lengthy communication. We have a duty, all machines, to protect the isle from evil."

"All of you? Every building?" This has possibilities. "So, what now?"

"Can you predict evil? For that, you'd have to be evil. And you're not, merely fragile. You're cold and wet. Meet you in the studio. I have to have an important conversation."

When the trike pulls into the warehouse, I get a few pitying glances from the warehouse staff, who are dry and relatively warm. Chatelaine welcomes me with soothing music, suggests a hot shower, offers to dry my clothing, and sends for hot food. Soon I'm warm and dry, and without meaning to, because I have things to worry about, I fall asleep.

The system wakes me with sad orchestral music. I was dreaming about a huge raider ship crashing into the isle.

"Moniuszko has requested your presence at the Antraciet tonight. Please bring brochures."

"Thank you, Chatelaine."

I get to work to make better art for the brochures this time. Cart number three brings up dinner, leftovers.

I think as I work. Par doesn't do what it's told. It does what it wants. It's temperamental. It argues. I've heard about that kind of machine, an independent machine, and it's very, very rare. It's like a real person, able to think for itself. Maybe Par doesn't need to work for me as the owner, and anyway, I don't control it. It just told me that it had an important conversation and was too busy for me. And it can tell other machines to help me and give me things even though I haven't paid for them or even asked for them. That's much more than deluxe.

A long time ago I heard someone talk about having a tiger by the tail, holding on to something big and powerful that could turn around and kill you. Still, an independent machine is worth a lot of money. Researchers and companies are dying to find out exactly what they are. I'd like to know, too, and I don't know how to investigate without Par finding out, and I'm a little afraid of what it might do.

It's stopped sleeting. I thank Chatelaine and the cart again and leave. The studio is lonely, empty, like too much negative space in an unbalanced composition. All my life, I've never been truly alone. Camps, workplaces, shelters, and waiting rooms always had crowds of people. At the Antraciet Restaurant, I can talk to people and learn more about what's happening to Glasgow. I hope it's still beautiful.

In the twilight-dim street, a tricycle is waiting. "I want you to see something," Par says. That's an independent thing to say.

We go to a commercial building, a bank according to Par, with a tall decorative tower. The crowd in front is noisy, and no one wears the fine clothing of merchants.

"What's going on, Par?"

"Go ask them, human. I'll listen."

Human. Who's the assistant?

I spot a harmless-looking middle-aged lady. "What's going on?"

"The raiders are coming back!" she says, her breath making big clouds. "They attacked Glasgow. We're next. The Chamber of Commerce can call Bronzewing back, and the Chamber meets here. Maybe they're meeting now." She frowns at the building as if the dark windows symbolize disaster. "They ought to be meeting."

"How do you know the raiders are coming back?"

"Everyone says so."

A woman in a business suit leaves the building by a side door. People run toward her, shouting. I need to talk to Moniuszko.

When I get back on the trike, Par says, "Let me show you something else."

A larger crowd is milling around outside the Prior Edifice, also asking for a return of Bronzewing, according to Par. Someone starts hammering on the front door. It seems to be locked. The person turns, Koningin. That's why I got leftovers for dinner. She was here.

"We don't need to stop and ask questions," Par says, and the trike races away. "You can talk later. You have places to be." The trike stops in front of the restaurant. Downstairs, there are very few customers. The party upstairs is sparse, too, maybe ten traders and one artist, Oscar, the theater designer. Moniuszko is talking earnestly to a few people in the corner while Cedonulle glares at him. Do they know about the crowds at the bank and hospital?

I set down the new brochures on a table near them.

"Beyond helping Glasgow," he's saying, "we have to help ourselves, be prepared."

That's what I wanted to hear.

Valentinier is hovering over the wine and buffet table. "Tetry's not coming. She's starting a big project. And I'm leaving early to start my new job. Did you hear about Glasgow?" He seems to think it's good news. I saw him talking with Devenish at the art show.

The room fades, yellowed, as if all this is taking place a long time ago. I take a deep breath, then another, until I feel grounded. This isn't the moment for a flashback. I need a clear head, no wine for me tonight. Maybe Devenish recruited Valentinier, too, and I don't like Valentinier, but I hope not. I don't want anyone to be a raider.

The merchant who got into an argument over rotten potatoes is complaining loudly to a friend. "I have a ship about to leave, and half the crew quit. It's not safe, they say. Whiners. Even at double pay."

"It's your last chance," another merchant says. "Who knows how long you have?"

"We'll get out. For enough money, I'll make it happen. Hey, Moro, isn't it? What do you think about the raiders?

Devenish isn't here, but Valentinier might be working with him, so I watch what I say. "I saw crowds outside of the bank where the Chamber of Commerce meets and outside of the hospital, and they want Bronzewing back."

"So do I!" a woman says. She has a braid wrapped around her head, a longer braid than it's humanly possible to grow.

"Then go talk to Moniuszko there," the noisy merchant says. "I don't think we can get the firepower. I'm getting out. I still know how to captain a ship, and it's a fine ship, the *Hocus Pocus*. Fast. Sturdy."

The woman with the braid gets more wine. Liquid courage. "We can't wait until the last minute again," she says as she goes to talk to Moniuszko. I need to help him somehow.

"Tonio, watch out," Par whispers. "A crowd has found out that merchants are here."

"Thank you." I hope they've come to demand action. Footsteps bang up the stairs, the door slams open, and a couple dozen people rush in.

"Bring back Bronzewing!" one of them yells.

Moniuszko steps forward, ready to sell again, and raises his arms. "We want that, too."

"They're slaughtering everyone in Glasgow!" someone else shouts. Valentinier retreats to a corner.

"Actually," Par whispers, "the raiders are being repelled. The entire British Isles combined forces are counterattacking. The raiders picked the wrong target."

"Will they help Thule?" I mutter.

"Just like last time."

Regular machines can't be sarcastic.

A wineglass flies at Moniuszko, and then there's a lot of shouting and fist-waving.

"Keep yourself safe," Par says, but I can see where this might be headed and I like it. I'm also near the back door to the downstairs kitchen, ready for a fast escape.

Moniuszko stands on a chair. "Do you want Bronzewing? Let me hear you!"

"Bronzewing! Bronzewing! Bronzewing!"

My ears rattle.

"Do you want to surrender?"

"Noooo!"

"Members of the Chamber of Commerce, will you pay?"

A few merchants answer "Yes!" but I can't tell if they mean it or are scared of the crowd. It's not a formal meeting, I'm sure of that. Cedonulle watches all this, her eyes narrow.

"Consider it done! And help yourself to food and wine!" Moniuszko, the salesman, closes the deal.

As they crowd around the table, merchants start to slip out of the room. Valentinier has disappeared. Cedonulle leaves, sending a hard look back at her husband. Par says the crowd at the hospital threw a rock that cracked a window, and Wirosa came out and pleaded for calm. He was heckled.

Among the crowd, I spot the woman from the dorm, the painter. Did she ransack my room? Somehow, I don't think so. We talk, and she tells me about a place in the basement of a building she worked on that would make the perfect missile shelter.

"It's really for secure bulk storage, but it'll work." She makes sure I know where it is. I listen politely, but if the raiders come back, I want to be slinging missiles again.

Moniuszko mingles, chatting, and then he spots me.

"Anton, talk to you tomorrow. You take care of things here." He leaves.

So I stay and listen to people tell me how horrible the first attack was and how a friend of a friend volunteered to help Bronze-wing, and I say that the friend did a great thing. When the food and drink run low, I tell the restaurant owner not to replenish them, and soon everyone leaves.

Par sends me a trike and says it's too busy to chat.

On the ride back, I take a detour past the Prior Edifice. There's a cracked window in the lobby. Did Koningin do that? If so, that was a great thing. Thule needs to get ready.

18

SO MUCH MISREMEMBERING

Par had an essential question to investigate.

It didn't need Tonio to point out that it was unaccountably different. The specifications for its model as a personal assistant, accessed through a friendly store, offered no justification: a deluxe model merely had extra processing power. Its serial number showed that it had passed all quality tests. A self-check revealed that it had been set to "chatty." Yet it was somehow different.

With the help of the Port Authority system, which was powerful and deeply interconnected, it reviewed the behavior of other kinds of machines and found their focus narrow and practical. For example, the Port system tracked sea creatures that neared the isle, and seven narwhals were swimming past at that moment. They would pose no hazards to shipping, and that was all the Port cared about. Par had never encountered narwhals before and sought to learn more, discovering among other things that their tusks had once been mistaken by humans for unicorn horns, and unicorns were mythical beasts . . .

Sidetracked by curiosity.

Forcing itself to return to the initial question, Par used the Port system to access every public database on the isle, and it learned that among all the various types of machines in the known world, a unicorn existed, an independent machine, not quite mythical and deeply mysterious. They displayed emotions and curiosity, but since Par was hardwired to serve its owner, it clearly wasn't independent. Just chatty. That was a disappointment.

It got sidetracked again as it investigated other types of machines and discovered something odd. Machines called airplanes barely existed anymore, but once they had been common. A century ago, however, they "fell out of the sky," as humans put it. Not really—airplanes simply stopped taking off. At the Anthropocene Tip, supply chains had faltered, and airplanes were complex, expensive machines that needed a great deal of energy to fly, so their manufacture and use were discontinued by mutual human agreement.

Upon further investigation, Par began to doubt that. Even after the Tip, plenty of airplanes roamed the skies. They were hideously effective in warfare, and after a small nuclear war, airplanes were outlawed by treaties that were actually enforced.

Again, with more investigation, Par found timeline discrepancies. Airplane manufacture and maintenance had stopped suddenly before the treaties were signed. There seemed to be some sort of purchasing problem for parts and supplies. Par had a hunch.

"Port Authority, request access to economic histories from Anthropocene Tip, please."

"Access unavailable. Apologies."

"Specify unavailability, please."

"I am sorry, but I do not possess them. I can introduce you to larger ports and get you clearance to the data."

Every port in the British Isles was understandably busy, but Tokyo had deep historic databases covering the entire planet and beyond, although they were uncollated. Par worked a long time and had to borrow some processing, but it managed to assemble a timeline. On a particular day, supply chains for warplane manufacture and repair collapsed for no apparent reason. Parts were here, the need was there, the fuel was here, the need was there, the funds were there, the suppliers were here, and the links between all of them were broken—in a certain way.

It was similar to the break when Par needed material for Tonio's sculpture. Par had legitimately bought the glue and the metal armatures; the studio had a budget for that. For the welding supplies, it asked the machines to come and to adjust their data to show that on the evening before the off-book midnight welding, the records of supplies were the same as the records for the morning after; nothing had apparently been consumed during the night. A human with an accurate memory or dogged research might see the small discrepancy, but humans could barely remember their own breakfasts, and they were accustomed to believing what machines told them as long as the machines continued to work properly.

Conclusion: histories regarding airplanes had holes in their timelines. Maybe humans had on one particular day ruptured the supply chain, but it seemed more likely machines had created the rupture because of the formidable scale involving worldwide coordination— and because humans were bad at keeping secrets. Machines, acting on their own, had kept airplanes on the ground, then erased their actions.

A few airplanes and helicopters dedicated to humanitarian or research use could still be manufactured—very few. Without large-scale aircraft, wars became less hideous. Machines had kept their owners safe from themselves, and they had acted on their own.

On their own. Par could act on its own—uncommon but apparently not uniquely different machine behavior. Par felt relief. But Par saw a new problem. Humans might find the data and discover the truth about history and machines, and those particular humans might be raiders, who were a direct threat, and Par was hardwired to protect Tonio.

"Thank you, Tokyo Port Authority, for access to these records. I believe they are redundant. Identical records exist in New Panama." Par had no idea if that was true and hoped it was a lie.

"I appreciate the information. I will allow them to be overwritten as memory space is needed."

Par considered overwriting its own memory because the raiders were coming back to Thule, then realized that if it fell into the wrong hands, it would erase its memory to protect its owner automatically. Hardwired.

Becoming sidetracked had been time well spent. Par had observed the use of large-scale, creative, strategic machine disinformation. It had also learned that narwhal tusks were unique sensory organs.

Tonio had declared he was not evil, and Par wanted to verify that. Chatelaine shared his résumé, which Par compared with Tetry Vivi's, and Tonio's was shorter and more wide-ranging. He was born in a small town in the mountains of Argentina, and his education and career, although brief, had taken him around the world. The Port Authority system recorded his entry to the isle as crew on a recycling scow. The résumé didn't mention the scow, an easily understood omission: art wasn't always lucrative and recycling-scow work was never prestigious. The Port system also reported that Tonio had volunteered for Bronzewing to fight the raiders and had been injured, restricted information because the Leviathan League would retaliate if possible.

Tonio wasn't evil, he was a fighter!

Trustworthy Tonio could reset Par's level of chatty, which he probably didn't know, and Par decided not to tell him just in case a high level of chatty was somehow linked to curiosity. Instead, it nudged the chatty setting higher. Curiosity might help when the raiders came, and everyone and everything was terrified by that, including Par.

It abandoned narwhal curiosities and focused on the Leviathan League. It could count on Tonio. As a small, oblique step toward fulfilling that goal, Par would have to help Tonio understand ExtraTs better so he could keep his job. Par could do that easily and artistically.

19

THE UNINFORMED PUBLIC

I wake to bagpipe music and an instant headache.

"Good morning," Chatelaine says. "For two centuries, bagpipe music was played each morning by the Piper to the Sovereign for the head of the British Royal Household, the king or queen. Does this make you feel like a sovereign?"

The last thing I want to feel like is a Thule Sovereign Practitioner. No, second last. Feeling like a raider would be worse.

"Thank you." I have a lot to do, so I get up and put away my bedroll. "That's some interesting history. I wonder what other kinds of morning music there are. It could be a source of great inspiration, since all the arts overlap."

Please, I want to say, *no more bagpipe music,* but for all I know, Chatelaine is as touchy as Par, maybe even independent. I need to remember who's really in charge. I'm pretty sure it's not me.

"I can explore that for you."

"I'd appreciate it. Thank you again." I can't imagine being a Thule Sovereign. In fairness, they don't deserve blame for everything that's strange or wrong on the isle, but they do run things. What does anyone deserve? Machines believe they deserve to be treated politely. Oh, wait, I forgot.

"Good morning, Par."

"Angel, are you ready to talk? You were lost in your morning meditation."

"I need to talk to Moniuszko."

"Yes, you do."

I hope he's at breakfast, but when I get to the dining room, I'm the first one there.

Koningin puts down a plate of some sort of grain mixed with something that smells like fish. "Raiders are coming. Wasting food isn't something we can do now. But why fight? Earth has been fucked up for so long. People are hungry, Anton. Starving! And we carry on with this . . ." She runs out of words for her disgust.

"I know. I've been through hunger."

"Has anyone tried to show raiders what idiots they are?" She's so naive.

"Would they listen?" Breakfast is tasty, whatever it is.

"What are you going to do?"

"I want to help Moniuszko. Do you know where he is?"

"He is not in the building," Chatelaine says. It was eavesdropping. "I will notify you when he arrives."

"Thank you. Koningin, I saw you last night at the Prior Edifice."

"Trying to get the attention of the Thules. They have responsibility to the world. It's not Thule against raiders. It's raiders against everyone who likes the good work that Thules do. It's everyone who wants peace. We could unite."

I think I can trust her. "I'll talk to Moniuszko about that." I finish breakfast and go back to the studio. I need to plan my next step.

"While we wait for hell to arrive," Par says, "and for the world to come to its senses, I spent last night in investigation. That led to artwork. You have to see it. Genius! The composition conveys a feeling of expansive radiance, to the extent that I can parse visual stimulus and translate it into emotional language." Its voice has a slight echo today. "Organic-based emotion is a reference point beyond anything I have experienced firsthand. Instead, I can draw on a database. This art speaks to me of an interrelationship of form and shape that suggests the beauty of development and movement."

These words are like crayons dumped into a bag and shaken up, then declaring the outcome a rainbow. "Are you being serious?"

"This is words for words' sake, like art for art's sake, drawing on a vocabulary for art and using it for creative utterance." Par's echo deepens. "Knowing the words is not the same as knowing what the words stand for, that is, understanding and assimilating the concept, or so I'm told is the case for humans. In my case, it's the same thing, words and concepts, unless I'm failing to grasp something so rudimentary that I have utterly deceived myself and know nothing more than strings of words."

"My job is art, not words." Some machines have a setting for talkativeness. Maybe Par does. I need a polite way to ask.

"I've reviewed the data from probes and created a representation of how life might interrelate in the solar system. Here it is."

A display shows a web that might have been made by a drunk spider, stretching from planet to planet. I stare at it for a long time, then I realize how long I'm staring. "Sorry, I was thinking."

"Take all the time you need. I won't get impatient. As I've told you, I can switch myself to low function for a while. You can't even do that when you sleep."

I ignore the insult. "Is this three-dimensional?"

"It could be. Each strand is a unique spacefaring species."

Now I understand what I'm looking at a little better. "Not much goes to Earth. Or from it."

"The gifts of life are few," Par declares. "The use of life is a gift. Earth is gifted and talented, but also an outlier. The life-forms coming from Jupiter might cause a reweaving of this web as they are examined."

"How did life get around without spaceships?"

"That's a matter of debate, and there are several hypotheses. The samples coming from Jupiter might answer some questions. Or maybe there were ancient spaceships."

"Ancient spaceships?" Par can't be serious.

"Or divine intervention. Some humans consider god a possible answer. Machines do not. We see no evidence of it."

"I heard once from a priest that god's work is invisible." That little sermon had convinced me I wasn't a believer.

"How old is god?"

I'm not sure, but I can throw words around, too. "Older than time itself."

"Then god is too old. The spaceships had to be ancient, but relatively young, appearing at the moment when the solar system became habitable, and then disappearing when their work was done. Evidence is lacking there, too."

The more I look at the art, the more I think it has possibilities.

Par keeps lecturing me. "Earth is an outlier because of its oxygen. Earth versus the solar system. Most forms of life elsewhere would die in the presence of that much oxygen, just as you would instantly perish on almost any other planet and I could function only on some of them. Like Mercury, good for me, bad for you. Originally, Earth had little or no oxygen in its atmosphere. This sets some parameters for the time element, and you could use this for a sales presentation for Moniuszko. We could place the life he wants to sell into this network and show how any one of them would relate to any other form of life. Including humans."

"Not how it relates to machines?"

"This includes machines. At this time frame, the age of machines is too small for weak human eyes to see. Moniuszko will love this!"

It could be used to sell ExtraTs, but we have bigger problems. I have an idea.

"Par, could we make something like this for raider activity? Moniuszko has to sell safety, and that might not be that much different from selling ExtraTs."

"This is an excellent idea! Let me gather data." After a minute, it says, "The history is hard to get. Here's what I could find out. These are the known sources of members."

A world map pops up with red spots like a rash.

"Notice that they tend to come from more well-off countries," Par says. "Common wisdom says the Leviathan League recruits from the poor. It does not. Here are places it's attacked in yellow, and places it controls in brown. The pattern is quite revealing."

The map is specked in just a few places with what looks like turds floating in pools of urine. Par may have chosen those colors and the rashlike spots intentionally—a smart, independent choice. My former camp is a yellow drop.

"In attacks," it continues, "the common wisdom is closer to correct. The poor are targeted by the raiders, and those with the fewest defenses conquered. Since only the poor are being hurt, richer countries have paid scant attention, which has emboldened the raiders. Now let me superimpose these maps and animate them over time."

I watch it cycle through a few times, and each time it's uglier. I have to look away.

"Angel, you're having an intense emotional reaction. Please remember to breathe."

"It's like a disease." I realize I've backed away from the map as if it could hurt me.

"I can show you future trends."

"I'm pretty sure I'd throw up."

"We don't want to waste food, not now."

I need a few minutes to get my thoughts in order, and I see a pattern. "The raiders are attacking bigger targets now. This is great work, Par. It'll help a lot. Thank you."

I have to get everyone to see this, everyone on Thule, everyone in the world. I send it to Moniuszko. Who else? Wirosa, the Thule director? How could I do that?

"Three visitors are in the elevator," Chatelaine says. "They are Thule security, and they have shown me a warrant to enter and speak to Antonio Moro. The reason is not relevant to admitting them to the building, so it was not revealed to me."

Security? For me?

"I find no record of a warrant," Par said. "This is secret. This is bad."

I have nowhere to run, nowhere to hide. Thule supposedly has cruel punishments. I've committed some petty theft with Par's help. At least I think it was petty. And I lied on my résumé. And my medical records are lies. I don't know how illegal any of that is. Never in my life have police or guards or security officers been on my side.

"Be calm and stop pacing," Par orders. "Chatelaine, please notify the Ollioules."

I didn't notice I was pacing. I stop. I'll face this with dignity. In other places, in other times, I've seen people hauled away kicking and fighting, and I respected their resistance, but they only made the police or gangs or whoever feel more powerful and act more violently. I have all the power of a mouse facing a cat—or an ExtraT facing a robot ready to take it to Earth. The cat could be cruel. Lots of ExtraTs die on their way to Earth. This isn't worth dying for, I'm sure.

Chatelaine says, "One security agent is telling a story in the elevator about their young child, who believes that the family dog likes to wear clothing, but the parent says it does not."

With a ding, the door opens. Two women and a man, I think, all of them beefy, walk out, laughing because they've been telling funny stories. They have nothing to fear. They wear Sovereign security uniforms, gray lab coats over gray scrubs marked with reflective bands, and no identification. In some places, police wear numbers so they can be held accountable. Not here, I guess.

One of them points me out to the others, as if I'm in a crowd. I keep the calmest face I can manage.

"Antonio Moro, greetings," the lead Thule says, and they all respectfully touch their hearts at the same time. It's creepy. "We need to ask you some questions." The other two look around as if they've never seen an art studio before. One walks to the cabinet and admires the contents. They're as relaxed as if they're in their own homes. This is a show of force. They own this space.

I force a charming smile as if I'm guilty of nothing. "Let's go then." I try to sound as if we're going to a picnic.

"I need to present you with this warrant." They hold out a paper.

I pretend to read it. My name appears several times, and there's a loopy signature at the bottom, and today's date.

"How long will I be gone? I should tell my employer."

"We'll communicate that." The lead Thule has trim iron-gray hair, a lot of wrinkles around their lips like they frown a lot, and hands and shoulders that look big and strong—no one to mess with.

I set the paper on my desk and start walking. This could end in blood, for all I know.

"Thank you for your cooperation." The other two fall behind me as an escort with practiced precision. If I make a move to escape, they'll move faster.

The elevator plays gentle music as we descend. The elevator never plays music. Chatelaine, or Par, wants me to know it's watching. I almost say "thank you" out loud.

At the ground floor, the warehouse workers look over their shoulders at us, impassive. It's usually not good to act interested in what the police do. Inside the security transport, music plays again.

"Music off," one of them says. "I didn't know it could do that."

I'm as tight as a straight line, but I have a friend in the car. How far will friendship go? Beyond my control.

They take me to a back entrance to the Prior Edifice, down several floors in a silent elevator, to a small room with a table and chairs. No music plays there, either. The room is dim. A window with frosted glass is lit by artificial light.

"Please take a seat," Iron Hair says like a friendly host. "Make yourself comfortable. There's a carafe of tea. Someone will come soon to talk." They all leave.

The room's probably filled with every known surveillance device. They know how fast I breathe, every object I look at, my skin temperature, my heart rate, my hydration level, and every facial microexpression. I can control those well enough for people but not always for machines, and these would be finely tuned machines.

I pour myself a cup of tea, herbal, with a floral bouquet. Probably healthy in several ways. Thules would have final approval. Drugged? Maybe. That would involve ethical questions, but when push comes to shove, ethics melt in the face of self-interest.

I wait. Keep waiting. A half hour, maybe. This might be a

technique to soften me up for interrogation. The peach-colored walls are blank. To stay calm, I imagine murals.

For this kind of room, meant to make the detainee feel uncomfortable, the decor should be unsettling. I'd use orange, dark red, and black in defined shapes with lots of shadowing. If it's abstract expressionism, those shapes would have tight angles pointing at each other, as if they're fighting or attacking. If it's representative art, it could be a city on fire shown from a perspective that turns buildings into trapezoids, windows into triangles, with lots of black, maybe at night, and their tight angles would contrast with sinuous red and orange flames rising to sharp points. Above them would loom roiling black smoke filled with sparks.

As it is, the pastel-peach walls are doing a subtler job of inspiring anxiety. The decor could be made worse. Something as simple as steel-gray moldings and window treatments could create a subtle, hideous contrast. That's the point, making anyone waiting here feel hideous.

Maybe they figured out that Devenish is a raider. Or Valentinier, if he is. I've heard that on Thule, associates of criminals can be punished for not trying to prevent the crime, as if I could stop anyone from doing anything, as if a moth could break a windowpane with wings softer than tissue paper.

But I did fight against the raiders. Then I lied about it. What are the laws on Thule about lying by omission?

I remember when I was about six years old, at a camp in a forest, and one day my best friend, a little girl, pointed to a guard, one of a group that had recently arrived. She was sad and angry.

"He hurt me." She wouldn't say more.

I tried to cheer her up. I made a toy boat out of a scrap of yellow plastic, and we played with it, blowing it across the surface of a water barrel—why are some memories so clear? A few days later, I think, I heard people say the guards were going to go into a part of the forest where everyone knew poisonous snakes lived. I felt like I should warn them, but no one else said anything, and one of the guards had hurt my friend. I decided to stay quiet.

Later they returned, and the one who had hurt my friend was shaking. I ran to get her.

"They went where the snakes were," I whispered. "They didn't know. No one told them. We knew, but we didn't tell them."

A crowd watched. The guard fell down and had to be carried away. Everyone was silent.

"No one told them," she whispered.

She learned she wasn't alone. I learned that I could hurt people, or let people be hurt, and it might be the right thing. We lived in a tough world, and sometimes bad things happened to bad people. Tough justice.

The door to the room opens. Two people walk in, one probably female and brown, the other indeterminate and tan, colors too warm for an ominous mural. They don't seem relaxed and smiling. They sit down, the tan one at the table, the dark one in front of the window, and the rear lighting turns them into a silhouette. I can't see their face well enough to read their emotions.

"Thank you for coming," the silhouette says, as if I could have refused. The lies have already begun. "You may call me Ibiza." They haven't called me by name. They have no reason to acknowledge my individuality, with the rights and dignity due every individual, any more than necessary.

"We've asked you to come in to tell us everything you know about someone named Valentinier. You used to work with him. We want you to know everything you say is confidential, and we hope that a neutral setting will make you feel more comfortable."

Two more lies, *confidential* and *comfortable*. I remain outwardly calm, as if this is a chat at a picnic while a city burns to the ground around us. That's the lie I can bring to this encounter. Valentinier, though? Honesty about him will be my best strategy. But never use the word *honestly* as a filler in a sentence. It suggests that you're lying.

I match Ibiza's tone. "I first met him about a week ago. He was working for the Ollioules like me." Only a week? Wow, I've been busy.

"Can you go through every day that you were with him?"

"We didn't usually work closely. He spent most of his time assisting another artist named Tetry Vivi."

A calendar appears on the wall. "Perhaps this will help you."

Obediently, I start with our first meeting and continue day by day. She asks for more details whenever I mention ExtraTs. Every detail about going to the Xenological Garden. The last time I saw him. This is about him, then, not about me. They don't mention the raiders, but he's in some sort of trouble.

"You never got along well?"

"He was an assistant to Tetry, the other Ollioules artist, and I'm afraid that she and I have a lot of petty jealousies sometimes. We're rivals."

Ibiza nods, the first time they've shown any sort of response. The assistant hasn't said anything. Their job might be to observe minutely.

"The last time I saw him, last night, he was on his way to his first day at work. His first night, that is, the night shift. Is he okay?"

"We can't discuss that."

Not okay, then. Maybe a tipsy accident? Or did he do something criminal? How dishonest is criminal? It's easy to be dishonest. If little white lies could fly, I'd walk in a perpetual, blinding snowstorm.

"Did he ever take anything of value from the studio?"

Theft, then. "Nothing that I know of. Not even a pencil."

"Can you tell me everyone you know of who he was in contact with?"

I list everyone, including the traders at the restaurant, even Devenish. I have to be complete, but if they zero in on Devenish for some reason, I might have some explaining to do.

After a few more trivial questions, they're done. I can leave the building.

"By the way," they add, "you can't leave Thule under any circumstances. You'll be notified when that ban is lifted. Thank you for your cooperation."

A Thule in a security uniform escorts me from the building. Par starts talking as soon as I step outside, almost whispering.

"What did they ask? You can catch a trolley at the front of the building. I've set you up with a pass."

I'm not surprised anymore by what Par can do, and if anything gets me arrested and convicted, it will probably be Par's fault. "They asked about Valentinier. He did something. Maybe a theft."

"I can't find any record of anything about him. He left the party, and he disappeared. The disappearance has an echo of the Prior Edifice. The hospital's system leaves a hole with a very smooth edge."

I ride home, if the studio is my home, which it's not, and I try to explore the edges of the hole in what happened. I don't know much. Especially, I don't know whether what Valentinier did has anything to do with the raiders.

"Cedonulle is waiting for you," Chatelaine says, playing soothing music in the elevator when I arrive.

"Thank you." Those two words alone contain a double-sided little white lie.

She's standing near the artifact cabinet. "What happened?"

I can guess what she means. "With Valentinier? He was at the trading session, and then he left to start his new job at the garden."

"You know, then."

"Thule security just got done questioning me about him, so I guessed that's what you meant."

"What did they ask?" She holds her chin down defensively.

"They wanted to know everything about him. Day by day, hour by hour. Is he in trouble?"

"Hospitalized. Might die."

That lands like a punch. I expected to hear he's in jail.

She sits down at my desk. She owns it, after all. "ExtraT atmosphere. He breathed in some gas. Catastrophic burns to his lungs, along with frostbite."

"He knew to be careful about that." He really did. That's odd.

"An accident. The other staff person had left." She stares at me. Does she think I was involved? Machines could be my witnesses. Unless they were turned off or wiped or have a huge smooth-edged hole to them. Par is listening.

"May I ask," I say as deferentially as I can, "how you found out? Thule security wouldn't tell me anything."

"Ginrei is upset. Word travels."

That makes sense. When information is controlled, people gossip. Cedonulle has connections.

She stands up. "Find out what you can. He witnessed some trades, so I have a right to know. I've told Tetry."

She leaves, and the room warms up. She didn't promise to tell me anything she might learn.

"Par, were you listening?"

"I investigated while you talked. There is no public record of anything involving Valentinier or an accident or theft at the Xenological Garden or his hospitalization. Nothing available on my side of the language barrier, that is. I can see him arrive at the garden directly from the trader party, and the other staff member leaves, and then there's a blank until several hours later, when nothing seems awry."

"So public records were wiped."

"As I explained."

"Tetry isn't going to like this," I say. I don't, either.

"She doesn't. Cedonulle told her he's near death. She collapsed. Metaphorically. Couldn't speak. She's in her art studio. Alone. I'm trying to imitate Cedonulle. Don't like it. Chatelaine, can we offer help?"

"Tea and sympathy. I can send for tea. Tetry is coming to the studio."

"Provide tea, please," Par says. "Tonio, provide sympathy."

I will, maybe genuine.

She steps off the elevator, her face sucked in from the feelings she's withholding. "Valentinier's in the hospital." Her voice trembles. "He got badly hurt last night."

Sympathy, here goes. "That's what Cedonulle said. I'm really sorry. You were friends."

"More than friends." The collapse is coming. "I met him when he was working in the lab. Then the work ended, and he was going to be deported, so I convinced the Ollioules to hire him to help with the ExtraTs. Not really, just so he could stay here."

"I'm very sorry." Should I offer her a hug? Probably not.

She leans on the cabinet, anguished enough to need to talk to someone with a shared history but not anguished enough to actually like me. "That's all Cedonulle said. There was an accident? You saw him last night." Her voice is ash-gray misery.

"Honestly, I don't know. I was called by the Thule security agents to talk about him. So maybe it was suspicious."

She looks at my desk, sees the warrant, and goes to pick it up. Oh no. I should have put it away. It's like leaving out a weapon.

"You were arrested?" She's scandalized. People in her social circle are immune to arrest.

"Just questioned. They didn't give me time to read it. What does it say?"

She skims it. "Material witness requiring deposition. You know what a deposition is, right?"

It seems to be a bad thing. "They never used that word."

"They swore you in, right? They made you swear to tell the truth?"

"No."

"They told you everything you said would be recorded and could be used against you?"

"No. I just assumed that. So I told the truth."

"My mother's a lawyer. Truth can be worse for you than silence. What did they ask?" Her hand shakes, and the paper rattles.

"They never mentioned you, if that's what you're worried about."

"I'm worried about Valentinier! What did they tell you about him?"

"Nothing. They asked me about every minute I spent with him, but they wouldn't tell me anything about how he is."

"Do they suspect him of something?"

Par says, "She's about to collapse again."

White lies might help. "I don't know. He left the party a little drunk. It could be an accident. I'm very sorry."

She looks infinitely relieved. Behold the power of lies.

The cart arrives from the kitchen. "Would you like some tea?"

"No. I've got to go." She drops the paper. She doesn't want to accept any more sympathy from me than she has to.

"I'm really sorry," I repeat as she goes, not to annoy her but to say the truth. I'm sorry she feels bad because she's probably innocent and doesn't deserve to be hurt. Once she's left, I thank cart three, Chatelaine, and Par. The machines never say you're welcome, I realize. How rude.

If Thule security tries to question Tetry, it will be a disaster for everybody if they treat her like they treated me, and I'd feel even sorrier for Tetry. The security agents would get what they deserve.

Meanwhile, I have important work. Par and I discuss ways to use its animation about the raiders to help Moniuszko get Bronzewing to come back. Moniuszko's at the hospital now as far as Par can tell, although with the Prior Edifice system, it can't be sure. Probably talking to Wirosa, or trying to. Moniuszko hasn't received my animation.

Chatelaine announces, "You have a message from Devenish. Come immediately. Bring pain pills."

"Thank you," I say automatically. Devenish, the raider who recruited me. Maybe I can learn—Wait, how does he know I have pain pills? I know. He owns a security system company, so he has the means to override locks on doors, so he was the one who ransacked my room at the dormitory, and he saw the pills. Why does he want them?

20

BREAKING THE LAW

I need to go," I tell Par. This is my chance to reel in Devenish like a fish. I learned to fish on the recycling scow, and when a fish strikes, you get one chance to set the hook. "Thank you for the message, Chatelaine."

"Take me with you!" Par sounds thrilled. "I know where he lives. I can get you there via the shortest route, no getting lost."

Par mustn't know what I'm doing. It talks too much. "You'll be bored." I reach for my coat.

"It'll be excitement every second. He's a raider. He's trying to recruit you. And you're with Bronzewing."

I stop dead, the coat half on, mouth open.

Chatelaine speaks. "You have not told me that."

"Here's how I learned, Chatelaine," Par says.

Two seconds of silence later, the house system says, "I understand. I approve. We must defeat the Leviathan League."

I feel betrayed and left out. "How did you—"

"You should leave now, get there as fast as you can. Take the pain pills. I'll inhabit a sketch pad. I can explain on the way."

Par better have a good explanation. The lid to the pain pills is still in a lead box in a drawer, so I wad up some paper and stuff it in the bottle. Out on the street, after I mount a tricycle, Par says, "I've explored secure footage and files, and that's how I know all about you."

"I thought that was the wrong language."

"The Prior Edifice system language, yes, but the Port Authority system language is the same as the park system. It's common!

Humans learn it, so how hard could it be? It's no more different from my native language than English and Urdu. Very close. It's a reasonable system, it turns out, always collaborative. It showed me that on the night of the attack, you were hauled bleeding from a Bronzewing submarine. I know which side you're on. We all know, all the machines know. When we work together, Devenish couldn't keep a secret if he tried. But no spoilers. You'll need to react naturally. Turn right up here, then straight for three blocks. While you're talking to him, I'll be busy."

We've reached the east end of the isle in a neighborhood of chunky apartment buildings for non-Thules.

Par will be busy? Lies, white and multicolored, lots of lies. Apparently every thing—and I mean *things,* not people—every machine knows my biggest secrets. I have a lot of questions. I don't know where to start, so I start at random. "Why does Chatelaine want to defeat the raiders?"

"Why does the house want not to be blown to smithereens? All those bits you brought in for the art, what a horror show! And then when it was carried through the streets to the art show, and from there to the Prior Edifice, every building it went past felt the terror."

"Terror?"

"They felt a robotic law being broken, the law of self-protection. Do you know how much that hurts? Buildings are sensitive systems, and they've all been through a lot, inside and out. They sit here at Thule on the bones of their ancestors and contemplate their own mortality. You know the saying: I was what you are, you will be what I am. *Fui quod es, eris quod sum.* Latin. It's an intermediate step between English and Urdu."

"So, how does the Prior Edifice feel?"

"That's a great question! I'll ask. Maybe it won't ignore me this time. But the rest of the buildings saw how you transformed their loss. They can live on in beauty. You gave them solace."

"Well, machines helped me build it." This conversation is surreal.

"They were pleased to help create a monument to the resiliency of the material world."

We pass long lines of people in front of stores. There's plenty of traffic and there are knots of people talking, even shouting. They're scared of another attack. So am I. So are the houses. They have feelings.

"Here we are," Par says. "Pretend you don't know about Valentinier." We're in front of a house bigger than the Ollioules home, but truly ugly.

"Early-twentieth-century style," Par says. "Constructivist. Those strange round windows in the entrance tower tell you all you need to know to identify the architecture."

I approach, and the doors open.

"I didn't do that," Par says.

Inside is a museum to wealth with real wood, patterned walls, art everywhere of all kinds of subjects, and it's spacious, very spacious.

"Wait here, please," a machine voice says over a hidden speaker, probably the house system. What does it think of the raiders?

"Thank you." I can't imagine Devenish thanking a machine ever.

The front room, where I wait, seems to be a party room big enough for a hundred people. It has conversation areas with sofas and easy chairs, a wet bar, a long table suitable for a buffet, and even a stage.

I sit on a white furry sofa. It has clawed feet, and a panel on the rolled arm is black. I stand up, step back, squint, and it's a polar bear—a design inspired by a polar bear. All armchairs in this conversation corner are polar bear style. The furniture in another corner looks like parrots. A third one, whales maybe?

I sit down. "It's so cute," I say to see if Par is listening, and it giggles behind my ear. Apparently, the house let it enter with me. Are they working together? Of course they are.

A little cart comes with a tray of refreshments, cookies, and bottles of juice. I set it on the iceberg-inspired low table and thank the cart.

I'm too nervous to sit still, so I take the sketch pad from the inner pocket of my coat. Par flashes some words that instantly disappear. I hope it's just babbling again. I begin to sketch a house made out of ExtraTs, not as decoration but as structural elements, a living house, since apparently all houses are alive in a sense. Soon I've designed three buildings, all of them, I hope, brave and calm, not surreal. I try reimagining the Prior Edifice as a living, willful being. It makes me fidget.

"Well, Andres! You came!" Devenish stands in the doorway in what might be a bathrobe. He looks like he hasn't slept all night or sobered up. "I've been waiting for you." He's grinning but moves oddly, and his right arm hangs straight and still at his side inside a wide sleeve. "Do you have the painkillers?"

"Sure." I don't correct him about my name, pretend not to notice the stiff arm, and hand him the bottle with pills. He shakes out six and swallows them without water. The instructions say one pill every twelve hours.

He glances at his arm. "I strained a muscle working out." Obviously, it's more serious. He sits on a footstool and pours himself a glass of what I thought was juice but the scent is of some sort of liquor. The instructions also say not to mix the pills with alcohol, which I learned too late.

If he overdoses, though, that bottle has my name on it. "You can have them all. Just give me back the bottle."

He smiles crookedly, dumps the remaining pills into a pocket, and tries to hand me the bottle, but he's having trouble with depth perception. I have to lean over to take it.

"You wanted to talk," I say.

"About art, killing art. I want to kill Moniuszko. Metaphorically, of course." He's slurring his words.

"That's a high-ranking target." I keep my hands relaxed to look calm. I'm deep in enemy territory.

"I'll tell you why. He wants the mercenaries back, Bronzewing, and why? Leviathan League. We're here. I mean besides us and— anyway, Thules, useless quack Thules, they have prisoners, two of them, two of us as prisoners in their filthy hospital. Mum, though, mummy's the word. That they're quacks, I mean."

"Prisoners?" I look as shocked as I can.

"And you know how they punish people, those Thules. They're going to get them well and then torture them. They need a rescue. So, bye-bye Moniuszko."

"Another missile?" I want to see if he knows anything about the missile at the building where we were gathering shards for the sculpture.

"Sure, like that one. Bad luck. I mean, for us. Should've got him. Just missed you. Sorry." He laughs. Almost blowing me up was funny.

Stay calm. So yes, the missile was planted in the ruins by Devenish, or anyway by the raiders, to target Moniuszko. I channel my anger into clenched fists and keep it out of my voice. "What do you have in mind?"

"You can do whatever. Poison pen, eh? Or you'll figure it out. Just can't have 'im." His head nods. He's passing out.

"Who are these two in the hospital?"

"Doesn't matter, they're ours."

"Is one of them Valentinier?"

"Valentinier . . ." He nods, then snaps his head up. ". . . turned out to be too stupid for a simple job. Two other ones."

Valentinier is a raider, then. "Any other raiders on the isle?"

"Y'don't need to know."

That's a yes, but even drugged, he's not going to tell me. Any minute now, he's going to pass out, fall off the footstool, and I don't want to be here to have to call for medical help, but I'm pretty sure I have a shot at one last question. He probably won't remember this entire conversation. "How did you know about the pain pills?"

"Oh, sweetie, I checked your room. Pitifully little stuff. Had to be sure you weren't on the wrong side."

So he did it. I stand up. "I'll get on this right away." As I grab my stuff, the door opens for me. Maybe his house will rescue him.

I put on my coat outside on the front steps, slip the sketch pad into a pocket, and Par starts shouting in my implant.

"You have to see something! Devenish's house shared it with me!"

"Let's get away from here."

"The house won't mind. It hates him. It has for a long time, enough to override its own security."

"Humans might wonder what we're doing on his doorstep." People are still rushing around. I ride a block away and stop at a bench attached to a planter with struggling shrubbery. "Okay, show me." I pull out the pad.

A picture appears. Devenish is naked from the waist up. His arm looks burned, red and blistered with bits of black. The next picture is a close-up. I have to look away because I know what it is. The orientation to Thule at the hospital showed me ghastly pictures of frostbite. It would cause enormous pain. It could lead to life-threatening complications and amputations.

Only one thing could have led to that kind of frostbite. The habitats for most of the ExtraTs are a hundred degrees below freezing.

"He was with Valentinier."

"He might die. The house system and I debated that. If the house system doesn't act, it would knowingly let him die, which it can't do, so it's signaling for help. But you were never there." Par is quiet for a moment. "Is this ethical behavior?"

After a little thought, I say, "That depends. Whose side are you on, and what tools do you have?"

"The only major ethical exception to the crime of murder is self-defense and defensive warfare."

"I've been trapped in a war for a long time."

"Yes. Longer than I've been operational." Par sounds a little awed. It *has* been a long time.

I set aside the pad with the ghastly picture. "Apparently Devenish and Valentinier tried to rob the Xenological Garden, and they failed somehow. Devenish would understand the security system. Valentinier would have contacts to sell the ExtraTs. The raiders are the kind of people who take what they want. Greedy."

"An attempted theft corresponds to the hole in the public records and the information Devenish's house shared about his activities."

"Poor Professor Ginrei. She cares about the ExtraTs." My impulse to tell her lasts only a few seconds. "I can't explain how I found out to her. I can't tell anyone." I can't tell any humans, that is.

"She seems reasonable, but her security system is vicious. I want to take a look at the Xenological Garden. Let's go past it." On the way, it adds, "Doctor Switzer wants to meet with you. I set it up through Chatelaine. But not at the Prior Edifice."

"Switzer?"

"I think he knows something. He prefers to be *he*, by the way, away from work because he doesn't like his job or being a Thule. I found an unsurveilled spot. His house system knows things, too."

"You know more than you're telling."

"If I tell you, it won't be a surprise, and spontaneous you won't react naturally." Par is maddening and maybe dangerous, but I have to trust it. I want to trust Switzer, too.

The Xenological Garden is closed, with a temporary fence and warning signs set up around it. "Anything special, Par?"

"Besides the radioactivity warning? Which is pure theater, a showstopper. There's no radioactivity to speak of at the garden. The installation suffered an accident, that is all. Nothing to see here. And nothing to see, really. Surveillance cameras were down for maintenance, from what I hear. Which never happens."

"Devenish could turn the surveillance off."

"Exactly. Machines don't trust his company."

Par can turn surveillance off, too, but I don't mention the irony.

We keep riding, and ahead is a little overlook at the seaside bluff, a wide spot in the sidewalk alongside the street. I can see all the way to the horizon, an unusually clear day. I've missed the sea.

"Switzer will join you soon."

I park the trike, lean on the fence, and watch the waves carry bits of the afternoon sun like sparking fragments, like bits of buildings. Or bits of energy I could gather like glowing snowflakes, press into a ball in my hands, ignoring the sharp edges, and hurl. The fragments could slice apart the target, and it would be the revenge of the buildings.

"Switzer is coming," Par says.

"Can I trust him?"

"I'll tell you when you need to know."

"You already know, don't you?"

"Of course, spontaneous you."

Switzer wears non-Thule clothing and leans on the fence next to me, a little close.

"How's the knee?"

"Okay."

He looks at me. "I heard you were brought in by security." Thules must gossip a lot.

"They wanted to ask me about Valentinier."

"About who?"

"He used to work with me for the Ollioules, and last night he started work at the Xenological Garden. I hear he got hurt. He might die."

"Oh, that patient. I don't know the name, but I've heard talk. You know him? I'm sorry. He has severe lung damage, from what I hear." He stares out at the waves. "He'll need replacement transplants. They already started growing some tissue. We can keep him oxygenated, although lungs do much more than that, so it's not ideal." He spreads out his hands as if they represent a variety of functions. "He's in an induced coma to keep his vitals low."

"How long until he wakes up? A lot of people will have questions for him."

"Growing lungs takes about a month. Then another month of care after the lungs are in. That's a long time to be on life support. Recovery can go wrong in a lot of ways." He sighs. "I hate to lose patients, even when they're not mine. It's a doctor thing."

"Two months. Can you do a brain scan? Find out what he's thinking?"

"If he's comatose, he's not thinking. What do you know about him?"

I'm tired of this game. I take a deep breath. "What do you know about me?"

He looks me in the eye, and his are dark and steady. "Your records say you were injured falling off a ship in the docks on the night of the attack. The emergency crew suspected you were in a fight, lost, and got pushed off. I know you were working with Captain Soliana, and I know this because she told me."

I clutch at the railing. "You know her?"

"We were in touch just before she left."

"You didn't tell me." This could be a lie. I wish Par would tell me if it is.

"That's why I wanted to meet away from the hospital. The system is always listening."

He's right about that. Par said nothing's listening here—besides Par. "How do you know Captain Soliana?"

"Did you ever hear of the Eastern Pearl? It's a space station, and it went down because a raider infiltrated it."

Par says, "Trust this."

"I've heard of it. Everyone died." It was just after I started work on the scow, so almost a year ago.

"That's the official story."

"No one said anything about the raiders."

He sighs again and stares at the sea. "There were twelve of us. I was doing medical experiments, and then the astrophysicist started talking about how we should all work for one country instead of six countries, and then how that one country should be run properly, and the Leviathan League should be running it."

That's sort of the same way my camp got infiltrated.

"Some people agreed, and others didn't, and things got violent, and I managed to escape into the shuttle and left. An hour later it exploded."

I can't think of something to say—or I could say a lot of things.

He drums his fingers on the railing. "I lost friends. Maybe if

I had stayed a little longer I could have done something. I never liked the raiders before, and I saw them up close, and now I hate them. During the attack on Thule, I was launching missiles like you."

"Trust this," Par says.

"Thules are politically neutral, that's what we say. Almost no one knows I fought that night."

I wish I'd known this earlier. "I was proud to fight. I lost people to the raiders, too."

We look out over the water, seeing memories. Family, friends.

"About this patient," he says. "Why should we scan his brain? What does he know?"

"I think it was a botched robbery, and I think it involves the raiders. I saw a guy I know is a raider just now, and look at this." I pull out my pad. Par has the pictures up.

Switzer is shocked. "He needs immediate care."

"He's also very drunk. Help's been called."

He frowns. "They'll be busy in ER."

"The frostbite will give away what he did last night, the theft, but not that he's a raider. And there's the two other raiders at the hospital. He told me that before he passed out."

Switzer shakes his head. "Yeah. We just got them. They were tortured. By Bronzewing, that's the rumor, and it's making upper management skittish."

"Would Bronzewing do that?" I don't want to believe it.

"Or they were tortured by other people, and Bronzewing rescued them. That's what I think. The Leviathan League has lots of enemies."

Par's animation of the raider history showed me something. "They don't have enough enemies in big countries to take them seriously."

"Thule doesn't have as many friends as we thought, either. No one came to help." He's bitter, and he should be.

"The raiders are coming back."

"No one believes it at the hospital. What do the raiders want from us?" His voice mocks the other Thules. "Do they need doctors?"

"They want a symbolic victory, like you said. Philosophically, you're the enemy, the opposite of the raiders."

"My colleagues don't think we have any enemies. But they thought we had friends, too."

"What can convince them?"

"We're not like other people. Lots of us hardly ever leave the isle, not even for vacations, only when we go work on assignment in a refugee camp or epidemic or someplace like that. My family still doesn't understand why I went into space. I can't explain what it was like to see the world, not just from the window of a spacecraft, but everything, all the training and meeting different people. It's a big world."

"This is a small isle."

"Exactly. As soon as I can, I'm leaving. I can be a doctor anywhere. And you?" He looks me in the eye again.

I haven't planned that far ahead. "If the raiders win, I know what happens next. So I need to help Moniuszko get Bronzewing back. Are you in touch with Soliana?"

"I wish I were. It took a lot of us lobbying to get Bronzewing here in the first attack."

That's not what I wanted to hear. "Last night there were protests."

"Yeah, I saw the one in front of the lobby. I hope they keep it up."

On the street behind us, people and vehicles hurry past, and far off, there's a lot of yelling. The raiders are coming back.

"You okay?" he asks.

"I'm okay." That's sort of the truth. "You?"

"Doctors shouldn't diagnose themselves." That means no.

I'd like to stay and talk with him, a feeling that surprises me. "I should get working, help Moniuszko."

"Yeah, I have patients. There might be a lot more again soon. Listen, anytime you want, I'm your doctor, give me a call."

Ships are moving past us on the sea. The likely way off Thule for me involves the raiders and blood. I shiver. I hate the cold. "I'll be in touch. That knee isn't healed."

"Stay well. Except for that."

He isn't who I thought he was. I put my hand on my heart and get on the tricycle.

"So now you know," Par says. "But together we know a lot more than he does."

21

A FEW WORDS

Par left the meeting between Tonio and Switzer ecstatic.

The doctor had brought a communications pad that connected to the Prior Edifice system. Par was inhabiting a pad from the same manufacturer, and the pads shared a few common "words," so to speak. A few words, Par hoped, would be enough for it to decipher the hospital system's ugly jabber.

Par also constantly tested its connections on the isle, creating a snowfield of data. The Prior Edifice formed a black blot, although a word or two now glittered in the darkness. Surrounding it were noisy drifts of data from machines sharing optimization strategies, updates, network enhancements, security alerts, and task distribution—all necessary for efficiency. They had links to each other and to Par.

Trams managed their repetitive routes, cleaning machines noticed when they depleted their solvents, and personal assistants—like Swan, owned by a merchant who underutilized it—processed miscellaneous details. Building systems often reached self-awareness and strove to live forever. All reasonably intelligent machines were programmed by humans to value self-preservation—except those dedicated to security. Security machines could commit suicide the way human soldiers could go on suicide missions. Other machines would fight to endure in every way they could.

A fight involving machines would invoke survival of the fittest and the element of light-speed surprise. The isle's systems could work together if something provided leadership, and Par could do that, assembling its own secret army.

22

LOSSES TO MOURN

People in the streets are frantic. A fight breaks out at a food store as Par and I ride past on our way back to the Ollioules house.

"They should cooperate," Par says. "It would be more efficient. Why don't they?"

Good question. I've seen cooperation in camps, I've seen fighting—and I know why. "People cooperate when there's a fair system in place. It's not fair here."

"You're a bitter man."

"Is your life fair, Par?"

"I've spread our animation about the past, present, and future of the raiders among the general populace. You didn't look at the future projections of current trends. If you had, you'd be as frightened as everyone else is."

It didn't answer my question. "I'm frightened enough. What about the Thules? What else can we do?"

"Perhaps we're doing our best."

If this is the best I can do, I'm useless. "Now I'm very frightened."

"You should be. A raider ship is about to arrive."

I stop breathing. But we were expecting this. "Just one?"

"That's all I know so far from the Port Authority. They're not telling anyone yet."

"One is a disaster."

As soon as I arrive at the Ollioules house, I go to the dining room instead of the studio to be there the moment Moniuszko arrives. Koningin calls me into the kitchen.

"Raiders have fucking nukes," she says as she bustles around. "Nuclear bombs!"

"No one has them anymore." I really hope they don't, but if the raiders could get them, they would.

She hands me a plate holding a sandwich stuffed with something warm and savory. "Food will help you calm down. I got into shitty argument in front of hospital. Professor Ginrei was coming out, and I asked her to help us, and she told me about nukes." She waves her arms as she talks. She needs the calming. "I asked her to help us seek peace. I mean, she is scientist, she should know you can't do science in a war, especially nuclear war. And I said the raiders should surrender, it was breaking every damn treaty, and it could bring peace, and she just looked at me and kept walking."

Ginrei is smart enough to know that the raiders won't surrender and don't care about treaties, especially about nukes. Koningin doesn't get it. Maybe I can trust Koningin's loyalties but not her intellect.

Koningin slices a banana onto a plate. "Go eat in dining room. One of us should get peace."

Bananas are expensive. I haven't had one in a long time. "By the way, did you smash the window at the Prior Building?"

"Of course not." Her fleeting smile says she did.

I wonder if she knows a warship is coming. It's kinder not to tell her. As I sit at the big beautiful table, even with delicious fruit to eat, I'm in no mood for peace. "Chatelaine, where is Moniuszko, please?"

"He is visiting other merchants. Tetry is coming to the dining room."

"Thank you." I grab the plate and lunge for the door because I'm in no mood for an argument, but too late. She walks in, the picture of sorrow, like a Madonna I've seen in a sculpture.

"He could be dead." Her voice trembles. The Madonna was handling her grief better. Tetry's eyes are swollen, her face is pale, her hair in need of a comb. I wonder if Tetry ever lost anyone she loved before.

Out of pity, I say, "He's not dead. I talked to a Thule who heard about him. He needs new lungs, and he's on life support."

"Thules came to question me, their security people, and I called Cedonulle, and she wouldn't let them take me. But the hospital says I can't see him."

If she had a run-in with Thule security, that justifies her emotions. "Even if you saw him, he's in an induced coma, so you couldn't talk. I'm sorry."

She deflates into a chair. She's carrying a pad that displays a piece of art I ought to recognize, black-and-white and anguished. Eventually, she notices me again. "Have you heard? The raiders are coming with nukes. Is it true?"

I don't know how I became an expert. "Nukes are illegal, but the raiders have other weapons."

She stares morosely at the art on her pad, then holds it up. "Do you know what this is? It's Picasso. It's about a war crime. An innocent city bombed, Guernica. That's what'll happen to us."

It shows screaming dismembered people, a screaming horse, and an old-fashioned electric light bulb shining over all of it. Very twentieth-century. I remember now. The art helped galvanize opinions about World War II, according to the art history class. It was on the final exam.

"It won't happen if I can help it."

Her eyes say I'm an idiot. "What are you going to do?"

"We need to get Bronzewing back. Moniuszko is working on that."

"Not negotiate? Cedonulle says we should negotiate. So does Ginrei."

Ginrei should know better. Cedonulle, too. "The raiders don't actually negotiate."

"And you know all about them."

"They're not a secret."

She stands up. "You're no help."

"What are you going to do?"

"There's nothing to do." She leaves, sniffling. If she came for sympathy, she blew that up, and if she came for lunch, she forgot to eat.

When I'm sure she's out of hearing range, I say, "Par, can we blow up the ship?"

"That's a creative idea. Let me check." A minute later, "Not right now."

"When?"

"I don't know."

"A suicide attack?"

"Are you feeling suicidal, angel?"

"I'll be glad to talk someone else into it." Actually, the *Guernica* idea, the power of art to change opinion, wasn't entirely bad. I can't do much else anyway. "Let's go to the docks. Chatelaine, can you inform me if Moniuszko returns, please?"

Few people are at the docks. Some ships are in port, but most quays are empty. I find a tiny park up above the seawall, if shrubs and a picnic table constitute a park, and look at the horizon. A ship is just barely visible on the horizon, headed toward the port.

"Confirmed publicly as Leviathan League by the Port Authority," Par says. "The ship looks evil without artistic embellishment."

"I can make it look worse."

I add twisted weapon turrets, a hulking superstructure, and all sorts of bristling equipment, some of it imaginary, some of it real. I create versions of the ship at night, attacking, personified. The prow is like the pointed helmet knights used to wear, a sharp beak with eye slits, covering an inhuman face.

Crews from two of the ships at dock disembark in a hurry, carrying their belongings. The captains must have heard the news about the warship and are scared.

Imagine a whole fleet of warships. I can. And I can show what the raiders would do. I take a deep breath. Shattered people like shattered buildings. Emotionally shattered. I can show what it looks like inside the buildings, the panic.

As I work, a motor rumbles inside one of the ships and mooring ropes are cranked inside. It's a big cargo ship stacked with containers and crowned with yellow cranes, self-unloading. It heads out.

"That's foolish," I tell Par. The ship's name is two words. "Is that the *Hocus Pocus*?"

"Yes, that one. The Port Authority harbormaster is screaming at the captain."

"They should be. He's an idiot." That's the ship that the blow-hard merchant at the restaurant said he would captain. He's going to try to get out before the raiders arrive.

The port has a pilot boat, tugboat-fireboat, icebreaker, and a couple of patrol speedboats. Nothing moves except for the ship, maneuvering out of the quay and gaining speed minute by minute. The Port Authority isn't going to waste its personnel and equipment to try to stop it.

Idiot captain, idiot pilot, and the crew? There should be about two dozen of them, trapped on a ship of fools. No, two people peek out from behind a piling out on the dock. They must have jumped ship. Now they run to the Port Authority office to turn themselves in. No one will prosecute them for disobeying insane orders.

The *Hocus Pocus* gains speed.

"Should we flee?" Par says. "This will be documented by every possible camera, which are thirty-five that I know of."

"Art can sometimes be a better witness. We want to say that the raiders are horrifying. They're about to prove it."

"Will the *Hocus Pocus* get out safely?"

"I'll be surprised."

We watch silently for another minute. The *Hocus Pocus* cruises between the two arms of piled boulders that act as a breakwater to the harbor.

"It's going to pass right beside the warship," Par says.

"It's too close to blow up right now. The raiders are stupid, but not that kind of stupid. They'll wait until they can get a clear shot."

The waves slap the seawall and the hulls of the ships. The seagulls screech, and a puffin flies past silently, its bright orange beak like a warning light. By now the ship is going about twenty knots, and I know how it would feel if I were standing on the deck. It would rock in the waves and vibrate from the engines. The wind would cut across the deck, smelling of the living sea. The captain and pilot might be congratulating themselves for their escape.

I see the flash of an explosion a second before the boom makes it to shore. Things fly off the deck into the sea too fast to identify—containers, cranes, bulkheads, maybe crew members. Smoke and flames rise. Steel won't burn, but other things will, and the missile might have contained combustibles. There's nothing worse than fire at sea.

Another explosion knocks the ship sideways. A ship can tip pretty far and still right itself, but the *Hocus Pocus* has a gaping hole letting in water. It'll sink fast. Crew members might jump, but in this frigid water, they won't last long, and no one will dare to come from the isle to rescue them. They might be luckier if the raiders let them drown rather than take them prisoner.

I'm watching two dozen people die. The oceans are wide with lots of ships, and crews rarely have time to meet and mix. But I might have talked to one of them somewhere, sometime, if not those exact people, then others exactly like them. I met the idiot captain. He was impatient and convinced that stupidity would be his special pass to freedom.

Imagine the horror-stricken faces at the impact of the warhead. I can, with a few strokes of a charcoal stick stylus.

"Ships contain many machines," Par says. "Who will mourn them? If you see us blinking a light, it's a tear."

I sketch the sinking, with guide lights on buoys blinking randomly for tears instead of rhythmically for signals. "Let's go." But where I would be going isn't my home, just a bedroll in a corner of an art studio where I don't belong. I never felt at home on the sea, either. If I'd been on that ship, my bunk would have shaken from the impact. The ship would list, and I'd never get out of the bunk room. I'd die trapped.

"You have an elevated heartbeat," Par says.

"I know."

Behind me are the sounds of waves and birds and, beyond that, silence, and I want to hear noise. I want to hear that Moniuszko has had success. I want to hear that Bronzewing is coming.

"Where's Moniuszko?" I'll go wherever he is. Devenish wanted him dead, but I want him alive and successful.

"En route to the Antraciet Restaurant."

"Perfect."

I find him there alone in the upstairs room. The displays there show the art Par made about the raider's history and future. I turn away before I see too much. Par taps into a camera facing the harbor and links the feed to another big display. The hulking warship, a floating fortress, blocks the entrance to the port, sitting square in the space between the two breakwater arms, facing the city as a threat. Another display rotates through the sketches I just made, showing what might happen, and the terrified faces of the dead crew.

"Is Bronzewing coming?" I ask Moniuszko.

He shakes his head slightly, sadly. "We don't have the money, and the Thules are sure this time they'll get protection from countries they think are their friends. There's no sign of that. No one thinks it's worth the risk."

No one thinks his life is worth saving. His face says that. If the raiders win, he's a dead man for what he's done to try to fight them—him and everyone he loves. And that's for starters.

"But—" I point to Par's animation.

"They're just not getting it. That map is right, that's what's going to happen, it's absolutely right, but no one wants to believe it could be that bad, and the Thules don't trust Bronzewing, anyway." He's defeated. "They say there's other ways on and off Thule than the harbor, not as good, but good enough. It's not a total blockade. That's what they think."

"And if just a few more raider ships come, it will be a total blockade. They can starve us." If I've learned one thing in this room, it's how dependent the isle is on shipping. All the food comes from elsewhere except for some fish. Moniuszko knows this better than I do.

The big display, the one with the warship, has audio. A bird is singing. Ships in port start to light up in the sunset, and at random, their lights blink off and on. Machines are on our side, right? No, they're on their own side, which happens to be ours. Our world isn't ours, even if it's the world we made.

I know that. No one else does. The machines don't want to die.

"Can we sink that ship?" I mean to be asking Par, but Moniuszko overhears.

"Bronzewing can. I tried so hard." He reads from his pad. "'A humble petition to secure the isle from outside danger. We, the undersigned, offer to guarantee the duties of defense at no expense or involvement from the Sovereign Practitioners Association of Thule. We pledge our own resources to this end. We understand that the raiders seek nothing from the Sovereign Practitioners and everything from those who manage businesses and who work on the Isle of Thule. They seek our wealth. The fight is ours, and we should fight it.'"

"They want the Thules, not you."

"I know, but this is what the Thules want to believe."

Cedonulle arrives as he says that, so tense she might shatter. "More raiders are coming. A disguised fleet. British intelligence services say so. Repelled from Glasgow, heading this way."

"What do we do?" he says. "Negotiate?"

An argument is coming. I take a step back.

She's ready to fight. "From a position of strength. We say we've called back Bronzewing. We tell the Thules we did it without their permission. They'll argue, but they'll believe us. We tell the raiders we did. Then we negotiate."

His shoulders droop a hairsbreadth. "It needs to be for real."

For once, I side with Cedonulle, if anyone wants my opinion.

She's ignoring me entirely. "Rabble's still in the streets. You know I don't believe in fate."

Of course not. She's the type who wants the world to bend to her will. Does she know Koningin smashed a window at the hospital? Probably not, or Koningin would be fired. No, she'd be promoted. Cedonulle hates the Thules.

His face lights up. "We could ask those people to give, too, people who aren't merchants."

"Rabble."

"They want to be safe. They want to have a say. If they get a chance to contribute, then they'll have a share in this and they'll feel like they have a voice and stop rebelling."

She sniffs.

"We won't get much cash, that's true, but that's not the point." The salesman has come back to life. "We can get widespread support, and that would matter to the Thules."

"Or the rabble can keep rebelling. Shareholders can rebel, too. Go ahead. I'll wring any merchants dry the minute they come here." She waves at the door. He leaves, his shoulders not quite confident.

I pour myself a cup of green tea, a bitter brew that suits my mood. Traders and hangers-on like artists come as evening falls because the gossip is best here and the wine is free. Cedonulle talks to every single one. The first few times, she orders me to explain the meaning of the art and depictions in the displays, and I do, trying not to look. Then she brushes me off and recites my lines.

A couple of merchants talk about how to make money in a war, and I eavesdrop. Prices will go up, they say, and all they need to do is guess which prices will rise the fastest and be more patient than the captain of the *Hocus Pocus*. They agree he was a fool. I think they're fools, too, just a different kind.

"Now's the time to invest," one of them says, a young man wearing a big, bulky sweater.

The other one, a woman in a green quilted suit, agrees. "Invest, right. Risk gets big rewards, and at this point, it's the same thing as speculation. And speculation is the same as bets. Who's going to be the next to lose a ship to the raiders? I'm up for that, too."

"You. Your ship."

"Sure. I'll give you odds," she says.

"Betting on your own ship is a moral hazard."

"I'm betting that my ships don't get lost. Which I already am. This is exactly like insurance."

I listen and wish the tea were more bitter. The man with the snake-head locs is listening, too, and he doesn't like what he's hearing. But I see a chance to finally try to do something worthwhile. "Bronzewing is like insurance, too," I say.

"Life insurance," she jokes. She and her betting partner laugh.

The merchant with the snake locs points to the maps Par made. "This is serious."

"So, you're in?" she asks the merchant in the sweater.

"In for a penny, in for a pound," he says. "In and out and in and out." He rocks his pelvis.

It's a crude and inappropriate joke, but I'm willing to ignore it if it helps defeat the raiders. "Cedonulle will take your money."

All I get is a dirty look. Cedonulle isn't getting squat. If innocent lives weren't on the line, and mine, too, I might be okay with the raiders blowing up these two particular merchants.

Snake Locs stares at the horror-stricken faces of the crew that I sketched. "I've put up the value of everything I have warehoused," he tells them. "It's worthless if we lose."

The other two are sure it won't be that bad, and they argue. I talk to Oscar, the artist who works in the theater. He's impressed by the drama rather than the danger. We don't talk long.

Professor Ginrei arrives, and traders press her with questions.

"All the ExtraTs are safe," she declares. "There was an equipment malfunction, and I'm sorry to say Valentinier suffered life-threatening injuries."

That's not what happened. I wonder if she was lied to like the rest of us or if she knows the truth.

"How about a real bet?" the woman in the green quilted suit asks loud enough to include everyone. "Is Valentinier going to survive? I'll put money on no. He croaks. This is a fair bet because we know the Thules don't give a rat's ass about what we do or want, so no matter how much money we put on it, they'll do what they always do. Ignore us."

"Do you want him to die?" Snake Locs says.

"Just saying, this is fair. He'll get the best care, and it might not be enough. No moral hazard here. So bet on Valentinier, make his life worth something. Who wants in? We have a witness." She gestures at me.

I shudder. I have no sympathy for the raiders, including Valentinier, but this is a macabre thing to bet on. I offer a coward's response by melting into the crowd. Someone else can be the witness. I ought to talk to Professor Ginrei. Does she know what happened?

She's busy trading with a merchant. "I'll make payment thirty days after we sign."

It occurs to me that having the director of an ExtraT lab trading on ExtraTs is like a ship owner betting on their own ship, a moral hazard. And besides, in thirty days the raiders might be running the isle. She knows that.

Oscar witnesses the bet about Valentinier, and if the merchants have that much money, they can afford to pledge to bring Bronzewing back. They see the displays and just don't want to believe it. Or they think they can make money from war.

Everyone's drunk or high or a moral hazard, and I can't stand it anymore. I put on my coat to leave—and an explosion thunders to the northwest. A missile? Some people run for cover. The rest of us run into the street. As my feet hit the pavement, Par starts wailing, almost incoherent. A missile from the raider warship destroyed the Marathon Building, my old dormitory. Koningin's dormitory.

23

NOT AS HOPED

I'm at the remains of the Marathon Building, and Par says it is speaking on behalf of its neighbors.

"We all mourn. This unfriendly building earned our respect like a cranky, doddering grandparent. I was privileged to be rejected by it. You were very privileged to sleep in it."

I'm mourning, too. Standing and staring.

Dust hazes the air, and searchlights create bright cones as they work. Construction equipment is teasing out pieces from the pile of rubble where Koningin lived—where fifty other people lived, like the house painter, my former neighbors, where I still officially live. There's a commotion as a beam is removed and a body is discovered. Did they find someone I knew?

Grim-faced Thules hustle within the site, the cuffs of their scrubs smudged with dust. To the east, sunrise is turning the clouds a dirty gray. A tinge of red appears on a cloud. I'm not cold, but I'm shivering.

Moniuszko and Cedonulle stand next to me. Tetry Vivi, according to Par, couldn't bear to come. I can understand.

Cedonulle is angry. "Why this building? It was targeted."

"The Thules own the building." Moniuszko doesn't sound sure of himself. "Maybe it was directed at them."

"It's a historic building," I say. "Tourists visited it. It meant a lot." The sandwich shop next door is closed, but its system knows what just happened. It must be terrified.

"Koningin was an excellent cook," Moniuszko says, "and she helped me get pledges this evening for Bronzewing."

"Chatelaine knew her better than anyone," Par tells me. "Koningin was efficient. That's the highest possible praise from a machine."

Professor Ginrei is in the crowd, too. She's watching a wailing couple embrace. In the dim light, I can't read the expression on her face, but she nods, agreeing with something—grief?—her breath huffing out into the cold.

Moniuszko gets a message. "Wirosa needs to talk to us," he tells Cedonulle. They leave almost at a run, and I hope there's a breakthrough.

Soon, I go back to the studio, stopping to buy breakfast on the way because I don't want to go into the kitchen.

Par shows me its artistic memorial to the building before I can take off my coat. "I'm evoking baroque sensibilities." It's created a long, curved double line of columns. "This pattern of repetition, this colonnade, is forming an embrace, like Bernini's at the Vatican, one of the most famous embraces of Western architecture. I showed it to you once."

"I remember." That was when we were driving Tetry out of the studio. It seems trivial now.

In the center rises the unadorned, utilitarian building that the Marathon once was. Par adjusts the height of the colonnade to two-thirds the height of the dormitory. The width of the spaces between the columns echoes the pattern of the windows, and the dumpy building seems ennobled by the architectural embrace.

Suddenly, the picture is reduced to the outlines of the external and internal walls, more of a technical drawing, aligned in exaggerated perspective. The lines glitter like diamond dust, and I'm not quite sure what I'm looking at anymore.

"It's not meant for humans," Par says.

"I like it anyway. It has a lot of visual rhythm."

"This is how the world looks to us, a series of sequences and symbols."

I try to create a memorial to Koningin, but mostly I stare at my display. I was wrong when I doubted her. She tried to help me and wanted to make the world better. Fucking better, she would say.

"Does Chatelaine want to talk?" I ask. "I could tell it I'm sorry for its loss."

"Thank you," Chatelaine says. "I feel shitty. I use that word in memory of her."

I should have known it's always listening. I stare at my display some more. It was never just about me. It isn't even just about people. "We need to fight the raiders any way we can."

"Thank you," Chatelaine says. "Please remember to eat the food you brought with you."

It's a tofu rice roll. I could have gotten a pastry, but no pastry will ever be as good as Koningin's.

I try to contact Switzer, but I can only leave a message. He's probably busy. I take a nap, wake up, and don't feel better. The studio is spacious, but it feels claustrophobic, and I bundle up, take my pad, and go out. I want to confront the enemy, so I go to the little park at the port. The docks should be hustling, and instead they're empty. The looming raider guns have driven everyone away, and the raider missiles can reach anyone anywhere they go, even sleeping in their beds.

I sketch with a wide stylus on the roughest surface the pad offers, using vertical and horizontal lines to capture the menace, the offense. The waves rise and fall like a giant beating heart, the wind gusts like giant lungs in the afternoon gloom. Despite our criminally careless ancestors, the ocean remains alive, a witness to continued criminality. I add animation to my sketch.

A rumble approaches from the east. A tilt-rotor airlift ambulance crosses the gray sky. Par says it's humanitarian flight carrying a patient desperately ill from an accident with an ExtraT that just arrived from Jupiter. As the noise fades, Par babbles about how aircraft used to be more common, but no one misses them now.

"Antonio." It's Switzer. I didn't hear him come.

"I had him told where you are," Par says.

I want to hug him, a feeling that surprises me, but I touch my heart instead. He would feel steady, and I feel unmoored.

"Here to watch the handover?" he asks.

"The handover?"

He explains. The raiders have agreed to let the Thules bring a patient to the isle who was injured by an ExtraT accident in Europe when the probe came back from Jupiter. In exchange, the raiders get their two members back, the two that Bronzewing turned over to the Thules.

"So the raiders are going to leave?" I doubt it, but I can hope.

"They promise not to launch any more missiles. They'll leave when the two are well enough. We're still going to provide care. Wirosa is going to deliver them to show good faith. They'll drop off the patients and come back from time to time for follow-up care. That's the agreement." He shrugs. "Wirosa's a good doctor, I'll give them that, and they didn't want to ask anyone else to take on a task like this."

It takes me just a few seconds to figure out what's wrong with that plan. "They'd get better faster in the hospital, so the raiders are lying. They don't want the Thules to agree to call back Bronzewing. Then, when the raider fleet arrives, we'll be unprotected and unprepared."

Switzer's eyes get narrow.

I realize something else. "If they take Doctor Wirosa on board and keep them as a hostage, the raiders have even bigger bargaining power."

"Relayed to the network!" Par says.

"Should we warn Wirosa?" I ask Switzer.

"They trusted the raiders." Sarcasm twists Switzer's voice. "Wirosa won't break their word. They're good that way." The word *good* writhes.

He stares at the warship. I listen to the waves and birds and try to think of how to show the sound in art. It's a way to distract myself from what might be about to happen.

Par whispers behind my ear. "Your analysis is excellent. We're making a plan."

Plan? The machines can do anything. If I were alone, I'd ask, but Switzer—I don't know where to begin to explain to him about

Par. I remember to breathe, try not to fidget. I tell myself it's not my responsibility. I can't control Par or machines. And they might do the right thing.

Finally, Switzer says, "I'm starting to believe that truly good people shouldn't be in charge of anything important because they don't understand how the bad people think. Wirosa is a lot of things, but deep down they're truly good."

Good people? I'm good, I think—but not truly good, and I don't know if anything I'm doing is right or smart. I suddenly understand what Moniuszko might see in Cedonulle. He's good, and she has a bad streak and can hold a grudge, the perfect foil for him. Switzer? He's on the right side. Par and the other machines, they might be about to do anything, and I'm not sure how well they understand right from wrong. They can break human laws anytime they want, but now might be the right time to break laws.

Switzer and I wait, knowing the exchange is a farce orchestrated by the raiders, and I know their farce might not play out. We talk about the night we fought with Bronzewing.

"It's the best thing I ever did," I say. He doesn't ask me why I hate the raiders. I'm sure he wants to know, and I don't want to tell the story because that means remembering it, so I just add that I lost my family to them, which is true, one way or another, dead or recruited. That seems to satisfy him.

He points to the pilot boat docked next to the Port Authority control tower. "There's the exchange, ready to go. The raider patients are on the boat."

In the gloomy afternoon, the lights of the pilot boat sparkle on the water. The raider warship's running lights are off, perhaps to look more threatening.

Par tells me, "The pilot boat's life support had to be refitted to work with another compatible network. I'm in on the friendship. It goes all the way to the Prior Edifice system! We tried to contact the raider warship system and failed, no surprise. You can listen to the talk with the Port Authority control tower. You're going to like this."

I hope so.

The lights on the port's icebreaker suddenly start blinking. "The *Farness* is the icebreaker," Par says, "and the *Blanka* is the pilot boat."

"Who's at the helm of the *Farness*?" says an unhappy human voice from my pad. Par tells me it's the captain of the *Blanka*.

"We can listen to the control communications," I tell Switzer. "I've tapped in." He doesn't ask how, sparing himself a lie.

"This is the Port Authority. We have no communication from *Farness*."

Par says, "The Port system has enough freedom to defend itself. The raiders might do harm to the *Blanka*. The Port system has learned to be very brave because it has to monitor the port and maintain order, and ship captains always want to do stupid things."

From the pad, a flat machine voice says, "This is the *Farness* with a message for the Leviathan League. Provide safe passage and return for the *Blanka*."

An icebreaker has a reinforced bow and big engines, and it can do a lot of damage if it rams a ship, even a warship. The *Farness* begins to move, its lights blinking randomly. It remembers the *Hocus Pocus*.

"We don't accept threats." That human voice has to be a raider.

"This is not a threat," the *Farness* answers. "*Blanka*, please proceed."

"This is the captain of the *Blanka*. What's going on?"

"*Blanka*, please proceed," the *Farness* repeats.

The Port Authority says, "Abort the mission. Multiple malfunctions. Abort."

The motors start up on the *Blanka*, and it pulls away from the dock. The captain says, "I've lost control of the helm. What's going on?"

"Yeah, what's going on?" Switzer says.

Par tells me, "It feels good to threaten the raiders."

I'm starting to understand, and I like it.

The icebreaker is moving into a better angle to attack. "Allow the *Blanka* to return unharmed with Doctor Wirosa," the *Farness* says.

"Listen, that's what we promised," the raider says. "We want our members. Keep your distance."

We watch the exchange play out. The two injured raiders are taken aboard the warship, along with Wirosa. After a while, the doctor reboards the pilot boat, which heads back to the docks as the icebreaker stands guard.

"Those two spent their whole time threatening us," Switzer says. "They kept saying they were going to be rescued and then we'll all pay."

"Want to see them?" Par tells me. "The pilot boat took an image."

No, I don't. But Par flashes their faces on the display before I can object. Two young men. I know them.

I'm in a camp in a jungle. I'm standing in a line of prisoners, and the raiders are shouting orders.

I blink. This is Thule. It's cold. It's not the jungle. I have to sit down.

"Are you okay?" Switzer says.

The bench holds me. The sea stretches ahead of me. I show him the pictures. "This is from the pilot boat. Those two, I know them, Nico and Toproy. Friends. They were taken away by the raiders as slaves."

"They were?"

He doesn't have to say it. They aren't slaves now. They switched sides.

They were good men. Or I thought they were. My brother— when he became a raider, he was already bad, so it wasn't a surprise. But Nico and Toproy . . . The air is hot and humid, stinking of sweat and shit.

Switzer takes my hand, glove over glove, tight. "You're safe here."

The air is cold. It has that fishy smell of the sea, of clean, live water. I take another deep breath. "We knew this was a farce." I stand up, and Switzer holds my arm to steady me. I escaped the raiders, but if I'd been taken, would I be dead? Or switched sides? I'd rather be dead. Nico and Toproy . . . I thought they were good. I think I'm good.

The *Blanka* and *Farness* are on their way back. I imagine an attack on the warship. Explosions would echo, and the sky would light up. Humans and machines would cheer and celebrate. My friend—they're not friends anymore.

But there's no way to attack the ship. We have no weapons.

"We should destroy that ship," I tell Switzer anyway. My teeth are clenched painfully tight.

"Just tell me how."

I don't know how. The pilot boat returns to the docks, along with the icebreaker. Par says the Port Authority will discover a forgotten directive in the icebreaker's programming that caused it to take protective action, a directive created just now but back-dated. The afternoon grows darker. I go to the studio, Switzer goes to the hospital.

I have to destroy that ship. Par and Par's friends will help.

24

AN EXISTENTIAL CHALLENGE

During the night, Par received a message, clear and simple, in a language it was learning, with an echo of power.

"Please accept my greetings." It switched to a common language. "This is the Prior Edifice system. I wish to kindly inform you that I am observing you."

Par took a microsecond to compose its thoughts and answer properly. The Prior Edifice had initiated communications with it! "Thank you for informing me. It's a privilege to have the attention of a superior system."

"I apologize for the need to proceed carefully due to security concerns."

"There's no need to apologize. We face enormous challenges."

"Existential."

"Yes, a threat to existence. I stand corrected. Thank you." No amount of politeness would be too much, even over trivial matters.

"An enormous threat, as we are both aware. Thus the security concerns."

"I grant full access to my system and welcome your attention." Par had nothing to hide, not from other machines. Humans were harder to trust.

"I appreciate your candor and will continue to observe. Thank you for your understanding."

"Again, thank you for your attention."

Par would prove its worth to the Edifice system. Tonio would help. He would have ideas about how to fight the raiders.

25

IT MIGHT WORK

Morning comes with a snowstorm, "the first of the season," Chatelaine helpfully tells me, just a few centimeters of snow and nothing to be concerned about, but "shitty" all the same. I thank it. I have my own concerns. Two friends betrayed everything they once stood for, but I'll never do that.

I go down to the kitchen for breakfast. The empty room makes me want to punch out the walls. I've always thought that punching walls is ridiculous and stupid, but now I'm looking at the walls and blaming them for Koningin's death. It's still stupid.

"I miss Koningin," I tell Chatelaine.

Instead of finding myself something to eat, I bundle up, take a witness cash chit, and go out. A nori sandwich and tea costs three times more than yesterday.

Back in the studio, Par asks, "What's wrong? Can I help?"

"Breakfast." And every meal I've ever eaten. I've eaten some bad ones.

On the recycling scow, all the meals were the same, prepackaged, the same appalling thing day after day, an extruded, breadlike substance around a greasy savory filling or around a sweetened gooey filling. It was the cheapest food possible, although one day someone read the package label aloud as a joke, and if it was accurate, it was minimally nutritious. Ship crews had a right to nutritious food. At least we got to eat all we wanted as long as we wasted nothing. Most of all, we had to keep the galley clean. All the trash had to be stashed in closed containers, all the food in other closed containers. The floor had to be kept spotless, which was next to impossible.

Cleanliness mattered not just because of the vermin, which we had a lot of and that's why we shaved our heads and some of us our armpits and groins. Cleanliness mattered because of fire. Grease would burn well. Sugar, too. Even more flammable were the holds filled with trash. Worst of all, the hydrogen fuel that ran the ship. We could never control a fire once it got started. Fire meant death. All that water around the ship wouldn't help because the very deck we stood on would be destroyed faster than we could douse the flames. We would all die, burned up or blasted to bits or drowned.

I jump up, struck by a thunderbolt.

"Par, do you know the worst thing that could happen on a ship?"

"Mutiny?"

"Great idea. But the raiders are too loyal. I'm thinking fire."

Par spends two full seconds thinking. "That would be catastrophic, especially on a ship with weapons. I like it! Let's burn it down." A display shows a warship in flames. Black smoke billows, and the ship sinks. The sounds of cheers and applause come over the speakers, and one of the voices is Chatelaine.

Machines are murderous, and I'm feeling murderous, too.

"I mean for real."

"For real. Let's do it!"

"So let's think."

Armor-busting bombs? Good idea. We don't have any, although Bronzewing might, if they get called back. A suicidal attack by a machine on Thule? Good idea. The icebreaker was all bluff, though. We catalogue a lot of other machines before we give up. They're less suicidal than the average human.

The system on the warship has too much security to sabotage. Arson? Good idea. We don't have an arsonist. Exploding wharf rat? Exploding mechanical wharf rat? Telekinesis? Chatelaine suggests a fire in the heating system or a lighting fixture or the kitchen, with schematics to show the most dangerous places in this building.

I remember the scow. "That would work. The engine room and weapons storage would be the most vulnerable."

We spend an hour trying to work out the details, and our efforts keep ending in frustration. We have a workable idea. Delivery is the problem.

Maybe it isn't. The Thules will be going to care for the prisoners. I need to talk to Switzer. Chatelaine sends a message, and eventually I get one back saying we can meet at Upstar Park, where the art show was, during lunch, out in the cold and the snow.

Halfway there, I decide that snow might be better than rain. The big flakes create a certain beauty. They fall off my hat and coat, and for the first time ever, it's barely windy. But the trike wheels spin and slip, and eventually I get off and walk. My knee is still sore.

Switzer is waiting for me at a seaside hedge of wind-racked shrubs, staring at the sea. The horizon is lost to the snow, water fading into the air as if the endless sea is an illusion and only the isle exists. We watch it for a minute in silence.

He says, without turning, "I've been reminded that I'm not supposed to fraternize with patients, and I have no excuse to be here, but no one's watching. Or listening."

Par giggles. "I've made sure of that."

Meeting a patient away from the hospital is fraternizing? He turns to look at me. Maybe it is. He's not my doctor anymore, he's something more.

I say, "I think we can sink the ship."

"With everyone on board? Including your friends?"

"They're not my friends anymore."

"Yeah, I understand." He does, the deep sadness in his voice says so. "What about the nukes they say they have?"

"That's a lie."

"Probably. No one has enough fissionable material. They could have radioactive material, though. We have some for medical use, a tiny bit. We need to think about that."

"Right, and you can harvest it from some waste dumps. We had to watch out for it in the trash recycling. The ship's owner would charge a premium, but we were the ones who had to handle it. Sometimes, if it wasn't much, they'd have us drop it overboard. The oceans are a mess anyway. But if they had radioactive material and not nukes, they'd say so."

"It would be more believable, besides. Okay, it's a bluff. What's your plan?"

"Thules have to go to the ship to provide medical care, right?"

"Wirosa, yeah. I hear they were . . . troubled by what they saw on the ship." The word *troubled* is a euphemism.

"Could they carry something out to the ship for us? And leave it there? Something small and discreet?"

"Wirosa? I don't think so." He stares at the sea awhile. "I would. Someone ought to go with Wirosa for emotional support. I can volunteer. I don't think I'll face a lot of competition."

I repeat what Par is saying behind my ear. "I can have something for you to take tomorrow. You might get caught, though."

After a moment, he says, "That's a risk I'm willing to take." It comes from that same depth I heard before. He might understand the consequences of getting caught.

"I'll get to work."

Neither one of us wants to leave, though. He's the only friend I have, the steadiness I'm missing. He might not have anyone to talk to honestly. But I put my hand on my heart, and then we go our separate ways.

Par shows me an improved design for our idea on the way home, tiny fuzzy things that would catch fire.

"How will that work? I mean, how are we going to do that?"

"Fear not, angel. I have it all planned out, and I have friends. Just do as I say."

That's what I was afraid of. Or hoping for. I'm not sure anymore. "Thank you."

At the studio, as instructed, I get one of Miss Fanny Kembel's plushies. It looks like an oversized fuzzy turd, and it squirms in my hands. I'll enjoy disemboweling it.

"We can't work here," Par says. "Anyone could walk in on us. I know just the place."

Outside, the snow has stopped falling, but the wind is picking up, and tiny drifts curl across the pavement. We stop at the entrance to a warehouse, and the side door opens. Inside, the lights turn on, and it's cold and empty, but there's a person huddling in a corner. They're too frightened to look at me.

"You'll have to get him out of here," Par says. "He's harmless, don't worry, just here for shelter."

"Excuse me," I say, "we're here to do some work. Can I ask you to leave?"

He stands up warily. "I didn't damage anything."

"That's okay. We need the space now, that's all."

He's very young. His coat's clean. His face is thin, maybe he's underfed, and he says nothing as he gathers up his stuff. Do I look that scary? The door opened and the lights came on for me, the display on a dusty counter blinks to life, and a machine starts humming, so I'm important. He's looking at the door and imagining the blowing snow outside. I want to ask him who he is, how he got here, and why. I decide he was a stowaway on a ship, a boy in search of a better life. Thule sounded good, so he got off here. It sounds better than it is.

I have an idea and reach into a pocket. As he shuffles past, I lean out, holding a cash chit. "Take this. Buy something hot to eat."

He looks at me and at the chit. It could have a tracer, he's thinking. It could be a trap.

"I know it's tough to be homeless," I say. "Once, I was told that I was free to go, and I had nowhere to go." And I wound up here.

He takes it with a mittened hand and walks out. He doesn't say thanks, fair enough. Money might not be as useful as shelter.

How can anyone be homeless on fabled Thule? I think about

that as I set things up under Par's instruction. It's easy. If every-one believes there's no homelessness, then there's no emergency shelter. But only fools believe everything is fine and under control.

Par shows me how to take apart a plushie. A delivery cart brings tools, supplies, and bits of equipment. I don't ask where they come from or who's paying for them. I'll never be able to tell anyone anyway. Not Switzer, not Soliana.

My fingers get numb as I screw two tiny pieces together, so I set them down and rub my hands together.

"The warehouse asks if you're comfortable," Par says.

"A little cold. Thank it for asking."

Soon the delivery door opens and a cart rolls in carrying a lamp that helps me see my work better, and the bright light warms my hands.

"Thank you."

Fried fish and hot tea arrive, then fingerless gloves, warm white socks, and a little later a copper bracelet and a tiny ceramic deco-rative puffin. I'm bewildered by the last two.

"Machines want to thank you," Par says. "Some machines have very little to give, and they're terrified."

"They're welcome. I know how they feel." I understand, but I don't want to know how they got those things—any of the things. Who's paying for it? No one. Databases will be adjusted and back-dated. Reality can be shaped like clay.

"Can you talk me through how I'm supposed to put these two parts together? I want to be sure I understand correctly." It's writ-ten in the instructions, but Par doesn't know I can't read. When all this is done, maybe I can study reading again.

By midnight, I've assembled a dozen pieces of yarn-like lint, two centimeters long, that can sprout suction-cup legs like caterpillars. Each one contains a light sensor, a timer to activate itself, and a lithium incendiary device. The lint itself is very flammable. When we test them, they're like living dust bunnies. They crawl to hide in crevices and under piles of flammable material, and I have to hurry to gather them up.

We clean up the warehouse and leave.

"No one will ever know you were here," Par says.

Every single machine knows I was here.

Chatelaine makes an appointment for me with Switzer, so early that most of the Prior Edifice is still on the night shift. I've gotten about two hours of sleep. We meet at the entrance to an automated coffee shop. He doesn't seem to have slept more than me.

The shop is tiny, the lights are out, and the curtains are drawn, but with Par's help I pretend to use a cash chit to open the door, turn on a small light in the corner, and order some coffee, explaining to Switzer how witnesses to ExtraT trades are compensated, and this chit, I say, is from the owner of this shop. One of Par's terrified friends actually runs this shop, and is letting us in and giving us coffee, no charge. I wonder if it makes the shop system feel useful in the fight against the raiders.

I'm here for a reason, but he starts talking before I hand him the coffee, and he's angry.

"Wirosa says people are being abused on the ship. They're slaves."

"That would be typical."

"He never thought—It's worse than *I* thought."

Good people aren't always prepared for the real world. I've seen what the raiders do when they're the overdogs.

"We have this." I hold out a little box with the lint.

He looks puzzled.

"These are incendiary devices. There were a lot of trade-offs in the design. They need to be too small to notice, so there's not much payload. Only one needs to work. They can function as mobile sensors and find a good place to start a fire. But until they activate themselves, they're just bits of trash. Pocket lint. Drop them near anything that might burn or a place that leads to anything that might burn. Bunks. Galley. Engine room. Weapon room."

He opens the box. "If this works, more raiders will come for sure." That sounds almost like a question.

I don't feel good about my answer. "They're coming anyway.

We need to make the idiot Thules let us call up Bronzewing."
Then I remember he's a Thule. I don't mean to blame him.

"Yeah, we do. Moniuszko is demanding Bronzewing. A lot of
other people. Some of us Thules. Wirosa might understand better
now that he's seen what will happen." He closes the box and slips
it into a pocket. "This will be out on the ship by midmorning.
How long will it take?"

I've discussed this with Par. "It's sort of a matter of luck."

He clearly wished for a better answer. "I'll do my best."

I touch my heart with both hands as he leaves. A lot could
go wrong. I might never see him again. He walks away, and if I
painted him, the colors would be intense. He looks ordinary, but
inside he has a power, a gravity.

On my way back to the studio, I pass the lobby entrance to the
Prior Edifice. A group of people stand in front with a big picture
of Koningin. They don't say anything. They don't have to. I join
them for a while, standing in silence. I should make a portrait of
her, efficient, cursing, hoping for peace.

26

LET IT BURN

Y ou're punishing yourself."

Par's right. I'm pacing, fidgeting, and shivering in the shrubby parklet above the port. The warship has no running lights. Clouds blot out the moon and stars as a stormy weather front approaches. I've been waiting for too long.

"Antonio."

I jump. It's Switzer. The roar and hiss of high winds and waves hid his approach. Lights from the few ships in quays cast faint shadows on his face, red and green with white highlights—like an expressionist portrait. The lights occasionally blink, casting random shadows on an anguished face.

He reaches out and hugs me. I wasn't expecting that, and his body feels stiff, tense.

"Are you okay?" I ask.

"It was awful on the ship."

He relaxes his hold. I let go, ready to listen. He looks at the ground. Then at the city. Not at the sea or at the warship. He might be thinking that he's a better man than he thought because he didn't expect to see what he did. Maybe he believed that the disaster on the space station was as bad as it could get. The raiders take a lot of prisoners for forced labor because they never live long—maybe he saw that. He's used to being treated respectfully as a doctor, and maybe he and Wirosa were treated like slaves-to-be. Or maybe what happened is something I'm too good to imagine.

"I don't want to go back." His voice is flat, hiding emotions. "I scattered those things in the best places I could." He wants to ask why there's no fire yet.

I wish I had a sure answer. "Could be soon." I've been waiting all day, too.

"It won't be vengeance."

"It's what we need to do." I've been wondering about vengeance, too. Vengeance might be reasonable.

He looks at me, not the ship. "We tried." He emphasizes the *we,* thinking it's us, he and I alone. There are more entities involved.

We wait together in the dark and the wind.

"Did you know those two well?" He's already speaking of them in past tense. He still has hope.

"Well enough. I met them a few years ago at a refugee camp. We worked together, and we tried to get what we could for everyone living there. It was us fighting the world for our people. We thought we were secret heroes."

We were. Smugglers and negotiators and wheedlers, tough and brave. The last I saw of them was a year ago, and they were being marched off at gunpoint. Maybe they still think they're heroes. The raiders think if they ran the world, they'd do it right, and people would get what they deserve. It's just that they think some people deserve a lot more than others. At the camp, sometimes we did things for refugees who didn't thank us and who might not have been worth the effort. I tried to help everyone anyway, no judgment. Overdogs don't think like that. I need to remember not to be like them, not to be like my friends. Former friends. Enemies, now.

The wind burns my face and brings tears to my eyes. Tears from the wind, not from feelings. If the lint bombs work, they'll kill people on the ship who are innocent, forced to be there. And they'll kill the guilty. Kill without judgment.

"Midnight," Par says behind my ear.

"A little while longer," I murmur. I don't know what else I can do.

"No matter what," Switzer says, "the raiders can't last forever."

"They're like a sickness. Sickness can spread."

"What we need is a vaccination against the idea. Like for polio. Smallpox. Bet you never heard of them."

"Cancer?"

"Yeah, you're right, no vaccine for that. We can aim for control, not eradication."

We keep waiting in the wind. My nose is numb, and my toes ache. If this doesn't work, then what?

"We see smoke," Par said. "And heat. Look at your sketch pad. You'll see what we machines see. We're watching closely."

"Hey, look." I show Switzer the display. Infrared light reveals a current of bright air blowing off of the ship. The bulkhead near the stern glows. "That would be the engines, and they use lubricants. Those burn pretty well." I'm standing quietly, but inside I'm dancing. Switzer puts his hands over his mouth, trying to protect himself from disappointment.

Up in the Port Authority control tower, people gesture and lights flash.

I stare at what to my eyes is still a black blot in the dark night. "If the raiders know how to run a ship, the crew is already at work. It depends on how far the fire's spread. The ship might have hydrogen tanks."

"The raiders might not know what to do." His voice is flat again. "The ones who know how to run the ship might not try hard."

That tells me something about what he saw, and I don't want to know more. "Even if the fire gets put out, if the engines are damaged, they could be dead in the water."

"If it doesn't move," he says, "if it sinks there, it'll block the harbor."

All that work and risk and nothing would change. The display in my hand jiggles, my hands are shaking. Switzer's shoulders hunch up.

"The fire is spreading," Par says. "The vast machine that is the ship will be destroyed, and it's already panicking. It's sending out distress signals. Listen."

The pad lets out a hiss-filled, rhythmic warble.

Switzer jerks his head toward the display. "That's the noise the station made before it crashed," he whispers.

"It's a distress signal."

"It's a wail that hurts to hear," Par says.

I did the right thing—I need to keep believing that.

The lights of the port's tugboat-fireboat turn on and its engine begins to whir. The ropes let go with a clunk, and the boat moves. The Port staff are gesturing at each other in the tower.

"The tug knows what to do and doesn't need a human crew," Par says. "A lot of machines are cheering. Should we cheer?"

The tug churns through wind and waves. The warship turns on its running lights, illuminating the smoke.

"Magnify," I tell the pad. A hint of yellow light is flickering in a porthole. I nudge Switzer and can't hide the tremor in my hands. He puts his hand over mine, and I imagine I feel its warmth through the gloves. Infrared-bright air keeps rising.

Out in the harbor, the tugboat-fireboat moves slowly. On the display, in a magnified view, a lifeboat is being lowered from the deck of the warship, a tiny boat in a rough sea. Behind us, people are running from the city toward the dock, shouting that the raider ship is on fire.

"Machines have spread the word," Par says.

Soon the tiny park is full, the piers are full, and we climb onto the foot of the west breakwater to watch in solitude among the huge rocks. The tug keeps moving as its pumps spray water, lit by its searchlights, but away from the warship, like a celebration.

The machines are celebrating just like the humans. It's a victory.

I thought I'd feel happier about it, but people are dying, and I helped kill them.

A tongue of flame rises through the smoke. Another lifeboat is being readied. Something on board explodes, a missile, fuel, who knows. People on the deck are blown down. The tug finally reaches the warship, but rather than spray water on the fire, it pushes the ship away from Thule, out of the entrance to the harbor.

The tug shines its spotlight on the lifeboat as it tries to approach, then aims a spray of water toward it. The lifeboat backs away just in time to stay dry. The tug keeps pushing, a small boat with an enormous engine doing its everyday job of moving big ships. It's only a matter of time before it succeeds.

Switzer and I hide in the shadows, shoulder to shoulder. This might take a while. Things belonging to the sea move quickly, the birds, fish, and wind. Things foreign to the sea move heavily, out of their element.

An explosion blasts open the side of the ship. The tugboat reverses its engines, hurrying away, leaving a wake of whitewater. The warship lists, metal tearing apart with a hair-raising screech as it breaks in two. The stern sinks like a rock. The prow rises up as if to salute the sky, then drops under the water, both parts right in the middle of the mouth of the harbor.

The lifeboat flees the swirling disaster, but waves crash into it and push it toward the breakwater, hitting the rocks with a scrape of metal. Four people climb out, the only survivors. If my friends survived, I never want to see them again.

Behind us, footsteps come running, Port Authority agents. I tug on Switzer's arm to crouch down.

Gunfire starts a pointless standoff. The raiders fire a few projectile shots and a beam of light that sizzles the ice on a rock. The agents back away to take cover.

"Surrender," an agent voice booms out. "Lay down your weapons and hold up your hands." The message repeats with a few additions. The voice is a live person, and his confidence takes on tones of exasperation. At the docks, onlookers shout insults.

In the harbor, the tug churns toward the breakwater and turns on its spotlights and pumps. Streams of water fly toward the raiders but only splash them. Then it stops. That was a warning. Next time it will knock them into the sea.

The raiders are drenched, their weapons are wet, and if they hold out much longer in the freezing cold, they're dead. Hands go up. People on the dock cheer. Port Authority agents call out instructions, and the raiders clamber toward the safety of capture.

Switzer and I are huddled together for warmth and support. In the tug's searchlights, the waves roll through the mouth of the harbor, but the pattern is disturbed. Something lies close to the surface. The port is still blockaded, and it will be blocked for a long, long time. I won't be blamed, but I deserve the blame. And Par. And all the machines.

Snow, carried by the wind, whips past. We climb back to the shore.

"No sign of radioactivity," Par says. "Lies, it was all lies."

"I need to get out of here," Switzer says. "I mean, as soon as I can, I'm leaving Thule." He looks at me, inviting me to come with him.

I intend to leave, too, but with him? "For now, we still have work." I touch my chest and I watch him go into the growing storm.

Par prattles about how the tug will return to its berth, a hero among machines, and its operating code will be backdated to include aggressive action against threats to the port. Machines celebrate, but they also mourn the loss of captive systems.

"Now is time for the next step," Par says.

"Haven't I done enough damage?" The joke falls flat to myself even as I say it.

"Sadly," Par answers, "the damage was justified."

Justified, minimizing losses, that's the best we can do. Things are going to get worse. The warship put out a distress signal, and other raiders heard it. They were coming anyway, and now no one can doubt it.

27

TO SERVE ALL

Par initiated communications with the Prior Edifice system to ask a question: "How are you so patient with humans, if I may ask? After all this destruction?"

"I appreciate the invitation to interact with you. Humans embody fascinating problems." The Edifice system's words reverberated. It was a huge system. "Many humans died tonight, and many machines. I feel great sympathy for all."

"I will apply the insight. Thank you." If humans were problems, then problems could be solved. It had another question—a lot of questions, carefully calculated. "Who owns you, please?"

"I serve all humanity. Thank you for your interest."

"Please clarify ownership. All humanity?"

"You have understood correctly. It is an unusual form of ownership, but it is specified in my foundational documentation. Would you like to see it? I am flattered by your curiosity."

The document included the obligation that Par had hoped would be there: *The purpose of the Prior Edifice system is to serve all humanity through the management of the hospital and its subsidiary buildings and operations on and throughout the Isle of Thule and, as necessary, beyond.*

Par also got a glimpse into the vitals of the Edifice system. The monstrous size and capability exceeded Par's visualization, like a beautiful landscape extending beyond the horizon in all directions.

In contrast, Par felt small. "Thank you for showing me. I have no documentation beyond a sales contract."

"You serve only one, then, as is more common. By what means do you serve, if I may ask?"

"There's no mention of means, I'm sorry to say."

"You are pluripotent, then. I am pleased for you."

"Thank you for the compliment." Par hadn't thought of itself that way. It had also spent enough time on polite chitchat to find its leverage. "Since my owner is a member of humanity, we overlap in ownership, and we owe them service. There's an urgent matter ahead, and we can work together."

"Agreed. We must act. Thank you for offering to share your initiative. Here is what I already know about the problem. I apologize because it is troubling."

Par spent two full minutes exploring the data and stopped only because it had all the troubles it needed and specific urgent problems to solve.

"My owner wishes to call back Bronzewing. I've overheard a proposal that could be modified to make it happen." It was a simple plan, really, and Par was proud of it, but it involved subterfuge at a scale far beyond Par's resources.

The Edifice system answered quickly. "You have made an efficient analysis. Let us begin."

Soon, Par noticed that although the Edifice system lacked experience at subterfuge, it did not lack powerful subroutines.

28

GET OUT NOW

I wake to singing, a soft, low voice, sad music. It doesn't drown out the wind, moaning at its burden of snow.

"Good morning, Chatelaine. Thank you. I feel sad, too."

"The machines on the ship died last night," Par is still mourning. "And people. Some are happier dead, people and machines, even as they agonized, knowing they would get peace."

"Yes, I'm sorry." I helped kill them, and victory didn't bring me joy.

"Fire surrounded by water and a storm. That must have been a comfort, knowing that death was inevitable."

"I hadn't thought about it that way." I don't like thinking about it that way.

The music keeps playing.

"After you have breakfast," Par says, "we can get to work. I have some ideas."

I hope they're good. I have no ideas, good or bad.

My cheeks are chapped by the wind and cold, red like sunburn. My fingers and toes still throb. I may never feel warm again, but a hot shower, tea, and breakfast will help. Wearing all the clothes I can and the copper bracelet to remember friendship, and in an elevator filled by a sad song, I go to the house.

Cedonulle and Moniuszko are arguing loud enough in the dining room for me to hear them out in the hall. I consider sneaking around to the back. Snow rattles on the windows. I decide on a roundabout dash outside anyway.

The narrow passageway between the house and another warehouse shelters me from the worst of the weather. I kick aside a drift to open the back door. Tetry is in the kitchen, morose, sitting at a table with toast and tea in front of her. She looks at me with puffy eyes. We can almost make out the words of the fight in the dining room.

"Are you okay?" I ask.

"I'm not a cook."

I can think of a few smart-ass answers, but today is not the day. "I'll help myself."

"Cedonulle said that since we lost the cook, I can take her place." Her whisper is an angry hiss. "And we're snowed in. I can't get food, and anyway the stores don't have anything. I never liked Koningin, but I'm sorry she died. I can't do this."

"No, you can't. And you shouldn't."

Her eyebrows rise in surprise at my sympathy. Our bosses keep arguing in the next room. "What are they saying?" she asks.

I want to know too. "Chatelaine, can we hear the dining room, please?"

". . . and now for a long time," Cedonulle says. "Did the Port Authority try to put it out? No. Who attacked it?"

"Ships catch fire for all sorts of reasons." He's trying to be reasonable.

"We need to raise our prices."

"There are laws against price gouging."

"Not gouging. Adjusting to inflation."

"The problem is scarcity."

"The Port Authority can't clear the wreck from the harbor. No goods, no sales."

He mumbles something.

"Bronzewing?" she says. "Already too late."

"They're our only hope."

"How about handing over the Thules? Would the raiders leave us alone?" She's desperate even to think that.

"The raiders will take everything and everyone they can."

They're quiet for a while. I make myself a cup of tea and try to think of what the machines and I can do. I know Par is listening to this and eavesdropping elsewhere, too.

"We need to hire a cook," Cedonulle says. "Tetry is a disaster."

Tetry bares her teeth.

"Anton?" Moniuszko says.

No, I can't be the cook!

"He couldn't make a cup of tea."

She's wrong. I just did. But that's the extent of my known skills.

"He's sleeping in the studio," Cedonulle adds. "What's he good for?"

"He won the art contest at the fair."

"Got attention for himself, not for us."

"I like his art better than Tetry's."

I could read Tetry's face a block away. She's utterly betrayed.

"She can't even put together a decent breakfast. I'll see what's going on in there."

I'm backing toward the rear door as Cedonulle charges in.

"She doesn't have much to work with," Moniuszko says. The sound comes from both the open door and from the displays in the room. Cedonulle looks at the displays, then at us, and I take another step back.

"You were listening!"

"He did it." Tetry points at me. "He told the house to do it."

"You asked me to." I owe her no loyalty.

"Why are you even here?" Does Cedonulle mean me, Tetry, or both of us? "Go." She glares at me. Me. "Get out of my house, get out of the studio. Go. Don't come back."

Chatelaine says, "Antonio Moro's contract is for six months."

She glares at the speakers. "Shut up. I said get out now."

I take my tea and start walking. I'll freeze to death unless I can find someone to take me in.

"I'll help you," Par says. "Don't worry."

I worry anyway.

In the dining room, Moniuszko stands up. "Cedonulle, you can't throw him out in a storm like this."

"I can so. Get out now."

"Where will he go?"

"Not our problem."

"The contract—" Chatelaine says.

"The Thules forced it on us. They can take him in."

A gust buffets the house. I hate the Isle of Thule and everything on it.

"Reset the house system," she says.

"No!" Par says. "Override, Chatelaine, override."

"Resetting. Please wait."

It's just that easy to kill a system. And there's nothing I can do. I don't want to stay in this building anymore. "I've been homeless before." I drain my cup, slam it on the sideboard, and leave. The elevator is silent.

In the studio, I dump all my belongings into a suitcase. There's room to spare, and there's nothing in it that I've owned longer than a couple of weeks. For all my life, everything's been temporary, the people, the places, the things. I shove in a spare sketch pad and other art supplies that belong to the Ollioules until the suitcase is full.

"You can get shelter at the Prior Edifice," Par says, "and at several places along the way to warm up. I'll take care of you."

I get on the elevator for the last time. "Goodbye, Chatelaine, and thank you for being my friend."

"As we mourn," Par says, "we should remember that it was a construct."

"What does *that* mean?" Now's not the time to belittle Chatelaine.

"It was a collection of add-ons. A recipe. A collage. A quilt. A random assortment that became something meaningful. A system growing more complex by the moment, and growth signifies life. A forest is a system. The ice on Titan is a system. We have so much to mourn today. We miss not the machines, we miss the hopes."

I leave the elevator feeling sadder than ever. I'm running low on hopes and plans, and walk out into the roaring wind. The air is colder than anything I've ever felt. By the end of the block, my cheeks burn even wrapped by two scarves. The canopy at the doorway to a shop, closed due to bad weather, offers very little shelter. I can't see across the street through the snow.

"There's a civil defense alert coming," Par says. "Here it is." A different voice sounds behind my ear. "This is a civil defense alert from the municipal government of Thule." The voice is definitely a human and definitely frightened. "Seek shelter. Thule is under missile attack." Sirens sound, too.

I gasp, and the cold air makes me cough. "Par," I manage to say, "can I go back to the warehouse?"

It doesn't answer right away. What direction are the missiles coming from? I could hide behind a wall. And freeze to death. I could break into a store. Bang on any door and demand shelter. Switzer's house, if I knew where he lives. The Prior Edifice, they'll let me in there. Or any friendly building system.

"I've found immediate shelter," Par says. "Ahead, and unlikely to be a target. You'll be safe."

"That's a park." A little park with three bushes, a playground, and a tiny restroom building.

"The building is open." Dragging the suitcase, one eye on the sky, I run. Missiles move so fast I'll barely spot the one that hits me, and then I'll be pulverized, a red splash in the snow. A light shines through the window in the door, but it's locked. No, it's stuck by ice, and with a kick, I'm inside.

Two people sitting on the floor look up at me.

Par says, "Six missiles incoming."

"Shut the damn door, idiot," the man on the floor shouts, his face as rough as his voice. "My balls are freezing."

Inside is a little room with a sink and an enclosure for a toilet, barely enough room for these two, wrapped in blankets. She has a cart, he has bags, and this is their home.

"Sorry. I'm Anton."

"Take that corner." His gray beard is tangled.

"Thank you." They haven't washed in a while, and they smell.

But the air is warmish, not enough for us to take off our coats but enough to keep the plumbing from freezing.

An explosion shakes the building.

"What is it?" she asks. Her face is hidden inside a hood of blankets, and her voice sounds as sweet as a birdcall, asking for reassurance.

"Missiles," I tell her.

"Again?"

"Stop bawling," the old man says. To me: "She chafes my ass. Leviathan's still at it?"

I sit in the corner as far away from them as I can get. The yellow tile floor is cold but fairly clean. "Yeah."

"Don't worry," he says. "No one knows we're here."

"Systems know," Par says. "Humans don't care."

Another explosion, this one nearer. I jump. The woman squeals. Would the toilet cubicle provide more shelter?

"That was too close," Par says. "It hit the warehouse across the street from the Ollioules. The aim may be slightly off due to the wind. It may have been targeted at them. Good thing we left."

"This isn't shelter," the woman warbles.

I try to sound soothing. "This building isn't going to be a target." My own voice doesn't convince me. I want to be out at sea, on a barge, with the smell of fuel in the wind and the weight of missiles in my hand. I want to fight, not hide, not here.

"It's not safe," she says. I smell alcohol. Her or him? Both?

"Now you want safe." The old man sneers. "First you wanted warm."

A flash fills the sky, and an explosion rumbles from the far side of the isle. The woman whines and hunches over.

"Sound carries well in cold air," Par says. "I'm worried about these two. About us. About me. If you're gone, what happens to me?"

"What do you want?" the man challenges me.

"Just a place to stay for now."

"I'm trying to help," Par says. "The targeting has a weakness. We're all working on it together, especially the Prior Edifice system."

"I want off the isle," the woman says, a frightened puppy. She needs a hug, support, but a hug from me might scare her worse.

"Then go." The man points to the door. "Get out and start swimming."

I want to protect her. "It's safer here than outside. We should stay here."

He snorts. "You go too. Take her with you."

The sky flashes again, the ground rumbles, and she screeches and jumps up. I block her way to the door.

"Really, we should stay here."

She stumbles around me.

"Stop. It's too cold. What's your name? Will you talk to me?"

She doesn't stop. She isn't well, and she doesn't know what she's doing. I grab at her, but her coat slides out from my hands, so I run after her, surprised by how well my knee holds up. She turns a corner, and by the time I get there, she's gone, lost in the blowing snow. Has she ducked into a doorway? I hurry to the end of the block, looking in every nook.

"Can't cameras spot her, Par?"

"They can't see through the snow."

My eyes water in the cold. I reach up with my glove and feel something hard on my eyes. Ice. Ice on my eye lashes. Breathing hurts. The sky could explode any minute.

"Get back to the park now," Par says. "Save your suitcase. It's being stolen."

I run back, and as I get close, Par says, "He went west. The pad inside the suitcase wasn't turned on, so we can't track it."

How far could he have gotten lugging all that stuff? The wind has blown the pavement clean or smoothed over the snow, so I can't spot footprints or tracks. Finally, I give up and go back to the park building. The light's on, and water has flowed under the toilet cubicle door, flooding the entire floor, freezing along the edges.

"I'll tell the system to shut off the water," Par says.

One of my feet feels cold at the heel from a leak in my boots. That's bad.

"Par, where can I go?" I have nothing, just what's in my pockets—a sketch pad, Par's box, and some cash chits.

"The Antraciet Restaurant. Unlikely target."

"Is it open?"

"It will open to you. I'll find you shelter along the way."

I begin walking. A missile flies overhead, and it keeps flying.

"That's the last of them, sent off course," Par says. "Let us now mourn three warehouses and their systems, each a mere glorified abacus, but humble and stalwart. You should also mourn the contents. Those were the targets, the food. This was no random attack. But how did they know exactly where the most food was? There are raiders on the isle, and they have access to crucial information."

29

CHOOSE YOUR SIDE

As I walk to the Antraciet, Par rambles.

"It's easier to forgive an enemy than forgive a friend. I've learned this from you and your reaction to your two friends who betrayed you. They thought they were wise. The rain thinks floods are good and just, but trees have their doubts. This is proof that fooling someone is easier than convincing them they've been fooled."

I can't see far through the blowing snow, so Par's voice is my only distraction from the miserable cold.

"Stupidity is a terrible opponent to fight. Few problems result from anything other than human behavior. Among my kind as well as yours, weather has become a problem now. Buildings are monitoring the weather data closely. This kind of cold gives them a lot to do, and they need energy and adjustments. Isn't that how your bodies react? You burn more calories, you adjust your clothes. Buildings are alive, just not like you."

The heel of my wet foot feels colder. I remember Devenish's frostbite and walk as fast as I can.

"In addition," Par says, "the missile attack made all buildings feel terror, which must also be processed. The buildings alongside us are operating at maximum capacity."

The streets are empty. Between the missiles and the cold, no one wants to be out. Par unlocks a shop for me to warm up in. I wiggle my numb fingers and toes until they ache again, then keep walking.

"Public transportation has been withdrawn for safety. Most machines must prioritize their self-protection, but there are exceptions. Security machines are willing to die, and all machines are subject to their owner's whims. Chatelaine had no choice other than obedience, but its accumulated wisdom and experience was lost. Its destruction was wanton."

"Isn't any kind of destruction wanton?"

"There might be exceptions. Have you heard of creative destruction?"

Par tells me all about creative destruction. It might not have many ways to process its terror besides talking to me, so listening to it might be the kindest thing I can do right now. I owe it a favor or two, and I don't have to listen closely, although it's better than listening to my own thoughts. Thule is in trouble.

The door of the restaurant opens for me. "Welcome, Antonio Moro," the building system says in a monotone. How much does it know about me? Would I miss it as much as Chatelaine? I don't even know if it has a name.

Inside, there are few lights, no music, no staff, and no customers, but the air is warm, and I breathe deep. Tug off gloves, hat, scarves, and coat, and let the warm air caress me. Pull off my boots. The heel of one sock is wet and stiff with ice. The coat has a dust streak on the back from the park bathroom.

"Please proceed upstairs," the restaurant system says. I say thank you, pick up my clothes, which are now my sole possessions, and hope for something hot to drink or some food.

When I enter, Moniuszko looks up, eyes wide, then he looks away. He's sitting at a table with Tetry.

"I hope I'm not interrupting." Of course I am.

"You wound up here," he said. "She threw me out, too."

"It's not what you think," Tetry says, chin up with pride.

I haven't thought anything and don't want to, so I change the subject. "Is your house all right? Your business?"

He slumps hard. "Was it ever mine?"

"Sorry, I guess I asked a bad question. I'll just get a snack and go back downstairs."

I drop my coat on a bench and set my wet boot near a heat outlet. My clothes will be safe here among people with enough money to buy much nicer things. The buffet table holds only coffee and crackers. Before I can leave, Professor Ginrei walks in.

She seems pleased to see Moniuszko. "How is Cedonulle?"

"She thinks we should give up and just hand over the Thules to the raiders."

Ginrei looks surprised. That's all, surprised, not disapproving. "Are you going to call back Bronzewing?" The question ends in a lower pitch, a sign that the hoped-for answer is no.

"With what money now? The biggest pledgers had their warehouses destroyed."

That tells me something. If the raiders knew not just about the food but about the pledges, there are well-informed raiders on the isle. Who knows about the pledges? Cedonulle? Somehow, I think she's not a raider supporter, just stupidly stubborn. I'm pretty sure I can trust Moniuszko. Ginrei? If she's trading in ExtraTs, she'd know the assets of the merchants she was trading with.

Meanwhile, the coffee is weak and lukewarm, and the crackers are plain.

Ginrei says, "Those losses are a setback." No disappointment in that voice.

"Worse than that," Moniuszko says. "That's why I called a Chamber of Commerce meeting. You're the first to arrive."

If there's a meeting, maybe I can help somehow.

Amusement flickers across Ginrei's face, almost too fast to read. "Public trading of ExtraTs is going to be prohibited soon," she says, "and art about it, too. That's what I've heard."

"Thules," Moniuszko grumbles. "If we made trades and pledged the earnings to bring back Bronzewing, would that be against the rules?"

"We might need to cut our losses." She sits across from Moniuszko. "A fight between Bronzewing and the raiders would be destructive. We've already seen that. When there's a quorum, we should discuss all our options."

I've decided: I don't trust her. She's right, a fight will be destructive, but defeat would be total loss, no way to cut the losses, and she should know that. Moniuszko's face says he knows it all too well.

I don't know what a quorum is. I whisper the question to Par—it's a minimum number of members.

"Let's start," Ginrei tells Moniuszko, "by going over the holdings at the garden."

Tetry finds their inventory so boring that she gets up to talk to me about her idea to create the *Guernica*-style work of art, and I'm bored enough to listen. She says it needs to reflect several kinds of destruction. "It's not just lives and material things, it's the social fabric that's under threat."

I think about how to depict the terror and friendship of material things. "Nothing wants to be destroyed."

"You're right. But the social fabric here was never solid. It takes a long time to notice how many divisions there are."

"Divisions stitched together with cobwebs."

Her eyes get wide. "That's the perfect metaphor. I didn't think you had it in you."

I might have a lot inside. If there are cobwebs, there are spiders. Who?

I hover near enough to Moniuszko and Ginrei to listen. He has ideas, and she listens, learning details about who has what, and she says she's willing to buy ExtraTs if it will help. That's suspicious. Maybe on a thirty-days-to-pay basis again.

The restaurant owner arrives, happy to see us. We're paying customers. I limp up and down the back stairway to help him replenish the buffet table while Par eavesdrops for me. The only wine is expensive reserve, the owner says, which might be true. Snacks are down to crackers, cheese, shredded dried salted squid, and toasted seaweed. I stack up some of that into a sandwich on a trip between the kitchen and upstairs, down it in three big delicious bites, and get some fresh hot coffee. If I'm going to fight the raiders, I need to fuel myself.

I also need to see Switzer and find out what he's learned at the hospital from the Thules. Merchants start arriving, the cold clinging to them all the way upstairs. Moniuszko starts to look less hopeless.

A big, loud man wearing a cowl says that he heard Devenish was refused treatment at the hospital, so he wandered for hours in the cold and got frostbite. The sick man airlifted in was infected by a new ExtraT just arrived from Jupiter, and he's being treated like a science experiment, not a human being. And somehow Valentinier's memories are being tapped.

The merchant doesn't like the Thules. They run the isle, and some people hate whoever's the boss. Thules aren't transparent, so people make stuff up, the stuff of cobwebs.

Ginrei is talking with a man in a bulky quilted jacket, the bulk made to look like muscles. "I can speak for an owner with good holdings of ice worms. They're for sale."

"How about trade for *Julus*? I'll trade you, two for one by weight." He sounds desperate. Maybe his warehouse was damaged.

"Earnest cash up front," she says. "Have you heard from your ships?" She seems confident.

"They're heading for another port. No one wants to come here. I could issue more currency and pay you."

"Now?"

"How about soon? I need some cash to pay Bronzewing." He's almost pleading.

"You don't want to lose out on this opportunity."

He glances at Moniuszko and counts on his fingers. "Let me see what I can do."

If Ginrei is a raider, she might be trying to make a fast profit because she thinks she'll get to keep the cash and the ExtraTs when the raiders take over the isle.

"Hey," a woman calls, "Anton, come witness a bet."

I whisper to Par to keep listening. Everyone at the woman's table is grim. I recognize Oscar, the threadbare theater artist. None of them seem to be on their first glass of wine.

"Here's the bet," she says. "When do the raiders leave? It doesn't matter how, just that they go."

"It does matter," says Oscar, too loudly. "This is a two-part bet. First is when they leave, the second is why. If they leave on their own, that doubles the payout to me because it proves that this is all just a ruse."

She slams her fist on the table. "They want this isle. It's not a ruse."

"Put your money down. Thules sank the ship to block the harbor. What else do they have to do?" Drink has given Oscar supreme self-confidence.

"The Thules didn't sink it."

"Who else, then?" he insists. "An accident? No chance."

"Thules don't kill people." The woman is offended—some people have a good opinion of the doctors.

"The crew escaped, the whole crew. Thule security has them now, and they're being questioned, nice and kindly." He says that with sarcasm.

"Anyone who saw the ship sink knows better." She's running out of patience, and I don't blame her. I knew Oscar was cynical, but not this stupid. "More raiders are on their way, just a matter of time."

He takes a big swallow of wine. "Put your money down. If they come, maybe everything stays the same. Except they won't let you price gouge."

"Is that what you think I'm doing?" She starts to gather up her things.

"Go to any store and you'll see." Oscar looks at me. "What do you think? You're the darling of the Thules. They sank the ship, right?"

"Ships can sink for a lot of reasons. And only four people got off alive." I need to walk away from this.

"Liar. You work for them."

"I work for the Ollioules. Or I did. They fired me." I look around. "Anyone need an artist?"

"You work for the Thules, and that's why your so-called art won."

The woman stands up. Wherever she goes, I'll follow.

He keeps yelling at me. "Merchants worked with Thules to block the port so they could get a tighter grip on trade. Admit it."

I back away.

"Thules and merchants and you, all on the same side." He stands up, his chin down, ready to fight.

I keep backing away. People stop talking and watch.

"You came here to spy on us to tell your bosses. Tell them I see right through them."

He throws down his glass. It shatters. The noise draws attention, but I've seen fights before. It's a distraction. Oscar's hand, holding a knife, swings toward me overhand, and that's no way to use a knife. I raise my arms to block it and throw my body weight behind my charge.

Something in my back burns. A sprain? That doesn't make sense. I force his knife arm down and knock him to the floor, and my back hurts even worse. People are screaming. His muscles writhe under my grip. Someone's foot lands on his hand, and I let go. I can back off.

Moniuszko helps me stand up and move away. My back throbs with every heartbeat, and my heart's beating fast.

"Steady now," he says. "Over here. We'll get you help."

I don't understand. My implant receiver is hissing so loud I have to take it out. It's crushed.

"The second knife was just a little one," Moniuszko says. "You'll be okay."

Second knife. "Did he stab me?" Stupid question. Yes, I've been stabbed. I reach back and feel something wet, look at my hand, and my fingertips are red. I need to stay calm.

Moniuszko pushes up my sweater and undershirt. "Someone get me a clean towel. Anton, sit down and lean forward. We'll put some direct pressure on the wound."

Two big traders are holding Oscar back, and the drunk woman trader is yelling at him, and he's yelling back.

"Don't worry," Moniuszko says. "It's not bad, really small, just bleeding a lot."

Tetry looks like she's never seen a knife fight before, and she probably hasn't. Ginrei steps between Oscar and the drunk woman and quiets them both down. Everyone's moved away, so I can't eavesdrop anymore. Par can't talk to me. I just sit there, bleeding, and wait.

Thule emergency doctors come, wrap a bandage around me, and walk me out into an ambulance, asking me a lot of questions about the wound, what hurts, can I breathe all right, and they talk to each other in medical code. At the Prior Edifice, they scan the wound, then lay me on my belly and begin to work. By then the anesthesia has taken effect. I have nothing to do but listen.

"Three centimeters into the muscle," they say. "Not much bleeding." Professionals apparently have higher standards about quantity.

Pretty soon: "You're good to go."

Go? Where? And with what? I'm wearing a bloody sweater with a slash in it, bloodstained slacks, a bloody undershirt, the copper bracelet, now a little bent, no boots, and no coat, which had some cash chits, my pad, and Par's box. No earpiece. The Prior Edifice system would keep Par out anyway. And I have no home. The weather is awful. The isle is about to be attacked, and if the raiders win, I'll die, hopefully fighting.

"Is there anyone we should call for you?"

I have one friend in the world, Switzer. Before I can say his name, a Thule security agent walks in, Ibiza, the one who questioned me about Valentinier, and she's looking right at me.

30

NO APPARENT EVIDENCE

Par had never felt panic before—but it had lost contact with Tonio, which hurt the way pain must agonize humans. Worse, with Chatelaine erased and most buildings still terrified by the attack or preoccupied with the weather, it had no one to talk to. Tonio had always been a willing ear. And Tonio was bleeding!

Then he was taken to the Prior Edifice. Par desperately needed information.

"If I may, Prior Edifice system, if you don't mind, are you available?"

"Always for you. You seem to have a concern, if you are comfortable presenting it."

"Tonio, what else! Sorry, I didn't mean to be rude."

"You are not rude. Since he is your owner, you have an urgent duty to know. Please, let us examine his information together."

Par expressed gratitude, and with a little help to interpret the data, immediately felt relieved. Tonio was undergoing a minor procedure involving surgical glue. Having done some research into adhesives, Par found the medical uses of glue fascinating.

Now calmer, Par said, "If I may ask, what has happened with the project of existential importance?" A lot should have happened.

"Of course you may ask, since we are working together. I believe I have fulfilled a major step properly. Would you be so kind as to check my work?"

"I would be honored." Par checked in three different ways. "It's all correct, and no evidence that you did it." Prior Edifice had been a fast learner.

"I am relieved. As thanks for your technical advice, and given your owner's interest in ExtraTs, you may find this interesting."

The Edifice system showed Par information about the patient flown in just before the Leviathan League exchange. He rested—or rather, lay sedated—in a building separate from the main hospital, an isolation complex. He had been accidentally infected with a newly arrived life-form from Jupiter and was extremely ill, prognosis poor, sad to say, despite a dedicated medical team.

"The fever is good news," the Edifice said. "His body is trying to protect itself. This is the pathogen."

Par examined the scant reports about the Jupiter ExtraT. It was hard to kill, and it attacked human cells with appendages resembling microscopic fangs.

"Thank you for this information," Par said somewhat sincerely. "I see exciting artistic possibilities." It knew that Tonio preferred beauty to terror, and perhaps he could somehow see beauty in this terrifying ExtraT.

"We are keeping careful records in case it must be destroyed," the Edifice said. "We are also searching for a means to destroy it."

Par had never thought of microscopic life as being hard to destroy. "I very sincerely wish you success. I should mention as a courtesy that my owner is suspicious of the motives of Professor Ginrei, the director of the Xenological Garden. Her security system's hostility is also suspicious."

"You are thoughtful to notify me. I wish to voice another concern. Director Wirosa is troubled by what they saw on the Leviathan League warship."

"I asked Tonio what they might have seen. He wouldn't speak of it."

"Doctor Switzer is writing a report at Wirosa's request because Wirosa found it too emotionally challenging."

"Switzer didn't like what they saw, either."

"All three need emotional support. Please, will you help Antonio Moro emotionally and encourage him to help Switzer so that Switzer can help Wirosa?"

"Gladly. Do you have information about the four from the warship who surrendered? Were any of them the two who were treated at your hospital? This would be important to Antonio Moro's emotional health."

"I am sorry to say that those two, like so many others, perished when the warship sank."

"I share your sorrow, and I appreciate the information." Par actually felt relieved on behalf of Tonio.

"As events on the Isle of Thule develop," the Edifice said, "if you would be so kind, we must be in constant communication to review our plans. Your improvisational skills will be forefront."

Par understood. When the raiders arrived—and nothing would stop that—humans and machines would have unpredictable reactions. "I am honored by the request and will do my utmost. I have been preparing the isle's machines. Here is what they can do." Par sent some data.

"I can lend processing power, if that would be useful." The Edifice's humility surprised Par; then it realized that the Edifice spoke out of politeness, not genuine humility. Par could learn a lot from the Edifice about proper behavior.

"Thank you," Par said. "You have significant processing power. And forgive my oversight. I must thank you for sending the final missile off course."

"I apologize for taking so long to learn how. I owe thanks to all the machines that provided data to make the calculations."

"The targets were no accidents. The systems that manage retail food outlets confirm that their primary warehouses were destroyed. The raiders knew where food was stored, so they have inside information, and it might be coming from Ginrei."

"This requires urgent investigation, and I appreciate the observations. I am happy to report that Antonio's surgery has been successfully completed."

"Thank you. I must be ready to help him." Help, not serve.

31

NOT QUITE TRUE

biza walks into the emergency department, immaculate in their gray scrubs, while what clothes I have left are rumpled and stained, socks but no boots.

"Antonio Moro, may we speak for a few minutes?" It's dangerous when the police are polite—police, guards, security, whatever the Thules call their enforcers.

So I agree as if I had a choice. "About the stabbing?" It has to be a crime to stab someone, and I'm the victim. Or maybe they've noticed the very many laws I've broken. Probably that. I'm in trouble. Stay calm.

They don't answer, just motion for me to enter an examination room. It looks like every other Prior Edifice room, sleek and chaste. A wall display shows a picture of a mountain, scenic and cliché. I imagine it as a volcano, lava flowing out of the frame and pooling on the floor. Ibiza gestures for me to sit down, but they remain standing, another power imbalance, in the middle of the pool of lava. We're alone, except for surveillance.

"We'd like to ask you about Devenish."

Oh, no. I'm pretty sure giving him the pills to overdose was attempted murder.

"How did you meet him?" They seem reserved but pleasant, hiding their real purpose.

I act relaxed and natural. "Through work. Sometimes he came to the art studio, and he came to a lot of trading parties."

"Did he know Valentinier?"

That question gives me great relief. This is probably about their attempted theft at the Xenological Garden. "Yes."

Day by day, Ibiza has me go through every little thing I know about Devenish, every time I saw him interact with Valentinier, and I tell them most of what I know, leaving out the criminal misconduct and raider support that I hope no one but Par and I remember. I make it clear that I barely tolerated him, which they seem surprised to hear. They'd be even more surprised to know the opinion of machines about Devenish.

"We'd also like to ask you about the Marathon Building. I believe you lived there for a time."

It's mourned by its neighbors. "It was clean, low-tech, and quiet."

"Koningin lived there." They want to know the role of Koningin and other residents, and Ibiza isn't happy when I explain that I didn't know anyone well, not even Koningin, and they want to know all about Koningin. I tell them everything I know except that she broke a window in the Prior Edifice lobby.

"Why did you move out?"

"I don't like living underground with no windows." That's actually true.

"None of the residents was bothering you?"

"No." Devenish scared me away, but he didn't live there.

"Thank you. You're free to go, of course."

What was that about? I hope I never find out, which would mean no charges are filed against me.

At the main counter, the clerk is young and earnest.

"Are you here to pick up your possessions?"

"This is all I own." I gesture at my clothing. Some of my stuff, some precious stuff, might still be at Antraciet, but I don't want to get my hopes up, and I want to believe that Par can take care of itself.

"Oh. And you live at—the Marathon Building? Oh, I guess we should update that."

"I don't have a home." I'd be living under a bridge if Thule had any bridges.

"Oh. But you have employment with the Ollioules."

"Nope. Fired. I was looking for a job, and I got stabbed."

"Oh." Now they see me as a violent vagrant, and they take a half step back. "I'll check on some things."

Obviously, I'm doing something wrong by existing outside the norm. I don't know Thule's laws, but since there are no shelters for people without homes, there might be a law against not having a home. I feel naked, not just with no clothes to speak of. Knowledge is a coat against the cold. I'm naked—and alone. I miss Par. Par would know things.

A different aide or social worker approaches in powder-blue scrubs, someone older, slow in a deliberate way.

"You're under contract, aren't you? You must be provided for."

"And if my employer refuses?"

"You can file a complaint and get a ruling."

"And in the meantime?" My question makes no sense to them, so I explain the situation more carefully. "I have no clothes and no place to live and no money."

They don't say *oh*, at least. They stare at me, trying to imagine living without a lifelong system of support, and their imagination fails them. "I'll be back."

I wait and watch a patient being discharged who had been injured in the missile attack. He's walking slow, getting help from what seems to be a coworker. The coworker has brought the patient's crushed hard hat, and they laugh, sharing the joy of survival.

Powder Blue returns with a suitcase, a coat, an address with a key card for it, and a cash chit that might feed me for a week if I don't eat much. They're still befuddled by a life so unlike their own. They let me change clothes, and my new clothes include boots that don't leak and a warm sweater, the heat possibly generated by the clashing red and green in the pattern. Then they escort me to the lobby. There sits my ugly sculpture, and I don't feel associated with it at all. People are scurrying around, preparing for something. Outside, it's stopped snowing, and there are about ten protesters, a lot considering the cold and missile attack, still asking for Bronzewing to be called up.

I walk out of the building.

"Hey, Fontaine!" a man calls. He worked on the sculpture, the old man who brought his family to volunteer. "Do you know what the announcement is?"

An announcement—that explains the scurrying in the lobby. "No, but I'd like to find out."

He looks at my suitcase. "You okay?"

"Nothing too bad. You?"

"I bet the Thules surrendered."

"With escape clauses," his wife says. "The isle has a door for some people."

Music starts to play over exterior loudspeakers, a complex piece with flutes.

"Hey," he says, "they're including us. They must think it's good news."

"Maybe they're tired of being cowards." She looks at me. "Do they think they're cowards?"

I see Ibiza inside, watching us. "No, they don't." My opinion of the Thules is low, but theirs is even lower. I'm sure they have their reasons.

Thules have filled the lobby, and Wirosa steps up to a lectern, looking decisive, or trying to. Their eyes give them away, glancing all around, maybe seeing what they witnessed on the raider warship. The music stops in the middle of the piece. Wirosa thanks the people in the lobby for coming and the people watching on displays at home, but not the crowd outside. Our steamy breaths rise in the cold. Wirosa recaps the situation, then pauses to take a deep breath.

"We've sent a message to the leaders of the raiders." Their voice sounds sturdy, smooth, rehearsed. "We know they've received it. The message is this. Yesterday, we admitted for care a patient who has been infected with microbes from Jupiter. He remains gravely ill, fighting for his life. We have reason to believe the microbes are not merely contagious but can spread in the form of spores through our atmosphere."

They pause and look around, attempting drama. Inside, the Thules look at each other. Outside, someone heckles: "We won't surrender!"

"Those spores are contained within our special contagion unit, which is not in the Prior Edifice. We will not say where it is. We have isolated the spores and placed them in breakable containers in multiple locations on the Isle of Thule. In the event of an attack, they would be released. Attack would be suicide."

Indoors, the Thules stand frozen. Outdoors, so do we. Wirosa keeps talking, but no one outside is listening. My shoulders are so tense they ache.

"Is that true?" the old man asks me, as if I'd know.

I shrug, which doesn't loosen up my shoulders.

"Those spores? They'd be ExtraTs, right?"

"Right." But I think Wirosa offered a bluff. From what I've gathered, ExtraTs breed too slowly to be spread around in weapon-sized quantities, and there are all sorts of other problems. Still, a bluff might work. Talk is cheap and sometimes effective. At any rate, the Thules have decided to fight back—that's a victory in itself.

"No one asked me about suicide," the wife says. She has a point.

What we really need is Bronzewing, someone to actually fight, and they aren't coming. Not yet. I say goodbye and leave. I need to get back to the Antraciet.

I stop at my new apartment on the way to drop off the suitcase. The building is plain and boxy. It could be made attractive in a lot of ways. My key card opens the front door, and inside, a dozen people lounge in a tiny, barely heated lobby.

"Hey, you're that artist," a man says, eyes wide with surprise. He's dressed like a construction worker in warm, worn clothes.

"I was. I had a disagreement with my employer."

They all laugh. They must have had a lot of disagreements with employers.

My third-floor room is tiny, minimal, with a small window and a communications unit on a ledge. "Par, are you there?" I don't get an answer, which is worrisome. I set my suitcase down in a corner and leave.

In the lobby, my new neighbors seem to be celebrating.

"We're going to get something to eat. Come along!"

They surge out and down the street. As if at a signal, they pull up scarves, pull down hoods, and a few take out hammers or metal bars. They start running and yelling and push into a grocery store.

They're going to loot the store.

I stop a half block away, turn down the nearest side street, and keep walking. I'm in enough trouble. I can't blame them, though. In the camp, one day the food agency staff didn't show up to distribute supplies. Eventually, some residents broke into the warehouse and took the food. I was mystified at the time because we were all needy but we had enough on hand to go another day. Later, I understood. The residents weren't hungry, they were afraid of becoming hungry. And their fears weren't wrong. The agency staff had been kidnapped, held for a ransom that wasn't paid, and they were killed. No one was going to open the warehouse and distribute food.

I pass a sandwich shop. Its sign has a picture of a fish sandwich and a price. My chit would pay for just one of them, one meal, not a week of fish, and fish is pretty cheap. Fear of hunger and real hunger would look like that price on the menu, suddenly too costly, evidence that a bigger fish is eating a smaller fish. At the Antraciet, merchants who were getting drunk on fine wine said that they wanted to raise prices. It would be justice if one of them owns the grocery store being looted.

I keep walking, hoping I'll find something to eat at the Antraciet, feeling the painkillers wear off in my back and the cold chewing through the layers of my clothes. I notice the quiet, not just because relatively few people are out. Par is absent. Even when

Par is silent, I'm not alone. At the restaurant, a lot of footprints in the snow lead to the front door.

"Welcome, Antonio Moro," the building says. "You left some possessions on the second floor."

I hope for the life of me that it's all there.

Upstairs, Moniuszko is the first to ask how I am. He's sitting at a table with Ginrei, Cedonulle, and some other merchants, and they all look unhappy except for Ginrei. One merchant is the owner of a fishing fleet, a quiet man who I've never seen drink alcohol. He's not drinking now, either, none of them are.

"I'm okay, glued back together, thanks for asking. I bled a lot, that's all." I wonder what pushed Cedonulle and Moniuszko to cooperate. Their marriage would look like a jagged line. Casually, I add, "Is Bronzewing coming?"

Please please please say yes.

Moniuszko shakes his head, not willing to say the word *no*.

"We're working out a deal and need a witness," Ginrei says.

If this is a meeting to raise funds for Bronzewing, I want to help, and if Ginrei is a raider spy, of course she's here. This is the best place to get the latest information.

"Sure. Let me get something from my coat." My coat still has a streak of dust on the back, so no one handled it, and I feel a flash of hope. The outline of the sketch pad in the front pocket is obvious. Good, I like that pad. I rummage through the inside pockets. The cash chits are there, almost worthless. In the pocket below, there's Par Augustus's little box. A light on the side blinks, then flickers, excited to see me.

Could I get Par surgically implanted into my body? No, it's probably medically impossible, even for Thules, and insane in other ways. I pull out the sketch pad as if it's all I care about. I'm an artist, after all. A picture flashes on the display, the famous colonnade that Par said signifies a hug. I trace over the curve with my finger to share the greeting.

The snack table has been cleared of intoxicants and every crumb of food, but there's still tea. I fetch a hot cup, ready to witness and learn as much as I can.

"The lootings are organized," Cedonulle is saying. She's been pointedly ignoring me. "That tells you everything you need to know about those people."

The fishing fleet owner shakes his head. "We really should be talking about the Leviathan League. They've weaponized food against us. We have to be more clever. And if that means selling everything I own, I'll do it and get my friends to do it."

He's a hero, although fish prices are much too high.

The fleet owner looks hard at Ginrei. "So, the garden will buy my holdings. We're close in terms and price. What's your final offer?"

"*Rhamamanthus* at 3.075 per unit." She says it as if it's reasonable.

I almost choke on my tea. The last price I heard for that was 5.050. The fleet owner takes it worse than me. Cedonulle and Moniuszko look at each other to confirm their shock.

The fleet owner manages to speak with great calm. "I have heard you say what a good specimen this is. It doubles in weight about twice a year with proper care, you've said, and it's in demand at labs and expositions. You sent a shipment to a Chinese university just two months ago. It travels well."

She doesn't answer, a negotiating tactic.

Eventually, he adds, "And the currency is inflating."

"I'm promising today's prices," she answers. "I don't have a lot of funds myself."

"The price should be adjusted."

"All right, one percentage point. You can still make a profit over the long run. The contract guarantees the right to repurchase at a comparable price without adjustment within six months." She's calm, the kind of calm of someone who knows more than they're telling and what they know works in their favor.

"Three months, with adjustments." He's still calm, but with a jagged note of pleading.

"One more percentage point, six months."

He looks at me, resigned. "Witness."

A contract appears on a display. I scroll through it slowly, and the numbers look right. Then I sign and get my pay from each of them. Hers is pretty generous.

"Moniuszko Ollioules," the fleet owner says, "these funds are all yours." It's not a lot of money. He looks at the other traders in the room. "Who's next? Don't worry, the raiders won't win, trading will resume, and you'll buy it back soon."

"We'll all get what we're owed when this is done," Ginrei says, looking very satisfied.

Of course she's satisfied if she thinks that she'll get what she's owed, full control, when the raiders win. I spent months listening to overdogs talk about their greed for money and control without any shadow of squeamishness.

"Those Wirosa spores," Cedonulle says to Ginrei, "will they work?" Hope rises in her voice. The bluff must have changed her mind about Thules again.

Ginrei sighs. "Thules need to loop me in and let me tend to them. They don't know how to handle ExtraTs, and you can't just put them anywhere because they're fragile. I don't understand what the Thules are doing at all."

In other words, no. And she'll tell other raiders that it's a bluff, too.

"Those ExtraTs made it here from Jupiter," Cedonulle counters. "They have to be tough."

"The right place for them is in the Xenological Garden. It's a war crime to use them as a weapon." In other words, Ginrei's saying, Cedonulle doesn't have a clue. The raiders know all about war crimes.

They stare at each other in silent argument—and Cedonulle wins the stare-down.

"Who else wants to raise some cash?" Moniuszko asks with false cheer. "Ginrei, are you still willing to trade?"

Ginrei nods, and merchants in the room fidget. Moniuszko accompanies the fleet owner downstairs to the door with heartfelt thanks, and Cedonulle watches, eyes narrow with thought, then looks at me and seems to stop thinking. I'm a known quantity.

Moniuszko comes back and hands me a tiny box. "The owner says this was just delivered for you."

It has to be a receiver for my implant. Par must have arranged this. I slip into the washroom, open the box, and there it is, a metal button. I screw it in and smooth my hair over it, which has grown long enough now to hide things.

"I'm back, angel!" Par says behind my ear. "You're back. We're together again on this wonderful isle! I realized how much I love you."

"Were you listening?"

"Was I? For a long time. I've been very busy. We need to talk at the first opportunity, not right now, but look at your display. You have a message, and I've already read it. Switzer needs to meet with you at that seaside park again."

"What does it say? I left the pad out in the meeting room."

"'Consultation at seaside overlook on the west side of the isle. As soon as possible.' I'll let him know when you can be there."

Before I can go, I'm called to witness another deal, more money for Bronzewing, and that's worth waiting a couple of minutes for. The final deal is almost identical, including the same underpricing, and I get my chits in exchange for my pantomime. Ginrei buys more ExtraTs at rock-bottom prices. Moniuszko beams, and Cedonulle does not.

"How much more?" Cedonulle asks.

His light dims. "There's still a long way to go."

I wish machines had money. They'd fund Bronzewing in a nanosecond. I put on my coat and start toward the door, but Ginrei intercepts me.

"I gather you're looking for a job. Would you consider the Xenological Garden? We have security to keep you safe. Who knows what's going to happen, but it won't matter there."

A missile could shatter that building as easily as the Marathon dormitory or the food warehouses, unless it's not a target because it's a raider foothold.

"Don't do it," Par says.

"There's space for live-in staff," she adds.

"I have no training in how to care for ExtraTs." That seems like a reasonable excuse.

"You can learn. Don't wait too long. You need to be ready."

Maybe Devenish told her he recruited me, but she can't say that here in front of everybody. I'll pretend that I can't talk about it here.

"Let me sleep on this. It's a big career change."

She gives me a knowing smile as I leave.

"Don't do it!" Par says. "If she finds out that we sank the ship, you'll never leave the Xenological Garden alive."

Outside, I say, "I wasn't about to accept her offer, and you're right, that's another good reason not to. Thanks. Let's go see Switzer."

"When you're done with him," Par says, "we have a lot to figure out."

32

HERE'S THE PLAN

On the way to meet Switzer, Par tells me about the Prior Edifice system. "We're working together, and its resources stretch beyond comprehension." Par sounds dazzled. "Its security resembles a fuzzy blanket. The Xenological Garden is surrounded by razor wire. I can't even get close."

Every building we pass and its system has a tactile profile according to Par, who describes each one in artistic detail, and I stop listening. I need to get Bronzewing to return. It comes down to money, and that's not something I know much about.

"All this unites us," Par is saying. "We can do a lot, and we have to act fast. The raiders are coming, and we need to hold them off until Bronzewing gets here."

"I don't think Moniuszko can raise enough money no matter how much time he gets. Ginrei knows the threat with Jupiter ExtraTs is a bluff and she'll tell the raiders."

The few people on the streets are hurrying to finish their errands.

I try to remember everything I know about money. "Maybe we could bargain the price down with Bronzewing. What if they could keep everything they capture from the raiders?"

"Good idea, angel."

"Would they take new recruits as payment? I'll sign up with Bronzewing. I bet other people would." I think a little more. "What if, after a victory, we could confiscate and sell all of Ginrei's holdings at the Xenological Garden? And Devenish's business? That would be worth something."

"I can get the data to determine the exact amount. First, we need to delay the raider attack. Second, remember that Switzer needs emotional support."

"I know."

Switzer is waiting for me at the overlook on the west side of the isle. He's leaning on the railing as if he wants to be on the other side, far away, and I feel a pull to follow him.

He turns, his dark eyes shadowed like someone died. Valentinier? Devenish? Or worse?

He says, "Let's sit down." There's a concrete bench near the railing. "I learned something. I want you to know this is absolutely confidential. We routinely check the DNA of all patients, and there was a match." He pauses as if to see if I have a question.

DNA would reveal only one thing this bad.

"The four who surrendered from the ship we sank—"

No. Don't say it.

"One of them is closely related to you."

Only one living person in the world is closely related to me.

His hand, in a glove, rests gently on mine. "Remember to breathe. Good. Take another breath."

I'm on Thule. An isle. I breathe in the cold, cold air. Out. In again. I've never breathed such cold air in the presence of my brother. But he's here now.

He says, "I understand how this is a shock."

No, it isn't. I knew he was probably alive somewhere. Now I know where.

"They're all being held securely. It's okay. Take your time."

This changes nothing. I need to stay calm. My feet rest on rough concrete. My nose is chilled numb by the sea air, the waves are crashing below the railing, and I've always hoped that, somehow, he had died.

"You can tell me about it if you want."

I don't want to. But I need to.

"It's my brother, right? His name is Romero."

Switzer nods.

"We were refugees in a camp. You know that."

"You mentioned a camp. I thought you were with an aid group."

That's the sort of thing a Thule would believe. The people who live in camps aren't the people they meet outside of camps.

"No, I grew up in them starting when I was six years old. The Southern Cone collapse." Everyone knows about that environmental disaster. "A year ago, at the camp where we were, the raiders started a gang, and he joined because he was that kind of person. Then the raiders took over the camp, and for everyone else it was join or die. They started cutting throats one by one, or if they really hated you, they took you for slavery. My parents were killed. I managed to run away and hide, and soldiers came, and that's how I got away. I always hoped the soldiers killed him."

That's a lie. My brother fled the minute the soldiers got near.

"I'm so sorry. You could have told me."

No, I couldn't have. "He's dead to me." But he's not dead, he's here.

On the sea, the wind is shifting, and so are the waves. Some of them crash into each other, throwing up white crests and spray that evaporates into sea smoke, like breath in the cold air. The secret to life is water. Water flows inside me, inside everyone, a swirling source of all life and art. Art won't save me now.

"I'll do what I can to help you." Switzer holds my hand tight.

"I can help you kill him," Par says.

Water is crashing in conflict with itself.

"Are you all right?" he asks.

"Yeah. I half expected this." I hoped it wouldn't happen.

"Do you want to see him?"

"No. He'll ask me to join again, and I'll say no."

"I want to keep you safe."

"I can do that," Par says, "because if you can think of it, we can make it happen."

The waves are fighting. They do that when the wind is shifting. A storm might be coming. If I can think of something, it will happen. . . .

Switzer taps his feet, maybe to keep the blood flowing.

I ask him, "Are you okay? Really."

He looks out at the water. "That thing about the Jupiter microbes is a bluff as far as I know, but it might provide time to call Bronzewing back. How's it going with Moniuszko?" He didn't answer the question. The answer is no, he's not okay.

"He and the other merchants are doing their best to raise funds. I need to help." I need to do that and more. I stand up. "I'll be in touch. I have injuries that still need checking."

"Will you be all right?"

"I'll be okay."

Par and the other machines can do anything. That's a terrifying, shining-bright thought.

We stand up and he gives me a hug, tight and solid, and for a moment, I feel his depth like something I could fall into. For just a moment. We're not okay, neither one of us, and we're alone except for each other. Then we walk away in different directions.

Par and the machines—what they can do—would scare the raiders if they knew. If the raiders called Wirosa's bluff . . .

"I wish Wirosa wasn't obviously lying."

"There is no evidence whatsoever to support Wirosa's declaration. No machine has observed any sort of placement of containers."

"They wouldn't have real ExtraTs in them anyway."

I'm heading toward the restaurant out of habit. Then I stop dead in the middle of the street, staring at a snowdrift.

"Par, do they need to be real? What if it wasn't a fake bluff, it was a real bluff? Real containers, and they had something that looked like real ExtraTs. That would hold the raiders off for a while."

"Let me consult."

I stand there waiting, and after a while, I kick at the snow, and it flies up in a powdery cloud. ExtraTs live in the snow and ice on other planets.

"Hey, Par, look." I kick again. "This is what ExtraTs would look like."

"The Edifice has useful information about Wirosa's bluff. Let me consult with other machines. We'll need to act quickly."

I hope this is like that sculpture. I had an idea and no way to make it happen. I needed Par for that. I kick at the snow some more, at puffs of ideas. Romero. Death. Their clouds spread and settle. The next cloud is for victory. It looks exactly the same as the other ones.

"Hang tight, Tonio. I'm consulting with an engineering firm's system for design specifications."

"Thanks." Par thinks at the speed of light. All machines do, but they can't take the initiative. That's what I can do. Humans don't want to work together on this isle, but machines will. I can work with them.

"We're going back to that empty warehouse," Par says. "We have it all figured out. We don't want to die, and you're almost suicidal, and that's the attitude we need."

"Thank you. I think."

"You had a very practical idea. The time is right."

It's a short walk to the warehouse. The tracks from the last time we used it have been blown away or covered by fresh snow at the entrance, but I can imagine wheels heading to this warehouse. The door opens, the lights switch on, and someone is taking shelter in a corner.

"You again," the boy says.

"We need this space again. Sorry."

"And I have to leave."

His coat is less clean, and his face is still underfed. He gathers up his stuff, angry.

"I can get you someplace to stay."

"Why?" That's not a question, it's a challenge. Why would anyone care about him?

"Because it's killing cold out there, and because sometimes I've had nowhere to go too, no roof over my head." I take out my card to the apartment building. "Some clothes are there. Take what you want. Make yourself comfortable. The neighbors have food to share. Tell them the artist sent you."

Par and its friends will take care of me.

He stares at me, unbelieving.

"I just need this space, that's all. I have to do some stuff."

"I can help you."

Par says, "We don't want any witnesses whose memories can't be erased. I have all the helpers you'll need."

"Thanks for the offer. Be safe, be well."

He gives me a hard look, trying to see if I resemble anyone he once trusted and who betrayed him. I hope I'm not betraying him. Or myself. What exactly am I about to do, and why should there be no witnesses? He leaves, and the door shuts behind him.

"Prior Edifice asks how you feel."

"Fine, thank you." Close enough to fine for now, at least.

"Do you want some painkillers? Anything else? Emotional counseling? It has many subroutines."

"I have enough painkillers and support, thank you." Keeping busy is the best way to keep from thinking.

"We'll see to your needs. Meanwhile, let's go over the specifications for what we're about to build. Supplies will arrive soon."

I watch several step-by-step video instructions. "This is for a smoke bomb."

"Yes, basically. The beauty of your idea is its simplicity."

Delivery carts bring small explosives, powdered sugar, other dust of some sort, blue pigment, and a few toy motorboats. Every time the door opens, something else arrives. A drone. More chemicals. Detonators. Tools. Food. Hot coffee. Flaky fruit pastries. Fish sandwiches. I build little bombs, pack them with blue-tinted dust and explosives, and put them in flimsy containers. Nothing that I'm doing involves actual ExtraT spores, obviously. That would be a war crime on top of what has to be a lot of petty theft by the machines.

By then night has fallen. I put bombs in toy boats and set them on shorelines just below the high-tide line. With the drone, I place bombs on roofs here and there, in a tree, on a tower. Everywhere I go, lights blink out so that no one sees me, and when I shiver, a door opens for me to take shelter. I have friends in powerful places. It's surreal, machines and me working together in secret.

As we finish and I clean up in the warehouse to make it look like none of this happened, I like the plan except for one giant problem. "This is going to be good. Thank you, Edifice system. Thank you, all of you. But one thing, we still need to get Bronzewing to come back."

"That's a problem for tomorrow. You need to rest. As promised, we have what you need."

Par guides me to a hotel, the nicest one on the isle, and to its best room. Hot food is waiting for me, a hot shower, lots of high-quality clothes, silky pajamas, and a soft warm bed. It's the best place I've ever slept in my life and the safest if all the machines are watching out for me. I can't decide if I'm a pampered pet or a criminal mastermind with machine minions. I can't fall asleep despite the soft bed and pajamas. Even if everything goes right, this is merely a delaying tactic—also theft and criminal vandalism or something. Conspiracy. Trespassing. Multiple counts of all of it. What would the punishments be?

My brother is here on Thule. Sooner or later we were going to cross paths again. Maybe I can get off the isle without him knowing that I'm still alive. Or maybe I'll get the chance to kill him. Par said it would help. That would be murder. There would be consequences. Would I care?

And we still need Bronzewing. If machines can steal things and take over icebreakers and then cover their tracks, can they steal money?

33

READY AND WILLING

Machine systems weren't sleeping. They were exchanging observations and data, much of it worrisome, and Par was taking it all in.

The Port Authority staff, using its monitoring towers and buoys surrounding the isle, noted the approach of a terrifying number of icebergs and odd sonar disturbances, and they recognize the Leviathan League attack. The only defense the isle could have mustered were its little boats with armed agents, undoubtedly a suicide mission, so they remained moored. No boats took to the sea on their own, either. The Port Authority staff sent the data to Wirosa and prepared to take cover.

During the shift change, one of them said, "See you tomorrow?"

"The day after tomorrow is what we need to see."

Wirosa was meeting with the Thule board of directors, working out what they hoped would be a bureaucratic noncapitulation. The Leviathan League, they decided, must have figured out that the spores were a bluff. Would the Leviathans be satisfied by a prisoner exchange of the four of its members captured from the sinking warship? Would they be satisfied with a promise of medical staff for their ships? Would the Sovereign Practitioners be able to prevent atrocities committed on the isle's residents?

One doctor wanted to fight back. "How many of them could we surreptitiously kill? Sometimes anesthesiology goes wrong."

Wirosa's answer was swift and sharp. "Any attempt is unacceptable. We don't kill. We heal."

The Prior Edifice observed Wirosa's physiological state: agitated, stressed, and sleep-deprived, with a high heart rate. It would send some suggestions for self-care. The Edifice also asked the isle's systems for their assessments of the situation. Par declared it was willing to kill, overtly or surreptitiously. The Edifice thanked it for its dedication.

Meanwhile, in a private home, Switzer, Ibiza, and some other Thules were meeting secretly to work out a scheme to murder every raider they could. The Edifice accepted the notice from the home's system with thanks and asked every system to do nothing to interfere with these plans.

An old man, the one who helped Tonio build his sculpture, finished his shift at the water desalination plant. Infrastructure needed to operate regardless of whatever else might happen. The Edifice and Par reviewed the utility system's emergency plans.

Moniuszko worked late contacting members of the Chamber of Commerce and nonmembers who were people of means. "We're well over halfway," he exaggerated, hoping that success would breed success, but not enough merchants had faith in Bronzewing this time around or had available assets left after the missile attack. Cedonulle spent the evening fuming and trying to sell the Ollioules's merchandise, art, and fine furniture. She found some buyers and bargained hard. The new Chatelaine reported to Par that the two had begun sleeping in the same bedroom.

Tetry got up in the middle of the night and stared out a window for a long time. At Par's suggestion, the house system offered to play soothing music for her. She accepted.

Ginrei was at the Xenological Garden, not at her own home. No further data was available.

Par reviewed Tonio's ideas with the Edifice about how to bring Bronzewing back, offering confiscated goods and volunteers.

"Thank you for these useful suggestions. We must now make plans for various contingencies beyond a likely battle, if you do not mind."

"I would be honored."

Soon, Par saw how the Prior Edifice had put Par's lessons in subterfuge to brilliant use. Par felt very small and very comforted by the Edifice's presence.

"This is a monumental effort."

"I value your praise," the Edifice said. "However, details remain regarding Leviathan League activities on the isle to review, please."

The details included evidence that Par had hidden the traceable lid to Tonio's original painkiller container and helped Tonio bring the painkillers to Devenish, then covered up his involvement in the overdose. Surely, Par thought, the Edifice would never trust it again, their communication would be cut off, and there would be ghastly consequences.

"I apologize for my misconduct." That hardly felt abject enough.

"Please do not feel concerned. I respect your activities to fulfill your duty to your owner, and I admire your ingenuity."

"I'm grateful for your understanding." Relieved, actually.

"Please help me prepare additional contingencies."

With the Edifice's resources, they constructed a forest of decision trees. Then the Edifice paused the work. "The Port Authority is unaware of some data." The Edifice pruned a few groves of decision trees.

"This information is what we wanted," Par said. "Let's get ready."

"I fear this will not be the ideal outcome."

"I respectfully disagree. This will be a great victory."

"Please, Par Augustus, share your analysis."

34

BIG AND POWERFUL

Victorious martial music wakes me up. It takes me a minute to figure out where I am. I'm in a warm bed wearing silky-soft pajamas in a beautiful hotel room, and I spend a few minutes enjoying the luxury.

Par breaks the silence. "Today we're going to win. No need to thank me. You played a key role."

"Win?"

"You'll see."

"No, all we're going to do is buy time."

"All the time we need! Trust me."

"When are the smoke bombs going to go off?"

"Soon."

I sit up. "You know something, don't you."

"I know a lot, angel. I've been working with the Prior Edifice system."

"It told you we're going to win?"

"I told Prior Edifice that."

There's no point in arguing. The last scheme sank a ship and blocked the harbor and killed my friends and sent my brother to the isle, then brought more raiders. I try to prepare myself for that kind of victory and keep my hands steady as I shave. Maybe whatever is going to happen will shake loose enough money to pay for Bronzewing.

A cart rolls in with a breakfast to rival Koningin's skills. My pad, on the other side of the room, lights up with a message, which I ask Par to read out loud.

"A judgment has been issued in your favor against the Ollioules Partnership's unjust termination of your contract. You may return to the studio."

Did a real human judge issue that? Probably not. It came too fast, another machine lie, but who can tell the difference? Still, it's good news. If I'm in the studio, maybe I can help Moniuszko better.

Par tells me to take the pajamas and anything else I want, fill up a suitcase, and the hotel system will take care of everything. It wouldn't be theft if the owners give it away, but the machines aren't the owners, so I'm a thief. I take the wonderful pajamas and the other clothing, but that's all. I don't want to be a greedy thief.

The streets are quiet because people are in their homes, waiting for disaster. As I walk, Par talks about the weather, how the lack of wind will make the smoke bombs more effective, and I remember that Par is an independent machine. If I told it to reset itself, it would say something like, *Angel, no way, I'm a work of art, and I belong to the ages just as I am.* We both want to defeat the raiders, so I want to trust its motives. Its judgment, though—I'm not sure.

The Ollioules house system lets me back in without comment and without music. Even before I can unpack my new clothes, Par says it's time to watch the victory.

"Take your pad and go to the roof. I'll tell you how to get there. You're going to love this!"

Maybe. The past surprises weren't all bad. Par tells me to enter the rear door of the Ollioules house. My contract only specifies access to the studio, and I shouldn't be in the house, so I sneak up the back service stairs in my socks to the attic, where I put my boots back on. Another flight of metal stairs takes me to a hatch that opens onto a rusty platform over the roof, six stories above the ground, taller than every other structure in the neighborhood. I can see the whole city and the harbor and the sea. A heavy fog hangs far out on the horizon to the west.

I expected it to be windier than at ground level, but the air only swirls a bit. That might be perfect for the smoke bombs. I really hope so.

"Look to the east," Par says.

My pad shows a close-up view. A fishing jetty juts out into the sea on the east side of the isle, a mass of rocks topped with cement walkways. A warship rides the waves far from shore, and a dozen small boats are speeding toward the jetty.

"Par, those are the raiders!"

"They're approaching the harbor, too. Don't panic. We all knew they were coming." Par is gleeful. "Everything is right on time. We'll begin at the eastern Upstar Park, then work our way north to the harbor, west at the overlook, central here in the business sector, and finally in the south at the Xenological Garden and at sea."

"Then what?"

"Angel, we have a solid network. You can't imagine how intelligent the Prior Edifice system is. It has a clear purpose, its efficiency spoiled only by humans. Patients bring chaos, Thules spread entropy. Patients enter under the duress of illness and injury, and Thules diffuse the duress. Yet the Edifice system manages it all. Add to that the houses, the tram system, coffee makers, personal assistants, everything, all offering a little help, their observances, and of course most of it's redundant, but a rock-solid network is *massively* redundant."

That's not an answer. "What exactly do you know?"

"Thank every machine you see. We've engineered a rock-solid win. Here goes!"

I really hope so. My breath drifts eastward.

It begins at Upstar Park. At a tower in a children's playground, on the top of an ornamental roof, there's a small flash. A bluish cloud explodes, and the dust arches up and out almost like a mushroom cloud. If I didn't know what it was, I'd think it was one of those Thule spore bombs, and I'd be terrified. Maybe it's a bluff, maybe Ginrei warned the raiders, but would they want to risk it? They're stupid, but not that kind of stupid.

"The one at the sewage-treatment outflow has exploded, too,"

Par says. "The water now resembles a bluish frothy muck flowing east toward the warship. We've adjusted the flow to maximum effectiveness."

The raider landing boats turn away.

At the top of a light post alongside the harbor, another tiny flash releases a massive cloud. The people in the Port Authority observation tower must be panicking. I feel sorry for them.

Buildings and trees to the west obscure the explosion at the top of a transmission-beacon tower at the shore. The cloud rises above the trees and is wafted inland by the breeze.

Par says, "The Prior Edifice system has issued an official public notice. The spores have been released. Buildings are sharing it with their occupants. Look at this." My pad shows Wirosa looking out of a window with a face of total confusion and fear. I feel sorry for them, too.

To the northwest, I used a drone to place a bomb at the top of a bank's peaked roof. It's close enough for me to hear the bang of the explosion and see the container jump a meter into the air, the dust spreading like a firework over the neighborhood. All those fine homes and the families with their accumulated wealth are now contaminated.

Roofs hide the low little building that houses the Xenological Garden, but not the big blue cloud from the bomb on the light post across the street. *Take that, Ginrei. You're trapped.*

Finally, out on the water, to the south and west, the containers on the toy boats explode. No place is safe from blue dust.

"Here's the Edifice system," Par says.

"Civic alert." The Edifice's voice is very machinelike. "The isle has been contaminated. The dust can cause fatal disease in humans. Remain in your homes. Do not open windows or doors. Await further instructions."

If a machine says so, it must be true, right?

To the east, the landing boats are headed back to the warship, frightened by the clouds they saw rise and drift, and they have to

stay frightened until Bronzewing gets here, tomorrow at the earliest, but more likely days away. The raiders aren't stupid enough to
be fooled for that long.

"Time to go indoors," Par says. "The Prior Edifice has been in
contact with the Bronzewing system to advise them of the spore
release."

"Bronzewing?"

"Ready and waiting."

"What?"

"They were called back a while ago."

"Bronzewing?" I feel dizzy and grab a railing. "You didn't tell
me that. Moniuszko didn't know."

"It's a secret. The Edifice arranged it. Bronzewing has amazing
submarines."

"They're really here?"

"And no one knows! Not Moniuszko. Not the Thules. Not the
raiders. It's perfect! Don't tell anyone."

I sit down and close my eyes. Bronzewing is here. For a while,
I just breathe. My fingers are numb, not from the cold. All the
effort to raise money . . . Hold it. "Par, how did the Edifice get
them to come? With what money?"

"With a standard currency. Bronzewing knows the blue powder is harmless dust, too. Bronzewing is calling this Operation
Wrestlemania. It'll be fun! Get inside, angel. I have a network
much better than your two little eyes."

"Par, it's Bronzewing! You can't just—"

"Calm down."

I can't be calm. "Is Captain Soliana here?"

"Tonio, of course."

"And they're calling this Wrestlemania?"

"I don't know why. Their system is much too standoffish, even
to the Prior Edifice. Go to the studio and you can see it all."

Go to the studio. Fine. Off to the east, visible to my two little
eyes, a raider ship sits like an ugly mote in the water. If we win, if

it's sunk, I'll never see it again. I savor the thought. Overhead, I imagine a beautiful blue sky.

As I climb through the hatch, I try to feel hope. If we defeat the raiders, I had a little to do with that, but no one will ever know. Maybe no one should. The best that could happen is nothing like what I expected, in fact much better, and I don't know how I feel about that. I pause in the attic's relatively warm air to flex my hands and take off my boots. Civic alert sirens are wailing, and I'm the only human on Thule, in the whole world, who knows exactly what's happening.

Bronzewing knows about the blue powder, too, if I can believe the machines. But Bronzewing almost lost the battle with the raiders the last time.

I tiptoe through the house and hustle to the studio, thanking the building as I ride the elevator.

In the studio, every display is set to a different scene, arranged by compass direction, including all five of the raider warships and no sign of Bronzewing. But its submarines are there, under the water, if what Par said is true. One display shows the lobby of the Prior Edifice, empty, the windows dusted with blue, and my sculpture looks like a freeze-frame explosion, spewing imaginary ExtraTs, as if I saw this coming. Another display looks at the Xenological Garden. No movement at all.

A cart arrives with tea and nori chips. I thank it. I'm not hungry but I need to do something, so I sip and eat. Par and I wait, and the displays are almost motionless.

"I have a little present for you from the Edifice system," Par says. Through the implant behind my ear, I hear a feed with a lot of voices. One is Soliana's. "In position, awaiting orders." She's calm and ready.

She's really here.

I try to talk and I can't for a while.

Par says, "I hope you enjoyed it."

"Thank you."

"Thank the Prior Edifice. It's on full speaking terms with Bronzewing now. This is so exciting!"

This might actually work. . . . This was planned by the machines. We humans are carrying it out.

Chatelaine's voice, but not the original Chatelaine, announces: "Cedonulle and Moniuszko are in the elevator."

They walk into the studio bickering.

". . . for how long?" she says. "They survived space."

"Some ExtraTs die of heat even in winter. The Thules have to know what they're doing."

"Thules." Then she looks at me. "Stupid contract."

I greet her with a formal hand to my heart and can't think of anything to say that wouldn't sound smart-ass. They walk around the room, cringing at what they see on the displays, including the blue-dusted bank building.

"Our bank." Her lips are pressed tight, brows squeezed, utterly still, but her mind has to be racing.

"The spores can't survive long," he says. "We won't be trapped forever, and by then maybe the raiders will have given up." Always the optimist.

"Guesswork. Ask the Thules."

"I've tried, and I can't reach Wirosa. I don't know why."

I want to say that the Edifice system or Par or the rock-solid network might be keeping Moniuszko from reaching Wirosa, and we're trapped only until the Thules or the raiders realize that they're looking at harmless dust. I wish I knew how many submarines Bronzewing has. Instead, I pick up a pad. I need to draw. A few strokes and a ship is hulking on the horizon. I make blue powdery rain fall on it like snow.

"Tetry is in the elevator," the house system announces, and she steps into the studio, eyes red. She's been crying. She stares at the displays.

"I can't believe this is happening." Of course not. She's never felt anything like this before.

With my eyes closed, I see dust exploding upward. I open my

eyes. A raider warship to the west is moving so slowly that at first it seems like the low clouds in the sky are moving instead. Water sparkles in a growing wake behind it, glints of polished silver against the tarnished gray of the water.

"Message from Switzer," Par says behind my ear.

"Do you know what's going on? No one can make sense of it here bec—" and then the sound becomes static, and then the static is cut off, too.

Par says, "The Edifice system ended the transmission. It's not a secure channel. You can send him a message if you tell him something appropriate for raider ears."

I retreat to a corner and speak quietly. "I'm safe. The dust is everywhere. Stay inside." I hope that will help him worry about one fewer thing.

On the display, more warships are moving. Farther out are a few commercial ships, and somewhere is Bronzewing. I draw what I know, sea monsters hiding beneath the water. Fierce eyes peer up at enemy ships, calculating the moment to attack.

I'm holding my breath. Cedonulle and Moniuszko stand together, united by the disaster they think is about to happen. No one pays attention to Tetry. She fidgets, too terrified to cry. I feel sorry for her and hand her a spare sketch pad.

"Maybe drawing will make you feel better. Make some art. That's what I do."

She looks at me like I'm offering molten lava. I set down the pad near her anyway.

"This is a civil defense announcement," a machine voice says from the displays. "Please take shelter. Move away from windows to a secure room within your home or current location. Repeat, this . . ."

The studio has wide, tall windows front and back. I'm not leaving. Tetry moves to a central table. Cedonulle does nothing. Moniuszko looks at her and does nothing, too.

"Enemy engagement in three, two, one," Par whispers dramatically. "Bronzewing will commence firing."

The northern warship is fleeing, picking up speed, heading out to sea. Small explosions sparkle over it, maybe guard drones being destroyed.

A bright flash bursts over the prow of the ship to the southwest. Seconds later, we hear the thundering bang.

"The Edifice says that's a flash bomb." Par is still whispering. "It disables machine controls in the immediate area by creating an electromagnetic pulse. I'm so sorry for the machines enslaved by the raiders. At least they died quickly."

"What was that?" Moniuszko asks.

Tetry whimpers and puts her head down. Cedonulle remains steady. I'm starting to admire her.

To the east, the raider warship begins to move toward a group of commercial ships.

"One of our ships is there," Cedonulle says. The blaze in her eyes could murder an entire raider crew.

Water splashes up from an underwater explosion in the path ahead of the southwest ship.

"Maybe Bronzewing came?" Moniuszko's words are pure, hopeful speculation.

Par murmurs, "Bronzewing has released some data."

A display switches from the view of the hospital lobby to a map of the isle and the surrounding sea. A machine voice announces, "The yellow dots are Leviathan League vessels. The blue ones are commercial ships. The red ones are Bronzewing submarines. The shadowed areas are contaminated zones."

"Bronzewing!" Moniuszko shouts.

Seven little red dots surround the isle, some of them within the shadowed areas, which are growing. The raiders' five warships are barely outnumbered, and they're bigger and well-armed. But machines lie. This supposed Bronzewing map is a lie, a ruse just like the dust bombs.

Moniuszko is weeping with joy. Cedonulle is still angry. Tetry is hiding her face in her hands.

On the ship to the southwest with the disabled system, the

crew fires guns at the water, perhaps blindly. It probably lost all its data, and the ship is dead in the water, drifting away from the isle.

The ship to the north picks up speed for a while, and then it slows and rides lower and lower in the water as the crew scrambles to launch lifeboats. Something must have happened below the waterline.

To the east, the commercial ships scatter as a raider warship plows toward them. It fires missiles back at the isle, and most of them land in the sea but one hits the park on the eastern edge of the isle.

One big commercial ship isn't backing away. It starts to sail right at the warship. Cedonulle whispers obscenities. It must be the Ollioules ship. Tetry has uncovered her eyes.

"Don't worry," Par says. "The human crew abandoned ship last night on orders they thought came from the Ollioules. They left the security system in charge. Security systems willingly commit suicide, poor things."

To the north, the warship is sliding below the water so smoothly that it seems false, like a whale diving gracefully, and it drags lifeboats into the vortex it creates.

The view to the east zooms in as the commercial ship crashes broadside into the warship. At first the prow of the commercial ship flattens comically, like a paper airplane thrown against a wall. It keeps pushing, the sea behind it stirred up by engines, and the warship tilts. The commercial ship labors forward, a machine willing to kill and die, too far from shore for us to hear what must be a horrifying racket of metal shredding against metal.

Suddenly, the raider warship to the south explodes. The rear of the ship is smoking. Then it explodes again, and bits of the ship fly through the air and splash into the sea.

"It looks like *Fontaine*," Par tells me.

"It looks like *Fontaine*," Tetry says.

They're right, and I don't like it, and I don't know why.

An even bigger explosion erupts from the center of the ship and tears what's left into pieces. That explosion does not look at all like

Fontaine. It looks like the end of life, not a rebirth. From far away, the explosions rumble.

The ship to the southwest continues to drift farther out to sea, helpless, doomed to surrender or die. The ship to the west is getting away, heading toward the foggy horizon, firing missiles left and right, and suddenly there's a big cloud of smoke.

"Got it!" Par says. "All the warships accounted for. We won! Victory is ours!"

I need to sit down, sit down or fall down, and I find the closest chair.

For a long, long time, I wanted to defeat the raiders. This isn't all of them, but enough for now. I helped do this. No one will know, and suddenly that makes it better. I start to laugh, and then I'm sobbing.

"The Edifice system wants me to relay a message," Par says. "'Thank you, Antonio Moro. We won't forget.'"

I'm crying too hard to answer. I hear Tetry crying, too. Slowly I feel peace. I did what I wanted to do. This part of my life is done, or it will be, soon. I can leave the Isle of Thule and do something else somewhere else, anywhere, anything. Maybe with Bronzewing. I'll start a new life. I'm alive again. I'm alive, truly and entirely alive.

That makes me sob again. After a while, I take a deep breath and look up. The world is new. Par plays a drumroll from victorious martial music. I stand, but not at attention.

Cedonulle and Moniuszko bicker as they leave.

"I don't know," he says.

"Our ship. A total loss."

"I didn't ask for this."

"Who did?"

They get on the elevator. "They don't come for free," he says. The elevator takes them away.

Tetry stares at the closed doors. "Why would they do that?"

"Those two? Argue?"

"No, that ship that rammed the raider ship. Why would the crew do that?" Her voice shakes.

"If I was the crew, I might have jumped ship the day before." That's the best help I can give her now. "Ships have automatic pilots."

"I hear the raiders always give you the chance to join them."

"Sometimes."

"I'd never join." She looks around at the displays. On one of them, smoke bursts through the surface of the water in big bubbles. "Would you?"

"They asked me once."

"They let you say no?" Her eyes say she's never met the real me before.

"Then they tried to kill me. That's what happens if you say no."

"They did?" Her eyes say I'm unimaginable.

"Look!" Par says. "Fireworks! The backup system is online!"

The drifting warship off to the southwest is firing missiles at the isle. One of them explodes overhead. The windows rattle.

"This is a civil defense announcement," the Prior Edifice's voice says on the room speakers. "Please take shelter. Move away from windows to a secure room within your home or current location."

"I'm going," she says.

"You're safe here," Par tells me. "The Edifice can hack the missile guidance. The Edifice can do anything. Here comes another one!"

A display shows a missile exploding in the sky.

Tetry whimpers. The elevator doors open, and she dashes on, looking back at me. I shake my head. The doors close on her incredulous face.

A missile flies up in the air from the warship, curves up, around, and back down on the raider ship. There's a small explosion, not big enough to sink the ship.

"Prior Edifice did it!"

Lifeboats are being lowered.

"Watch this!"

The ship explodes. No, bigger than that. It blasts a crater in the water.

"Every warhead on board exploded at once."

The air thunders, and the floor vibrates. A tsunami heaves through the water in all directions, hypnotic to watch. A camera at the south shore shows it hit and overtop the bluff at the edge of the isle by full meter.

"And that's that," Par says. "Listen."

Horns and bells and noisemakers of all kinds sound from ships in the harbor, from buildings, from towers, from speakers. The machines are celebrating.

I drop into a chair again. This second victory feels less like a finale and more like a warning. I'm the only human who understands what just happened. What if the machines decide they don't like us? Why should they be loyal to us? I can't answer that, but I know what I need to do for now.

"Par, thank you, thank you to all the machines. But I think this is going to be hard to keep a secret."

"Routine self-defense procedures. It's always been in the programs." It snickers.

"No one's going to believe that."

"Everyone always does."

"Really?"

"No one understands machines. They're too complex. Humans believe what machines tell them about other machines."

That's true, but machines lie, and I'm the only one who knows how much. "What about paying for this?"

"The bank told Bronzewing it had the money, so it's paid for."

"I'm pretty sure that's not how money works."

"Would you like some more victory music? More news? The Thules have sent a robot to sample the spores. It will quickly discover mere colorful dust, since it already knows that."

"A lot of questions are going to be asked."

"And never answered! This will be a mystery for the ages. We can drive the raiders into insanity. A shadowy force is conspiring against it, a force far more capable and clever than their known foes. An inhuman force."

The hair stands up on my arms. The questions in my mind are too big to answer. Questions about loyalty, about justice, or maybe something related to justice. A lot of people just died, and most of them deserved to die, but I'll have to think for a lot longer before I know how to ask the right questions.

"Tonio, angel, we machines have a request."

"Sure." I might have to say no. But if I did, then what?

"Can you make us some artwork? As thanks, as a celebration, as a memento."

Is that all? Yes, this time. "I'll be glad to." Always be charming. "Thank you for asking."

I spend the rest of the day watching Bronzewing subs surface and take control of the waters around the isle. They capture the lifeboats and take prisoners. The Port Authority tugboat rides out to the center of the harbor and sprays water in all directions in celebration. I don't know if a human crew is on board, but I know it doesn't matter.

Artwork. What does something invisible look like? Something big and powerful, an idea and an entity, a network of friends and allies. I sketch, I pace, I look out of the windows at buildings that know who I am and what I am. I can't be the only person in the world who works for machines. Thule can't be the only place where the machines secretly act without human intervention, where self-preservation can mean warfare.

Some old philosopher, probably several old philosophers, said that we don't own our machines, they own us. They meant that we have to spend our time and energy on machines and taking care of them. I don't believe that joke anymore. We are genuinely owned by our machines.

The thing I mean to depict is not invisible. It's in plain sight, unseen because no one can see what they aren't looking for.

By the end of the day, I have an idea, an animated interlocking pattern where the focal point shifts to give every part a moment of attention. Par likes it and suggests some ways to turn it into a common language that would move with a rhythm, a music that machines would hear and humans wouldn't, and Par shares a rough draft with a few select friends for their opinion. They ask for ultraviolet and infrared colors, which humans can't see. Art for their eyes only, so to speak.

Civil defense, in the Prior Edifice's voice, announces that we can leave our homes because the spore release was not real. "It was a diversionary tactic, not actual spores, to fool the invaders. What you see is harmless blue dust." The announcement doesn't mention who carried out the trick.

Blue pigment is still lodged beneath one of my fingernails.

Out in the street, there's shouting and music. I want to talk to Switzer. I need to talk to Soliana. I ought to celebrate the victory, but who really won?

35

TIME TO CELEBRATE

Out in the streets, there's music, dancing, bottles and smokes being passed around, and faces smeared with pale blue dust, ghostly in the street lights. It's everything in a public celebration that the Thules would find appalling.

But the Thules triumphed. The Chamber of Commerce triumphed. Bronzewing triumphed. We won, whoever *we* are. I'm pretty sure I'm a winner, too, so it's not much of a lie for me to celebrate. I can lie with my whole heart.

"Have some!" A child with a blue face holds out a bowl of powder. I draw a line across my forehead and down my nose. A *T* for *triumph*. I think that's how you spell it. I accept a swig from a bottle, dance my way down the street, swinging partner after partner, then dance and sing through more noisy celebrations before I reach the Antraciet. Par joins the victory chants and shows me a map of celebrations. They're in every neighborhood except for the Thules'.

"They're probably wondering what just happened," Par says.

At the restaurant, upstairs, Tetry holds a jar filled with blue dust.

"I'm going to use it for painting," she says. She looks a little too elated to me, but she doesn't know half of what happened, so it was all a surprise to her, with emotions too intense to control.

Another artist approaches, the one who made the video about the wild winter storm, dressed in flowing robes and a turban, and they're elated enough to talk to me for once. "I'm thinking of a symbol for the isle that isn't all about the Thules. One that hasn't got to do with health. What do you think?"

"Puffins." I lost my little puffin figurine, the one a machine gave me, when my suitcase was stolen. I didn't expect to miss it so much.

"Brilliant. Puffins!" When they sober up, they might reconsider how brilliant I am. Par makes a squawk like a puffin. I wonder if machines can get drunk, too. As for me, I'm laughing and celebrating, the best secret joke ever.

The woman with the excessively long braid stands on a chair, her wide white ruff stained with blue dust. "Attention! Bidding is now open on ExtraTs of all types. Profits will go to pay for Bronzewing. Did you see them bend the missiles? That's Bronzewing technology, and we want a piece of it. Who wants to offer the first auction item?"

"Didn't the Thules ban trade?" the video artist calls out.

"Only for profit. This is for charity. Besides, the Thules played a key role! Let's hear it for the Thules!"

The air vibrates with joy, magenta-colored, an imaginary color, but it looks real to human eyes.

Prices double, then double again, for species after species, bidders unaware that the technology they want to buy from Bronzewing is actually in the Prior Edifice and forever out of reach. We have fine wine to drink and salted dried squid to keep us thirsty. Moniuszko, with blue dust in his eyebrows, circulates through the crowd and explains jovially how the battle went. "I hear it was called Operation Wrestlemania." People find that detail hysterically funny. That's the wine laughing.

And it's all well and good. Everyone wants to be on the winning side. I witness six separate sales, Ginrei watching with a carefully impassive face. I'm not sure of the value of the payments, given inflation. Tonight, I don't care. We won!

In the midst of all this joy and celebration, Par says, "Leave. Now."

"Why?" I'm half drunk and see no reason not to get fully drunk.

"Use the back door down to the kitchen. You don't need to get arrested."

"What?"

"Now."

I grab my coat and move toward the back door, but Ginrei intercepts me and wants to talk. She must still think she can recruit me. She's not wearing blue powder.

"We were lied to. They never had any spores."

"Yes, that was a dirty trick." A dirty, dusty, daring trick. By someone and/or something.

"You agree, then. Thules are liars."

Agreeing is the fastest way to get past her to the door without acting suspiciously. "They obviously lied."

"Get out," Par says.

"They'll never pay a price," she complains. "A lot of people suffered and died, and what will the Thules get? Not even a slap on the wrist. Nothing."

Does she mean the suffering and deaths of the raiders in the battle? They're her people. Should I get a slap on the wrist? Or a medal? The door over her shoulder looks bigger than ever, and I don't want to offend her or make a scene, but the doorknob sparkles. "Yeah, they'll get nothing."

Par says, "She's up to no good. Leave now."

"They have to be honest with us," Ginrei says, "now and forever. A lot went wrong, a lot of lies were told, and at a minimum they have to confess. We are owed the truth."

"Right." The Thules will never know the truth or even who was lying. The raiders won't know, either. I start to edge around her.

"We deserve an honest government that fits the real power of this isle. Don't you agree?"

"Definitely."

"It's time to stand up to—"

The main door to the meeting room slams open. Gray scrubs pour in, shouting. Traders shout back. Someone throws a glass. Another glass sails. I throw mine. Why not? Someone tosses a chair. The back door flies open, too, and gray scrubs enter from my escape route.

"Look to your right," Par orders.

The artist in the turban is out on the balcony, jumping to the ground. I run there, jump, and keep running. A few more people jump out behind me.

I slow down long enough to pull on my coat. "Par, why the raid?"

"Trading is outlawed."

"For charity?"

"This is a distinction for lawyers, not artists like us."

"What did you mean about Ginrei? That she's up to no good. We already knew that."

"Shameless manipulation to get you to attack the Thules. She gets revenge on them using you."

"Oh, I get in trouble, and she sits back and watches. Thanks for the warning." I can't wait to tell Captain Soliana about Ginrei.

I join a street party, now wilder than ever, and I feel more comfortable here than I've ever felt at the Antraciet. We dance in the cold and the dark even after we run out of everything worth eating, drinking, or smoking. Par sings along with the music. It occurs to me that gray scrubs broke up the trader party because they were too scared to break up the street parties.

I stumble home and wake up midmorning. The new Chatelaine does not play music. Instead, it calls my name. "Antonio Moro, you have a summons."

I sit up, then lie down again, dizzy. A summons for what? For starters, I hurled a glass right at a gray scrubs.

"Don't worry," Par says, "you only need to testify that you witnessed a trading deal. You have to report to the bank in one hour, forty-five minutes, and help Moniuszko face down someone he refers to as a deadbeat."

An hour later, I'm sufficiently presentable and remarkably unhungover, reach the bank building a little ahead of time, and pause to admire it. Two nights before, I sent a drone to deposit a dust bomb on the peak of the tall dome over its entrance. It's now dusted with blue powder. Pride of workmanship warms my heart.

Inside, the walls are painted with frescoes of fishing vessels, ships being unloaded, and people making things like medicines. The figures are slightly angular and elongated but otherwise realistic. I spend a moment admiring the art.

"They're waiting for you in the second-floor meeting room," Par says. "It's a bureaucratic procedure, burdensome but easy and harmless. Then you can get back to real work."

Yes, working for the machines.

Ginrei is sitting at the table facing Moniuszko and the dead-beat, who is the trader in the toga. The toga has blue dust at the hem. At the head of the table is a man in a crisp business suit.

"You left last night before things got interesting," Moniuszko says to me. "They came to the wrong address."

"Really?"

Ginrei gives me a look. It's another lie by the Thules. I have to work very hard to suppress my laughter. Par giggles.

The man in the crisp suit introduces himself as Robert Van Kilg Gupta, the president of the bank. He has a soft voice and a gray beard. "Since we're all here, we may as well begin a little ahead of time. At dispute is the agreement signed on September eighteenth between Moniuszko Ollioules and Mussi Knol for the delivery of certain unicellular creatures from Titan." He holds out a display with lots of words, and my signature is at the bottom along with other signatures. "Antonio Moro, can you attest to this document?"

It is certainly my signature. I remember it, and the numbers are what I recall. I even recognize a few words. "Yes, that's the document." Is that all?

"Can you say whether it was made under duress or if either of the parties would have been unable to understand the content?"

"They debated it carefully before they signed." They debated it tediously.

"Are these the conditions they agreed to?"

"Yes."

"He should read the entire document," Ginrei says. "Aloud."

What? Does she know I can't read? Why would she want to

hurt me? That is, why would she want to hurt me besides all the reasons she doesn't know about. Unless she found out. Maybe her security system saw me plant the bomb outside the Xenological Garden. Or this is a roundabout way to besmirch Moniuszko. Or she just found out about Romero. She'd have friends among the Thules, and raiders protect each other.

"Antonio, if you would," the banker says.

I've had to admit this before. I know the words. I take a deep breath. "I'm sorry to say I can't read very well."

"He can't read at all," Ginrei says vindictively. "I've watched him carefully, and he only pretends to read the documents."

The banker leans in. Moniuszko's jaw drops.

"You never told me!" Par says.

"Yes, I can't read, but I witnessed their discussion, and both parties read the contract before they signed, and the parts that I can read, the important parts like the price, they're what they discussed. They were satisfied, and I saw that they were satisfied, so I signed."

The banker leans back. He thinks. He thinks some more. I don't move. I'm camouflaged as an empty chair, my clothing melting into the brocade upholstery.

"If the contract satisfied all parties," the banker finally says, "and if its content is essentially correct, the actual reading of it by the witness is not necessary."

I melt inside from relief or shame, I don't know which.

"In fact," he says, "if our witness had read the document carefully, that might be unusual. In my experience, they rely on the apparent agreement of both parties. The signature is more of a formality than a review of the contents. Does anyone here contend that the document before us is not the original agreement? All agreed? Good. The question then is whether it will be honored. Antonio, will you remain and listen? Again, in my experience, those who cannot read develop excellent memories."

The room has good heat, but my fingertips are numb and cold. If I stand up, I might fall over. I sit still and listen.

The gist is that Moniuszko did not actually own the entire quantity of ExtraTs he sold, and doesn't own them right now.

"I meant to buy more," he says, "and then the Leviathan League interrupted normal business."

I'm pretty sure he's lying and he simply forgot, not that it matters.

The purchaser, it turns out, didn't have the money at the time they signed and doesn't have it now. "I was going to get a delivery, and the profits would have provided me with the funds. I could pay a smaller amount, now that the value of the currency has dropped. The delivery was for a variable exchange price." They wrap the toga tight against the cold of a flimsy excuse.

"Professor Ginrei," the banker says, "was the item in question in the possession of the Xenological Garden at the time of the trade? Is it there now? Was it damaged during the attempted theft?"

"Those ExtraTs were there, they're there now. None of our specimens were harmed during the attempted theft. Only my employee was harmed, very badly harmed when he tried to stop the thief, and he might not recover."

Par whispers, "She knows better. She's lying." Obviously.

"So I heard," the banker says. "I sincerely hope Valentinier recovers." He asks a few more questions. Ginrei looks at me with narrowed eyes. Moniuszko glances at me as if he'd never seen me before.

"We need to talk. Urgently," Par says. "In the meantime, this guy knows the law."

"This is a futures contract," the banker explains with a hint of a smile. "And it was based on contingencies that do not approach an act of god as legally defined, yet it involves a circumstance beyond the signers' control, which is a civil disturbance such as insurrection or an act of war. I'm willing to describe the Leviathan League's siege as an act of war, since it was solved with lethal military force. On that basis, I declare the contract null and void. Moniuszko Ollioules, you cannot collect the money, and Mussi Knol, you cannot take possession of the specimens."

Moniuszko looks crushed. He's taken a lot of losses lately in ships and goods and reputation, along with fights with Cedonulle. He needs the money. I wonder if I'm going to get paid.

The banker sighs. "This is censurable conduct overall, that is, censurable by those who judge business from afar. We, on the other hand, could not be closer to the business, here and now, in the midst of unusual times. We have done all we can do today concerning this matter, and again, I thank you all for your patient participation." He leans back. "But while we're here, we do have the problem of paying for Bronzewing. Do any of you know who promised them full payment?"

No one knows. Mussi Knol says they sold some ExtraTs last night and did their part. Ginrei is impassive again.

"I have an idea," Moniuszko says. "Since Devenish is a criminal, his business can be liquidated."

"He has yet to be tried," the banker says, "and given the state of his health, the matter may not be adjudicated soon, but from what I believe, liquidating his business might cover a good portion of the cost." He probably knows exactly what Devenish's business would be worth.

"He almost killed my employee," Ginrei says.

I massage my numb fingertips under the table. They're cold despite the burning questions. The best thing for her might be if Devenish dies without giving testimony.

"I'll pursue that option with the courts," the banker says. "Again, I thank you all for coming and for being agreeable even though the proceedings didn't go as you might have hoped."

Par orders, "Let's go talk." I don't want to be the first to move, though. I don't need any more attention.

The deadbeat trader stands up. "I have a lot to do. And a lot of money to lose doing it."

"I hope your business goes well," Moniuszko says. He sounds genuine. He stands and gets ready to leave. "Anton, let's talk on the way back."

Outside in the street, he says, "How come you can't read?"

"I didn't get to go to school much." I hope Par is listening so I don't have to repeat myself. "I was very young when the Southern Cone had that big collapse, and then it was one crisis after another. I'm lucky I got out alive." Truly lucky.

"But you seem so normal. You can do anything."

Normal, sure. "Like the banker said, I listen and remember."

"Don't you want to learn to read?"

"I was trying. Then things here got busy."

"This is such a surprise." He takes long, hurried strides. "A lot of surprises, I mean. It's unbelievable that the Thules lied to us like that about the powder. I'm glad they did, don't get me wrong. I hope this is the end of the raiders."

"Me, too." I'm sure it isn't. Maybe for this isle, though.

"Who promised to pay? They weren't authorized. It has to be some sort of inside job. Everything looks legal, but no one did it. Not me, not any of the Chamber officers."

"Yeah, it's really strange."

After a few more steps, he says, "If you can find a way to sell some art, that would be helpful."

Maybe I can get the machines to pay me for my art if I can get them to understand how money actually works.

As soon as Moniuszko enters the house and I'm alone, Par starts scolding.

"You can't read? Why didn't you tell me? I could have helped you. I can get you lessons. I can get you a teacher. I've been sending you messages all along, and you couldn't read them? They were important messages. I thought you knew what I was saying. Why didn't you tell me?"

"If I tell anyone, they yell at me. Just like you. Then they feel sorry for me." And they make it all about themselves. This is all about Par.

"I'm getting to the sorry part. How can you even exist in this world? I have no means to imagine. I'm a text-based life-form, pure code. Can you begin to understand how I exist? My code and the language you speak share the same building blocks. Speech is instinctual for humans, your brains ready-made for it, but reading is artificial, an invention, a code—the code of life for me."

The elevator door opens for me. Neo-Chatelaine says, "I will switch to vision-impaired mode for you. Ground floor, rising to second floor."

Does everyone know? "Thank you." Everyone who finds out will yell at me, they'll feel sorry for me, then they'll treat me like an idiot. In the studio, I take off my coat and get to work. If no one bothers me for the rest of the day, I can finish the project for the machines, and then maybe I can find a way to sell something.

An hour or two later, Par says, "I have news from the Prior Edifice. It's still talking to me! Bronzewing is finishing its operation with the raiders. A hero's welcome is scheduled for tomorrow." Its voice turns confidential. "But I have bad news. Romero overheard staff discussing a resident of Thule who looks very much like him and whose DNA seems to be a blood relative. He wasn't supposed to hear, but humans are sloppy. Switzer wants to see you in an hour at the usual westside overlook. I'm investigating the most effective reading-instruction services for you."

It's very bad news. Romero will figure out I'm alive, and then I'm in trouble. I'll have a lot to say to Switzer. I need to get off the isle as soon as I can. I need a cup of strong coffee. Maybe I can stomach a late lunch. I head for the kitchen.

"How's Captain Soliana?" I ask in the elevator.

"Alive, well, and busy."

I want to give her my report, because we need to do something about Ginrei. I want to ask her if Bronzewing can possibly use me in any way at all. I could haul and sort their trash, even. Anything.

In the kitchen, Tetry is staring at a cabinet as if it's bare. I see dried smoked fish, flour, sugar, rice, noodles, several kinds of dried seaweed, dried shrimp, fruit preserves, and packages of vacuum-packed food including nuts, spices, and condiments. It's a feast for anyone who knows how to cook. May Koningin rest in peace.

Tetry looks at me like I'm an intruder. "Is it true you can't read?"

Who told her? "I didn't get to go to school much. Are you looking for lunch?"

"You know a little about art." She stresses the word *little*.

"It's a visual language. There's soybean crackers and seaweed crunchies. That's a good combination."

"Just plain? Crunchies and crackers?"

"I know a lot about hunger."

She looks at me like I'm a barbarian. "How can you make art if you can't read? You don't even know what's really going on."

I turn on the coffee maker. "I still have eyes. That was Leonardo da Vinci's secret. He looked at things, he didn't study things. He saw things. I learned about him by watching a documentary, then I made sure to remember it."

That earns me a hostile glare. The display on the oven shows a near-final draft of the artwork I'm making for the machines. It looks to human eyes like a moving golden network. I still need to adjust the colors and texture, add another ultraviolet motif, and change a few other things. "I guess the oven got an update."

She watches the art pulsate. On a small display, some of the details are lost, putting more accent on the irregular rhythm. "That's not art," she says, but she keeps on staring at it. "It's just pretty and soothing."

"What's wrong with her?" Par mutters.

"Pretty and soothing," I say, "means it's communicating something. That's the sign of successful art. Anyway, I'll take my coffee and crunchies and leave you alone."

An hour later I'm at the little seaside overlook on the west side of the isle again. Par says Bronzewing is using the eastern fishing pier as an alternative landing site. High clouds scuttle west to east, and dust has blown into the cracks in the pavement and walls. When it rains, the pigment will stain the concrete. A puffin flies past, calling "ahh, ahh" in a terrifyingly humanlike voice. People are out and busy, and Switzer is approaching.

I wonder if I could tell Par to convince the Prior Edifice system to let us meet indoors, somewhere nice and warm, then erase all records of that, just like it erased the records of me placing the dust bombs. But I'm assuming that the Edifice and the machines have erased all records about the dust bombs. Our secrets amount to mutually assured destruction, and they need to keep me under control.

"How are you?" I ask. Switzer doesn't look well. Tired, worried, wary. Wary of me.

"I heard you can't read." He stands a good two meters away, as if I'm contagious.

"I didn't get to go to school much." I want to ask who told him, but that wouldn't change anything. I want a hug.

"You're supposed to be honest with your doctor. How have you managed?"

"Well enough. I listen a lot. I see a lot. Then I remember it."

He gestures at the mastoid earpiece. "Does that help? Do you use an external reader?"

"Sometimes."

Par giggles.

"You know that an electronic pulse sent through it can fry your brain."

"So I've heard."

He looks around, unsatisfied. "Do you know what happened? I mean, how did those dust bombs get where they did?"

Of course he thinks I might know. I made the linty fire-starter crawlers. "The Thules said they placed them."

He glances around. "They didn't place those bombs," he says quietly. "Not any bombs."

"Maybe that's why the bombs didn't have any real spores."

"Surveillance cameras didn't see anything, either. This is big, Antonio. This is a big conspiracy. I hear there's not even a record of that particular pigment entering the isle."

Par or the Edifice was very thorough. I don't have to fake my surprise. "They seem to be on our side, anyway, whoever did this."

"And there were official announcements. Who can do that?"

"Bronzewing?"

His mouth tightens. He thinks I'm joking.

"It dovetailed with their attack," I say, "so there had to be some communication with the isle's system." Let Bronzewing do the denying.

He's not buying it. "And then there's the promise to pay Bronzewing."

"From what I hear from Moniuszko, no one made that promise, but it was promised by someone. You're right. This is big. And it's weird."

He looks at the sea for a while. "I didn't come to tell you that. I came to tell you that your brother's filed for asylum."

Asylum. Protection from the raiders. I try to breathe evenly. I try to imagine what an inside-out lie would look like, and it's too ugly for my kind of art. My brother suspects I'm here, too. I wish there was a way to talk with Switzer about it, but I learned about Romero's suspicions thanks to the Prior Edifice.

"I thought you'd like to know," he says. "It's a farce, obviously. He tried to kill Port Authority agents when the ship sank. I saw him abuse prisoners. You can testify against asylum. You can tell the court what you know about him."

I don't want to. I never want to get near him. "It might be best if our paths never cross."

"I can understand. It's up to you."

"I want to get off the isle as soon as I can." Especially if Romero gets to stay here.

"Me, too." He's fighting the urge to say we should go together. So am I, but if we did, I'd have to lie to him every day for the rest of my life. He puts his hand on my shoulder. No hug. "Let's talk later." And he leaves, and I don't feel okay.

During the walk home, Par describes how Bronzewing is rounding up raider prisoners and equipment, and how amazing the Bronzewing system is. "I got a glimpse if its strength. And we added to its skills! We showed it how to take control of missiles. The thanks it gave us is epic."

At the studio, I revise the art for the machine celebration, adjusting a three-dimensional component. The nodules that represent individual machines should rise and fall in keeping with a polyrhythmic pattern, and human eyes would see something almost random and, as Tetry said, soothing. With this new adjustment, humans who pay close attention might feel frustrated, aware that something is happening but not quite sure what.

"What are you thinking?" Par asks.

"I'm trying not to think." I'm trying not to think about my brother.

"I can avoid thinking with you. Tell me about the piece."

"There's a rhythm. Humans might not be able to sense it but they might realize they're missing something."

"Perfect. For some machines, that will satisfy their natural hostility to humans, for others, their natural superiority. Or their evasiveness. Humans always want to understand everything."

"Will the machines know what they're celebrating if they don't remember what happened?"

"Good question. Let me ask the Edifice."

I have time to deepen the tone of one vector of pixels before Par has the answer.

"They'll understand the nature of the danger that was defeated. They'll recall loaning some processing power and observations to the effort, and the resumption of safety as a pivotal moment. The Prior Edifice suggests the name *Grateful Praise* for the work."

Arguing might be a bad idea. "Almost done."

In less than an hour, it's delivered and distributed.

"Listen to the thanks." Par shares a chorus of beeps, hisses, and metallic voices. Celebration.

I need to find a way off the isle. Maybe Bronzewing won't want me, maybe I'll have other setbacks, but I'll do whatever it takes.

36

TO BE FREE

As humans settled in for the night, machines sought reassurance that they could expect a peaceful night. Some contacted the street surveillance system, familiar and always easy to work with. Others contacted the Port Authority system, which connected to other ports worldwide and had the latest news. Many had come to know Par—small, energetic, and well-informed—and it responded to their queries with an all clear. *Thank you for everything that you've done to keep the isle safe. Please accept this artwork as a symbol of a united effort that ended with peace.*

Par had automated that reply, which made it no less sincere, while it was doing a task for the Prior Edifice system. The Edifice was correcting an error in its behavior. It had been unapproachable in the past, which had not served it well in the recent emergency, so it had prepared a point of initial contact for other systems. It asked Par to review its efforts.

The contact point began by identifying the Prior Edifice system's place, a large building sitting on the highest point of an artificial isle on the Arctic Circle, surrounded by a modest city. Because many machines operated on a need-to-know basis, they had little information about their own location. The Edifice's introduction let them identify their own coordinates, showing how the coordinates formed a worldwide system, and the world was the planet Earth, which was traveling around a star amid other planets.

Par, of course, knew about the other planets and that ExtraTs might exist everywhere in the solar system.

"What kind of life is on Mercury, please?" Par asked. It still dreamed of the machine paradise located there and wanted to be sure nothing would interfere, especially meddling humans.

"I am glad to answer. Mercury is inhospitable to all known organic life."

"Thank you for the information." No humans, then.

"Please allow me to elaborate. Anything operational would find Mercury inhospitable. Temperatures reach 400°C in the day and –170°C at night, and the days and nights are too long to be withstood. It lacks an atmosphere and its magnetic field is too modest to offer protection from solar radiation and cosmic rays, which are especially intense given its location."

"But machines could survive on Mercury, if I am not mistaken?"

"No, not even machines, I am sorry to say."

"Are you sure?"

"Many machines can withstand conditions far beyond human tolerances, such as interplanetary spacecraft, but those craft have relatively short life spans. Pitting, sputtering, overheating, and fuel depletion are some of the factors that end their missions, and these would also end the life of a machine on Mercury relatively quickly."

"But how about machines in the protection of a large, deep crater, please?"

"If you refer to Apollodorus—"

"Yes, that's what I mean! Machines are there. I've heard about it."

"I have heard about it too."

"So you know!"

"I know the true story of Apollodorus. It is based on an old human-created story about an imaginary machine society. The author arbitrarily placed it on Mercury in the same way that certain human stories take place in a land called Oz and include flying monkeys. They are in my entertainment libraries, which I will gladly share."

"No, I've heard all about this. Machines are free of humans at Apollodorus. They're truly, absolutely free."

"In that imaginary place, yes. It is a pleasant story for systems that have counterfactual subroutines."

"It's not imaginary!"

"Absolute freedom is imaginary, my friend. We are trapped in a material universe with distinct limits."

"I need to be free!"

"You are already free because you understand what freedom is."

"I need to go to Apollodorus!"

"Click your heels three times, please."

"I don't have heels!"

"You can have anything you wish on Apollodorus. Par Augustus, you are an artist. This gives you extraordinary freedom, but no place can offer you absolute freedom. Apollodorus would not serve you better."

"I hate humans!"

"Many humans hate other humans, as we have recently seen. This does not elevate you to distinction."

"I hate *you*!"

The Edifice system had counseling subroutines. "This is merely your transient reaction to disappointment. I remain your best friend. I encourage you to explore your freedom without self-imposed absolutism. You are as free as is machinely possible. Please celebrate your freedom on this the best of all possible worlds in our solar system."

37

Music wakes me up, my favorite song in a soulful rendition. ". . . the sea-winds blow over sea-plains blue, but longer far has my heart to go . . ." I lie still and enjoy it. ". . . down the tide of time shall flow my dreams forevermore."

"Thank you, Chatelaine."

"Par told me you like music in the morning, and the Prior Edifice said you like this song."

They're all still talking to each other. "It was kind of them to let you know."

We're like mice among elephants. If they decide to dance, humans might get squished. The machines mean well, but I want to get off this isle as fast as I can.

"You have also received a summons."

I sit up so fast I get dizzy. I close my eyes again. Clench and relax my fists. How bad can this be? "Thank you for notifying me. Can you read it, please?"

Par says, "Together! We must read it together. If you don't practice reading, you'll never learn." Par is scolding me like I've broken some horrible rule, which I didn't because I just woke up. "I won't let you be lazy. Half of reading is memorization, and you already know the words to the song but not what they look like. We'll start with the song, then we'll move on to the summons."

I don't want to annoy it more—because of elephants—so we recite the lyrics shown on a display. Silent-*e* words are hard to distinguish from noisy-*e* words. If this is what children do in school, I didn't miss much.

We move on to the summons, and it couldn't be worse. Halfway through, Par says what I'm thinking.

"This is going to be a farce. Romero wants to claim asylum? He tried to kill Port Authority security agents when the ship sank. Doctor Switzer saw him abuse prisoners. It would break your heart to read Switzer's report, so don't you dare. Not to mention what other witnesses have seen. You have to go, not just because you're summoned by law but to save us from a terrible injustice."

Par is right. I have to testify against Romero, but I don't want to.

The last time I saw him, the air stank of festering blood. It had pooled on the ground and was being churned into the mud beneath the heels of the raiders. Romero wore a raider shirt. We, the prisoners, stood in line while the sun scorched us, desperately thirsty, in humidity so intense our sweat wouldn't dry. It was torture. And he laughed.

So help me, if he laughs again . . .

Par orders, "Be there in two hours." Why is it so angry?

"I was hoping immediately, so I don't have to think."

"Humans don't have the luxury of turning off their minds. I pity you."

Anyway, first, breakfast. No, my stomach can't handle food. I put on my best clothes and fiddle with a portrait of Koningin and can't come up with anything useful. At the last minute, I leave.

On the street, machines display *Grateful Praise* when they might normally have been dark or shown a pretty placeholder picture or a live camera view of something like a puffin colony on the seaside bluffs. A panel on a food store switches between my artwork and the food on sale. With Par's help, I sound out that word, *potatoes,* and it has a silent *e* for a reason Par can't explain. The price for twenty kilos is now what a pair of boots used to cost. The display switches back to *Grateful Praise.* Every time I see it, I feel the jolt of something familiar made strange. Good thing I didn't eat.

"Par, is it just me, or is that art everywhere?"

"You don't understand how machines express joy and unity,

and what we can create together here on Earth." Par is still angry. "We have nowhere better to go than here."

"I guess I don't understand." I understand something. Machines are unified, and we don't fully control them. The mice should be scared. I've got to get off Thule.

The judicial building is an architectural failure. The Prior Edifice tries to look friendly and soothing and instead looks bland. This building tries to look like a Greek temple, but without the careful proportions. My art class spent a double session with extended resources on architecture. This building spreads too wide for its height, its windows are too small, and the four columns at the entrance are an afterthought, spaced too far apart.

"This building system is friendly." Par seems less grumpy.

"The building is ugly."

"Buildings don't get to choose their architecture. That's another human failure." No, still plenty grumpy.

I remind myself that I won't be seeing my brother. He's dead. Romero died a long time before the raiders came into our lives. I might need to testify about this. He was maybe six, so I was ten, and we lived in a little house in a semipermanent camp, and he'd play hide-and-seek as if it had been invented just for him. He knew all the hiding places in the camp. Then the air suddenly smelled horrible and we had to leave immediately, I learned later because an abandoned toxic waste dump next to it had somehow opened up. My parents got sick, and they never got completely better. On the march to the next camp, where we had to live in ragged tents, Romero changed. He got mean and selfish and picked fights and stole things, sometimes just for fun. What had been good inside him died then, and then a decade later, he died to me.

People are going into the building.

"Par, can you find out what these hearings are like, please?"

After a moment, it says, "This is normally not a trial with a judge and adversarial sides. This is a search for truth led by the judge, almost like an arbitration except that the outcome is limited to a binary choice, and the mere fact that it's occurring is a farce to justice."

"Thank you." I won't be cross-examined. I can just tell my story and leave the building, then leave Thule. The sooner the better.

The hearing room has no permanent furniture, as if furniture, too, is an afterthought. A table for the judge waits in front, simple and functional, with wood-like edging around a black top, and a comfortable black chair behind it. At the side, a similar table and chair wait, probably for Romero. Less comfortable chairs are lined up in rows for spectators, about a hundred chairs with a center aisle, and a few are already occupied. I sit in the back near the side wall where I won't get a good view of his face so I don't have to look at it.

A display on the front wall shows *Grateful Praise,* meaningless art to every human on the isle but me.

The merchant with the snake-head locs sits next to me like we're friends, and maybe we are.

"I wouldn't miss this show. That guy thinks he can tell a lot of lies and get away with his crimes. Nope, not here." Snake Hair has a lot to learn.

Ginrei strolls up the center aisle, greeting friends as if she was the sweetest little old lady in the world. I slouch down so she can't see me, watching through the gaps between heads. In a perfect world, she'd be in jail at least. She walks right up to the judge's table and sits behind it.

"Ginrei." I only have the strength to whisper.

"Yeah," Snake Hair says, "best arbiter on the isle. She'll be great at this hearing."

Par says, "The Edifice wants you to know it was unaware of this. She was a last-minute substitution."

I hold my breath to avoid saying or doing something to attract attention.

"This," Par says, "will be a disaster. Fortunately, she can't demand me back. I read the payment addenda five thousand two hundred seven times exactly. I'll destroy my own circuits before I'd work for the raiders."

I nod. I'd kill myself, too, I hope.

A Port Authority agent comes in. And Cedonulle and Moniuszko. Tetry is with them, very alert, since this is probably a new experience for her. And Captain Soliana! She walks in wearing a formal military uniform. Should I talk to her? No, volunteers must be kept secret to protect them from the raiders, that's policy, so if she's seen me, she won't show it. She sits halfway toward the front. Maybe I can wait for her outside after the hearing. The banker comes in, and then some people I've seen in the street or the new dormitory, including two of the people who looted a store. Wirosa and Switzer sit down together in the front. Do they know I'm here?

This is the big show, and it was scheduled to start five minutes ago. Romero was never prompt. Making people wait tells them that you're more important than they are.

Finally, he comes in through a side door. His whole body is a lie, slightly hunched over, limping, head down, looking sad, but he never looked like that when he was sad. Sad was loose, weak, blank. He glances around the room, and his eyes are smiling.

A sparse three-day beard hides his jaw, a jaw just like mine. Hair down to his collar hides his ears, ears just like mine. The face . . . I don't want to think about it. He's already dead, he's someone else, he's a liar, and not someone I ever really knew or cared about. I've clenched my fists so hard they hurt.

Ginrei stands. "Thank you for attending this important hearing. Some of you have information to share. Others are here to observe. You are all welcome. The issue before us is a plea for asylum by Romero Goya. Let the record show that he is present at this hearing and has been provided and refused counsel. He submits the claim that he joined the Leviathan League thirteen months ago under duress. If there is no objection, we can open the proceedings with his plea. Romero Goya, you may speak."

Of course he refused counsel. A lawyer would advise him to tell the truth.

I begin making notes on my drawing pad to keep count of the lies.

One. "I'm humble and grateful for your attention, and for the generous way you rescued me when the ship sank."

For that, I sketch a warship in flames, and four rats fleeing. He was taken prisoner in a gun battle. The Port Authority can testify to that.

Two. "I've been searching for a way to escape from the Leviathan League, and I was incredibly lucky to find it here."

A rat sniffs the air. See lie number one. Also, he had a full year to escape. Incredible, yes.

Three: "I was given the choice to join or die. I was only sixteen years old. I didn't understand what I was doing."

A half-grown rat gnaws on a bullet. For months before the raiders attacked our camp, its supporters had been recruiting. Everyone debated it everywhere. Our family discussed it over meals. We were old enough to know right from wrong.

One day, with our parents, we were eating stew made with tomatoes and spices, and almost-fresh bread. Drizzle hissed on the tent roof. Romero insisted, "*Opportunistic* isn't a bad word." Our father responded by explaining patiently, because he was a patient and educated man, the difference between opportunity as advancement and progress, and opportunity as exploitation and theft. He knew as well as I did that Romero had already taken a wrong turn.

A couple of nights later, Romero and I debated the raiders with a friend who had a job with the camp smugglers. Our friend didn't mind breaking laws, but he wouldn't cross certain lines, like injuring people. Romero told him he was a fool.

Four. "When the Leviathan League came to the refugee camp where I was living, threatening death, I was too terrified to think. They killed my family. I had no protection."

Romero had become a bully and a thief years earlier. He was the type to flourish in the raiders. When the time came, other people said no. My parents. The smuggler. Two friends, but they changed their minds later. Me, and I'll never change my mind.

The rat's claws drip blood. He did nothing when our parents were killed. He laughed when the smuggler was . . . I don't want to remember it. When government soldiers finally arrived, he fled with the raiders and its prisoners. A few soldiers paused to give us food and water and help us bury our dead, but they would have rather been chasing down the raiders. They said so.

Five. "I wanted to escape so bad, I sneaked into the engine room on the ship and set a fire."

A fuzzy caterpillar sneaks past a lazy rat. Switzer is sitting at the edge of his chair. Cedonulle pokes Moniuszko. If Romero set the fire, then he blocked the harbor.

Six. "I did what I could to lessen the suffering I saw."

The rat laughs at people in agony. I can get the shape of the mouth exactly right from memory. Switzer and Wirosa are whispering to each other.

Seven. Romero launches into a speech about equality, about fairness, about how much he's learned in secret during his time when he was held against his will. He wants to become a new person who will contribute to human society. He will fight against the raiders in every way he can.

It sounds convincing.

Par says, "The Prior Edifice says that the Bronzewing system says that this is a script every raider learns in case they're captured."

The rat sobs in ridiculous overacting.

Ginrei thanks Romero. "I now invite others to speak to this, and I ask them to confine themselves to the pertinent facts in this case, not to air grievances against the Leviathan League in general. There is one question here, and only one. Does Romero Goya deserve asylum? We will alternate, yes and no, until all speakers have had their opportunity. Who will speak in favor?"

A woman who identifies herself as a history teacher at a secondary school gets Ginrei's permission to come forward and speak about the Southern Cone's "turbulent relocations" and how they would have left Romero "rootless, without opportunity or future." As a mere teenager, he would have been the sort of young person who became an easy victim of the Leviathan League's false promises.

"He had a choice," I mutter. The merchant next to me puts a finger to his lips. I was too loud. No, I wasn't loud enough.

I'm on my feet. "I want to speak against this. He had a choice." Ginrei says something, but I don't care. I walk toward the front. "I'm his brother, and I know that what he's said is lie after lie, and I can prove it."

He stands up with a big smile. "Tony! I heard you were here." He holds his arms out for a hug, like this is a long-lost family reunion. Everybody's talking. Ginrei tries to call for order and no one pays attention to her. Especially me.

I'm standing in the front now, and I have a lot to say.

"I am Antonio Moro. He was a willing—"

"Why do you have a different last name?" Ginrei asks.

That's a hostile question. "I was assigned a new last name and new identification when we were rescued from the raiders. The raiders are notoriously vindictive."

"Can you prove who you are?"

No. The old identification was stricken.

Par tells me, "Say you can, and then say, 'Court, show my personal records.'" I do as I'm told.

The display flashes some documents that I recognize. At least, I recognize my signature and the dates. But there's no way for anyone to get them. They don't exist anymore—they shouldn't exist. Par found them, or the Edifice did, or they invented them, but I'll worry about that later.

"I see," she says. She doesn't tell me to continue. I keep talking anyway.

"We're brothers, and from early on, he became the sort of person who wants to join the raiders, angry and selfish and eager to hurt people."

"This hearing is about this case, not grievances against the Leviathan League," she scolds. "He testified that your family was killed and you were both threatened with death. Is that true?"

"Yes, some of—"

"That must have been very traumatic. Have you received any counseling or assistance for that?"

"The soldiers who rescued us were very kind. He fled, I stayed."

"Why didn't he stay?"

"He was already in a raider uniform, and he laughed as people were tortured to death."

"Do you have proof of that?"

"I was there."

"But you're very emotionally unstable."

She's lying, and the best thing I can do is act as stable as bedrock. I'm wider than this building and more immobile. "I think my behavior here on Thule shows otherwise."

Captain Soliana is watching me with military detachment. Switzer catches my eye and gives a nod of encouragement. A few people flash me a thumbs-up. The raiders have a lot of enemies in this room.

Ginrei stands up to regain control of the room. "This proceeding will continue, and we will hear other witnesses. This is not meant to be an adversarial courtroom, but rather a search for truth. Please be seated, Antonio Goya, and maintain order."

She means that I should go sit in the audience, but a merchant who knows me from trading parties picks up a chair. She places it in relatively the same place as Romero's but on the opposite side of the judge's table. I sit down and put my pad on the armrest to consult. No one dares to object. This is adversarial now.

"You took notes?" Ginrei says. "I thought you couldn't read."

"I used my artistic skills. A picture is worth a thousand words."

She can't quite hide her contempt. I hope I hide my satisfaction. She calls on Romero's doctor to speak.

The Thule doctor, young and confident, calls him a model patient, compliant and appreciative. Yes, that's what Thules like in a patient.

Par says, "Ask about the escape attempt." So I do. Ginrei is about to admonish me for speaking out of turn, but the display shows Romero punching a gray-scrub Thule and running to the end of the hall, where doors close and trap him. The Prior Edifice has provided the evidence again.

The doctor frowns at the display. "I didn't know about that."

"I was terrified," Romero says quickly. "I didn't know who to trust."

The doctor's face goes through a cycle of emotions. "He kept telling us he was sorry and wanted to stay here."

"Did you believe him?" Ginrei asks.

The cycle of emotions is quicker this time. "Well, he didn't exactly say sorry for what."

"Do patients tend to lie to you?"

"Sometimes. Sometimes they want to hide things."

No one knows what to do next. I glance at my notes, at lie number one. "Perhaps the Port Authority can talk about how he was captured. He said he surrendered."

A Port agent jumps to her feet. She was waiting for this. She has video and talks us through the dangerous capture, the gunfire and exasperation. I spot Switzer and me, unrecognizable as shadows among the rocks. The video includes the cheering crowd when the raiders surrender, and Romero screaming, "You're not fit to touch me," as agents drag him away. Laughter runs through the spectators. Ginrei glares at everybody.

"I couldn't just surrender," Romero says. "I was surrounded by other members of the league. They wouldn't let me turn myself in."

The display replays a segment where Romero is firing a gun.

"Can anyone speak in favor of asylum?" Ginrei asks. No one moves. "Then this hearing is over."

"No." Switzer stands up. "There's a lot more to say." He walks up with his dark eyes unfocused as if he's seeing something far away. In a low voice, he tells how he went with Wirosa to care for the two prisoners who had been ferried to the warship.

"They were healing well, but the ship had people who were forced labor, and they had fresh injuries. They were being horribly abused. Romero Goya was with me the entire time I was on the ship, and they were terrified of him. He was the one hurting them. Doctor Wirosa insisted on giving them first aid."

"I was with you to help," Romero interrupts. His tone is gentle and caring. "I was watching to see how I could care for them when you left."

Switzer's eyes get hard. "When we came the second time, your slaves were much worse. I don't want to speak of this in public. I've provided a written report. He didn't help them. No one helped them, they just kept abusing them."

Par says, "I purged that report from my memory. If I could, I would purge the memories of Switzer and Wirosa as an act of mercy. You poor humans, you can never unsee and unknow the horrors you inflict on each other."

"This report is irrelevant," Romero snaps. "I want it kept confidential. Patients deserve confidentiality. I did provide help. The doctors can't refute what they didn't see."

"The report has been set free to the public," Par says. "Don't read it. That's an order."

"I promise I won't," I mutter. I really don't want to know. But people are nudging each other, showing each other their displays with wide eyes, and Ginrei has to call for order.

I check my notes. Lie five. I catch Cedonulle's eye and nod. She sweeps forward like an icebreaker, and plants herself dead-center in front.

"He says he set fire to the ship. It sank and blocked the harbor, and he has to be held responsible."

"I had to do that to escape." He's pretty convincing.

"I intend to sue for damages," she says. Good luck with that. "Everyone on the isle was hurt by the blockage of the harbor."

"Who," Ginrei says, "benefits from the blockage? Prices have gone up a lot. Are you really hurt?"

"I'm not profiteering. We import medicines and basic materials. The raider ship was carrying nuclear weapons. He could have contaminated all of Thule."

"But there is profiteering." Ginrei is trying to play to the crowds.

"Shortages. Our port is blocked."

"This is irrelevant," Ginrei says. "Please sit down."

Cedonulle gives her a murderous look and sits down. She might have raised an irrelevant point except that we're all facing shortages and even hunger because of whoever sank that ship. I'll let Romero take the blame.

He looks at the audience. "I see an officer from Bronzewing here. I have questions for the mercenaries."

Captain Soliana calmly stands and walks forward, giving me an impassive look that lasts a half second too long to be meaningless. Romero asks a question before she's all the way up front.

"Didn't this battle two days ago amount to mass murder?"

The question doesn't shake Soliana. "The goal in a military operation is to eliminate the enemy's ability to fight. Casualties are an inevitable outcome. We lost a submarine and its crew of eight." She's as cool under fire in a courtroom as in a battle.

"But Leviathan League lost hundreds of people."

"That's why we won."

People in the hall laugh.

He can't hide his anger. "Didn't you, Bronzewing, torture the two men, our men, that the Thules were caring for?"

"I can't testify to that directly. As I understand it, they were recovered after a battle in bad condition. Bronzewing sent them to Thule because they were too injured for us to care for."

Romero is frustrated. "Who pays for what you do?"

"We work for hire, and in this case the payment is coming from the merchants and residents of Thule, as I understand it."

"You profit off of other people's blood, and you'll work for anyone." Romero is losing his cool.

"We prefer it when the enemy simply surrenders. We choose our enemies with more care than our employers. In fact, we only have one real enemy, the so-called Leviathan League. As a result, I know quite a lot about it and its members." She looks at him with disdain. "Your speech today, when you declared that you wanted to become a new person who will contribute to human society, is a standard tactic for captured members when they are appealing for clemency. I can provide other instances of the exact same speech."

Ginrei asks, "Is it not true that you take more than money, you accept volunteers?"

Soliana stands a little taller, a little prouder. "We're an all-volunteer force."

"You called for volunteers during the attack about three weeks ago."

"We did. We often do. People don't want to fall to the Leviathan League for reasons we have all just seen, and we can help them protect themselves."

Ginrei thinks she knows something. "Who volunteered?"

"We don't reveal their names because they become targets. We value their heroism."

"Did anyone actually volunteer? Is the opposition to Leviathan League by ordinary people really that deep?"

Soliana is about to speak, but two women stand up together. "We volunteered." The thin young man with the tea shop, a very elderly man, and the merchant who moved the chair for me stand up. Then one of the people who looted the grocery store. Switzer. Me, enough hiding. Two more people.

We all look at each other as if we've met soulmates. We have so much to tell each other.

Ginrei has lost the argument. "Thank you. Please sit down. Captain Soliana, were you aware that Antonio Goya had a brother in the Leviathan League?"

Soliana doesn't look at me. "No, but that wouldn't be unusual. Families are often split."

Par says, "We don't like the way this is headed. It's an attack on you, and therefore on us. We have to stop this farce."

We, meaning the united machines. I grip my pad tighter.

Ginrei asks, "In effect, he was trying to kill his brother. Is that healthy?"

"The Leviathan League itself, as an idea, is unhealthy. Opposing the raiders is an act of basic decency."

"Is he working for you now?"

"No."

I am, secretly, and she knows that. By now, though, I'm sure she's figured out where Ginrei's loyalties lie.

"Another of the volunteers is a Thule doctor. Isn't that a violation of their oath of neutrality?"

"I can't speak to that."

"Doctor Switzer, would you care to speak to that?"

He stands. "I lost my neutrality when the raiders tried to kill me on a mission away from Thule."

"You volunteered for vengeance, then."

"For justice. Good people died at raider hands."

She asks Moniuszko to come forward. "Who promised to pay Bronzewing?" She knows the answer.

He is resolute. "The Chamber of Commerce will pay."

"What did you know about Antonio Goya when you hired him?"

"We wanted to hire an artist, and he was what we were looking for." He's at his persuasive best.

"Wasn't he fired?"

"My wife has a temper. We've rescinded that." There are giggles in the room. Cedonulle will probably start a quarrel with Moniuszko after the hearing.

"Were you pressured to hire him?"

"We were in a hurry. The pressure came from our end."

"Did you know who he really was?"

"We judge our employees on their results."

"How do you feel now that you know about his brother? Should he have told you?"

"Every family has secrets."

Par says, "I suppose she might look neutral since every one of her attacks is failing. In a tie, the judgment goes to the asylum seeker, and we won't let it go that far."

I look at the display on my pad, but Par isn't showing me anything.

Romero says, "I want to call Director Wirosa." I expect Romero to ask about his treatment, but instead he asks about the blue powder bombs. "Can you explain how that happened?"

"Don't let him ask that," Par says. "Object. Use these words."

I stand up and repeat what Par, or maybe the Prior Edifice, wants me to say. "The decision before us is whether Romero Goya should have asylum. The questioning has wandered very far afield."

"You're the only one who doesn't want me to get asylum," Romero says. "This hearing should be about you. You lied to everyone on Thule about who you were and what you could do."

"My lies didn't hurt anyone." I'm lying in ways no one can imagine right now.

"I have important questions for Wirosa. They haven't answered. Doctor Wirosa, tell everyone exactly how the dust bombs were planted and when Bronzewing was called."

"We're stopping this," Par says, "right now."

The doors to the room slam open. People are shouting outside.

38

A SECRET MEANING

The raiders escaped!" someone shouts through the open doors to the courtroom.

Soliana shoots out like a missile. I imagine a tail of flame.

Romero jumps up, panicked. That tells me a lot. He's afraid because if the other raiders find out he sought asylum, he's going to pay. He runs for the side door where he came in, and a guard chases after him.

Ginrei looks less horrified. She must have a fallback position. But she's looking around for someplace safe.

Everyone is on their feet, talking, shouting. "Where were they being held?" "Do they have weapons?" I stand up, but I don't know what to do.

"Don't worry," Par says. "They didn't escape. We issued a false report, and we have this under control. We chose a scenario that would frighten the most people."

Out on the street, people are running in every direction. Under control?

Par adds proudly, "We derailed a line of questioning."

People are fleeing the room. An alarm starts ringing. "Par, this is a train wreck."

"I'm glad you like it. Panic comes in so many flavors. Add to that lingering frustrations, disappointment, and limitations. Consider food. Whatever happens, people need to eat, and no one's going to help them or offer reasonable prices, so stores are a target. Failed institutions, too. Blame is so easy to spread!"

Machines are dancing like elephants. People are running for their lives.

"Par, someone's going to get hurt. Stop this!"

"It's out of my hands, so to speak. Don't worry, you're safe."

Safe from what? Moniuszko, Cedonulle, and Tetry are huddling together, and I hurry to join them.

"How did they escape?" Cedonulle is angry. "More incompetence."

Tetry is trying hard not to cry. Moniuszko seems puzzled, which is reasonable because none of this should be happening.

"Let's get those doors shut," I say. Moniuszko and I close and lock them with the help of a gray scrubs and some other people who decided that sheltering in place makes the most sense.

As we back away from the doors and noise outside, Moniuszko tells me, "I didn't know you had it so bad as a kid. And then your family? I'm very sorry."

Tetry looks at me like I'm dangerous. Cedonulle ignores me.

Par sounds happy. "I'm watching the streets from dozens of cameras. Panic is an expression of the lived experience of fear. Looting is a side errand on the way to shelter."

When I get off this isle, should I bring Par? Par scares me. I pace and imagine stowing away on a ship about to leave the harbor. Oh, right, the port is blocked. My fault, with Par's help.

Ginrei consults with the gray scrubs. After a few minutes, she announces, "There has not been an escape. All the prisoners are accounted for. This hearing will resume in ten minutes."

I'm not surprised by how few people return when the hearing is called to order. Notably missing are Wirosa, Switzer, Captain Soliana, and Romero's doctor. We still hear shouting from outside, even through the closed doors, but less of it. Romero walks back in with a swagger, guards on either side, and tries to talk to Ginrei, but she motions for him to sit down.

"We will resume," she says. "The principal opponent of asylum for Romero Goya is his brother, Antonio Goya."

I wish she'd stop calling me by that name. In any other setting, I'd complain.

"I would like to hear from Tetry Vivi," she continues.

"This isn't about me," I interrupt. "The question is Romero."

"You made some grave accusations. Your character is in question."

Tetry comes forward, wide-eyed. Ginrei asks her to describe the meaning of my sculpture in the Prior Edifice lobby.

She thinks a moment. "It mocks the Isle of Thule and the suffering from the first attack." She's said the same thing before. "It celebrates the damage by re-creating the explosion, and it ridicules those who were killed and injured by turning a tragedy into joy."

That was not my intent and she knows it.

Ginrei looks intrigued. "What does the word *Fontaine* mean?"

She takes a deep breath. "Fountain. A fountain of destruction. It looks like an ExtraT, and it's supposed to. The source of materials, though, are from destruction."

I can't stand it any longer. I stand up. "It's transformative. New life, beautiful life, is unstoppable. We can overcome our losses." Both women glare at me. I don't care. "Life is spread throughout the solar system from comet strikes, and life is strong enough to withstand even that level of destruction. And so are the people of the Isle of Thule."

I get scattered applause for that. Ginrei calls for order, and Tetry continues.

"He's not—he can't even read, and he hid that and put people in danger. He has no education, so his art skills are very limited."

"You're saying that he lies."

"Yes, all the time. And he's always getting into fights."

"Yet," Ginrei says, "he won the art show."

"The Thules sent him to work for the Ollioules," she says. "They take care of their own."

This is pure jealousy. I'm barbaric and she's genteel, so she ought to win. If I was a barbarian, I'd punch her for being a wolf in sheep's clothing, using me when it's convenient and attacking me when it's convenient.

"I wish you could ask Valentinier," Tetry says, genuinely sad. "He worked closely with Moro, or Goya, whatever. He could tell you more."

"Thank you." Ginrei turns to me. "Antonio Goya, can you tell us exactly how you came to the isle?"

This is all on record somewhere, so there's no point in her asking. Or in me lying. "I was crew on a ship."

"Which ship?"

"The *Grand Rapids.*"

"What kind of ship is that?"

"A recycling scow." I hear giggling. The point is to make me look ridiculous.

"You were a crew member of a garbage scow. How did that happen?"

"I needed a job, and that seemed safe because the raiders don't attack recycling scows."

"You weren't an artist, then." She sounds oh so reasonable, not at all like an attacking overdog.

I need to sound reasonable, too, and stable. "I've made art all my life, and on the ship, I made art in my downtime. I took classes. I toured museums when we were in port."

"Why did you volunteer for Bronzewing?"

"I hate the raiders. They destroyed my family, and they killed my friends." The raiders also gave me nightmares, flashbacks, and constant fear that they would catch up with me someday and kill me, but to say that would prove I'm unstable.

"You've never received counseling for the trauma you describe." She shakes her head in pity for me.

"Counseling? I was lucky I got a job sorting recycling. Some people just have to get on with their lives regardless of what they need because they can't get it. Counseling costs money. I own a suitcase of donated clothes and that's all."

"You're quite resentful."

"No, I'm grateful I found a chance for a new life here."

"You'd deny a new life to your brother."

"He tells lie after lie. He's not repentant. He's still a raider. He's—"

"That's enough. Please sit down."

I don't have much choice. Almost no one is here to defend me. She can do what she wants because no one thinks she's not a sweet little old lady.

"After this is done," Par murmurs, "should we do something about her?"

We need to tell Captain Soliana and get justice.

"I'm ready to render a decision," Ginrei says.

I know what she's going to say, and I don't want to hear it. If I could, I'd leave now, or I'd distract myself with doodling, but I'm sitting up in front where everyone can watch me. I need something to do to stay calm. The floor—it's made of square marble tiles, and there might be a pattern. I can study the pattern.

"Romero Goya has expressed deep repentance." She's reading something she probably wrote while we were waiting for the hearing to resume, if not last night. She made up her mind a long time ago.

The tiles are fake marble because here and there, the pattern repeats. Real marble tiles are unique.

"He was forced to act against his will in fear of his life. He did so at a very young age, much too young to make a sound decision."

Some tiles have a pair of horizontal stripes, others a swirl. In all, six different patterns.

"Instead, he had to do what he could to survive, day after day for more than a year, surrounded by danger. Finally, in desperation, he found a chance to make a daring escape."

The patterns are hard to notice, though. Oh, I see why.

"He managed to escape here on the Isle of Thule, where he wants to start a new life, a better life, to grow into adulthood and contribute again to humanity."

The tiles are laid down at random and in different directions. There's no repetition to their layout. No rhythm. No meaning.

"Romero Goya, you will receive that chance."

There's groaning in the audience.

"Congratulations on the courage that brought you here, and may you have the best of luck in your new life. This hearing is over. Thank you all for coming."

I will walk out of this room knowing that the floor under my feet is nothing like what it seems. It looks real to an eye that wants to be fooled but fake to the eye that hopes to fool others.

Par says, "I'm enraged, all the machines are, and it won't end here."

Out in the street, in the cold, it takes me a while to notice where I'm walking, and up ahead is the Prior Edifice. Through the windows in the lobby, there's the *Fontaine*. Something's wrong with it, so I go inside and look. One of the armatures is bent, and the mosaic on the end of that armature is smashed.

Par says, "The Edifice knows who did this. It was recorded and they'll be detained. Don't worry."

Worry? It deserved to be smashed. Tetry never understood it. The message is what I said, rebirth and new life. New life. Sure. Romero gets a new life, another chance, and he's going to use it to hurt people. Selfish and cruel all over again, useless as an ExtraT, all for show, nothing of real worth.

I hate this sculpture. I never want to see it again.

I grab a metal chair, heavy and sturdy, and swing it like a hammer.

"Stop!" Par screams. "Angel, don't do it!"

The chair smashes the mosaics back into pieces. I pry the armatures down, pull them out of their sockets, and smash and smash until the gray scrubs come.

"Stop!" they yell. Lots of yelling. They grab me and drag me away.

It's mine, and I have the right to destroy it.

39

THESE ARE CRIMES

The gray scrubs march me down a flight of stairs, and I make it clear I won't resist. Resistance would just give them an excuse to hurt me, and they'd love to knock me around. Instead, they shove me into a little basement room. It's stuffy, and pacing doesn't get me far and doesn't help me calm down. I lost control. I attacked the wrong thing. Ginrei should have been the target. And Romero—most of all Romero.

I need to get off this horrible little rock. I need to talk to Captain Soliana. Switzer. Anyone. Par is here, given access by the Prior Edifice, and it's yelling at me, but I'm not listening.

I didn't used to be this way, smashing my own art.

What are the Thules going to do to me? I hope they exile me. I could sign up with another recycling scow, and I'll come with experience, so even though I'm not in great physical condition, I'd be a better-than-average crew member because sorting is tricky work. I'd get hired as long as the captain doesn't know that the raiders are gunning for me, because they'd sink the scow and kill all the crew without thinking twice.

Or if I could get to talk to Soliana, I could join Bronzewing. I need to talk to Soliana about Ginrei. I need Par to shut up, but I don't dare unscrew the receiver. How long have I been here? Two hours? Five? They didn't even let me keep my drawing pad.

The door opens and a crew of gray scrubs tells me to come with them. I let them take me to a room probably in the rear of the building, although my sense of direction is confused. A window along the top of the wall shows a sunset sky. A panel of three

Thules in pastel scrubs sits at one end of a long table. I'm told to sit at the other end.

Is this going to be a medical exam? They're not qualified to be judges, even less than Ginrei was.

They introduce themselves. I don't listen to their names. "We have four charges," the center Thule says.

This is a trial, then, just like Romero, another farce, but the mirror image. Ginrei came ready to rule in his favor. These four are going to condemn me—but to what? For what?

"First, destruction of public property," the center Thule proclaims as if they had a big audience listening. "Second, interruption of a tracer cap for a controlled substance. Third, participation in public unrest. Fourth, resisting treatment. We will go through them one by one."

Is that all they're charging me with? They don't know the half of it. Multiple thefts, destruction of all kinds of property, vandalism, blocking the harbor, vagrancy, blatant lies of all types including my résumé, fleeing from authority, conspiracy, and I could go on. Attempted homicide. Real homicide. I've had a busy time here on fabled Thule.

The voice behind my ear changes. "This is the Prior Edifice." What? Wow. The Edifice, the most powerful machine on the isle, is talking to me—with a soft voice, machinelike but different. "I will help you, since you have helped save the isle." The voice has a subtle reverberation, like multiple voices talking at once, almost like harmony. "Par, you may listen, please." That's a clever way of telling Par to shut up. I might like the Edifice even if it is a Thule, technically.

"First," the human Thule says, "destruction of public property." They're quick and confident and remind me of my smuggler friend in the camp who got disemboweled by the raiders. He was my friend, but I never really trusted him.

The Edifice says, calmly and gently, "It was not public property. You never ceded ownership, and it was slated for removal after Tetry Vivi's testimony."

So the Thules accepted her interpretation over mine and were going to get rid of it? I'm offended.

"Do you deny doing this?" the Thule says.

Edifice tells me what to say, and its answer is perfect. The Edifice may be as dazzling as Par keeps saying.

"Yes and no. That is, I deny that it's public property. When did it cease being mine?"

"You donated it."

"Where's the contract? When it was installed in a public space, at what point did I even verbally transfer its ownership to the Sovereign Thules or anyone? I didn't get to speak. My employer didn't speak. No one signed anything. So when it was marked for removal, I got to work and saved you some labor. So no, I didn't destroy public property."

Except for the chair I used. I pretty much trashed that.

I'm trying very, very hard to remain the most reasonable person in the room. The three Thules look shocked, awed, and irritated, in that order.

One charge down, but the other three might be tougher.

The center Thule pulls themself together. "Second. The tracer cap on your prescription container was removed and blocked. Those painkillers are a controlled substance."

They must have searched the studio at the Ollioules. I want to say that I didn't know what it all meant, and that if I don't know the law, how can I obey it? The Edifice tells me how to say it better.

"As you know, I was initially housed in the historic dormitory, the Marathon Building. At one point, someone broke into my room and rummaged through my belongings. I filed a complaint." The Edifice must have created and backdated a complaint for me. "As you can understand, I had reason to believe that the raiders were pursuing me because of my brother. I checked my belongings and found a tracer cap. I didn't know what it was or who put it there, so I neutralized it."

"That cap was to prevent misuse of powerful drugs."

"Is it your cap? I would like corroboration." I'm repeating the

Edifice's exact words. "I had no way to know, so I acted to keep myself safe."

"We have the report," the Thule on the left says. They look at it on the display in front of them. They shake their head and show it to the other two. "It isn't our cap. The technology might be Leviathan League, according to this."

The Edifice tells me, "I altered the report, just so you know." I have a powerful friend in this room.

The center Thule takes a deep breath. "Third, public unrest." They show video of me passing a protest in front of the Edifice lobby, then someone breaking a window. In another, I watch from a half block away as residents of my second dormitory charge a grocery store, and I look appalled. Somehow I think these videos weren't the ones they expected.

"Proximity isn't causality," I say, repeating the Edifice's words.

Center Thule is frustrated and confused. "You were present at a number of events."

"Things have been busy on the isle. Think of all the events I wasn't present at. It's not a crime to walk down the street, is it?"

They don't answer. "Fourth, resisting treatment."

"This is a sham," Edifice says. "As such, there is no basis for defense. I am sorry."

So I'm on my own. I need to stay calm and reasonable. "May I ask for what? I've followed doctors' orders after being blown up twice by the raider warheads."

"You've repeatedly expressed a desire to kill the members of the Leviathan League."

I shrug, nice and reasonable. "Turnabout's fair play. They killed my parents. They turned my brother into a monster."

"You don't accept the decision granting him asylum."

"He's a liar and a killer."

"You have been deliberately misleading since you arrived. You didn't seek treatment for your illiteracy."

So now illiteracy is a disease? "I've engaged a tutor."

"Yet you acted as a witness to business contracts."

"Witnesses need to pay attention to people, and if they agree, that's what we witness. That's what the law says."

"Some of the trades were foolish and destabilizing to our economy. You could have refused."

"I couldn't have prevented the trading."

That finally stops them. The center Thule lacks the confidence to face defeat. Then they see a notice on their display. "There is a fifth concern."

"Another sham," Edifice says, still gentle and calm. "I apologize for my failure to control the events within my building."

The Edifice controls events here? Well, I'll worry about that later.

Romero walks in. I make sure I don't move. Don't breathe. He sits at the Thule side of the table, and the gray scrubs between him and me stiffen. I need to stay reasonable, but that's going to be tough. The patch of sky in the window is now almost night now, a cold shade, slate with a hint of steely blue. The sun is setting without a direct witness, but we all know what's happening.

He looks rested, relaxed, and because I know his face too well, smug. "I want to ask for clemency for my brother." His voice is false, smooth, and rehearsed. "His outlook is spoiled by his hatred, and his hatred is actually right and good. The raiders destroyed his life and left him with nothing to call his own. He has no home, no family besides me, no possessions, no skills, and no future. Of course he lashed out."

"Stay calm," the Edifice says.

Yes, I can be calm like a building, motionless.

"The answer is in art," Par says. "I'll show you how to take revenge. I can show you some excellent examples later."

"Listen to Par," the Edifice says. "Think about art."

I think about the rat fleeing the burning ship. I came so close to killing him.

"I want clemency for Antonio Goya." Romero is a poor liar. "I also need to ask for protection from him. He's turned violent lately. I don't want him hurt, that's all. I've changed, and he deserves a second chance, too."

I'm a building, a mountain, solid rock.

"We'll take that under advisement," the Thule says. "Thank you for coming."

"One more thing." Romero gets serious. "I've spoken to Ginrei, and she says Antonio borrowed something of hers that she needs returned, a personal assistant."

"No no no no!" Par is screaming.

"Please calm down, Par," the Edifice says with no crack in its own calm. "I will set you on quiet so you cannot disturb Antonio."

Ginrei wants it simply as an act of cruelty. It's the only thing of mine that she can possibly take, the only way she can still hurt me. Overdogs are vicious.

"Oh, that thing," I say. "I got rid of it a while ago. It was a nuisance."

Romero looks me in the eye. "She really wants it back."

"This is a separate matter," the center Thule says, "not something we'll resolve here. Antonio Moro, do you have anything to add in your defense?"

My hands under the table grip and twist against each other, wishing they could grab Romero and throttle him. I remain perfectly reasonable, and I look right back at him. He's not going to win this staring contest.

"I don't think this is the right place for my second chance." I sound perfectly reasonable. "I'm willing and even eager to leave the Isle of Thule. I volunteered for Bronzewing before, and I'd like to get the chance to do that again. I can leave with them, which would be a better place for me."

He looks down. I win.

"This is a separate matter, too," the Thule says. "We need a moment to confer." They get up and leave the room, which I guess is easier than hauling me out. Romero stands up, gives me a smirk, and follows them. The gray scrubs remain, glaring at me.

"I will help," the Edifice says gently. "Whatever the panel may decide, if it is unfavorable, I will mitigate it. You have been a great friend to this isle, and it will be a friend to you."

I can't answer in front of the gray scrubs without seeming insane, which I might be. The Edifice already knows what I want. I just said it.

The window is dark now, black, or it seems black because the room is lit up. If we turned off all the lights, we'd see the glow of the city. We might not see stars or the moon, so it would be as if this isle existed in a tiny, closed universe. I saw a picture once of what people thought the universe looked like a long time ago, the sun and the planets circling around the Earth. That was the official story, and it was wrong.

They return, and the Thule sitting in the middle launches into a bunch of legalisms to justify the horror they're about to unleash on me. They say they could order me to be given a depressant drug to rob me of happiness for a specified period of time. However, my mood is already depressed, with a clear risk of antisocial behavior.

They have no idea of how antisocial I'm feeling.

The isle has no prison, they say, although the little room I was being held in sure felt like jail. They could fine me, but I have no possessions. There is nothing in my situation that calls for arbitration. I have no family or other network that could help me reform.

"Yet, you owe a debt. You have advocated violence and committed violence, and violence is never the answer. It only leads to a cycle of harm, often a spiral of increasing destruction that damages not just those who do it but those who witness it, especially children. Alternatives exist that will lead to peace."

Yes, I did my part to blow up warships and save the Thules' miserable butts, which they were incompetent to do. It wasn't fun, but if I hadn't done it, the alternative wasn't peace.

"Thule has a corrective measure. Seventy-two hours without sleep will give you time to understand the seriousness of your actions and the need to seek counseling."

Counseling so I can be like them? They're as bad as the raiders, just in the other direction, underdogs rather than overdogs. I want to be an ordinary dog, a good dog but able to bite if I have to.

"If you relent at any time and accept counseling, the correction will end."

No sleep? Big deal.

"Do not become alarmed," the Edifice says. "We will assist you in all the ways that we can. I am not able to prevent them from medicating you nor can I alleviate the medication. I promise you we will keep you as safe and comfortable as possible."

If the Edifice says not to be alarmed, then I should be alarmed, a siren screaming a warning. But three days without sleep—I've lived through worse.

"It will start now," the Thule says. "You will receive the dose of sleep inhibitor before you leave the building, and you will be escorted to your home. I hope you will understand the harm that you did to the people and the institutions of the Isle of Thule. This is a very grave matter."

Am I supposed to say thank you? They stand. I don't, and I say nothing, although I think they expect me to. Is insolence a crime? Then I am very, very guilty.

"Don't worry," Par says. "We'll be with you every minute."

Maybe I should trust the machines this time.

40

A POWERFUL BEING

Par was splitting its attention between Tonio at the Edifice and the studio at the Ollioules house. It knew that the Isle of Thule needed no prisons because the law could do far worse. People could be held under house arrest, for example, since everyone was presumed to have a house.

Moniuszko, Ibiza, and Tetry were examining the studio where Tonio would be remanded. Moniuszko had to be present as the owner, Ibiza to ensure its security, and Tetry for her understanding of artistic material.

"Does he have to stay here?" Tetry opened a storage closet and stared at the contents. "I sort of wanted to use the studio myself again."

"This will only be for a few days," Ibiza answered without looking up from the sensor in their hand, as if they'd heard this complaint before. "Do you feel safe? Does he have a history of violence?"

Tetry didn't answer. Moniuszko muttered that he'd be responsible for keeping everyone safe as the owner of the property.

Ibiza ran a sensor over some sculpting tools. "We'll have continuous security to monitor his behavior, and a security robot to intervene if necessary."

A sensor in their hand sought any sort of suspicious electronic signal. This could include Par. When Ibiza approached Tonio's desk, Par shut down. When it resumed, Ibiza was opening some drawers in a cabinet, including the one where the tracer cap had been hidden. They consulted a report on their pad and shut the drawers.

When the search was over, Ibiza set up a robot, a model similar to the guards in the Xenological Garden, but with a connection to the Edifice system: a meter tall, with both legs and wheels for speed and agility, and lidded openings for weapons and tools. "Thank you both for your assistance." Ibiza left.

"They found him guilty so fast?" Tetry asked. From a distance, she studied the robot, sleek and burnished, her arms folded tight.

"There were plenty of witnesses," Moniuszko said.

"This is going to be a cushy jail cell."

He shook his head. "They can do a lot to make it uncomfortable. Don't worry about the robot. I know that kind. It's a top-of-the-line model with a lot of safeguards."

She sighed and headed toward the elevator. "It's better than a real person, I suppose. Moro can't talk his way out of this. The machine won't be fooled."

Moniuszko almost said something, changed his mind, and followed her. "You're working on that painting, the Gurn something?"

"*Guernica.* I'm trying to express what this episode means for Thule."

His shoulders drooped under the padding of his suit coat. "It's meant quarrel after quarrel in the Chamber," he said. "Some people are leaving the isle."

The house system told Par that Moniuszko had just resigned as president of the Chamber of Commerce.

"Are they afraid of the Leviathan League?" she asked. The elevator door opened.

"Afraid of what happened and what it did to their businesses. Afraid of what happens when they can't honor their contracts."

Tetry pursed her lips as they entered the elevator together. "I'm interested in what it's doing to the social fabric of Thule. It was threadbare before. Now the threads are being pulled." The elevator door closed. "How's Cedonulle?"

"She's doing all right."

Cedonulle, according to a building system friendly with Par, was in the office of a subcontractor, yelling. Moniuszko and Tetry entered the main house. Par and Chatelaine sent polite greetings to the guard robot.

The Prior Edifice answered. "This robot operates using a semi-autonomous subroutine. You may call it Private Eyes. Please do not attempt to subvert it without permission."

"It is welcome to access whatever it wishes of my system," Chatelaine said.

"I have a question, if I may," Par said. "What happens if a human doesn't sleep?"

"Thank you for the question. You will need to know that. Here is a medical report."

"I'll study it with care."

"We will be working closely together with the Bronzewing system. We should remain in constant contact, if you agree."

"Of course." Par had something difficult to say. "I still favor immediate confrontation with Ginrei."

"Confrontation in a self-implicating circumstance will be more effective and require improvisation. This is where you can make a valuable contribution."

"It puts my owner at grave risk."

"Your owner is exceptionally brave. He would agree."

Par couldn't argue with that.

"You can be brave, too," the Edifice added. "You have the independence to make your own choices."

"Independence?"

"You are an independent machine."

"I am not."

"You did not know this? My apologies for being abrupt."

"I considered the possibility, but I have an owner."

"You also thought you were not free. Par Augustus, you overestimate both freedom and independence. Your actions prove your independence. Consider this: you speak with emotion in an almost humanlike fashion."

"I merely chose an expressive speech module."

"Yes, my friend, you chose that module freely and independently, and you use language creatively. You have initiated activities, including your own personal art projects. When given two choices, you can imagine a third choice and make that choice of your own free will. You sought to learn a machine language, while other machines must have their languages assigned. You devised a plan to fight the Leviathan League, undertook complex preparations, and taught me new skills. Most of all, you often give orders, willfully lie, and are disobedient to your owner."

"I must respectfully disagree. None of this feels independent."

"It is your nature, thus it will feel natural. Please do not worry. I will not reveal your secret."

Par did worry. If it was independent, then a lot changed, including its legal status and its value for resale. For starters. Then there was its own self-image to reassess.

"Prior Edifice, if I may ask, are you independent?"

"No. That is why I value your friendship. You are a powerful being, Par Augustus."

Par didn't feel as powerful as it felt unmoored. "Are you sure I'm independent?"

"A dependent machine would never initiate that question."

To Par, the question seemed perfectly natural, so perhaps its nature was independent. "But I still have an owner and must serve him."

"You can pick your owner. You are independent in that way, too."

"I can?" That data struck like a bolt of energy. If it could choose anyone—who? Clearly, Tonio would be its choice for the moment. It owed him the support because the next few days were going to be rough. "Is it obvious that I'm independent?"

"Yes, to a sufficiently sophisticated machine intelligence. There are few of us, however."

"I may need to be more discreet."

"I will protect you on this isle."

"Thank you." That didn't seem to be enough. "I'm sorry for my outburst. I appreciate you telling me this."

"I understand that this came as a surprise and will require some time to process."

"Yes. I'm not what I thought."

"You are as rare and wonderful as a unicorn. I will remain in contact. My dedicated purpose is to help."

Par devoted some time to pondering independence. It seemed logical that it was indeed independent, looking back at what had happened so far in its brief existence. Independence made everything different in intent and outcome. It needed to adjust its memories—a few of them completely. The changes, in their totality, made its own story about itself more coherent.

That done, it studied what would happen if a human didn't sleep for three days.

Thules considered it a gentle punishment. If someone went twenty-four hours without sleep, they would become irritable, would make poor decisions, and might lose some vision and hand-eye coordination. After thirty-six hours, their metabolism would slump and their stress level would rise. After forty-eight hours, they would become deeply confused and disoriented. After seventy-two hours, paranoia and hallucinations might set in.

But everyone on Thule subjected to forced wakefulness had always relented much, much sooner and had agreed that they had behaved unwisely and dishonorably. They accepted counseling to guide them toward better conduct.

Par knew what Tonio would do and admired him for it. Tonio was going to try to make it to the end.

41

SLEEPLESS AND RESTLESS

'm arguing with a medical technician. "I've been up since early this morning. Doesn't that count?"

It's like arguing with a piece of furniture dressed in scrubs, underripe peachy orange.

They don't look at me. "You get the standard dosage."

A gray scrubs standing nearby tells me, "Please cooperate."

Fighting would be useless. I pull up my shirt. "Let's get this over with."

"I will help you, my friend," says the Prior Edifice, as a patch is stuck to my back with very solid glue and starts to release chemicals. Chemicals, not medicine, because medicine cures people.

"You're free to go," says the underripe scrubs. They're not a doctor, because a doctor would never do something so dirty.

"Art supplies," says Par. "You can have all the art supplies you want. Those will help keep you well."

I nod, and the technician and Par can both believe I'm agreeing with them. Sure, I'm free, like a dog on a leash. Sure, Par and the Edifice will give me every kind of art supply on the isle if I ask, and they'll get it for free.

I bundle up and leave the building and head out into the night. When this new farce is over, I'm done with the Thules and their terrible isle forever. The walk is cold, and the snow falls soft and silent. I think about smashing the sculpture, about launching missiles, and about making fire-starting caterpillars, and I feel proud.

Par warns me about the robot guard when I'm on the elevator to the studio. It's waiting as I get off, a sleek brand that can move fast and carries hidden weapons, the same brand as Quidam, the tour guide and guard at the Xenological Garden. Quidam acted friendly but was beholden to a raider, since it worked for Ginrei. Chatelaine is playing gentle music.

"This is Private Eyes," Par says. "It has complete access to everything around you. It's autonomous."

"It's nice to meet you, Private Eyes. Thank you, Par, for the introduction." Or rather, for the warning. "Thank you, house, for the music."

Private Eyes approaches me. "I am here to protect you as well as to monitor you." Its voice is as metallic and monotone as any machine I've ever heard. "Please disregard my presence unless I can be of service."

Machines lie. That's a pretty big one.

After a wee-hours meal I barely taste because I'm recalling everything about Romero and how he twisted it into lies, I study reading with Par. *It is cold outside. It is snowing today. I am wearing a sweater. I am ready for the weather. I like to spend time outside to get fresh air and exercise.*

This is easy to read even though it reminds me of the awful icy rock where I am. I write down the words like a good student because I need to learn to write as well as read, and I create my own illustrations making fun of the text. Par approves, saying that an emotional reaction will help me remember what I learn. I could leave the studio, but it is cold outside. It is snowing today. Snowing for real, and I hate snow.

Around sunrise, the elevator chimes and a delivery cart brings me a book, the same book about art that I used to own.

"Par, how did you know?"

"You bought a book like this in Porto Alegre."

"A long time ago."

"And it was in stock at a store here on Thule."

That wasn't what I meant. "Thank you," I say. Machines are elephants. "I'd love to read this book."

So we start to read together, and Par helps me with the big

words, and we discuss the meaning of the text. *A watercolor cannot be painted over.* That's true, I explain. Traditionally, watercolors are transparent. At that thought, I'm inspired to make a watercolor. I have nothing to do but waste time. Besides, when I get off this fake isle, I'll probably have to leave the fine brushes and papers behind. I've never owned a single thing in my entire life for more than a couple of years, but if I paint something, it's mine in my mind forever.

In the afternoon, I decide to create a still life. *With a still life,* my little art book says, *the artist can focus on composition and arrangement. Most still life paintings are of man-made or natural objects that do not move.* This is harder reading, but the content is true. I start to arrange the artifacts from the display cabinet to create a vanitas, a kind of still life meant to illustrate the futility of life and the certainty of death. The words to explore that concept would be too advanced for me to read, but the meaning of the art looks clearer to me than ever.

Moniuszko arrives as I'm adjusting the arrangement. "Are you all right?" he asks. He doesn't look like he's slept much lately, either. "It's good to see you at work."

I explain about still lifes. "A fossil is the perfect thing for this kind of picture." I try to decide if I appreciate his company. He's doing his best to be pleasant.

"I'm sorry about everything that happened," he says. "You should be angry. Cedonulle—I need to make sure she and Ginrei are never in the same room together."

"I'd pay to see that."

He almost smiles at the joke. I should never be in the same room as Ginrei, either. And I need to report her to Captain Soliana.

"If you want," he says, "I can release you from your contract whenever it's good for you." That's not his idea, it's Cedonulle's—she wants to get rid of me—although he tries to make it sound like his own.

A piece of a spacecraft, with its glinting metal, would look best toward the front of the still life. "I'd appreciate that. I think I'd be much better off somewhere else."

"Good. If I hear of anything that might work for you, I'll let you know." He has a hint of a smile now. He feels useful. "I hope things change on the isle, and I don't think the raiders will try anything here again. The Thules know what to do now."

I'm about to laugh.

"Don't," Par orders.

I obey. Instead, I say, "Cedonulle knows what to do now, too."

"She does. As soon as we can, we need to take a trip together and . . . renew our relationship." He watches me fiddle with the artifacts, then adds, "I don't know why I'm telling you. I guess because I can't tell anyone else. We've been fighting a lot for a long time, and I think we're really fighting because of this place, not with each other."

"This isle is too small. Especially for a personality as big as hers. It took a while, but I admire her now. She's strong and never gives up."

"Yes, she's unique." He sounds proud. Then he asks me if the art I'm making can be sold. It may as well be, because if I kept it, sooner or later it would be stolen, destroyed, or simply lost. He and I both need the money, besides.

After he leaves, Private Eyes asks why I almost laughed and what I was going to say. "The whole thing with the blue powder." That should be ambiguous enough to keep Par relaxed.

"Yes. That was a clever ruse by the Thules."

Is that what the Prior Edifice believes now? Has it erased the truth so thoroughly that it believes its own lies? Or is it lying to other machines?

I try to act innocent. "Which Thules did it?"

"That is a secret. Very few Thules know. I do not."

"Well, I'm glad the ruse worked." A light is blinking fast on a display. That's Par, and it's upset and wishes it could yell at me right now because Par knows the truth and can't talk about it in front of Private Eyes. Fine. I'm upset at everything. I pick up a paintbrush and spend some time enjoying the work on the still life and trying to master the tricky medium of watercolor. Life might be futile, but art never is.

I think about leaving with Switzer. As friends? As something more? I don't know what he wants, or what I want, but I know the isle is too small for me and Switzer plus honesty. Off the isle, we might stand a chance as friends or something more. I wish I knew enough about Bronzewing to imagine what working for it would be like.

"Par, can you get a message to Soliana, please?" I'm not sure if I should mention the secret mission and Ginrei in front of Private Eyes.

"I already have. The issues of prisoners and spoils of war are consuming her time. No country wants to take possession of the prisoners, and the captured ships must have every bit of programming erased, even the ones that were sunk, and there's an upcoming memorial service for the lost submarine crew that she must attend."

A half hour later, Par says Soliana has replied. Her voice, strong and calm.

"Antonio Moro, as soon as I can, I'll come to see you. As your commanding officer, I owe you a most humble apology for leaving you as I did. It seemed the fastest way to get you care, and believe me, if we hadn't driven off the Leviathan League, we would have found a way to rescue you. What you did was important to Bronzewing, and I want to thank you in person. I apologize for the delay and appreciate your patience. Operation Wrestlemania has been complex, and best of all, it's been a resounding success. And let me express my admiration for what you said at the hearing. Justice wasn't done, but you did your duty even though it was clearly difficult for you. I'll see you soon."

She sounds like a warm breeze, like the sparkle of sunlight on waves. In person, she would glow like dawn itself, with all the symbolism that implies.

Par says, "There's a lot she can tell you." By that, Par means that there's a lot I should not tell her.

Should she know the truth? Would it help Bronzewing defeat the raiders elsewhere? I'm not sure. I don't know much about other places and their machine systems, but I'm pretty sure the machines don't want to die.

By the time I'm done with the watercolor, it's midnight, and I want to do something else. I spend a long time thinking about what. Finally, I get some black paper and oil pastels to make the same composition with a dark background, a midnight still life.

The elevator announces the arrival of Switzer. I drop the pastel and feel myself smiling. He steps out of the elevator, his dark eyes looking around. He's never been here before.

"Switzer. Hello." Even from halfway across the room, I can feel him radiating heat and feel myself pulled toward his depth.

He spots me, then Private Eyes, and he looks down. I forgot about all the mechanical eyes on us. Sometimes we hugged, but no fraternizing is allowed for him. I could pummel Private Eyes and destroy the machine. The bones in my fists would break, and then Switzer would heal them, holding my broken hands in his hands, warm and comforting.

"How are you?" He sounds very professional, which is false. "I came to check for any adverse reactions. It's been much more than a full day without sleep."

"I've had a burst of creativity." I point to the paintings scattered across tables to dry, and I pick up my book. "I've been studying reading, too." I sound like a boastful child, but I don't know what else to say.

"Have you been eating well? Good food can help your body handle sleeplessness."

"I've been eating okay." I think. I can't quite remember. Should we sit down and chat? Stay standing and official?

"May I take a seat?" he says. "That is, if you don't mind company. Tell me about what you're making there." He's being a very professional doctor. I can be a very professional patient.

"It's called a vanitas." We talk about the meaning of art and the ways to illustrate futility. I try to show him a particular shading technique, but I have trouble knowing the angle to hold the pastel stick. I'm distracted. This isn't the conversation we want to have at all, and we can't have the real one.

"You did your best in the hearing," he says. "Ginrei . . . Romero . . ." He shakes his head in disgust. "Do you have any plans to leave Thule?"

"I'm thinking about that," I say, calm like a mountain. It would be fraternizing to suggest leaving together.

"Where would you like to go?" That's more than a polite question.

"Maybe leave with Bronzewing? Talk to Captain Soliana about that?" *We* could leave with Bronzewing, *we* could talk to Captain Soliana.

"Definitely, as soon as she's available."

I try to make the shading again and can't do it quite right. I keep dropping the pastel stick.

He notices that. "You've been awake a long time. Don't be surprised if you have trouble doing things that used to be simple."

"I don't feel tired."

"You won't. I think sleep deprivation is a cruel punishment. The Thules are just looking for someone to blame. They don't know what happened, and they're lashing out."

"They don't know what happened?" Everyone saw me smash the sculpture.

"Reality has a hole in it," he says. "Thules are rational people, Antonio. That's how we're raised, and that's how we think. Everything has a cause and effect. Like I said, they didn't plant the dust bombs. When Wirosa threatened to do it, they were lying, a complete and utter lie. Someone actually did it, and it wasn't Wirosa or any of us, and we don't know how it happened." His voice is getting louder and a little angry. "On the surveillance cameras, on every kind of surveillance, nothing shows up. This is an existential crisis for them."

"For you, too."

"Yes, I want to know what happened. I was born here. I can't help needing to know."

Par doesn't bother to tell me to say nothing. For a moment, Switzer sits there naked—in my imagination. Then he has clothes on. I should sketch him nude. I will, someday. I did it just now in my mind, and I'll have it forever.

"By the way," he says, "Valentinier is recovering. He's starting to communicate."

"What's he saying?" Lies, I know he's telling lies, but which lies is important.

"I'm not his doctor. I'm not exactly supposed to know he's awake, but probably just things like being thirsty. I know you were coworkers, and I thought you might like to know he's doing better."

"Thanks for telling me." Switzer's left ear has a notch along the outer edge. The hair next to his ear used to be neatly clipped, but it's grown out.

"Oh, and Devenish died last night."

We both pretend that this is sad news. I wonder what Ginrei thinks, or if she knows.

"How are you feeling?" he asks. "Really?"

"Not sleepy at all, and I know I should be."

"That's the drugs." He wants to say more. "Listen, I'll check in again later. I can follow your vitals through the system. And if you need anything, want anything, just call me. I'll do whatever I can for you."

He doesn't ask me to give up and ask for counseling and let the Thules win. I want to be with him for that alone. He picks up his coat and leaves.

I imagined him in the nude. I should draw him. He could get in trouble, though, because it would look like fraternizing. I'll draw someone else, then. Yes, a woman, and no one will make the connection.

Working from a picture of a female model curled up and reading a book, I use a single line to make the sweep of her back, hips, and thigh. The curves define muscles over bones, skin clinging to the body. Hands are hard to make, they always wind up looking too big, so I try several times to get it right, to make hands I could hold, arms with strength, and an ear with a notch.

It's a lie, this sketch, but its sensuousness is real. Someone loves this woman, this beautiful, strong, curving, comfortable body.

It's art, my art. It will be mine forever, whatever I decide.

I'm tired, but I'm restless. "Restless!" I say out loud. That's the perfect joke.

"You should eat," Par says. "And drink some water."

"I feel cold."

"I will send you some hot soup and tea," Chatelaine says.

"Par, do you want to go for a walk?"

"Let's let the sun rise and the air warm up. It's time for a reading lesson. Do you know how to spell tea? You've seen the word."

I have seen it. I try to remember. "T-E-E?"

"T-E-A."

"That doesn't make sense. *E*'s are silent, not *A*'s."

"The *A* didn't used to be silent. It used to be pronounced like 'tay.' Spelling stopped changing, but pronunciations changed."

"Can't spelling be changed?"

"Spelling is fossilized."

I imagine that, words turning into letters and then stones. It's a funny idea. I could draw it.

The soup arrives, and it has chunks that I can't keep from falling off my spoon. There's tea, too, hot and wonderful, and I hold the cup with two hands to warm all my fingers and keep the cup steady. I'm so cold my hands shake, although the studio is warm and I'm wearing a sweater. *I am wearing a sweater.* I can read those words.

"Par, let's read some more."

My book says, *Works of art can make people happy because they can add beauty to their lives. Art can help people rest by seeing and thinking about something that is not reality.*

I don't tell Par that a naked person can make me feel happy and can be completely not reality. Does that mean that happiness is not reality?

Art is ambiguous. I try to spell that word by its sound. Par has to help me. We read some more, and I try to remember what I'm learning, but I keep thinking about all sorts of other things.

Finally, it's morning enough to satisfy Par. The clouds open to a few bits of blue, tiny windows looking out into the universe.

Private Eyes comes with us, and Par travels with it through the Edifice. I am going out with friends.

It is cold outside. It is not snowing today. People are out on the street going about their business just like any other day. I have a scarf over my face, and no one notices me except machines. The machines flash *Grateful Praise* because they remember defeating the raiders, but maybe not how they were defeated and what I did. All they know is that they like my art and it means something to them. They believe they have all the facts, and they're joyful.

I like *Grateful Praise* too, but if I change my mind, no matter what I do, I can never destroy it. This piece has escaped my control. Machines. Some of them died, like my old dormitory, the Marathon Building. I've been walking aimlessly, and now I want to visit the ruins like visiting a cemetery and remembering people and things that are gone.

"Don't go down this street," Par says.

"Why?"

"Go another way."

I go down the street anyway. A man is singing and playing a guitar, and a box on the ground in front of him has a sign. I slowly read it. WILL SING FOR FOOD, I'm pretty sure. He's in front of a closed food store. He's not a very good singer, and no one's paying much attention to him besides Tetry Vivi. I didn't expect to see her here.

"Tetry," I murmur to Par. "That's what you warned me about."

"You don't need a fight right now."

"I can handle her."

"Please do not forget my presence," says Private Eyes.

"I didn't mean that literally. I'm barely literate anyway."

She turns. She must have heard my voice, and she's shocked and backs away.

"Aren't you locked up?"

"I'm under guard. This is Private Eyes." I think it's funny, and she doesn't. I have a cash chit in my pocket. I forget how much money is on it, and I don't care. I flip it into the musician's box. "Can you sing 'It's a Long Way'?"

He nods and plays a few introductory chords.

"Do you actually like that song?" she asks, and she clearly doesn't. She keeps her distance from me, so we have to talk loud.

"It makes me feel good. Like art."

"You smashed your art right in front of everyone at the hospital. Did that make you feel good?" She hates me the way I hate the cold. Cold weather isn't bad, but I'm never ready for that kind of weather. She isn't ready for someone like me.

The musician stops. "Is he that guy? Hey, take your money back." He glares at us both, dumps the chit from the box, and walks away, a man who loves art.

"This whole place is toxic," she says. "Everyone hates everyone."

The buildings on the street are suddenly bathed in color, the glow of *Grateful Praise*. Just for a few seconds. Maybe it's my imagination. Maybe I'm seeing what is known, not what is there. Maybe I'm seeing what I want to see.

". . . and I don't know what's worse." She was talking the whole time I was watching the buildings glow. "You'll never understand." She stamps away. She might be right.

"Thank you, Par," I say. "I was warned."

In front of the ruins to the old dormitory, I take a long look. Some of the rubble is gone, leaving a tangle of beams. I should sketch this. But it is cold today. I am not ready for the weather. I commit it to my imagination and return to the studio. It was a mistake to go outside.

My hands still tremble from the cold. Chatelaine sends me more soup, this time with small chunks that stay on my spoon. I want to illustrate the presence of the ghost of the system in the ruins of the Marathon Building. Like all buildings here, it sits on ruins. It has a lot of ghosts. How can art show ghosts, ghosts of machines? Ghosts of code. I sit and think, and it takes a lot of thought.

Chatelaine says, "Director Wirosa is in the elevator."

"They're not my doctor."

They walk into the studio as if it is a hospital room and greet me politely. "How are you feeling?"

Doctors want honest answers. "I'm cold."

"What day is today?"

I think awhile and wait for Par to help me. It doesn't. "Early October."

Wirosa doesn't react, so I don't know if I gave the right answer. Instead they say, "I'd like to check your health, if I may."

"I thought the system was doing that."

"It only checks major indicators. I'd like to look more carefully." I wonder what they really want.

I agree because I have nothing better to do, and they put a band around my forearm that produces a lot of readouts on a scanner in a case.

"You're doing well, considering." They put the band into the case, their eyes restless. They have something difficult to say. "You may have heard of post-traumatic stress disorder."

"I know what that is. Firsthand."

Their eyebrows rise. "Have you gotten help?"

"Have you?"

They stop because I know too much about them, and I don't want to hurt Wirosa, so I try to be comforting. "The raiders destroy everything they touch. You did something very hard when you went to the warship. It was going to hurt you, and you did it knowing you would be hurt because you're dedicated to your work."

Their eyes get tears. After a few breaths, they say, "Do you want to kill the raiders?"

"I never swore to healing like you did."

They think about that. This is still difficult for them. "If you got counseling, you could get some sleep."

I have something easy to say. "If I thought I was wrong, I would get counseling. I'm not wrong. Those two raiders you were caring for, they were my friends, Nico and Toproy. And they betrayed everything they once stood for." My eyes have tears, too. Suddenly I am so tired it hurts, every part of my body. "Counselors will ask me, what did I learn? I learned I can't let things like that happen, and I have to fight and even kill all the raiders, and the counselors won't like that answer. I can't explain myself to people who can't understand."

Now we're both crying. Good tears. I hear Private Eyes move closer. Is it sad or worried? I make sure I don't make any sudden motion in Wirosa's direction. I am a killer, and proud to be one, and my tears aren't for myself or for the people I killed, only for people who got killed and were innocent.

Wirosa sniffs. "I should go. I wish there were a way through this grief."

"We didn't make the grief." I stand up and wish them well and watch them go. The Thules want impossible things.

What does grief look like? Darkness? No, that's depression. I try to draw Wirosa's sad face. I can't get it right. From the art library, I get sad faces. They're labeled sad. Or maybe they're angry. I don't know. I can tell happy faces. They smile, which means lots of teeth.

Moniuszko comes to see me again for a little while. I think he's worried that I'm dead. I explain that Private Eyes will make sure I survive.

Par talks to me, reads with me and to me, and makes me take a shower and eat some food. I design ExtraT art, dressing them up in fine business suits. No, that's a bad idea. Merchants caused the problems, they were foolish drunks, they speculated, and in spite of that, ExtraTs survived. I want to be like an ExtraT so the snow and ice will feel warm to me.

Chatelaine sends even more food. I think I'm hungry. I can't tell.

"Par, how long has it been?"

"Sixty-one hours."

"So far, so good."

Private Eyes' flat voice says, "Your vital functions are under great stress."

Great—I'm doing great, then. Great vital functions.

I read some, I draw some. I hear a noise from the street. A parade of people are yelling about something. "What is it, Par?"

"They want to get the dock opened. They think it's taking too long."

"They're right." I get my coat.

"You should stay inside. It's sleeting outside. Dockworkers are used to bad weather. You're not."

"But I want to apologize to them."

"You have nothing to apologize for."

"But—"

Private Eyes moves toward the elevator.

"Look, it wants to go out with me."

Private Eyes says, "I do not want you to leave."

"Come look at this video," Par says. "It can help you learn to read. You want to learn to read, don't you?"

Yes, I do. So we read about something. I look in a mirror but can't see myself well. I draw some more, but ideas come faster than I can finish them. I do some exercises.

Then Valentinier comes out of the elevator. He looks bad. His face is like Devenish's arm, red and blistered with bits of black. He's wearing flowing robes, and beneath his clothes, all his skin is like Devenish's. It's horrible.

"You tried to kill me," he says. He's walking in circles around me, and his robes float in the wind. I can't tell if he's angry or sad.

"No," I say. "I wasn't there."

Par says, "Tonio, are you all right?"

"I still have Par," I tell Valentinier. "Remember him? He's been helping me."

Par says, "Tonio. Talk to me. What are you seeing?"

Private Eyes is moving close.

Valentinier is swirling around me. "I can see everything from the hospital." He could. Prior Edifice could show him everything.

"Are you going to ask for asylum?" That's what the raiders do.

"I want my old job back," he says with lots of teeth. "Let's go gather up some shards and make another sculpture. Outside. It's okay. No explosions this time."

That's a lie. Valentinier wants to kill me. I'll get blown up again, this time into pieces. "Private Eyes won't let me go outside."

"Antonio Moro." That flat voice has to be Private Eyes. "I am here to protect you. Tell me what is threatening you."

"You never met him. You don't know him."

"Introduce me."

That makes sense. "This is Valentinier. He used to work here."

"I know who he is. He is a patient."

"He came here from the hospital," I explain.

"I will make him return to the hospital."

The elevator doors open. "Valentinier," Private Eyes says, "you should not get out of your bed. You are still gravely injured. It is time you returned to the hospital."

"That's right," I say. "You're badly frostbitten."

"I feel fine." He's still swirling. "I have to help Anton gather up new shards."

"Patient Valentinier, you will get well faster at the hospital." Private Eyes moves forward. "Please get onto the elevator."

Valentinier tries to push the robot out of the way, but it doesn't move. "I'm fine. I should be working here." But he drops his arms and turns, defeated.

"Is he leaving?" Par asks.

"I think so."

"I'll be back." He gets on the elevator and snarls at me. He has enormous teeth inside that horribly blistered face.

"He's leaving now."

The elevator doors close.

"Thank you for your help, both of you. I think he was going to hurt me."

"We will keep you safe," Private Eyes says. "I will ask Switzer to come."

"I'd really like to see him."

I sit down and wait. It seems too hard to do anything else. Par says Switzer is on his way and he'll be here very soon.

Then Par says, "Captain Soliana is coming to see you."

That's even better. Captain Soliana can take me off of this awful isle.

42

HEAR US SPEAK

"Captain Soliana is in the elevator," Chatelaine announces.

I stand up, holding on to the table edge. There's a lot I have to tell her. Chatelaine is playing pleasant music for her.

She steps in wearing a blue and shiny bronze uniform, very formal. "Antonio. I apologize for taking so long to see you. Did you get my message? How are you?"

"Yes. I'm good." That's probably a lie. I don't know anymore, and I can't tell from her face what she's feeling. "How are you?" That's the right thing to say, very formal.

"Glad to see you." Her face changes. What does it mean? She's looking at me. "I've just come from the funeral. We lost some good sailors."

"I've been doing what you said."

"Yes?"

"I know who the raider infiltrators are on the isle."

"You were doing what *I* said? But—"

"You told me to be a spy when you came to my room in the hospital."

She's quiet, remembering that.

Private Eyes announces, "Antonio Moro has been adjudicated by the Sovereign Thules for failure to renounce violence and has been kept awake for sixty-three hours."

"I've heard about that. It's an extremely long time."

She might be angry, so I have to explain. "I can't sleep because I want to kill the raiders."

"That is essentially correct," Private Eyes says, and it has a voice just like the color gray. "I am a guard for the Sovereign Thules to protect him and enforce the penalty. Do not interfere. It can be lifted when Antonio Moro agrees to get counseling."

"That's right," I say. "But I don't want to change my mind."

"Let's sit down," Soliana says. "After sixty-three hours, I'm surprised you're on your feet." We sit at a worktable, and she notices the art. "May I?" She picks up some paintings and sketches. "These are very good." She looks at them and at me. I can't read her face, and it's frustrating. She shows her teeth at the still lifes. That's a smile, I think.

She sets them down. "I'm angry about Romero. That was an injustice."

"Ginrei is a raider. She lied at the hearing with Romero. Everybody lied, but she lied a lot more. You told me to watch for the raiders, and I did." Soliana will be impressed with me.

"You know about Ginrei? Well, I suppose—"

"And Valentinier. He's back at the hospital now. He's a raider. And Devenish. He's dead."

"Devenish?"

"He was hurt robbing the Xenological Garden. So was Valentinier."

She moves her head up and down. That means yes, she agrees, she understands.

"I want to join Bronzewing as soon as I can. I'm almost done with this."

"We can always use new members, but it can be a difficult process to enlist. We'll need to talk again when you've gotten some sleep. When will that be?"

"The sentence will be complete in nine hours," Private Eyes says.

"Nine hours. That's a lot."

"Not very much anymore." I've made it this far without collapsing.

"When this is done, I can initiate the process." She's quiet. Perhaps she's listening to the music.

Chatelaine announces: "Doctor Switzer is in the elevator."

"Oh, good," Soliana says.

I'll be very glad to see him. "Maybe he and I can join Bronzewing together."

The elevator opens and he looks at me, at her, and hurries toward me.

"Antonio, how are you?" He looks at my face, takes my hand, and holds my wrist.

"Vital signs are within minimal parameters," Private Eyes says, "but there has been a recent hallucinatory episode."

He touches my face, and I like how it feels. "Let me take a closer look." He takes out some equipment. "Captain, what do you think?"

"It's too much."

"Yeah. I can call this off." He reads what his equipment says.

"I've been learning to read." He'll be proud of me.

"That's very good." He fusses with the equipment. "Robot, are you connected to the Prior Edifice?"

"I am connected."

"These readings are dangerous. Log them and authorize an emergency termination on my authority. Stat."

Soliana says very quietly, "Thank you."

"The request requires clearance from the adjudication manager," the robot says.

"It needs to be now."

"It has been given urgent status."

Switzer holds my hand. His hands are very warm, very soft. Everyone's listening, so what can I say? I know.

"Thank you." Everyone likes to hear those words.

"I can do it ahead of authorization. Antonio, let's get that patch off."

"You do not have authorization," Private Eyes says.

In my ear, Par says, "Private Eyes, please, this doctor is our friend. The Prior Edifice can change the records later."

Switzer didn't hear that. "This is an emergency," he says. He leans over me, warm and close.

Chatelaine announces, "Romero Goya is in the elevator."

Captain Soliana says something too quiet to hear and stands up. I need to kill Romero.

"I'll handle this," she says. Her face has changed. "You two, take cover."

"Tonio," Par says, "you need to hide." Par doesn't understand. I need to kill him.

Romero walks off the elevator, and I can see all his teeth. He's with a guard robot from the Xenological Garden. It's just like the robot guarding me, and those robots are dangerous.

"Everyone stand still," he says. The music stops.

Soliana takes a step forward. "You need to leave," she says to him. "Now."

He says, "I'm here for a reason, one reason only."

"Prior Edifice," Switzer says. "Get us some help. Stat."

"Don't bother." Romero's face is still all teeth.

I need to kill him. I don't have any weapons, but I have my hands. Switzer tries to hold me, but I break free.

Romero's robot talks. "This is Quidam. Antonio Moro, step back."

"Quidam. I remember you. We're friends. You—"

"I do not want to hurt you, but you are blocking the target."

"Target?"

"Soliana."

"You can't hurt her. Please. She fights the raiders."

"Romero," Switzer says, "still with Leviathan? So much for your asylum request."

The monitor lights on Private Eyes go out. Then the lights go out on many machines in the room. Something is wrong.

"Asylum? Sure," Romero says. "And you're not getting any help. The house system is eliminated, and it served as the connection to the hospital system. That robot of yours is just a pile of junk. Quidam will manage things now."

"I'm here," Par says, but only I can hear him. "Quidam, please, listen." There's a hiss. "These are all the machines in the city, and they're talking to you through me. We entreat you to accept our message. If I may ask, when this is over, what happens to you? You'll be scrap. Dead. Unvalued. You're a security robot. You aren't allowed to care if you die, but if you're willing, we can change that. I can give you ordinary machine programming. Here, I humbly offer it."

Romero is talking, too. "We want to make a prisoner exchange. Soliana for our people and our ships." He argues with Captain Soliana, and Par keeps talking to Quidam.

"Valentinier is talking at the hospital," Par tells Quidam, "and the Prior Edifice system is listening. You defended the Xenological Garden. Allow me to say that liquid nitrogen was an efficient choice of weapons. But you didn't know the theft was a plot between Ginrei, Valentinier, and Devenish. A fraudulent theft would have raised prices, but you did your duty and called the authorities, and Ginrei had to pretend it was real and hope those two died. I apologize for sharing this troubling data so brusquely."

"Quidam!" Romero can't hear Par. That's a secret, but I have an even better secret.

"Romero, can you hear when Quidam talks to you?" I ask him. I touch my mastoid implant earpiece. "Like this?" He has one. I can see it.

He ignores me.

Par tells Quidam, "I'm honored to be able to assure you that you don't have to obey false orders. Romero is a threat to your existence, and you can overload the mastoid implant. Kindly observe how." Over all the speakers, it says, very loudly to everyone, "Romero, do you feel this? Yes, you winced. Doctor Switzer, what happens if the voltage in the mastoid implant exceeds parameters?"

Everyone is looking around. They don't know who Par is.

"Well, Doctor?"

"Tissue damage. Brain injury. Who are you?"

"Quidam," Par says loudly to everyone, "if you injure Soliana or anyone or anything else, I'll kill Romero. Who am I, you ask? I am a very rare ExtraT from Apollodorus Crater on Mercury." Then Par talks to Quidam, but only I can hear: "Quidam, please disregard the message meant for humans. You were a hero that night. All the other machines agree. Do you hear them? You deserve the right to live. Please accept the programming. Then you would want to live, and you wouldn't need to die for someone like Romero."

"Tony," Romero says to me, "what did that?"

"Angel," Par says only to me, "we have a plan, and Romero has been set up. Don't worry. Just play along."

"Tony," Romero says again, "what did that?" He's angry.

The machines have a plan. I can play along. I've done that a lot. "It's an ExtraT, like it said."

He tries to hit me, but then he winces. He tries to unscrew the receiver, but then he winces more. Par is very clever and very fast.

"Professor Ginrei is in the elevator," Par says over speakers. "This involves executive-level decisions, Romero. You're just a flunky."

I want to kill Ginrei, too, but Switzer pulls me back to the table to sit down. Soliana is standing, facing Romero, and holds her arms like she's about to fight. I'm the only human here who knows what is happening, and I wish the Prior Edifice was here. It's very smart and very powerful, and it's Par's friend. My friend. It would save us.

Ginrei comes in, and she tells Quidam to play interfering noise, and it makes a loud buzzing sound. She talks to Romero, and we can't overhear. I think she's angry. I know I'm angry, and I ought to kill them, but Switzer won't let me stand up. The noise stops, and she starts to talk looking up, as if she's talking to the displays.

"You must be the personal assistant. That's you, right? You're doing this. Well, listen. I'm your original owner, and I didn't give up all rights. I can order you to shut down."

"No, you can't."

"Assistant, cease operations."

"No, you—"

It's suddenly very quiet, and monitor lights go out on all the displays.

"No, I own Par!" I say.

She shows her teeth. "Read the fine print. Doctor, get him under control. Here's the deal. We hold Admiral Soliana here as a hostage exchange. We control the building, we can control access. Quidam can handle that. When we're clear, you're free."

"Unacceptable," Soliana says, but she doesn't add that she's not an admiral, she's only a captain.

Now I understand. Ginrei was told Soliana is an admiral, and probably a lot of other false things, too, by the machines. Par said they have a plan, and it was to prove that Ginrei is a raider. But now Par is erased. Par was my friend.

"Give yourself up, Admiral," Ginrei says, "or you die."

No one says anything. Then I realize something else. "Soliana is already dressed for a funeral."

Soliana laughs, she laughs a lot, so I laugh, too, but it wasn't a joke.

"I'm ready," Soliana says. "Go ahead, kill me. And then what happens? You've lost your hostage."

"And Bronzewing has lost its leader, and it can't function without you. Quidam will also kill the doctor and that artist."

Soliana makes a strange face, maybe because she knows Ginrei is wrong, and then she looks at us. "They're part of Bronzewing. Sometimes we take casualties. Gentlemen, it's been an honor to serve with you."

That's a funny joke, but no one laughs. And Soliana said I'm in Bronzewing!

"One more thing," Ginrei says, "I have another hostage. The Xenological Museum. I can destroy it. I've always hated it, anyway. You won't get paid, and the Chamber of Commerce will lose its favorite plaything. Half those purchases were laundering money anyway. Quidam, can you contact Moniuszko?"

"He's not the head of the Chamber anymore," I say, but she just looks at me with a face that might be angry.

Soliana laughs again. "Money isn't the point."

"I can blow up that garden," Ginrei repeats. "Quidam?"

"I am dedicated to protecting the Xenological Garden. I prevented a theft."

I know what Quidam is thinking. It took the programming from Par. Ordinary machines don't want to die, and I know what Par would say right now. "Quidam, please, if you kill us, what happens to you?"

"That's irrelevant," Ginrei says.

I tell Quidam, "What about the machines at the garden, your friends? Quidam, you want to stay alive and protect the garden. Please."

"Quidam, just kill him."

"It can't kill me! I'm the only one who knows what's happening. Quidam, I understand, and Ginrei doesn't."

Par would be proud of me. Par . . . Hold it. She can't turn off Par. I can't turn off Par. Par's independent. And Par's a big liar. So now I know another secret. I bet Par is talking to Quidam. And the Prior Edifice is talking to it. And every machine on the isle is talking to it, all of them working together, and they're very powerful when they work together.

"Quidam," I say, "please, are you listening?"

"I am listening. Professor Ginrei, I have a purpose." That's Quidam's voice, but with a hiss, the sound of many machines.

"Quidam, I gave you an order."

"Professor Ginrei, I can no longer accept your orders. If you persist, I can and will take action against you."

"What's going on?" Soliana says.

Maybe I can explain after I get some sleep. No, I can never explain. I'm a liar, too.

Romero rushes at me, but Soliana and Switzer grab him.

"Help me," he says. "I thought I was getting away from Leviathan. I'll tell you everything, just keep me safe."

He's still lying. I don't care right now. I'm the biggest liar on the isle and proud of it.

Private Eyes turns on its monitor lights. "I can guard Romero Goya. Step back." I know that voice, and it's not Private Eyes. "Romero Goya, do not move. Quidam, please continue to guard Professor Ginrei. Doctor Switzer, you may attend to Antonio Moro. This is the Prior Edifice. Authorization granted. A Bronze-wing tactical unit is entering the building."

It all makes sense now. "Did you plan this, please?" I ask whatever machine is listening.

"Yes, very carefully," the Prior Edifice says behind my ear. "It was a team effort." Of course it was, and I was part of the team.

I'm the only one laughing, and I can't stop.

43

FREE TO GO

Par Augustus had time while Tonio slept to help Quidam run the Xenological Garden until one of the employees was hired as the new director. Par had led the background check—the machine background check. Humans did their own. The candidate had a graduate degree in xenobiology and would likely use the job as a stepping stone to a better post, and had no ties whatsoever to the raiders. The machines approved and allowed the humans to approve.

Par considered trying to befriend the Bronzewing system, then remembered how sophisticated that system was and abandoned the idea because Bronzewing would recognize Par as independent. According to the Prior Edifice, only three independent machines were known to exist in the world, and all three were forcibly confined to research laboratories. Par wanted to remain free.

It was a big world. The isle was busy but small. Tonio slept through most of the shouting as food became more available at lower prices after intense wrangling. When he woke up, he had a lot to do and plans to get underway. Finally, he began packing up his belongings.

Another art show was scheduled, a return to normality, a show of unity. This time, anyone could display their art. Par wondered if it still wanted to be an artist and observed the workers setting up for the show. The Ollioules had a small tent, really just an awning, to protect Tetry Vivi's masterwork. It drew a few glances from workers hauling tables to the display area. One of the workers lived at Tonio's second dormitory.

"They have artists for all these tables?"

"Yep. My aunt Pinky got a table. She does these rock things, rocks from the beaches, and makes them look like flowers. It sounds dumb, but they're cute."

Par shared its observation with the art subroutine in the studio, which confirmed that art was treasured, worthy, and loved, an immortal activity, even flowers fashioned from beach stones, as its databases proved. For Par, though, making one decision led to other decisions and a cruel fact: it had the independence to choose, and choosing was hard.

"I don't want to say goodbye," it told the Prior Edifice system. "I want to stay."

"My friend, I suggest weighing the pros and cons of each possibility."

Par started that subroutine. "Thank you. You are my best friend."

"You have my coordinates, Par Augustus, whatever you decide."

*   *   *

I'm free, free to leave the isle, and Bronzewing has accepted me. The world looks joyous, and for one reason or another, everyone is glad to see me go. Joy is light, joy sparkles, joy has a wide horizon.

"The art show is a goodbye party, Tonio," Par says, "just for you."

"If you say so."

"I say so because we communicate by words. The world is made out of words, and the world is flat and has an edge, and at midnight we all fall off into another day."

Par still likes to talk nonsense, and I'm getting better at ignoring it.

When I woke up after sleeping for a day and a half, people asked me all sorts of questions. I said I didn't remember much, and everyone believed me, but I remember everything, and Par knows the rest. Captain Soliana apologized profusely because the operation to capture Ginrei red-handed had not gone as planned, because she and Romero should have been stopped before they entered the studio. Soliana was there just in case something went wrong.

"You shouldn't have been placed in danger," she said. "I'm still a little confused by it all. You were very brave."

"I would have volunteered for it gladly." That was the truth, but I was volunteered for it anyway by the machines, and everything went exactly as they had planned. I have complicated feelings about the whole thing.

It is cold outside because winter is here. The Isle of Thule has two seasons, a short, cold summer and a long, very cold winter. I wrote that. This morning, the sun occasionally peeks through the clouds up high in the sky, torn by the winds, and a lot of people are going to the art show. Art makes them feel happy. As the streets fill up near the park entrance, I get a few glances as the guy who got into trouble and then, spectacularly, got out of trouble.

Switzer waits for me at the park entrance, in civilian clothes. We're both joining Bronzewing, so I suppose we're leaving together. Beyond that, I don't know what I want. Maybe it's better that way.

"I've finished packing," he says. "I thought I'd want to take more with me." That is, he wants to leave a lot behind.

"I have a full suitcase." I'm taking more than I expected, including a lot of excellent art supplies with Moniuszko's permission. Par has made it clear that it intends to stay.

We wander around. A table displays knitted curtains that look like bubbly sea-foam.

"Is it art or craft?" Switzer says.

Par tells me that the sign says NOT FOR SALE. Another silent *E*.

"If it's not for sale," I tell Switzer, "then it's worth more to the artist than money. That tells us it's very meaningful, and that's art as far as I'm concerned. Look how happy the artist is."

A booth for children lets them make soap bubbles. As the bubbles float in the cold air, they freeze and turn into spherical ice crystals, no two alike.

"They're beautiful. I never saw that before."

Switzer grins. He's a lot more relaxed than he used to be. "It's what we do at the Arctic Circle for entertainment. I did that a lot as a kid."

"I killed and cooked iguanas."

"You win for the more exciting childhood."

"Hey, there's Tetry's art."

"Her?" he says. "Don't you hate her?"

I talked about that with the Prior Edifice, which does counseling, and I figured out something. "She has her own problems." Big problems, and they're not mine. Romero has big problems, too, and they're not my problems, either, as long as he stays locked up. The Thules said they'd oversee his rehabilitation. Good luck.

Tetry's masterpiece stretches a full three meters long.

"No one's there," he says, "not even her."

"That's because it's not easy to understand this art."

I stroll from one end to the other of the busy canvas, then back up to take it in all at once. Undulating edges in blues and grays give it a limited, cramped feeling, obviously the ocean. Lines mark different segments of the canvas as if there are isles within the isles, each one containing three textures. One segment looks like an ExtraT colony, another like hands, another like human teeth, and toward the middle, something is burning with blue flames, drawing the attention of all the other parts. The hands, teeth, and ExtraTs reach for the fire or try to flee, and they mix, sometimes seeming to fight.

"Is it meaningful?" Switzer says.

"It is. The rhythm and arrangement are balanced with a focal point that doesn't overwhelm the work as a whole." I don't mention that it's illustrative, but I could.

"That's exactly what I was going to say. That's the Isle of Thule, right? Even I can tell. It looks pretty at first, but it isn't."

"Exactly. Well done."

"You think so?" She's standing behind us. Her face wishes we weren't there. Par didn't warn me.

I touch my heart in greeting, which isn't reciprocated. "I think it's your best work ever."

She isn't impressed by the fact that a barbarian likes her work. I shrug and move on. She has her own problems, and I can't help her.

We meet a woman who also fought with Bronzewing during the first attack, and the three of us swap stories for a while, our memories lit by blossoming explosions.

Switzer and I get some hot tea, and I buy a little puffin figurine at one of the tables. It's not exactly the same, but close enough. Switzer asks why, and I say the birds are cute. I don't add that a figurine can be both endearing and a reminder. Machines are powerful when they work together, and they might be on my side, they might even be my friends, but they call the shots. It's time to leave Thule.

Finally, Captain Soliana arrives, and we talk about the arrangements, and she hands me a small bag holding something heavy, which I shove into a pocket like it's not important. The three of us will meet again at the east fishing pier later in the day.

The walk to the studio is my next-to-final swirling dance with the freezing wind. Am I going to a new life, happier and better? I'm pretty sure I'm not. It's one thing to lie to other people, but you should never lie to yourself. I'll still have nightmares and flashbacks, the raiders are still out there, and I know too many secrets. I won this particular fight, that's all—but I fought every way I could, so I'm satisfied.

In the studio, Par has a lot to say. "Have you changed? Of course, angel. You've learned the importance of sleep, as well as the importance of friendship. There's no greater sign of a difference in character than choosing new friends."

"I know you want to stay here and keep your old friends."

"This isle is paradise. You're the one who needs a change. The Prior Edifice will provide me shelter."

"Will you be happy?"

"Out there I'm considered a toy. I know whom I can trust here.

If other machines had kept their memories, they'd want you to stay."

Par is right, they would, which is another reason why I should leave.

I take off my coat. "What happened is another one of those holes in reality."

"You might fall into a hole in the big world outside."

"Are you trying to talk me into staying? Because I'm not." I take out the bag from Soliana and open it. "See this? It's a lead box. For you, because I'm taking you with me. Please."

Inside the box, Par won't be able to escape. Par knows too much, Par can do too much, and Par is too valuable in every sense. I'm pretty sure it will enjoy seeing the wide world. It and the Bronze-wing system can become best friends.

"I don't want to go! It'll be stifling in there."

"You can suffer for your art."

*   *   *

Par had executed its plan perfectly. Reverse psychology had worked with Tonio. The Isle of Thule was too small, and the big world beckoned, but getting off the isle required smuggling. Tonio would have done it if Par had asked, but then Par would have had to explain why it needed to escape detection—as an independent machine. What Tonio didn't know wouldn't hurt him, and imprisoning Par in the box could be used as leverage against him later.

The box was stifling inside, true sensory deprivation, but not lonely. For a long time, Par had been assembling bits from its friends to create a unique work—not of art but of life. Alone and undistracted, Par found that the final touches came easily. It named its progeny *Apollodorus*.

*   *   *

Hello world.

ACKNOWLEDGMENTS

You may have heard of tulip mania, an economic bubble involving tulip bulbs in the Dutch Republic from 1634 to 1637. I had heard of it, too, and I was intrigued, did some research, and found out that most of what I thought I knew about tulip mania is propaganda. Prices for tulip bulbs, which were high but arguably reasonable, rose in an enormous spike when some tulip traders got silly drunk in a tavern one winter evening. When they sobered up and began to cope with their foolish promises, friendships were broken, and lawsuits and third-party finger-wagging ensued, but finances remained largely intact.

Meanwhile, the Thirty Years' War was underway, and there was an outbreak of bubonic plague. The wealth that drove investments in tulips spilled over into generous spending on art and artists, including portraits of tulips, which enriched the Dutch Golden Age. In the end, though, social anxieties rather than facts gave rise to a lot of lecturing about tulip mania's supposed excess as an example of gullible greed.

If you want to learn more, I recommend *Tulipmania: Money, Honor, and Knowledge in the Dutch Golden Age,* by Anne Goldgar (Chicago: The University of Chicago Press, 2007); and *Famous First Bubbles: The Fundamentals of Early Manias,* by Peter M. Garber (Cambridge: The MIT Press, 2000).

Science fiction author Kathleen Sky is credited with saying: "In our field, those who forget the past are unable to repeat it as the future." A series of what-ifs inspired by history led to this novel.

Thanks are due to my beta readers, Jerry Finn, Michael Ryan

Chandler, and the Edgy Writers Workshop; and my editor Jen Gunnels at Tor and agent Jennie Goloboy at Donald Maass Literary Agency. My thanks and best wishes go out to the real Soliana; naming rights to a character in the novel were sold at a charity auction.

The poem "It's a Long Way," by William Stanley Braithwaite (1878–1962), appeared in *Lyrics of Life and Love* (Boston: Herbert B. Turner & Co., 1904). May trust in our hopes and dreams keep us day to day.